Praise for *Deadly Play*

"Bravo! Like the stage and television actors she writes so expertly about in this most engaging suspense novel, M.K. Perkins weaves tenderness with heart-stopping drama into a book impossible to put down. I just finished DEADLY PLAY and already want whatever's M.K.'s writing next!"

— National bestselling author Shane Gericke, TORN APART

deadly play

mk perkins

LANGNER PRESS, LLC

This book is a work of fiction. Names, characters, businesses, organizations, places, events, and incidents either are the product of the author's imagination or are used fictitiously. Any resemblance to actual persons, living or dead, events, or locations is entirely coincidental.

Copyright © 2012 M. K. Perkins
All rights reserved.
Published by Langner Press, LLC

ISBN: 0983733325
ISBN-13: 9780983733324
Library of Congress Control Number: 2012935183

North Charleston, SC

Cover design by Patti Manzone

Dedication

This book is dedicated to:

John E. Perkins
and
Natalie Kellner

Words cannot express how much I love you both. My heartfelt thanks for reading countless drafts and never once giving up on me, not even when I asked you to read one more.

Acknowledgements

My sincerest thanks to Yasmin Assef, Judith Brush, Debbie Conover, Mark Feldman, James King, Joanne King, Lynn Malat, Christine Manzone, Patti Manzone, Edward Rutherford, and Sharon Watroba for giving generously of their time, reading many drafts and providing invaluable feedback. I'm also indebted to Lieutenant Rob Green of the Meriden Police for allowing me to observe a precinct in action and for introducing me to my first gun store. Lieutenant Green chose the Walther PPK for Kate, 007's preferred gun and now Kate's weapon of choice. Special thanks to Shane Gericke for his support and kindness. And last but not least, my love and gratitude a second time to Patti Manzone for her spectacular cover design.

Chapter 1

Andrew gripped the steering wheel tighter and leaned in closer to the windshield. The sun shower was tapering off, but a low-lying fog made it difficult to see the road more than a few feet ahead. There were black spots dancing in front of his eyes that he had to keep blinking away.

"You gonna ask her to go?" Luke took a deep drag and reached over, offering the joint to his friend.

"Nah, she's too straight. Wouldn't work out." Andrew turned his head towards the younger boy as he grabbed the joint and the car swerved right towards the trees.

"Watch it!"

Andrew jerked the steering wheel and the car straightened out. "Relax, man. I know how to drive." He'd been driving Luke around for almost an hour now, and the kid was really getting on his nerves.

"I feel sick," Luke said in a whiny voice, "but I can't go home like this."

Andrew eyed Luke with disgust, making sure that he wasn't about to puke all over his car. He seemed all right, but just in case, he eased the car into the next curve more gently. "Wouldn't want little Lukie's mommy to get all upset."

"Stop being such a prick."

Andrew was two years older than Luke, but only a grade ahead. He knew he never should have agreed to hang out with him. The kid was such a major wuss. This was the last time. From now on he'd stick to guys his own age.

"I feel sick," Luke said again in a small voice.

"Fuck it, man. You're such a pussy. Grow up."

The road snaked in and out. Andrew had to concentrate on holding the car steady in the right lane. He wasn't feeling so great himself. His stomach was queasy and he was feeling lightheaded all of a sudden.

He checked his rearview mirror and the spots in front of his eyes almost made him miss the black car behind him in the distance. It seemed to be coming awfully fast.

"Shit. Could that guy drive any faster?" He stepped harder on the accelerator pedal and the car speeded up.

Luke sat perfectly still looking out the window, as if he hadn't heard him. Thin with round shoulders and stringy brown hair, he seemed a lot younger than his fifteen years.

Andrew punched him lightly on the arm. "I'm sorry, Luke. Okay? I didn't mean it about your mother."

He glanced in the rearview mirror again and saw that the black car was gaining on him. If the driver didn't slow down, he was going to plow into them. *What had his drivers' ed instructor said to do if a car is coming too fast from behind? Slow down and let it pass.*

The road made a sudden curve and Andrew skidded on some wet leaves. His pulse quickened as he managed to straighten out the car. He eased into the breakdown lane and drove slowly so the guy could pass him, keeping his eye trained on the other car in his side view mirror.

"Jesus – what's he doing?"

The black car had followed them into the breakdown lane and was barreling down on them.

Luke looked behind him to see what Andrew was talking about. "Go faster - he's gonna hit us!"

Andrew turned back onto the road and stepped on the accelerator, but the black car caught up with him, staying a few inches off his rear bumper. He stepped down harder, but the other driver speeded up as well and bumped his rear with the front of his car. At first he thought it was an accident, but then the other car did it again.

"Shit, man. What's he want?" Luke sounded like he was on the verge of tears.

Seeing that no one was coming in the opposite direction, Andrew yanked the steering wheel to move into the oncoming lane and get away. Instead, he whirled around in a 360-degree spin. He jerked the wheel back and forth, frantically trying to remember what his drivers' ed instructor had taught him to do in a skid. A tree flashed in and out of his vision as the car spun out of control. Finally he gave up and let go of the wheel as the airbag exploded in his face.

Chapter 2

Andrew was pinned to his seat by the airbag, too dizzy and nauseous to call for help. He tried, but the words died in his throat, as he tasted vomit and swallowed it back.

Someone yanked the passenger door open and pulled Luke to safety. Through the open door, a man's voice, hoarse and gravelly, said something to Luke who responded in a high-pitched voice. Andrew tried to focus on what they were saying, but couldn't seem to manage it. He closed his eyes and felt like he was being pulled underwater.

A noise brought him back awake. His heart pounded in his chest as he fought the dizziness like a drowning man struggling to break the surface of the water. The airbag felt like it was crushing his chest, and he tried to maneuver out from underneath it. *What was that sound?* He lay still, straining to hear through his shattered window.

There it was again; only this time he recognized it: the sound of rustling leaves. He froze, suddenly remembering that a black car had tried to force him off the road. *Had that really happened or had he dreamed it?* Andrew heard something moving towards him, but the dizziness was so overpowering that he barely registered it when someone pried him loose from the car and tossed him roughly onto the ground. He felt someone rifling through his pockets and fought to stay calm. *Maybe he's just looking for identification.* But Andrew didn't really believe that.

The man shook him by the shoulders and was saying something in that hoarse voice of his. Andrew tried to concentrate, but the man's face kept swimming in and out of focus.

A siren in the distance seemed to draw the man's attention. He turned his head towards the sound and started to stand up. Andrew closed his eyes and stayed still, praying for the man to go away. Instead, he crouched back down and whispered something into Andrew's ear. Andrew's eyes shot open as if they were disconnected from his body and had a will of their own. An overwhelming panic shot through him and this time he failed to swallow back the vomit as the sound of the siren grew louder.

Chapter 3

In retrospect, I should have sensed something was wrong. Evil lurking in the shadows. A malevolent spirit waiting in the wings, preparing for violence. Unfortunately I sensed nothing until suddenly I was standing in its path, as unaware as the blind person crossing the street at exactly the wrong moment, neither hearing nor seeing the oncoming bus. But in defense of myself, I was too wrapped up in rehearsals to notice anything other than the looming disaster awaiting us all on opening night when the critics submitted their reviews.

Most of the time good plays come together suddenly. Actors stop acting and begin talking like real people. Costumes transform into clothing and sets become dwellings as characters take up residence.

None of this was happening on the stage set of *Wait Until Tomorrow*. We were two weeks away from opening night and the leading man, Brad Simpson, still argued non-stop with the director over interpretation.

Energetic and loud, Brad Simpson was a talented egomaniac who had made a comeback by playing the endearing grandfather in a popular movie that had come out earlier in the year. Although he hadn't won, he'd been nominated for an Oscar for Best Supporting Actor. Before that, he'd primarily been known for his starring role on a sitcom that was in its fifth year of reruns.

I had a show in reruns too - a nighttime TV drama for the teenage set that had once been one of the most popular shows on television. Fortunately, it had recently captured the imagination of a whole new generation of young people, and I was praying that my stalled career was about to rise from the ashes like a phoenix.

My name is Kate Sachs and I played the ingénue in *Wait Until Tomorrow*. I'm a few years south of thirty, but this was one of the few age-appropriate parts I'd ever landed. Casting directors couldn't lay eyes on my strawberry blonde hair and freckles without thinking teenage drama queen. From Hollywood to Broadway, I was the acting world's oldest teenager. Not that I was exactly in demand on either coast.

Brad, on the other hand, looked somewhere between fifty and death. It was impossible to tell. After the film's success, he'd apparently decided to have work done on his face. Although you couldn't see it from the audience when he was onstage, he had almost no facial expressions – not when he laughed, not when he was angry, not ever. Everything on his face was botox-frozen except his mouth, which never stopped moving. Presumably none of this was permanent or he'd have trouble finding work in film or television again; his lack of facial expressions would look positively scary in close-ups.

If Brad looked like he just stepped off the cover of an AARP version of GQ, our director was just the opposite. Cy Williams had dark circles under his eyes from constant sleep deprivation. He seemed distracted all the time. I didn't realize it then, but he had a lot on his mind that had nothing to do with the play.

In his early forties, he was handsome in a boring sort of way. Bland and blond, he fidgeted a lot during rehearsals, with an asthma inhaler appearing from his pants pocket every now and then and a small vial of smelling salts constantly at his side. He claimed they cleared his sinuses. The man was a physical wreck. Together

Cy and Brad were a disaster. When they weren't bellowing at each other, one of them was bellowing at someone else. Cheerful work environment.

That morning's rehearsal was slow going. If Brad didn't like someone's interpretation of a scene, he'd jump in ahead of Cy and tell the actor how to fix it. These interruptions provoked Cy into screaming fits that made his asthma spiral out of control. At one point, I was afraid he'd stopped breathing.

At last, we arrived at the scene in which I came rushing into my parents' house late for dinner, my boyfriend already there. Before I could get more than a few lines out, Cy leapt onto the stage and interrupted me.

"Kate, I want you to take it from the top. But this time, fall into the room like you just ran ten blocks to get there, throw your arms around Paul, and give him a long, passionate kiss."

Maybe this wasn't really Cy. Maybe this was his clueless twin brother.

"Suzanne would never do that, Cy. She's way too conservative. It's completely out of character."

I was wasting my breath. The man wasn't listening.

Cy hadn't always been like this. He'd directed me in an Off-Broadway play while I was a student at NYU. His instincts had been flawless back then. Thanks to him, I won an OBIE for Best Actress – Off-Broadway's equivalent to the Oscar. Not bad for a college freshman.

But that was years ago. Our paths didn't cross again until my agent called to say that Cy wanted me to play one of the leads in *Wait Until Tomorrow*, a new play by Jake Ormond. The producer, David Sobel, was testing it on summer audiences at Omnibus Playhouse in Westport, Connecticut for a possible Broadway run. That's producer-speak for "come see our show now before ticket prices soar on Broadway."

But most shows never make it and I was afraid to count on this one being any different. Just in case, I had an ironclad clause written into my contract guaranteeing that if the show moved to Broadway, I'd go with it. I wasn't born yesterday. I knew the original cast would be replaced with big name performers, most of whom couldn't act, to the detriment of the play. No wonder so many Broadway shows closed quickly.

I tried doing the scene Cy's way, but it wasn't working. "Suzanne would never act this way," I said, stopping. "Not in front of her parents. Paul wouldn't stand for it."

I looked around for Jake and spotted him in the back. "Jake – what do you think?"

Jake Ormond was tall and lanky with unruly dark hair and a prominent nose. In his late twenties, he was an up-and-coming writer who had written brilliant material that had been staged by smaller theaters around the country. This was a big break for him, so he never missed a rehearsal, and rarely interfered. I'd put him on the spot, but he didn't disappoint me.

"Kate's right, Cy. Suzanne wants to marry Paul. She'd be afraid of embarrassing him…"

"Shut up, Jake." Cy's voice turned shrill. "No one gives a damn what you think."

"Who do you think you're talking to?" Jake stood up abruptly and started moving towards the front. As he got closer to the stage, I could see the fury in his face.

"Get back in your seat!" Cy's tone was still aggressive, but I detected a note of uncertainty.

"You have no right…" Jake's voice trailed off. He froze in place and pointed at something over our heads. "Look out!"

I looked up and saw a light fixture dangling from a long cable attached to the ceiling. Cy and I were standing directly in its trajectory. It made a squealing noise like the wheels of a train grinding to a stop as it slipped another foot or so.

"Move!" I shoved Cy out of the way as I leapt to the side.

He fell to the ground and started wheezing. He pulled his inhaler out of his pocket and shoved it into his mouth, drawing in a deep breath without removing his eyes from the dangling light. "Who's up there?" he yelled.

I looked up, but saw no one.

"Dammit," Cy yelled again, "I've had enough - come down here!"

The rest of us were so stunned that at first no one said a word. Finally, Brad sprang into action and for once I was glad to see him intervene. "Cy, there's no one up there. It was an accident."

Cy shook him off. He was so agitated that he was gasping for air. He took several more drags on his inhaler, but it wasn't helping. Panic showed all over his face. I thought it was because he couldn't breathe. If only I'd divined the truth, maybe I could have prevented what happened. But I'm getting ahead of myself.

I put my arm around his shoulder and helped him down off the stage, guiding him to a seat in the front row.

"Someone get me his smelling salts," I said.

One of the stagehands picked up the bottle from where it had fallen to the floor and handed it to me. I waved it under Cy's nose. He jerked his head back as the smell of ammonia hit him. After a few minutes, he seemed to revive.

"Okay folks," Russell Duby, the stage manager, got everyone's attention. "Let's wrap it up for the morning. We'll pick up rehearsals at two o'clock."

Jake turned abruptly and stormed up the aisle. He left through the back of the orchestra, slamming the door to the lobby behind him.

"Asshole," Cy muttered.

"No he's not, Cy," I said. "You humiliated him for no reason."

Cy looked from me to Brad. "I'm sorry."

"Apologize to Jake – not us!" Brad said, jutting his chin at the lobby where Jake had disappeared.

Cy took another drag on his inhaler, but it was clear that it still wasn't helping.

"Why don't you lie down for awhile?" I asked.

"Okay, I'll lie down in the Green Room."

I'm not sure why, but in the entertainment world, the actors' lounge is usually called the Green Room. The one at Omnibus was painted the color of pale moss. I helped Cy navigate the walkway linking the theater to the new wing where the Green Room was located on the second floor.

When we got there, his eyes swept the room from the doorway as if he wanted to make sure it was empty. He seemed nervous as he finally crossed the threshold. Instead of sitting down right away, he walked straight to the back, disappearing momentarily when he turned right into the kitchenette that was located in the L-shape part of the room.

"What's wrong?" I asked when he finally reappeared.

He collapsed on the sofa. "Nothing."

"Cy, what's gotten into you? How would you like it if someone yelled at you that way?"

"I know. You're right. But he's driving me crazy. Just sitting there, rehearsal after rehearsal, judging me."

I said, "He's nervous about the play. It's his baby. He's not judging you."

But Cy had a point. Directing and writing require entirely different skills. A lot of experimentation takes place during the rehearsal process. I could see why Cy might feel inhibited with Jake watching all the time.

"You're probably right – I'm over-reacting. I just need to lie down for a while."

I closed the door and was about to head downstairs when Carla Manzetti, the costume designer, stuck her head out of the wardrobe room.

"Kate! Mind trying on a few things for me?"

Carla was too nice to refuse. I followed her into the wardrobe room where dozens of costumes hung from racks on wheels. One of Carla's assistants, an older woman who spoke mostly in Italian, was bent over a sewing machine in a corner of the room. She looked up and smiled as I entered.

Carla walked over to the coffee machine, poured two cups, and handed one to me.

"You look like you need reviving."

I told her about the fracas during rehearsal.

"Sounds a little out of character for Jake," Carla observed. "Cy, on the other hand, is just plain mental." She removed a coat from one of the racks and helped me into it. "Wait 'till you see the getup he wants me to put you in at the top of Act II." She grabbed a short, transparent dress off another rack and held it up for me to see.

"Suzanne would never wear that!"

"You're preachin' to the choir. I told him, but he won't listen."

She strode over to the closet and rummaged around. "I just got an idea."

Carla emerged from the closet with an evening jacket draped on a hanger.

"Whaddaya think?"

I tried it on and looked in the mirror. "You're a genius. Most jackets make me look so short."

"That's 'cause you are short. Now turn around slowly." Her trained eye examined me head to toe. "That'll work. The green's fabulous with your red hair. Just don't let Cy see you before dress rehearsal. He'll be fine with it once he sees you onstage."

The rest of my costumes needed only minor alterations. It hit me how close to opening night we were and I felt a sudden knot in my stomach.

When Carla and I were finished, I decided to look in on Cy and ask if he wanted me to pick up lunch for him. The door to the Green Room was open, but when I looked inside, he wasn't there.

I heard him braying at someone down the hallway. He was in a spare office with the door closed.

"How dare you? I told you I'd do it."

Another male voice replied, but it was too low and muffled to identify the owner. I put my ear against the door to hear if Cy was at it again with Jake. Suddenly all hell broke lose, with lots of banging and what sounded like furniture scraping against the floor.

"Stop!" Cy yelled in a panicked voice.

The other man grunted something back, but he was so hoarse that I couldn't make out what he said. I realized that it couldn't have been Jake, not unless he'd developed a raging cold within the past half-hour.

There was a loud crash as if someone had thrown a heavy object that shattered against the wall.

"Please!" Cy begged.

"You piece of shit!" The man's voice cracked as he tried to shout. It sounded like he had laryngitis.

Something thudded against the door. Then I heard Cy give a loud groan followed by an alarming silence.

I wrapped on the door and tried to open it. It was locked. "Cy, open the door! What's going on in there?"

Cy groaned again and I banged on the door even harder.

"Something wrong, Ms. Sachs?"

I leapt back from the door and crashed into one of the stagehands on the lighting crew. "Jesus – you scared the hell out of me."

"Sorry - didn't mean to startle you. What's going on?"

"Cy's in there fighting with someone."

"So what else is new?" He looked at me with an amused expression. Short and powerfully built, he was attractive, except that he reeked of cigarette smoke.

"It sounds serious this time." I rapped on the door again. "Cy – open up."

A series of muffled blows sounded through the door. After each one, Cy gave a loud moan cut short by the delivery of the next blow.

The raspy voice hissed something on the other side of the door, low and threatening. We heard Cy pleading, "No – don't!" and what sounded like a slap followed by more furniture being shoved around.

The concern on the stagehand's face heightened my anxiety. He banged on the door. "Mr. Williams, it's Art Desmond. Is everything all right in there?"

The door opened abruptly. Cy stood in the doorway, blocking our view into the room.

"What?" His eyes cut from Desmond to me. He looked frightened and disheveled and had a red mark on his cheek.

"Are you all right? What's going on in there?"

"Everything's fine, Kate."

He forced a smile, but the fear in his eyes never wavered. I expected him to throw open the door and introduce whoever was in the office with him. I've never forgiven myself for not insisting.

Chapter 4

I left the theater, barely registering how beautiful the day was outside. I couldn't stop thinking about the fight I'd just heard and what a mistake I'd made in accepting this part. When my agent had first called to say that Cy wanted me for it, I'd been flattered that he'd even remembered me. But I'd hesitated to take a role in a theater that was frankly one step up from summer stock, for all David's talk about a pre-Broadway tryout. It felt like my career was sliding backwards, but I needed the money. Besides, David had promised to let me direct for him in New York once he found the right script. But so far the "right script" hadn't materialized and I was starting to think it never would. Whenever I asked him about it, he responded evasively and hurried away.

Not that I wanted to give up acting altogether, but I was sick of being typecast. Directing gave me an alternative career to pursue along with the thrill of bringing a play to life. Over the past few years, I'd been paying my dues whenever I wasn't acting, working my way up from assistant director and then directing in regional theaters. I felt ready to tackle New York; so when David promised to let me direct an Off-Broadway production, I'd been elated. Now I felt like going into hiding somewhere.

I clicked open the locks and climbed inside of my red Audi TT convertible. It was six years old and occasionally needed coaxing, but for the most part it still ran like new. I lowered the top, revved the engine, and backed out of the parking space. The Audi picked up speed and I welcomed the feel of the wind in my face as I headed towards downtown Westport.

I thought about Cy. He had arguments all the time, but the one I'd just overheard had turned seriously violent. Maybe I should have called the police. Who had he been fighting with? Why hadn't he wanted Art Desmond and me to see who it was?

I made several frustrating circles around Westport's municipal parking lot near the river before finally finding a spot. I cut through the Gap to Main Street and tried to forget about everything as I strolled along, looking in all the shop windows. You could find whatever your heart desired, providing your taste ran to mainstream mall.

Westport hadn't always been like this. Before the new Mc-Mansion building epidemic spread throughout Fairfield County, Westport had been a quaint New England town with mom and pop stores that sold everything from clothing to antiques and books. But as housing prices soared, store leases were quick to follow, and all the mom and pop stores were pushed out by the major chains.

The one holdout to all this modernization was Oscar's Deli. Oscar's was a Westport institution. Long and narrow, it had a deli counter that took up the front half of the store. A sign on the wall read, "Never trust a thin deli person."

A crowd had gathered in front of the register for take-out or to pay the check. I eased my way to the back past baby carriages and briefcases spilling into the narrow aisle that divided the tables crowded against opposite walls. I found a free table and grabbed it, sliding inside to sit on the red cushioned bench.

"Hi Kate. Coffee?" the waitress asked.

"Thanks, Pam, that would be great."

I'd been coming to Oscar's all my life. I grew up one town over in Weston where my parents still lived in the same house. Some actors were known at Sardis on Broadway and 44th. I was known at Oscar's Deli.

I sipped my coffee carefully, feeling the stress of the morning dissipate. Facing me was a big painted mural of life-sized Oscar's regulars from days gone by – men sporting an assortment of beards, work clothes, and hats. I recognized some of them from my childhood and, of course, Lee, the owner, still looked the same, only older. My attention wandered from the mural to the people around me. Chicly clothed professional types out on their lunch break mixed with mothers and kids sporting Ralph Lauren casual. The contrast from the sixties characters in the painting was emblematic of how the town had changed.

My thoughts drifted back to Cy. I replayed the entire morning in my head from the time I arrived at the theater until I left for lunch. I wracked my brain trying to match someone I knew to that odd hoarse voice I'd heard through the door. Images of different people flowed through my mind like a film in fast-forward, but in the end I came up empty-handed. I could think of no one.

"Hey gorgeous, mind if I join you?"

I looked up to see my father standing in front of me, a wide grin on his tanned lean face. He looked tired, albeit extremely dapper in an open-collared navy shirt and white slacks, his mass of curly hair wild as usual.

"Dad!"

"Waiting long?" he asked.

"Just got here."

He folded himself into a chair and crossed his legs, his white Sauconys peeking out from under the table. "How're rehearsals?"

I sighed. "Lousy."

He laughed. "Care to elaborate?"

Before I could answer, Pam came over to our table and we ordered our usual - corned beef on rye with mustard, coleslaw on the side.

My father reached for a pickle. "So what's up at the theater?"

I told him about the disastrous rehearsal and the fight I'd overheard Cy having.

"Should I have called the police?"

"That's really up to Cy – don't you think?" Dad said.

"I guess so."

I lowered my voice, realizing that an old lady at the next table was eavesdropping. "So what's up with you, Dad? You look beat."

My father, a family practitioner with the greatest bedside manner in medicine, had a tendency to take his work too much to heart.

"I am beat." He leaned in closer and spoke quietly. "They brought two kids into the ER after a car crash. One was DOA. The other was so doped up on a cocktail of drugs we had to put him in detox."

"That's awful."

The old lady was straining to hear. He stole a glance at her and she looked away quickly, picking up a half-eaten sandwich from her plate.

He started to tell me something else when our sandwiches arrived and we dug in.

"When's the last time you ate?" Dad asked.

"You're just jealous." One of the traits I've inherited from my mother is that I can eat like a horse and never gain weight.

He smiled. "We on for tonight?"

"Absolutely."

On Friday nights whenever possible, the Sachs family congregated for dinner at my parents' house in Weston. My grandfather, Max, and his brother, Abe, came up from their apartment in the city and I drove over from my loft in Norwalk. It was a tradition we enjoyed because it brought us all together. It was also an opportunity for my family to grill me on whom I was seeing and whether I was ever getting married.

Oscar's was packed by the time we finished eating. Not wanting to tie up Pam's table, we headed up front to pay the bill. My father waited on line while I took a side trip to the ladies' room. When I returned, he was talking to a man standing with his back to me. When he turned around, I was surprised to see my producer.

David Sobel had green eyes shaded by long lashes that many women spent fortunes on mascara trying to imitate. He was tall and slender with an olive complexion and thick, wavy dark hair that formed a widow's peak over his forehead.

My father spotted me and waved me over. "Kate - look who I ran into."

David extended his arm to shake hands. He exuded a self-confidence that bordered on smugness. "Hi, Kate. How's it going?"

"Fine David. Good to see you."

Glancing at my father, I saw him trying to gauge my reaction to David's good looks. My family never gives up.

Just then a baby carriage narrowly missed swerving into me.

"Why don't we move outside," Dad suggested.

We stepped out onto Main Street. People were milling about in shorts and T-shirts. The outside tables were all taken, so we continued talking on the sidewalk.

"Are you still planning on moving the show to Broadway?" Dad asked.

"Definitely. But a lot will depend on how things go up here. And whether I can raise enough money."

I wondered if David was aware of how badly rehearsals were going.

"My wife's uncle is a genius at raising money," Dad said. "He might be able to give you some advice."

David looked as though he doubted it, but responded politely. "I'd love to meet him sometime."

Dad's eyebrows shot up and I had a sudden feeling about where he was going with this. My mind raced for a way to head him off at the pass.

"Are you busy tonight, David?"

Too late.

David looked at my father as if he hadn't understood the question.

"If you'd like to meet Abe, why don't you join us for dinner?"

"Dad! I'm sure David has other plans."

David grinned. "I don't have any plans for tonight, Dr. Sachs. I'd love to come for dinner."

Chapter 5

We said our goodbyes in front of Oscar's. I agreed to meet David at the end of the day and drive him to my parents' house since he'd commuted from the city by train. I had to pass the station on my way home, so dropping him off after dinner would be easy.

I was parking my car behind the theater when movement at the far end of the lot caught my attention. Cy was unmistakable from the slouch of his shoulders and the drab beige pants and white shirt he wore every day. He was deep in conversation with a teenage boy in a red polo I recognized from the crew. Cy helped some of his acting students get summer jobs at the theater and this kid was obviously one of them. Although I couldn't hear what they were saying, I could tell the kid was upset from the way he was flapping his arms around and scowling. Cy threw his arm around the boy's shoulder and spoke to him at length with an earnestness that made me smile. He'd talked to me in much the same way when I was a fledgling actress, helping me through more than one crisis I was certain I'd never survive.

I started to leave when the boy looked up and saw me. He said something to Cy who turned around and shouted hello, waving at me with a big smile. The boy waved also, but less enthusiastically. Cy practically had to drag him over to meet me. As Cy got closer, I was relieved to see that, except for a bruise on his forehead, he didn't look hurt.

"Kate, I'd like you to meet Billy Cole, one of my star pupils."

Billy smiled at me sheepishly. He had large brown eyes and shaggy dark hair that fell to below his collar, covering his ears. I guessed he was around fifteen or sixteen.

"I watch you on television all the time," he said.

"Thanks. Are you an aspiring actor?"

"Director."

Cy looked at him proudly. "You two have something in common."

I explained, "I'm a director too."

"Cool," Billy said.

My eyes shifted from Billy to Cy. "Are you okay?"

His frown coupled with the slight shake of his head as he darted a look at Billy was enough to stop me from saying anything further.

"I feel great," he said. "Just a little tired."

I left them talking in the parking lot and entered the theater through the stage door. Russell Duby, the stage manager, was waiting for me inside with a smirk on his face, tapping his watch and tsk-tsking. "You're late, Kate."

I must have looked like I was going to deck him because he quickly added, "Just kidding. Cy asked me to stand in for him this afternoon so he could go home and rest."

Russell was short and thin with a pointy nose and pasty complexion. He stepped towards me, his face so close to mine that all I could focus on was the big pimple on his chin.

"You know I love you." He pursed his lips together and made kissing noises.

I took a giant step backward.

Don Harrison, who played my boyfriend in the play, had arrived just in time to catch Russell acting out his bizarre mating ritual. Don was half a foot taller than Russell and stepped in between us.

"Sit down, lover-boy. The lady's not interested."

Russell sat.

To be fair, Russell was a good stage manager. He knew where every piece of scenery was supposed to go, which props were used in which scenes, and he'd committed every lighting cue and costume change to memory. An aspiring director, he was always the first to arrive and the last to leave. He was just a dork when it came to women.

That afternoon, most of his attention was on the commotion behind us. Carpenters were hammering scenery; the lighting crew was stringing lights; and stagehands were scurrying everywhere with props that needed to be in place for our first dress rehearsal on Monday.

I noticed Art Desmond on the topmost catwalk with Billy. Apparently they were tightening the light fixture that had almost fallen earlier. Alphonse Billings, the lighting designer – a.k.a Sparky, God help us - supervised from below. An older man with a penchant for dressing in pastels, Sparky had coarse bottle-blond hair that made him look like he was wearing a Beatles wig made out of straw. The bottom rim of his large black glasses - ten years out of style – rested halfway down his cheeks.

Don and I worked well together. We concentrated on our more difficult scenes, making sure to stay far downstage out of the way. Occasionally, Russell helped us get back on track if we forgot a line or needed a lighting or special effects cue.

Around 3:30, David arrived to see how things were shaping up. He looked past me to Russell, asking why Don and I were rehearsing onstage in the midst of so much construction. He was clearly annoyed and wanted to know where Cy was.

"Cy's not feeling well," said Russell, minus the supercilious tone. "He asked me to rehearse Kate and Don, but we're constructing the set today…"

"Okay, okay," David cut him off and walked away.

I could have kicked myself at how rejected I felt that he hadn't even said hello. Fine with me. The last thing I needed was a complicated relationship with my self-involved producer.

Don and I resumed rehearsals. We were working on a particularly difficult scene in which my character entered her boyfriend's apartment late at night. Mistaking me for a burglar, he hit me over the head with a vase. The prop was jury-rigged to break easily without hurting me, but this time, it didn't work. The blow made me disoriented and I toppled to the floor.

A crowd gathered around me. Sparky kept calling my name and asking if I could hear him. Then someone yelled, "Watch out!" and the light that had almost fallen earlier came crashing down in a hail of glass.

David came running onstage. I looked up at him, on the verge of assuring him that I was okay. But instead of looking at me, he was focused on Sparky, his face contorted with anger.

"You stupid old fool! Can't you even hang a light fixture properly?"

The theater fell silent. A forty-year veteran of the theater, Sparky had won an Oscar and three Tony awards for lighting design. As he rose to his feet, I watched him struggle to maintain his dignity, willing his face into a neutral expression.

"I realize you're upset, David, but I won't be spoken to that way."

In the meantime, Art and Billy had come scrambling down from the catwalk. Art stepped forward, holding a piece of cable.

"If anyone's to blame, it's me, Mr. Sobel. There was a second weak spot near the ceiling that I didn't catch." He bent the cable so that David could see what he was talking about. "See? There's another deep gash here, but when the cable is hanging straight, it's hard to see."

I tried to get up to look, but sat back down, dizzy.

David's attention shifted to me. Something in my expression must have registered with him because his face softened. He looked from me to Sparky. "I'm sorry. Please, I…"

Sparky raised his hand in the air and interrupted him, "No need, David. This never should have happened. I take full responsibility." He turned towards Art and continued, "Let's clear the stage and examine all the cables before we let anyone back out here."

I tried standing up again, but found that I was still too dizzy.

"Don't try to move, Kate." David's green eyes looked concerned as he bent over me.

"I'm fine – really."

"Let me help you." He gently lifted me off the floor, holding me in his arms while the cast and crew gave a round of applause.

"Please put me down." My cheeks felt like they were on fire.

David lowered me to the ground and guided me towards the back of the theater. "I need to talk to Russell. Then how about us getting out of here? Bet you've had enough of this place for one day."

He smiled and I felt something stir. *Probably indigestion.* I agreed to meet him in the parking lot after I freshened up.

While I was dusting myself off in the dressing room, I wondered about the light fixture and whether Sparky and Art would find any others that had been compromised. A chill went through me as I thought about how close I'd come to turning into the late Kate Sachs. I sat down on a small chair and waited for the sudden shakiness I was feeling to pass.

Chapter 6

The air turned cooler as David and I drove north into the country. I put some tunes on the radio, trying to cover up the ambivalence I felt towards him. I couldn't shake the image of him ranting at poor Sparky, a theatrical icon whose advanced age alone should have commanded more respect. David had apparently put the incident behind him, however, because he kept glancing sideways at me, grinning. He was noticeably more relaxed than I.

"This is fantastic," he said.

I forced myself to smile. "You mean the car? Or the scenery?"

"All of it!"

The countryside was dense with foliage. Huge oaks and maples mingled with the occasional pine, shading the lawns of houses spaced well apart. We passed a stream where kids were knee-deep in the water fly-fishing.

"Did you grow up here?" David asked.

"Yup."

"It's beautiful."

"How long have you lived in New York?"

What I wanted to ask was whether he lived in New York with a woman. I was trying to remember the name behind the face my mind kept linking him to. I was almost certain I'd read about him and some model. Maybe it was an actress. The guy was handsome, admittedly, but something about him irritated me. He was so self-assured. And a little too well groomed. I hated the way he kept touching his hair.

"Kate?"

"Huh? Oh sorry – what did you say?"

"I said I've lived in the city for ten years. Then you seemed to drift away."

"Sorry. My mind wandered off. It's back now." To my great relief, we were approaching my parents' road. The small talk was starting to make me anxious.

My parents lived at the end of a quiet cul-de-sac in a vintage white Victorian with a wrap-around porch. It wasn't the biggest house in the neighborhood, but what it lacked in size it compensated for in warmth and welcome. We stepped through the front door into a foyer that led to the family room in one direction, and the dining room in the other. My parents had lived here all of their married lives. I was their only child, so the walls were covered with my pictures at different stages of development, all taken by my mother.

Except for the scrumptious aroma of brisket of beef wafting from the kitchen, the house seemed empty.

"Anybody home?"

No response.

"Hello?" I said, louder this time.

"In here, sweetheart," Grandpa Max's voice sounded from inside.

David followed me into the kitchen where we discovered my grandfather pulling the brisket out of the oven. He stood up and gave me a hug, then shook hands with David, eyeing him with approval. Gramps explained that Uncle Abe was on the phone in the library clinching a deal to buy some company in Nebraska. Or India. He wasn't sure.

Hearing this, David seemed more eager to meet him.

"Where's Mom?" I was fairly certain I knew the answer.

"In the studio," Gramps said. "She forgot the brisket."

When she was working, my mother tended to be absent-minded about everything else. Such was the case that day.

"Where's Dad?"

"Still at the hospital. Big emergency."

When my grandmother died of cancer, Grandpa Max was devastated; he and my grandmother had been happily married for over 50 years. My mother, his only child, begged him to move in with her and my father. But Grandpa Max refused, insisting he couldn't take the quiet. Tall and wiry with a bushy white handlebar moustache, he went to the gym every day and hit the ski slopes most weekends in the winter. Hardly the sedate country type.

So instead of moving in with my parents, Grandpa Max sold his dental practice on Long Island and moved into Manhattan to live with his brother on the Upper East Side. Uncle Abe's idea of a good time was to take in all the shows on Broadway and then prowl the jazz clubs until the sun came up. Abe routinely invited two female friends along, although Grandpa Max insisted they weren't dates.

Uncle Abe appeared in the kitchen, snapping his mobile phone shut. Shaking hands with David, he said, "Nice to meet you, David."

Uncle Abe was different from his older brother in every way. Short and dapper, he'd been married and divorced three times from successively younger women. At 60, he'd finally sworn off marriage. A brilliant financier who claims he's retired, his cell phone is still constantly pressed to his ear as he makes one last deal too good to pass up.

Before David could respond to Uncle Abe, my mother swept into the kitchen. She kissed me hello, and then spun around to greet David.

"David, meet my mother, Annie Rosenthal."

"The photographer?" David asked.

"The same," my mother said smiling.

My mother's work hangs in some of the world's greatest museums. Her photos have appeared on the covers of most major magazines and she's photographed the front lines of two wars plus scores of natural disasters. Worrying about her is a family occupation.

She shook hands with David.

My grandfather saw the look of surprise on David's face and let out a hoot. "They look just like sisters, don't they?"

My mother and I share the same strawberry blond hair and freckles. We're both small with athletic builds, although my mother is half an inch taller, as she delights in telling everyone.

"Like twins," David said. "It's an honor to meet you, Ms. Rosenthal. I'm a big fan."

"Thank you," she said. "And please - call me Annie."

When we were all settled in the family room with drinks, my relatives pounced on David for information about his plans for bringing *Wait Until Tomorrow* to Broadway. As usual, David was evasive.

" I'm exploring some options now."

"What kind of options?" my mother asked.

"Financial, for the most part. As you can imagine, it takes a lot of money to bring a show to Broadway these days."

I noticed a silent communication pass between Grandpa Max and Uncle Abe. It wasn't a happy one. Over my protests, they'd invested in a play I did a few years back and had lost their shirts. It was not a mistake they were likely to ever repeat.

David apparently misinterpreted their exchange because he looked hopefully at Uncle Abe. "Dr. Sachs said you were in finance and might be able to give me some advice."

"I was in venture capital," Uncle Abe said. "What sort of advice are you looking for?"

"Actually I was hoping you could recommend some investors who might be interested in backing a Broadway show."

"Possibly," Uncle Abe said without enthusiasm. "Do you have any financial projections?"

David sat up straighter in his chair. "Yes, but not with me. They're in my office at the theater." He looked at me. "Would you mind stopping by tonight so I can get them before you drop me at the station?"

"I guess I could," I said.

"Problem solved then," Gramps said. "We'll get them from you tomorrow."

There was a lull in the conversation until my mother broke the silence. "Is your wife in the theater too, David?"

I groaned inwardly. The inquisition was upon us.

"I'm not married," he said. A spot of color appeared on each cheek. "I was, but I've been divorced for over two years."

My mother looked sympathetic. "I'm sorry to hear that."

"Katie's never been married," Grandpa Max said.

"She came close though," Uncle Abe said. "But he died. Terrible tragedy."

"Uncle Abe!" my mother said, her tone incredulous.

Years ago I'd had a serious boyfriend named Robert Bennett who died while he was on a business trip, although his body was never found. He'd flown out of Athens on a private jet that disappeared shortly after takeoff. My family was convinced that this lack of closure prevented me from becoming romantically involved again, even after all this time. But my psyche really wasn't that complicated; I just hadn't met the right guy. My family, champion over-analyzers, found this explanation too simplistic.

David looked like he was about to offer me condolences.

I glared at my mother, silently imploring her to change the subject.

"How did you get involved in producing?" she asked David.

"After graduation, I helped my college roommate raise money for a play he wanted to direct. I was a lowly analyst at Goldman Sachs back then."

"No kidding." Uncle Abe was clearly impressed.

David nodded. "I got hooked on show business from that point on. Gave up investment banking a year later and never looked back."

Uncle Abe looked appalled, but before he could say anything, we heard my father's key in the door.

Chapter 7

It was past eleven o'clock when David and I pulled up to the theater. I was exhausted and wanted to get this over with so I could drop him off at the station and go home. I got out of the car and clicked my remote. Two chirps signaled that the doors were locked.

As we walked towards the side entrance leading to the new wing, David's hand brushed against mine. I moved over, widening the gap between us. He stepped sideways and closed it again. An image of Russell Duby, our aggressively amorous stage manager, popped into my head and I almost laughed out loud. David's hand stretched across my back and rested on my shoulder. He stopped walking and gently turned me around to face him. He leaned down and kissed me lightly - his lips feathery against mine. I returned the kiss, my only excuse being that the full moon reflecting off the river was creating a lot of atmosphere.

His lips parted and he kissed me again, harder this time.

I broke away. "You'll miss your train."

The main floor of the new wing was dark, save for a few dimmed emergency lights that cast shadows along the walls. David led the way up the winding staircase to the second floor. He grabbed my hand as we walked down the long hallway leading to his office. As we got closer, we noticed a small strip of light shining from under the Green Room door. I offered to turn it off while David went into his office to get the financial report for Uncle Abe.

I stepped into the actors' lounge and clicked off the small table lamp next to the door and started to leave. A rustling noise made me pause in the doorway. I grew conscious of a metallic taste in my mouth as my muscles tensed and I tried to figure out where the noise was coming from. Moonlight streamed through the glass sliders at the far end of the left hand wall, casting light onto the closet alcove facing them where a few coats and jackets were hanging. The L-shape of the room prevented me from seeing around the corner to the right into the kitchenette. I turned the table lamp back on, but it didn't cast enough light to see much beyond the doorway. I took a step further into the room and listened carefully. Then I realized what was making the noise. The sliders were open. A breeze drifted in, causing the curtains to rustle as they billowed inward.

As I crossed the room to close them, I noticed something I hadn't seen from the doorway. There was a pair of white sneakers on the floor of the closet alcove. I looked above them in a straight line until I locked onto a pair of disembodied eyes. Like a black cat perched on a shelf way over my head. Only there wasn't any shelf and this was no cat. Peering at me through slits in a black mask was a tall man hiding in the shadows.

Neither of us moved at first. Then my instincts kicked in. I quickly scanned the room for every item I could use as a weapon. I reached to my left and ripped a table lamp cord out of its socket, and hurled the lamp at his head. It shattered against the wall.

The man rushed at me, but I dived out of the way, banging into the sliding doors. He reached for me and grabbed me by the hair. I screamed and kicked him in the shin, but that only made him angrier. He held onto my hair and tugged harder, wrapping his other hand around my throat. I couldn't breathe, let alone yell for help. I brought my knee up hard and connected with his groin.

He gasped and doubled over, letting me go. I ran between the open sliders and escaped outside onto the deck.

Bad move. He ran after me.

The deck was no more than twenty feet long and half as wide. I got into a crouching position and ducked out of reach each time he tried to grab me. We faced off like that for a few seconds, moving around the perimeter of the deck like two prizefighters. I thought about vaulting over the railing, but it was a ten-foot drop or better to the embankment below. I hesitated and he lunged, catching me by the arms, his fingers digging into them so hard that I screamed.

The man slammed me against the railing, calling me a bitch in a hoarse voice that I instantly recognized. Cy's sparring buddy. His body odor was nauseating. With the black mask over his head, he looked like a trick-or-treater on steroids. I reached for it, but before I could pull it off, he grabbed me around the neck again and bent me backwards over the rail. My muscles strained against him, but I was no match for him. No sound came out when I tried screaming for help.

A light came on inside and I heard David shouting my name. The man loosened his grip. I stomped on his foot and broke away. He started to come after me but stopped suddenly when David shouted my name again, closer this time. Then he leapt over the railing and landed with a thud. I heard him groan and looked down just in time to see him limping away along the embankment.

"David." I was so winded that it was an effort to speak loudly enough to make him hear.

He came running out onto the deck. "Kate - what happened? I heard something crash."

I gasped for air, my lungs ineffective as fish gills on dry land. "Man. Tried to kill me." My whole body started to shake and I couldn't manage another word.

David put his arms around me and held me close against his chest. "It's okay. You're safe now." He kissed the top of my head. "Come inside. We'll call the police."

He guided me to an armchair. "You're shivering." He grabbed a trench coat from the closet alcove and draped it around my shoulders.

I told him what happened, but had trouble getting the words out.

"Want a drink of water?" David asked.

I nodded.

I heard him flip a wall switch and another light came on. Then he shouted something incoherent and I jumped up and ran to the kitchenette. David reached for me with both arms, trying to prevent me from seeing whatever had caused him to cry out.

I maneuvered around him and gasped at the sight of Cy splayed out on the floor face up, glazed eyes partially open. His face was bruised and puffy and blood trickled from his nose. I forced myself to kneel down beside him and touch his neck with my fingertips. He still had a pulse.

Chapter 8

I didn't argue when David insisted that I keep his cell phone so the 911 operator could stay on the line with me while he waited downstairs for the ambulance. Her name was Karen and she had a professionally soothing voice that I found reassuring nonetheless. She used my name a lot; I had the feeling she'd been trained to do that.

"How're you doing, Kate?"

I told her I was doing fine. Cy, on the other hand, was a mess. One eye was almost swollen shut and his nose was still bleeding. I thought I should get some ice for it out of the freezer, but Karen told me not to touch anything and to wait for the paramedics.

"Is there some place comfortable you can sit and still keep your eye on him, Kate?"

"Yes." I started to sit on a kitchen chair, but opted for the sofa near the sliding doors instead.

Cy groaned.

I ran over to him. "Cy! It's Kate." I crouched down and gently touched his arm. "Who did this to you?"

He didn't respond.

"What's happening, Kate?" the calm in Karen's voice wavered.

"I thought he was coming around. But he's not responding."

Cy started wheezing.

"He's having trouble breathing," I said louder than I'd intended. "He's a bad asthmatic."

"I want you to stay calm, Kate. Can you do that for me?"

"Yes."

"Good," Karen said. "Does he use an inhaler?"

"Yes. Also smelling salts."

"Okay, Kate. I want you to check his pockets and see if he's got them."

Cy's pockets were empty. "My God, where are they? He's never without them."

"Calm down, Kate. Maybe they fell on the floor."

I probed the rug with my fingers, methodically feeling the area around his body. "They're not here." I crouched even lower to check under the sofa.

"What are you doing?"

I stood up abruptly and bumped my head on a floor lamp. A huge man eyed me curiously from the doorway. He was well over six feet – he had to be at least 6'4". He strode into the room followed by two uniformed policemen. Their deferential attitude made it obvious who was in charge.

A young woman with streaked blond hair and a burly middle-aged man pushed past him. They carried a stretcher into the room and hurried over to Cy.

"I was looking for his asthma inhaler," I said to the man.

"Who are you talking to, Kate?" Karen asked.

"The police just got here," I explained into the phone.

"What about the paramedics?"

"They're here too," I said.

"That's good. May I speak with one of the officers please?"

I handed the cell phone to the tall man. "The 911 operator wants to talk to you."

The woman with the stretcher finished placing an oxygen mask on Cy and looked up at me. "Do you know if he takes any medication?" She had a kind, reassuring voice.

"He has bad asthma. He always has an inhaler with him. And smelling salts."

The woman began searching for them until I said, "They're gone. That's what I was looking for."

The tall man handed David's phone back to me. "I'm Detective Matt Warren. I've asked Mr. Sobel to wait in his office so that you and I could have a chance to chat. Step into the hallway, please."

I rolled up the sleeves of the oversized trench coat David had given me and entered the hallway. Warren glanced at the bruises on my arm and frowned.

"It's okay," he said in a gentler voice. "Just tell me everything you can remember."

I told him what had happened and about the fight I'd overheard Cy having with the same man earlier in the day.

"You're sure he's the same guy?"

"Pretty sure. He had the same voice. Hoarse. Like he had bad laryngitis."

"No idea who he was?"

I shook my head. "But I think Cy suspected he was hanging around the theater."

"Why?"

I explained about the falling light fixture and Cy's strange suspicion that someone was up on the catwalk.

"You're sure no one was up there?"

"Not that I saw."

Warren was silent for a moment as he jotted some notes in a small spiral notebook. Then he said, "I know you couldn't see his face, but how about the rest of him? For example, was he tall or short?"

"Tall," I said.

"Tall as me?"

"A few inches shorter," I said. "I'm guessing maybe six feet."

"What color was his skin?"

I tried to picture him as he pinned me to the railing. "It was so dark. I can't be a hundred percent certain, but I'm pretty sure he was white. Maybe Hispanic. His skin was on the darker side. Sort of olive."

"Did he have an accent?"

I shook my head again.

"What happened after you fought him off?"

"He jumped over the railing. I looked down and saw him limping, so I think he was hurt."

Detective Warren removed a walkie-talkie clipped to his belt. "You there, Al?"

A voice came on following a burst of static. "Affirmative."

"Perp jumped from the second floor onto the embankment. Check for footprints."

Glancing indifferently in my direction, he raised his index finger and left me standing in the hallway as he stepped back into the Green Room. "Check the local hospitals. Witness saw a tall male limping, so he may be hurt."

He rejoined me in the hallway. "Do you know any reason why someone would want to harm Cy Williams?"

I shook my head again. "Look – can't we sit down somewhere?"

"Sure. Sorry - tough night, huh?" He smiled and I noticed his dimples for the first time. "Follow me."

He led the way to David's office and rapped twice on the open door. Without waiting for a response, he stood to one side and gestured for me to enter in front of him.

David rose from his desk and joined me on the black leather sofa. Detective Warren made himself comfortable in one of the armchairs. He directed his first question at David, "What can you tell me about Cy Williams?"

"Cy is Director-In-Residence at Omnibus," David said. "He also runs a teen acting program during the school year."

"Could one of the older kids have had it in for him? Maybe someone who's graduated?"

David and I both shook our heads.

"Cy has great rapport with the kids," David said.

"Someone in the cast?"

I shook my head. "No one has a raspy, hoarse voice like that."

"Did you notice anything unusual in his behavior lately? Besides what happened with the light fixture."

"Only that he's been very up and down emotionally," I said.

"Meaning?"

"Cy's always been temperamental. But lately … there've been more outbursts than usual. And some of his interpretations seem a little … off."

"What kind of interpretations?"

"Artistic. Character motivation, wardrobe – that sort of thing."

"Are you saying the play's not ready to open?" David interrupted.

"It needs a lot of reworking."

I looked at the detective and explained, "Cy's a brilliant director - everyone knows that. Which is why some of his decisions seem a little out of step."

David started to ask me something else, but Detective Warren motioned for him to keep silent.

"Ms. Sachs, besides the argument you overheard today, have you ever heard Cy Williams argue with anyone else?"

I laughed. "Cy argues with everyone. He's … eccentric. Opinionated."

"But who does he argue with?"

I wanted to be truthful, but I hesitated for fear he'd blow what I said out of proportion. "All of us. I argued with him myself today - over one of my scenes."

"But specifically - who else have you heard him arguing with?"

I didn't like where this was headed. "No one in particular. Like I said - everyone argues with him." I had no intention of giving him Jake's name. Jake didn't have a hoarse voice. Nor did anyone else. And we all had arguments with Cy.

"Ms. Sachs - please. Whatever it is you're not telling me - I'll find out anyway."

I stood up and spoke quietly, reining in my emotions. "Detective Warren, I have nothing further to tell you. I'm tired and I want to go home. If you think of any more questions, feel free to call me in the morning."

From the look on his face, I could tell that he knew he'd pushed me too far. He stood up and looked at David. "Mr. Sobel, I need the addresses and phone numbers of everyone connected with the play."

David opened the top drawer of his desk and rifled through some papers. I recognized the contact list as he handed it to the detective.

"When's your next rehearsal?" Warren asked me.

"Monday. We're off for the weekend."

He scribbled something on two cards and handed one to each of us. "If you think of anything else, call me. My home phone and cell number are on the back."

Chapter 9

The last train to New York had departed hours ago. It was past 2 AM and I didn't have the energy to look for a hotel. Grudgingly, I offered David a spare bedroom. As we walked towards the car, I felt too warm in the trench coat I was still wearing and tossed it into the back seat before driving home.

We drove the short distance from Westport to my loft in Norwalk. A bunch of kids were hanging out in front of a bodega on South Main, smoking. Most were teenagers, although some looked even younger. We drove past them and rounded the corner onto Washington Street where a string of restaurants and bars filled with yuppies even at this hour lined the street. At the end of the block, I turned right onto Water and continued down the dark alleyway leading to the parking lot underneath my building. The parking attendant had gone off duty.

"Is it safe here?" David asked.

"No. I get mugged every night when I get home."

"Sorry. I didn't mean …"

"Don't worry about it."

We parked the car and entered the building through the basement. Fluorescent lighting ran down the middle of the ceiling, illuminating the cracks in the cement flooring. The elevator took us to the top where my loft occupied the entire sixth floor. When the doors opened, I shoved my foot in between them so they wouldn't close until I'd finished turning my key in the lock next to the sixth floor button.

"What's that for?" David asked.

"So the elevator won't open on my floor unless I buzz the person in. Discourages unwanted visitors."

"Oh."

I fumbled with my keys and unlocked the top and bottom bolts on my front door.

"Had any problems?" David looked around as if he expected one to materialize.

I shook my head. "Paranoia from living in the city too long."

I flung open the door and held it for David.

"Wow! This is some place."

This was true.

My living room was an open space with a spectacular view of the Long Island Sound. The lights from the boats on the water reflected off a mirrored wall to the right of the door that made the room look bigger than it really was.

"Was this all here when you bought it?" David asked.

"Nope - raw space. I bought it after I landed a couple of commercials. A friend of mine is an architect. He designed it for me for free."

"Impressive."

It was. Unfortunately so was my mortgage, and I worried constantly that I'd be forced to sell. Keeping up with all the bills was becoming increasingly difficult. Not that my family wouldn't have been willing to help me had I asked, but I would have rather died than let them know I was having trouble making ends meet.

I kicked my shoes off. "Make yourself comfortable."

"Thanks." David wandered around the room admiring the photographs on my tabletops.

The living room was painted a gray-blue. Brown leather armchairs provided seating opposite two burgundy chenille sofas sitting catty-corner to one another. In front of them within easy reach stood a glass coffee table.

"Want a drink?" I asked.

"Vodka and tonic, if you've got."

"Mmmm. I think I'll join you." I walked over to the bar. David followed.

I fixed his drink and handed it to him. We clinked glasses. David stepped closer and kissed me lightly on the mouth. In one swift movement, he relieved me of my drink, placing it on top of the bar next to his. Then he folded me in his arms and kissed me harder, running his fingertips up and down my bare arms.

I shivered. David was a very good kisser.

When we finally separated, he looked at me with a distinctly amorous gleam in his green eyes.

"Let me show you to your room," I said.

He looked extremely disappointed.

"I'm too exhausted to do you justice."

He smiled. "I can wait."

I opened the windows before getting into bed and switching off the light on my night table. The lapping of the waves was soothing. My thoughts drifted to David. *What was I thinking? He's my boss, for chrissakes. Plus he's arrogant and vain. The man can't pass a mirror without looking at himself.* I closed my eyes and concentrated on relaxing each muscle in my body starting with my toes until finally I drifted off to sleep.

Robert and I were walking through Central Park in early spring. The trees were covered in white and pink blossoms, and the grass smelled freshly cut. We held hands and walked uptown towards the 72nd Street boat basin. Robert stopped and pulled me towards him. I felt his breath on my face as he leaned in close and kissed me.

We were passing a playground when a horde of schoolchildren, no older than seven or eight, swooped down on us. They ran between us, deliberately forcing us to separate. I laughed at a small girl who dared me to chase her. She wiggled her fingers in her ears and stuck her tongue out at me until her teacher intervened and warned her to mind her manners. I waved goodbye and then turned back to Robert. He was gone.

I heard the planes before I saw them. Then one by one, I watched them crash into the elegant apartment houses lining Fifth Avenue to the east. The buildings burst into flames before imploding in a cloud of debris.

I ran out of the park towards the wreckage, finally catching sight of Robert who was helping an elderly woman retreat from the rubble. I ran towards him, but as I got closer, he morphed into the man in the black mask with the hoarse voice.

I awoke with a start, my heart pounding. I switched on the light, relieved to find myself in my own bed surrounded by familiar yellow walls and a Chagall poster I'd purchased years ago in Paris. The digital clock on my nightstand said it was 4:50 AM.

I'd had these nightmares before, especially when I was attracted to someone. Okay – so maybe my family wasn't completely off the mark about the lack of closure thing with Robert interfering with my social life. But the guy in the mask was a new touch.

I thought about his odd voice. Then my thoughts wandered to the people I knew who'd had fights with Cy. None of them had laryngitis. But given Cy's record at Omnibus, there were probably lots of others he'd antagonized that I didn't even know about. One of them could have hired Hoarse Voice to take Cy out. *Take him out?* I was starting to think like a hackneyed crime writer.

I got up and went into the bathroom, splashed cold water on my face, and brushed my teeth. As I was rummaging in my closet for running clothes, I noticed some things I'd forgotten to take to the cleaners neatly piled in one corner. I placed them on the bed so that I wouldn't forget them again. Then I dressed quickly and scribbled a note to David before quietly letting myself out of the apartment, double-locking the doors behind me.

I tossed the cleaning into the back seat and got into the Audi. The garage was deserted, save for one other car that exited behind me. A few early morning commuters drove in the direction of the

Norwalk train station. I headed the opposite way and drove the short distance to Compo Beach in Westport, parking near Joey's By the Sea. The snack bar was closed this early in the morning. The crowds would swarm later on, but for now all was serene.

I walked to the water's edge and did some yoga stretches and other warm-ups, enjoying the briny scent of the sea. The sunrise was spectacular. I stood there admiring the pink and lavender ribbons that streaked the sky. A gust of wind came up suddenly, and I felt goose bumps prickle my arms and legs. It was time to get moving.

I jogged along the beach, slowly at first, until I found my rhythm and picked up speed. My foot caught on some shells and I almost twisted my ankle. I slowed down and walked up the steep incline until I reached the boardwalk and resumed running. The sun was rising in the sky as I passed the playground and rounded the cove, running under a grove of trees where wild green parakeets chattered noisily. Legend had it that they'd escaped from a pet store years ago and had managed to adapt to Connecticut's climate, a freak of nature admired by everyone.

As I headed back towards my car, I noticed a man fishing out on the jetty and a few more joggers working their way along the coastline. A woman in black biker shorts and a sleeveless bright orange T-shirt zoomed past me. My competitive nature kicked in and I forced myself into overdrive and ran faster.

By the time I got near the changing area, I was exhausted and drenched in sweat. I did a cool-down walk and some stretches before heading inside for a drink of water.

I entered the changing area and reacted to the sudden stillness by scanning the maze of whitewashed lockers, making sure that no feet were visible under any of the doors. Then I stepped around the corner to the water fountain and let it run for a while, angry that I'd allowed the events of the night before to unnerve me this way.

By the time I grew conscious of the foul body odor, it was too late. I was bent over the fountain taking a long drink and started to turn around to investigate. A hairy arm grabbed me around the neck and jerked me upright. Something sharp pricked my neck and I froze. He tightened his forearm against my windpipe, making it hard to breathe, and forced me to stand with my back tight against the front of his body.

"If you want to live, don't say a word until I tell you to." The hoarse voice was unmistakable. "Nod if you understand."

I did as I was told.

He lowered his arm from my windpipe, gripping me around my chest instead in a tight hold. With his other hand, he held the tip of the knife to my neck.

"You have something that belongs to me..." He pricked my neck with the knife for emphasis in a staccato rhythm as he completed the sentence, "and I - want it - back."

I was frozen in place, too terrified to move. But then I felt his sweat seep through the back of my shirt and his penis harden against me. *In your dreams, asshole.* I kicked back, aiming for his groin. I couldn't reach it and caught his shin instead.

He spun me around and I saw that, like the night before, his face was hidden by a black mask. His arms and legs were visible, however, through black running shorts that had deep pockets where he must have hidden the mask before entering the changing area. He backhanded me hard across the cheek.

I stumbled backward into one of the stalls. The door gave way for me and then slammed shut in his face. I pulled it open again and banged it into him as hard as I could. He swore at me as I sprinted past him out of the locker room.

I ran towards my car, feeling for my keys in the pocket of my running shorts. When I was within a few feet of it, I looked behind me. No one. I got in, locked the doors, and backed out of the space. I started to drive away, but then changed my mind. *Show yourself, you bastard. Let me see your face.* I waited with the car idling, checking all the mirrors in a methodical sweep. Several men went by, but none of them even glanced in my direction. As the rush of adrenaline slowed, my thoughts came into clearer focus. I'd managed to escape him twice. The next time I might not be so lucky. Whatever had happened between him and Cy, he thought I was involved.

The woman jogger I'd noticed earlier ran past me towards the changing area. She jolted me into realizing that if I didn't call the police, someone else might get hurt. I reached for my cell phone sitting in the ashtray and, without taking my eyes off the road, punched in 9-1-1. Then I waited for the police to arrive in a replay of the night before.

Chapter 10

When I entered the apartment, David took one look at me and sprang to his feet like I was Jack The Ripper.

"My God, what happened?"

"He was at the beach," I said.

"Jesus. Did you call the police?"

"Yes." I hurried into the bedroom and examined myself in the mirror over the dresser. My cheek was swollen and red, and there was dried blood on my neck. Just the look I was aiming for on opening night. I continued into the bathroom and turned the water on in the sink.

David followed me to the bathroom doorway. "What did they say?"

"Nothing. They just wrote down what I told them."

"Are you hurt badly?" David asked. "Maybe you should go to the hospital. Or at least have your father check you out."

"No! Don't you dare call him."

The hurt expression on David's face made me continue in a more solicitous tone. "I'm fine, David - really. It looks worse than it is. I'm more shaken up than anything else."

"Well at least let me call that detective - what's his name?" David rifled through his pockets and withdrew a business card. "Warren. Matt Warren."

"David – please. Not now. I'm sure the police will fill him in."

David looked at the floor a moment before continuing in a quiet voice. "Did you see his face this time?"

"No. He had the same black mask over his head."

He watched while I splashed cool water on my face. "What happened?"

I looked at David's reflection in the mirror and saw that he was steeling himself for my reply. "He didn't rape me, if that's what you're thinking. Just beat the crap out of me."

David came up behind me and wrapped his arms around me. "You smell like a skunk."

I broke away and gave him a look, then turned on the shower. "He thinks Cy gave me something."

"He said that?"

"Not in those words exactly."

David looked confused. "Then what did he say?"

"That I have something that belongs to him. But that makes no sense unless it's something that Cy gave me last night."

"But Cy was unconscious!"

"You and I know that, but he may not." I pushed my hair out of my eyes and noticed David look at my hand. It was shaking.

"We need to get you to a hospital," he said, frowning.

"The only thing I want to do now is take a shower and wash that man's sweat off me."

David grinned. "Can I watch?"

"No."

I ran the water in the shower as hot as I could stand it and scrubbed myself raw. In a moment of weakness, I leaned against the shower wall and allowed myself a good cry. It made me feel a little better. Leaving my hair wet, I threw on jeans and a T-shirt before joining David in the dining room. He'd made a fresh pot of coffee and had toasted some bagels he'd scrounged up in the kitchen. He handed me a towel in which he'd wrapped some ice that I applied to my cheek.

I wolfed down a bagel. While I was toasting another, I realized David had something on his mind. "What?"

"When you're through eating, I'm taking you to the hospital."

"I feel fine."

"You don't look fine. Give me your keys. I'll drive," he said.

"You're just dying to get behind the wheel of my car."

"Nothing gets past you." He held out his hand. "Keys."

I handed them to him. "One scratch and you're dead."

Chapter 11

A disadvantage of being a doctor's daughter is that everyone knows you in the hospital. The minute I set foot in the Emergency Room with David, the entire staff converged on me to ask what had happened. I even skipped triage; the admitting nurse whisked me into an examination room ahead of the other patients who shot me withering looks.

Inside, faded floral curtains were all that separated me from the patients on either side of my bed. To my right, what sounded like an old man called to the nurse in a pitiful voice.

"Aw shut the hell up," the woman on my other side snapped.

"Hey," I said, "the man's sick. Show some compassion."

"I'm not talkin' to you. I'm talkin' to him, dumb-ass."

I lifted my head off the pillow. "What did you call me?"

"You heard me. That old coot's been moanin' since he got in here."

"He's probably in pain," I said.

"Yeah. Yeah."

The old guy groaned again and the woman told him to shut up again, and on it went until I finally managed to tune them both out and fall asleep. I had no idea how much time had passed when a doctor came in and woke me. He introduced himself as Dr. Silver. In his late twenties, he was short with dark hair and tired brown eyes. Every time he touched my cheek, I moaned and the woman made tsk-tsking noises that I tried to ignore.

"You're lucky," Dr. Silver said. "Just bruises."

If he thought this was luck, his life had to be a real mess. He was writing discharge instructions when my father walked in. He took one look at me and I thought I was going to have to give him the bed.

"How'd you find out I was here?"

"Every nurse in the ER called me. What did you expect?" He picked up my chart and read through it carefully.

"Did you hear about Cy, Dad?"

"David just told me. Why didn't you call me?"

"It was late and I didn't want to worry you. I'm sorry."

Dad shook his head. "Thank God you're okay."

"Any chance we could get in to see Cy?"

"Are you sure you feel up to it?"

"Absolutely."

He smiled. "Get dressed and I'll use my influence."

David joined us as my father led the way down a long white hallway with red and yellow doors that should have made the place seem more cheerful, but didn't. The scent of cleaning fluid and antiseptic followed us onto the elevator, overwhelmed momentarily by the smell of greasy fries. A large woman in the back of the elevator was carrying a McDonald's bag. My stomach growled, which everyone pretended not to hear.

Intensive care was on the third floor. On our way to the nurse's station, we passed a grim waiting room where a couple sat on a torn vinyl couch without talking. A nurse directed us to a cubicle around the corner.

Cy looked dreadful. A plastic breathing tube protruded from his mouth. His breathing sounded ragged, punctuated by a snorting sound he made every time he inhaled.

My father picked up the chart at the foot of Cy's bed. He was wearing his *don't worry everything's fine* doctor's face, but I knew better.

"Can he hear us?" I asked.

"I doubt it. He's in a coma."

One of the nurses came in to check Cy's IV and take his temperature.

"What's his prognosis?" David asked my father.

"Hard to say, but the longer he stays unconscious, the worse it is."

David cleared his throat. "He's not coming back to work anytime soon, is he?"

My father looked at David over the top of his reading glasses. "If I were you, I'd look for a new director."

Chapter 12

I dropped my clothing off at the cleaners before driving over to Starbucks. It was 11:30, but judging from the line, the whole town had just woken up. David ordered a latté and I asked for a large regular coffee. We found a seat in the back with a view of the river. People pretended not to notice my bruised face, and then glared at David with loathing. I thought it was funny, but he was mortified.

David took the lid off his cup and stirred the foam into the espresso. "Just how bad is the play at this point?"

I took a deep breath and plunged in. "The staging is awkward and the way Brad's playing his part doesn't make sense. Some of the costumes are wrong for the characters. Carla's aware of this, only she hasn't been able to convince Cy."

David stared at me like I'd just told him he had six months to live.

"Is it fixable?"

"Yes, if everyone pulls together and starts playing the scenes the way Jake wrote them. It's really a fabulous play."

Poor David. He looked at the river as if he wanted to jump in. "Where am I going to find a director to take over this late?"

"David…"

He turned away from the river and looked at me questioningly.

"Let me do it."

From his expression, it was clear that I'd taken him by surprise.

"It's not that I don't have confidence in you, Kate. I do. But you don't have enough experience as a director. Besides, you need to concentrate on acting your part in the play."

I leaned in closer across the table. "I have experience directing. Maybe not a Broadway tryout, but I have directed in regional theaters before. Please, David. I know exactly how to fix this show. No outside director can possibly come up to speed in time. And as for my part in the play, stop worrying. I can handle both. I wouldn't offer to do it otherwise."

David looked at me dubiously.

"Give me a chance, David. You won't regret it. You have my word."

He regarded me in silence for a moment. Finally his expression brightened and he smiled. "Okay. But I have to clear it with Jake first. Assuming he agrees, what can I do to make things easier for you?"

I thought about this for a moment. "Brad is going to have a lot of trouble taking direction from me. He argued with Cy all the time and interfered with the other actors. If I'm going to whip this play into shape, I'll need everyone's cooperation. And a chance to bring some of my own interpretations to the play - providing, as you say, that Jake agrees with them."

David nodded. "Done."

Chapter 13

I was poring over the script and jotting down notes on changes I wanted to make when the downstairs buzzer sounded. I wasn't expecting anyone, so I hesitated before pressing the *Talk* button, instantly irritated with myself for feeling so jumpy.

"Who is it?"

"It's me," my mother's voice said. "I'm with Gramps and Uncle Abe. Can we come up?"

The family police.

I buzzed them in and ran to the bedroom to check myself out in the mirror. Makeup? There wasn't enough makeup in the world to help me. My cheek was so swollen that my eye was practically hidden. No wonder I was having trouble reading.

The doorbell rang. I popped my collar up in an attempt to hide the cuts on my neck and went to answer the door.

My mother sat next to me on one of the sofas, obviously trying to hold herself together. Gramps took one armchair and Uncle Abe took the other. Three pairs of the same deep-set blue eyes stared at me expectantly. My mother was so tense I could see the outline of her jaw muscles as she ground her teeth. She looked like she wanted to bite someone. Uncle Abe tapped his foot up and down while Grandpa Max stroked his moustache thoughtfully.

Finally Gramps said, "Do the police have any leads?"

Uncle Abe shook his head as if the question had been directed at him.

"They must have by now," I said.

Uncle Abe jumped to his feet. "You can't depend on the cops. We're hiring a bodyguard."

"No you're not," I said. "Let the police do their job. They'll catch him."

Uncle Abe shook his head again and began pacing the room. He was used to being obeyed – just not by me. I don't like taking orders; in that way, we're a lot alike.

"It wouldn't be forever," my mother said. "Just 'till they catch him." She turned to my grandfather. "Right, Dad?"

"A bodyguard's a good idea, Katie." Grandpa Max stood up and reached under his jacket for something that seemed to be attached to his belt. "But I'd feel better if you had one of these." He held out a black pistol, carefully pointing the barrel at the floor.

We all stared at him.

"Max - how long have you had that thing?" Uncle Abe asked this with so much admiration in his voice, you'd have thought my grandfather had just won the Nobel Prize.

"Since I moved into the city."

"Where'd you get it?"

"Remember George Cornwall? Used to sell me dental supplies?"

"Sure," Uncle Abe said.

"George sells guns now."

My grandfather fiddled with the gun, apparently removing the bullets, and then handed it to me. I took it by the handle, careful not to touch the trigger nonetheless.

My mother inched further down the couch, looking at my grandfather as if he'd lost his mind.

"Here, let me show you." My grandfather took the gun from me and pointed it at the wall, planting his feet on the floor parallel to each other. He looked like he was auditioning for *Law And Order*. "You hold the gun in your right hand and support it with your left. Then aim at your target and squeeze the trigger firmly."

"Careful!" my mother said.

"It's not loaded."

He handed the gun back to me and I held it the way he'd demonstrated. It felt heavy in my hand, but powerful. Like a tennis racquet with just the right grip. "This seems a little drastic," I said. "My luck, I'll shoot myself with it."

"Not if you know how to use it," he said.

A few shooting lessons together with my kickboxing classes - I'd be all set.

We were interrupted by the downstairs buzzer. My apartment was starting to feel like Grand Central Station.

"Who is it?" I yelled into the intercom.

"Jordan."

Jordan Hollis and I met in Brownies at the start of second grade and have been best friends ever since. Our families are separated by a cultural chasm that's as wide as the Grand Canyon. She went to Cotillion; I got Bat Mitzvahed. My mother traipsed the world photographing wars; hers set fashion trends at Vogue. But over the years we've managed to build a bridge nonetheless. We've celebrated one another's successes, commiserated over failures, and helped each other recover from dozens of boyfriends.

I went into the hallway to wait for her by the elevator, grateful to escape my family, if only for a moment. When the doors opened, Jordan was stuffing something back into her bag. Tall with pale white skin and sculpted features, she liked dressing in all black - a reaction to her mother, the Fashion Nazi, who preferred bright colors. That day she was wearing black Capris and a black T-shirt.

She stepped off the elevator and papers tumbled out of a messenger bag she tried unsuccessfully to hoist back onto her shoulder. Jordan could be a bit clumsy at times. A leather Coach bag was twisted around her elbow, perilously open at the top. Some of the contents spilled onto the carpet in slow motion. First a comb, then a lipstick. She righted the bag momentarily, but it slipped again, this time ejecting a collection of pens, pencils, a micro recorder, and a Metro North schedule. What the schedule was for, I'm not sure since Jordan always made the trip from New York City in her car, a racing green Mini Cooper with a black top and thin white stripe.

I helped her retrieve everything from the floor and stood up.

Her eyes widened as she took in my battered face. "My God, Kate! What happened?" She bent down to examine me more closely. "Are you in a lot of pain?"

"It looks worse than it is. I'll tell you about it inside."

She didn't move. "What's that for?"

I followed her line of sight until my eyes rested on the gun I was still holding in my hand. "Long story." I gestured towards my front door. "Family's here."

Jordan followed me inside where I handed Grandpa Max his gun back.

"What a wonderful surprise," my mother said. "Are you up here on assignment, Jordan? Or just to visit?"

"I'm here because of this." Jordan removed the New York Post from her messenger bag and unfurled it for us to see.

The headline read, *Director Near Death in Westport*. In smaller letters underneath: *Actress Kate Sachs Held For Questioning*.

I grabbed the paper out of Jordan's hand and opened it.

"What's it say?" Uncle Abe asked.

I read out loud, "Actress Kate Sachs was held for questioning last night in the attempted murder of director, Cy Williams. Williams has been directing Sachs in a new play about to open at Omnibus Playhouse in Westport, CT, a town located along Connecticut's fashionable gold coast. A source that asked not to be identified told the Post, 'Sachs had plenty of motive. She wanted to direct and now the way's been cleared for her to take over.' Producer David Sobel confirmed that Sachs is jumping into the role of director…" I stopped reading. "This is unbelievable. They think I tried to kill Cy?"

"Stop worrying," Jordan said. "I convinced Al to let me cover the story. Who'd believe the Post?"

Al Harper was Jordan's editor at The New York Times where she worked as an investigative reporter specializing in high profile stories. She'd even won a Pulitzer for her coverage of a well-known politician indicted for embezzling campaign funds.

"Besides," she continued, "it gives me a professional excuse to keep my eye on you – and judging from how you look, you could use a bodyguard."

Uncle Abe shot me a look.

I glared at Jordan, running my finger across my neck in a gesture that told her to cut it out.

Throughout this exchange, my mother had been searching for something in her handbag. She pulled out a small digital Nikon she keeps with her at all times and started taking pictures of me, framing close-ups of my face.

"Stop!" I said.

"It's evidence," my mother said. "You didn't beat yourself up."

"Your mom's right," Jordan said. "It'll make a great counter-story to the Post. Not to mention the credit I'll get for the Annie Rosenthal photos."

The phone rang and I sprang to the kitchen to answer it, grateful for the escape.

"Hi Kate. It's David."

"David! How could you do this to me?"

Everyone stopped talking in the living room.

"What are you talking about?" he said.

"Have you seen the Post?"

"No."

"It says I had a motive for wanting Cy dead so I could take over as director - and that you confirmed it!"

"I did not." He was practically sputtering. "They asked what I planned to do about Cy being in the hospital and I said I'd asked you to direct in his place. Period."

My mother and Jordan had crept into the kitchen and were almost standing on top of me.

There was silence on the other end of the phone. Finally David said, "Kate, I'm so sorry. I called to ask if you'd have dinner with me tonight."

"Sorry, my family's here and my best friend just came up from the city. Rain check?"

"Sure." He sounded extremely gloomy.

Chapter 14

By the time my family left, Jordan and I both needed a drink. We were hungry besides, so we opted for Donovan's where we could satisfy both urges without going broke.

Donovan's was an old saloon at the end of Washington Street with dark wooden booths along one wall and tables crowded close together in the middle of the floor and by the windows near the entrance. A bar extended nearly the length of the restaurant on the opposite wall with a television mounted above it at each end.

We stood in the doorway and waited for the host to seat us. It was early, so the crowd hadn't formed yet, but he looked harassed already as he approached us and led the way to one of the booths.

As I told her everything that had happened, Jordan took notes in a black moleskin notebook I'd seen her use a thousand times. It felt good to talk things over with her, especially the jitters that I couldn't seem to shake.

"Kate – you wouldn't be human if you didn't feel some kind of residual fear. Anyone would after going through what you did." She took a bite of her salad. "What I can't figure out is how he tampered with the light fixture without anyone seeing him."

I stopped eating. "But... that could have been just an accident. The other lights were fine when they checked."

The fear that crept over me must have shown in my face because Jordan looked sorry that she'd brought it up.

"Possibly," she said. "But let Abe hire a bodyguard - just to be on the safe side. Okay?"

As we walked back to my apartment, the bars and restaurants were filling up rapidly with yuppies ready to party all night. Around the corner, a group of teenagers too young to get into the clubs were hanging out in front of the bodega drinking beer and smoking cigarettes. From the acrid smell, cigarettes weren't all they were smoking. One of the girls gave me a shy smile. I smiled back, startled to see my downstairs neighbor's kid. She couldn't have been older than fifteen. I doubted her mom knew she was hanging out with these punks.

We stepped off the elevator onto the sixth floor hallway. I was fumbling with my keys when Jordan grabbed my arm and pointed to the front door. It was ajar.

"Do you have your mace with you?" I whispered.

She nodded.

Carrying mace was a habit we'd acquired after a friend had been mugged a few years ago. I fished mine out of my handbag, wishing that I had Max's gun instead. The door squeaked when I started to open it and we froze. When nothing happened, we squeezed through, not wanting to risk more noise by opening it wider.

My apartment was a wreck. The contents of my hall closet had been dumped onto the floor of the entryway. From where we were standing, we could see pillows and books strewn all over the living room.

I started to move forward, but Jordan grabbed my arm again and pulled me back. She whispered, "Kate – don't. He could still be here."

Had I been thinking rationally, I would have listened to her and retreated out the door and called the police. Instead I wrenched my arm free and lunged ahead, feeling violated and enraged and wanting payback.

There was no one in the living room and dining area. Nor was there anyone in the kitchen. However, my counters were covered in a sticky mess of coffee, flour, and sugar that had been dumped out of their canisters. Even my refrigerator had been rifled and my trashcan overturned.

We crept down the hallway to the bedrooms with our mace held out in front of us. Cautiously I opened the door to the first bedroom we came to and examined it from the doorway. Everything had been tossed. A ruffle made it impossible to see underneath the bed, and the door to the closet was shut. Jordan motioned for me to check under the bed while she stood guard in front of the closet. Stooping down, I lifted the ruffle with one hand, gripping the mace with my other, prepared to spray it in his face. No one.

I walked quietly over to Jordan who wrenched the closet door open. Again no one.

We proceeded more confidently to the next bedroom, which contained little else besides my out of season clothing that I kept in a dresser. The drawers had been emptied onto the floor and the bare mattress had been flipped off the box spring. The only possible hiding place was the closet, but the door was open and we could see that it was empty.

I almost lost it when I went into my bedroom and saw my Chagall poster torn off the wall with its back slit open.

Jordan put her hand on my shoulder. "You can get it fixed."

We made certain no one was in the room and then went into my bathroom. The violated feeling I'd had upon first entering the apartment had been mounting with every room we examined, but this was a real shock. Someone had emptied every item in my medicine cabinet and dumped out everything I kept in the shower: shampoo, makeup, vitamins, talcum powder, allergy pills. Everything was ruined.

We called 911 and for the third time in twenty-four hours, I waited for the police to arrive.

Chapter 15

Two uniformed police officers examined the chaos from the entryway. They introduced themselves as Sergeant O'Brian and Sergeant Perrone.

"What a mess," O'Brian said, shaking his head. He had a broad, open face and a receding hairline.

"Have you seen a doctor?" Perrone asked. "You look terrible."

I took a moment to process this. "I look worse than I feel."

Jordan broke in impatiently. "Do you have any leads?"

"Who are you?" O'Brian asked.

"Jordan Hollis."

"My best friend," I explained.

O'Brian noted something in his book, and then looked up at me with kind blue eyes. "Good you're not alone. Why don't you tell us what happened here."

We explained what happened from the time we left the apartment to go to dinner until we returned and found the door unlocked.

"Did you turn the security lock on in the elevator before you went to dinner?" O'Brian asked.

I wanted to kick myself for having forgotten. "No."

"Big mistake." Perrone hitched his pants up higher around the spare tire around his middle. He had bushy eyebrows that moved when he talked. "Anyone could've ridden right up to the sixth floor."

Jordan flashed him a look and I could tell she had to restrain herself from saying "duh" out loud.

He went over to the door and squatted down to examine it. "Guy forced the lock. You can see the scratch marks."

O'Brian walked over to see for himself. "Yup."

Perrone straightened up. "Did you girls touch anything?"

I watched Jordan struggle to let the "you girls" comment slide by.

"We went through each room and made sure no one was still here, but we were careful not to touch anything," I said.

"Pretty gutsy," Perrone said with a smile. He had a gold front tooth. He wandered over to the home theater in the wall unit opposite the sofas and gave a low whistle. "If this was a robbery, they missed some great stuff."

O'Brian frowned at his partner and then looked back at me. "Take us through the apartment and see if anything's missing. You up to that?"

I nodded.

To Perrone, he said, "Let's get a photographer and the print techs in here ASAP."

We started with the hall closet in the entryway.

"Anything of value missing?" O'Brian asked me. "Furs - stuff like that?"

I shook my head. Then I glanced at Jordan and noticed that she had this vague expression she gets whenever she's trying to wrap her mind around something. She wandered into the living room and we all followed. Her eyes scanned the wall unit and the coffee table. Then she bent down to look underneath a small table in the corner of the room.

"Something's under here," she said.

"Don't touch anything," O'Brian said, coming over to take a look.

My navy blazer was under the table with the lining slashed to ribbons. The gratuitous violence of it all was upsetting and I suddenly felt shaky. I thrust my hands in my pockets and walked over to the wall unit, waiting for the feeling to pass.

The wall unit contained mostly memorabilia from past performances. It had been searched, yet nothing was broken despite the obvious fact that everything was out of place. At least it was obvious to me.

"Anything missing?" O'Brian asked.

"I don't think so."

"Something outta whack then?" he said.

"Things have been moved around."

Jordan came over and stood beside me, scrutinizing the wall unit. "At least nothing's broken."

We continued to the kitchen.

"Holy cow!" Perrone said, "What a mess. Maybe he was hungry and couldn't find anything he liked to eat so he got pissed off." He barked out a laugh. "Really stinks in here. You should clean out your refrigerator more often."

I saw O'Brian shoot Perrone a warning look. He examined the mess with a grim expression.

"The next time I think someone's about to ransack my apartment, I'll be sure to do that," I told Perrone. Then under my breath, "Damn him."

"He was obviously searching for something," Jordan said.

"Any ideas what that could have been, Ms. Sachs?" O'Brian's kind blue eyes had turned to steel. The atmosphere had turned decidedly frosty.

"No." I was suddenly so nervous I could feel my heart fluttering.

"If you have something on your mind, Officer, just say it." Jordan's voice was a low purr, a sure sign she was about to boil over.

"I want to know what someone could have been looking for in these canisters," O'Brian said.

"You mean drugs?" Jordan said.
"Are you involved with drugs, Ms. Sachs?" O'Brian asked.
"No!"

I stretched my neck from side to side until it cracked and saw Perrone wince. Then he and O'Brian exchanged a look and seemed to silently agree about something. When O'Brian's eyes rested on me again, the steel was gone and I realized that he believed me.

We'd almost finished walking through the whole apartment when the fingerprint technicians arrived with the photographer. They went over every inch of the apartment during the course of several hours.

On his way out, one of the technicians held up a clear plastic bag with something inside. "You can have this back as soon as we've gone over it in the lab. I'd be lost without mine."

It was a white iPod.

"That's not mine," I said. "I own a black one."

O'Brian overheard us and came over to see for himself. "You've never seen this before?" he asked me.

I shook my head.

"Well whaddaya know," the technician said. "Maybe we caught a break."

By the time they left, it was past ten o'clock. I was so exhausted I could barely breathe. My aches and pains had retreated to the outer edges of consciousness. It was like I didn't have a body at all.

Unfortunately, going to bed before cleaning up the mess was not an option. I was constitutionally incapable of it. I donned rubber gloves and grabbed a box of trash bags from under the sink.

Jordan groaned. "You can't be serious. You're falling off your feet!"

We tackled the kitchen together. Jordan held a trash bag open while I scooped everything up and dumped it in. When we finished bagging the detritus on the floor and countertops, I poured antibacterial cleaner into a bucket and filled it with water.

"You're mopping the floor now? Are you crazy?"

"I can't leave it like this."

Jordan rolled her eyes and stomped out of the kitchen. Moments later I heard her putting things back in the hall closet, mumbling under her breath that I was nuts.

It was two in the morning by the time we called it quits and collapsed in the living room. A stiff nightcap in hand, we each took a sofa and I channel-surfed until I found an old Humphrey Bogart movie - *Casablanca.*

I was focused on the movie until Jordan broke the silence. "Maybe you should move in with your folks until this thing blows over."

"No. I'm not letting some thug frighten me out of my own apartment."

Jordan sighed. "I thought you'd say that."

Someone was trying to shake me awake, but I was too exhausted to get up.

"Kate – wake up."

I opened my eyes.

"A Detective Warren is downstairs," Jordan said. "He wants to come up."

Chapter 16

I was still struggling to wake up when Matt Warren stepped into the room. My first impression was of a big sloppy guy looking at me like I was a lab specimen. He dangled a plastic Stew Leonard's grocery bag from one hand, while holding a Dunkin' Donuts bag in the crook of his other arm. I tried to sit up, but toppled back over, at which point, the detective quickly handed his bags to Jordan, knelt down on one knee in front of me, and scooped me upright onto the sofa.

With his nose only inches away from my own, I had the opportunity to observe him up close. He was younger than I'd first realized and his smile was slightly lopsided, although his dimples and the cleft in his chin more than offset any lack of symmetry. His eyes were hazel – orbs of brown flecked with amber - unsettling in the way they stared at me without blinking. He was dressed in a medium-blue T-shirt over a pair of jeans.

"How do you feel?" he asked.

"Sore."

We stared at each other for a few moments more.

"Want to lie back down?" he asked.

I assured him I'd be fine sitting up.

Jordan had been standing off to one side without saying anything. She had that vague look back on her face and I wondered what she was thinking.

"Did you two meet?" I asked.

"At the door," Jordan said.

The smell of coffee wafted from the Dunkin' Donuts bag. As if reading my mind, Jordan handed me a container, passed one to the detective, and kept another for herself.

"Why don't you two chat while I put breakfast on the table," she said. Gesturing towards one of the armchairs, she invited Detective Warren to make himself comfortable before disappearing into the kitchen.

He lowered his huge frame into the chair and pushed back the tab on his coffee lid, commuter style. Then he stretched his long legs out in front of him, crossing his feet at the ankles. His scuffed white sneakers had seen better days.

"I know you've been all through this with O'Brian and Perrone, but I'd really like to hear it from you myself." Although he said this politely, it was an order, which I found irritating. But in the spirit of cooperation, I did my best to describe the events of the prior day.

Detective Warren's eyes never left my face as he listened to me without interruption, his expression inscrutable. His stillness was unnerving. He let a few beats go by after I finished speaking, and then asked me matter-of-factly, "Why do you think someone was looking for drugs in your apartment?"

That miserable question again. "Why does everyone assume he was looking for drugs?"

"Because of the way he turned everything inside out. Do you have another explanation?"

"No! I realize how bad this looks, but all I can tell you is what I told O'Brian and Perrone. I've never been involved with drugs in my life."

Jordan must have been listening from the kitchen because she bounded into the room and announced that breakfast was on the table.

Detective Warren sprang up and offered to help me to my feet.

We filed into the kitchen where a feast was spread out on my kitchen table. Orange juice, smoked salmon, bagels, and all the accompaniments.

"You brought all this?" I asked.

"Least I could do," he said.

"That was extremely generous. Thank you."

"Do you bring breakfast to the victims in all your cases?" Jordan wanted to know.

I gave her a look, although looks rarely deterred Jordan.

The detective flashed his dimples. "No – this is a first."

He seemed to realize that more explanation was expected. "I spent the weekend babysitting for my niece and nephew so my brother and his wife could go to a wedding. I got home late last night and found a message on my machine about the attack at the beach and the break-in. I wanted to get to you first thing this morning, only I was hungry. So I brought breakfast." He sat down at the table without waiting to be invited. "Turns out we're practically ncighbors I live over on Washington. Besides, it's not every day I get a case involving my favorite actress." He grinned at me.

"You're a fan of *Young and In Love?*" Jordan asked.

Young and In Love was the teenage television drama I'd starred in when I was still in college. Now thanks to reruns on cable TV and the show's resurgence in popularity, my fans seemed to be coming back, albeit somewhat older, and were watching the show again faithfully.

"I only watch it because of Kate." He flashed another grin. "I've seen every play you've been in."

"Oh."

"Salmon?" He offered me the plate.

"Every play she's done?" Jordan asked.

"Even the first one - Season's Greetings. You won an OBIE for best actress."

I'd been busy smearing my bagel with cream cheese and looked up, surprised.

"I told you - I've seen everything you've done," he said.

"That's very flattering," I said. *Weird. But flattering.*

Few appreciate the delicate art of preparing the bagel to receive the lox. Each side has to be layered with just the right amount of cream cheese, smoked salmon, red onion, and tomato - in that order. I was absorbed in layering my bagel to perfection when Detective Warren interrupted me again.

"I thought your apartment was ransacked."

"It was," Jordan said. "But Kate is obsessive-compulsive. She had us cleaning until two this morning."

I positioned the last tomato slice on top of my bagel. "Liking things neat and clean doesn't make me obsessive-compulsive."

"Did you wash the clothes you were wearing at the beach when you were attacked?" Warren asked.

Jordan dipped her chin to her chest as she looked at him. "What do you think?"

"Did you, Kate?"

I'd have bet his fingers were crossed underneath the table while he waited for my answer.

"As a matter of fact," I said, "I forgot."

He exhaled loudly. "I'd like our forensics team to take a look, if you don't mind."

I did mind. The idea of handing him my sweaty jogging clothes was extremely disconcerting. "Is that really necessary?"

"Kate - what's the matter with you?" Jordan said. "Of course it's necessary."

"Your clothing could be important," Matt said. "I have evidence bags in my car. I'll get them after breakfast."

"What will forensics do with the clothing?" Jordan asked. I could tell she was itching to take notes.

"They'll examine it for hairs, sweat, blood traces - that sort of thing," Matt said.

"Which DNA databases will they query for a match?" Jordan asked.

The detective had just swallowed a mouthful of coffee and it went down the wrong pipe. He had such a nasty coughing fit, I found myself mentally reviewing the Heimlich maneuver. When he finally stopped choking, he said to Jordan, "Now I remember who you are. You write for the Times!" It sounded like an accusation. I half expected him to quote Miranda rights to her.

Jordan's eyes narrowed. "Before you keel over from shock, Detective Warren, let me remind you that Kate Sachs is my best friend. So please – don't treat me like the enemy."

Jordan and Matt faced off across the table. I felt like a boxing referee waiting for the bell to sound.

The detective flashed a wise-guy smile. "I thought we'd advanced to first names."

Jordan smiled in spite of herself. "Look – Matt - if you say something's off the record, that's where it stays." She poured herself another glass of juice and gave a wry smile. "What's with everyone? Don't you think reporters have any integrity?"

Matt Warren left around noon, taking my dirty clothes with him. On his way out, he scrawled his cell phone number across the top of his card and placed it on my kitchen table. "Here's another card. Call me twenty four hours a day. I mean it."

I was bone tired by the time Jordan left a short while later. All I wanted to do was lie down and go back to sleep. But with less than half a day remaining before rehearsals resumed with me in the director's chair, sleeping wasn't an option.

I curled up with the script on the window seat in the living room and opened the windows. The sea air that drifted into the room made me feel calmer, and I got to work.

Chapter 17

I knew exactly what had to be done to make the play work, but as I made notes in the margin of the script, I kept worrying about tomorrow's rehearsal. Was it possible to make so many changes this late in the game? I consoled myself with the thought that most of the actors and everyone on the crew knew the play was in trouble unless big changes were made.

I plunged into making phone calls to my newly inherited team, starting with Carla.

"Tell me whatever you need and it's yours," she said.

Maybe this wasn't going to be as bad as I'd imagined.

We spent the next half hour talking about which costume changes to make, and agreed to avoid any that were too complicated. When we'd accomplished as much as we could over the phone, I mustered the courage to ask her to come in at seven o'clock the next morning.

"Kate – stop being so apologetic. Everyone knows you're under the gun. Believe me, anyone gives you trouble, they'll have me to answer to."

I hung up with Carla with renewed confidence. I called Sparky next, followed by Jake. Both expressed enthusiasm for the changes I wanted to make.

I saved the most difficult call for last, anticipating that our stage manager, Russell Duby, would be upset that David hadn't asked him to direct in place of Cy.

By the fourth ring, it occurred to me that he might have seen my number on Caller ID and decided to ignore it. I was about to hang up when he finally picked up.

"Kate, oh fearless leader, how's the sexiest woman alive? David called me with the great news."

He sounded so insincere I wanted to punch him.

"Look, Russell, please can the sexist remarks. We all know the show's in serious trouble. We have a lot of work ahead of us to fix it, so let's pull together as a team."

"Fine." His tone was frigid.

"I'm holding a staff meeting tomorrow at seven and I'd like you to join us."

"That's awfully early," he said.

"It can't be helped. Please be there."

I hung up.

An hour or so later, my phone rang. It took me a while to find it where it had fallen underneath the window seat.

"Hello?"

No response except heavy breathing. I slammed the phone down.

It rang again a few seconds later.

"Who is this?"

More breathing.

"Listen, you pubescent asshole. Stop calling me."

I hung up again and glanced at my Caller ID. I knew before I even looked that it would just say *Restricted*.

By the time he called a third time, I was really spooked. I went into the kitchen and found Matt Warren's card on top of the table where he'd left it.

He picked up on the second ring. "Warren."

"This is Kate Sachs. I just got some weird phone calls."

"How weird?"

"A breather. He called three times."

"Flair for melodrama, huh?"

"Glad you find this so amusing," I was having second thoughts about having called him.

"I'm sorry. That was stupid. Has this ever happened before?"

"No."

"I'll come back over. If the phone rings again, don't answer it."

"I need to get out of here for a while," I said.

"Fine. Meet me at the Daily Grind. Know it?"

"Yes, but that's really not necessary," I said.

"It's no problem. I live a few doors down from it. Just wait for me. In the meantime, I'll try and have the call traced."

Chapter 18

By the time I stepped off the elevator into the lobby, I felt a little calmer. In all the excitement I'd forgotten to get yesterday's mail, so I rounded the corner to the mailroom where a row of silver mailboxes, one for each apartment, had been recessed into the wall above a white marble ledge barely wide enough to sit down on. I slipped my key into the tiny lock and pulled out a couple of magazines, a bunch of bills, and lots of junk mail. There was also a pale blue envelope with my name and address written in a scratchy scrawl across the front. It must have been hand-delivered because there was no stamp on it and, when I flipped it over, no return address either.

"Get the letter I stuck in your box?"

I jumped.

My super, Vincent Rosario, was standing at the entrance to the mailroom. Middle-aged, short and stocky, he was bald on top with gray fringe around the sides of his head. He had an inky black moustache that always looked carefully groomed.

"Sorry. Didn't mean to startle you," he said.

"You mean this?" I held up the blue envelope for him to see.

"That's it. I found it in front of my door a little while ago. Somebody must've left it."

"Thanks," I said.

He gave me an appraising look. "The police talked to me about what happened last night. In fact, I'm waiting for the locksmith to get here any minute to fix your door." He shook his index finger at me. "You look after yourself – hear? And if anything else happens, I expect you to call me day or night - capice?"

Outside, people were strolling along Water Street, window-shopping. I took the letter out of the blue envelope and started reading it as I walked towards the corner. It was neatly typed on a sheet of blue paper that matched the envelope.

Kate –

You have property that belongs to me. Leave it in the closet in Cy's bedroom and all this will stop. The key to the house is hidden in a fake rock under the bushes to the right of the front door. If you fail to do exactly as I say - or if you go to the police - I will kill your family one at a time and then your friend Jordan. In case you doubt me, I will provide a little demonstration of my capabilities. I have no doubt that it will create a lasting impression on you.

I stopped walking and stared down at the letter in my hands. A man knocked into me and made a quick apology as he rushed past me. Without really seeing him, I looked up and almost at that exact instant, heard a loud explosion coming from the direction of my building. I jumped at the noise and tripped, falling on my side in the middle of the sidewalk. My right arm was pinned underneath me and when I untangled myself, I realized that it was bleeding.

A man and woman hurried over to help me, but stopped when I backed away from them. Another man stooped down beside me and asked if I needed an ambulance. Something in my expression must have warned him off because he straightened up abruptly and quickly moved away.

I managed to stand up and looked down the block at my building. Billows of black smoke seemed to be coming from the alleyway leading to my garage. *I have to get away from here.*

My legs felt like rubber as I crossed over to the other side of Water Street and hurried around the corner to the Daily Grind, scanning faces in the crowd that had formed. I found a table near the front and waited for Matt Warren to appear, sitting on my hands to make them stop shaking.

Minutes later, his giant body filled the doorway.

"There was an explosion on your block. Are you okay?"

I nodded, afraid that if I said anything I might start crying.

He sat down opposite me. "You look all upset."

My mind raced as I tried to think what to say. I wanted desperately to tell him about the letter, but with the threat to my family and Jordan, that was out of the question.

"Kate – talk to me. What happened?"

"I was walking up the block…"

"Water Street?"

I nodded. "I heard an explosion behind me and tripped. The next thing I knew I was sitting in the middle of the street."

"Jesus. Are you hurt?"

"Mostly shook up. "

"And?"

"And nothing. I came here to meet you," I said, trying to smile.

He looked at me without saying anything. The table vibrated as he tapped his foot up and down underneath it. "Why do I have the feeling you're not telling me everything?"

"I've told you everything I know." It sounded like a lie even to my ears.

Suddenly a fire truck came roaring down Washington Street, sirens blaring. I stood up on autopilot.

Matt reached out and gently touched my arm. "Easy does it, Kate. We'll find out what's happening together. I'll give you a rain check for the coffee. Okay?"

Crowds of people clogged the street, and I heard the words *terrorist attack* several times as we walked back towards my building. I didn't think terrorists had anything to do with it, and I found myself peering into faces, attempting to identify an attacker whose face I'd never seen.

As we approached my street, I saw a police barricade at the corner of Washington and Water. Two fire trucks were on the scene and several squad cars were parked at odd angles up and down Water. The smoke had subsided, and I was relieved to see that there was no damage to my building.

A uniformed policeman stepped forward to block our path. Matt flashed his badge, and the officer stepped aside, allowing us to maneuver around the barrier. We spotted O'Brian leaning up against one of the patrol cars and approached him.

"Glad to see you're all right," he said to me. "I thought about you as soon as they told me where the explosion was."

"What happened?" Matt asked.

"Fire bomb in a trash can over there." He pointed in the direction of my building. "No one hurt that we know about."

"Can I get back in?" I asked.

O'Brian shook his head. "Bomb squad guys are checking out the building. It could take a while."

Great. All the work I'd done on the play was sitting on my window seat. I must have looked upset because Matt asked me what was wrong.

"I left my script in my apartment and I have my first director's meeting tomorrow morning at seven."

"Do you have somewhere else you can stay?" Matt asked.

"I guess I could stay with my parents."

"Which reminds me - are you related to Dr. Jeff Sachs by any chance?"

That threw me totally off guard.

"He's my father. How do you know him?"

"He's been helping us sort out a few cases."

"Really."

"If you tell me where to find the script," he said, "I'll get it for you after they clear the building. I can drive it up to your folks' house later tonight."

This seemed beyond the line of duty. Was he hitting on me?

I decided to press my luck. "Can you get my car out of the garage for me?"

He opened his palm and grinned. "Give me your keys. While you're waiting, you can write out directions to your folks for later."

He started to leave for the garage when an enormous black woman appeared out of nowhere. She must have weighed three hundred pounds.

"Hey Matilda," Matt said to her. "How'd you get here? The street's blocked off."

"Hey yo'self. I told the cop on the corner I's lookin' for you and he let me through." She eyed me curiously. "Who's your friend?"

"This is Kate Sachs. Kate, meet a friend of mine - Matilda."

Matilda gave me a quick glance and turned back to Matt. "Could y'all spare ten dollars, please?"

"What for?" He was smiling as if he already knew the answer.

"Pizza. I hungry."

Matt pulled his wallet out of his back pocket and smiled as he handed Matilda a ten-dollar bill. "You're always hungry."

Matilda threw her arms around him and almost knocked him over. "Thank you! Thank you!" she said and then skipped away.

"Who was that?" I asked.

"She lives in a group home for adults. I go there a few times a month and just hang out. It's through an organization called The Friendship Sphere. They pair you up with someone with special needs and you make friends. I'm Matilda's special friend and she's mine. It means a lot to both of us."

His expression was so earnest that I couldn't take my eyes off him. I almost forgot about everything else.

Chapter 19

I called Jordan from the car and caught her just as she was about to leave the hospital. She'd gone up earlier to talk to Cy and find out whatever she could about the attack.

"Wait there for me, okay? I need to see Cy. He's the only one who knows what's going on."

She said, "He was still unconscious when I checked a half hour ago."

"Maybe he's come to by now. I have to talk to him."

"What's the matter with you?" she asked.

"I'll tell you when I see you."

Jordan was waiting for me at the entrance to the hospital. The color drained from her face as she read the letter.

"Kate, you need to show this to the police."

"Are you crazy? He's stalking me. He exploded a bomb near my building, for chrissake."

Jordan looked at me for a moment without saying anything. Finally she said, "When you got up after the explosion, did anyone seem peculiar to you? Or stand out in any way?"

"I was pretty shook up, but I don't think so. No one looked suspicious, if that's what you mean."

She looked down at the letter again. "I doubt he looks like a weirdo. You can tell he's probably educated from the letter."

"How?"

"It's well written. No grammatical mistakes. No punctuation errors. Whoever he is, he probably blends in with the scenery," she said.

"Except when he's wearing a black mask over his head."

It was dinnertime on the third floor. The smell of overcooked fish and green beans filled the hallway as orderlies pushed rolling metal carts from room to room. I shoved open the heavy glass door that separated the ICU from the rest of the floor. Silence greeted us, broken only by the beeping of equipment and occasional hushed conversation.

The door to Cy's cubicle was open; but his bed was hidden behind a curtain that Jordan pushed to one side. Billy Cole was sitting in a chair next to Cy's bed with his head buried in his hands, crying. He looked at Jordan blankly, but then recognized me standing behind her and stood up. He seemed shocked by what he saw.

I had forgotten about my bruised face. "It looks worse than it feels."

I introduced Jordan and explained that she was covering the story for The New York Times.

Billy gave her a worried look.

"How do you know Cy?" Jordan asked him.

"I take theater classes with him after school. He gave me a summer job at Omnibus Playhouse…" His words choked. "This is so embarrassing."

"No it's not," I said. "It's human." I moved closer to Cy's bed. "Has he come to at all?"

Billy shook his head. "The nurse told me to talk to him. She said people come out of comas sometimes when you talk to them." He offered me his chair next to Cy and pulled another one over for Jordan.

Cy looked like he was in a deep sleep. I touched his hand. "Cy, it's me – Kate."

His eyes flickered for a moment.

"Did you see that? He acted like he heard me."

Billy thought so too, but Jordan looked at me like I'd just told her I'd seen a monster under the bed. I tried a few more times to get Cy to wake up, but to no avail.

"What happened to your face?" Billy asked me.

"I got mugged at the beach."

Billy looked at his feet. "That's awful."

Several moments of awkward silence went by.

"Cy must think a lot of you if he gave you a summer job," I said.

Billy smiled for the first time since we'd entered the room. "I guess."

Jordan and I stood up to go and Billy did the same.

"Headed home?" I asked.

Billy shook his head. "I want to visit my friend. He was in a car accident with another kid."

"The boy who died?" I said.

"How do you know?" Billy asked.

"My father was the doctor on call when they brought your friends in. I'm so sorry."

"How old was the kid who died?" Jordan asked.

"Fifteen," he said.

We didn't know what to say, so we didn't say anything.

The gravel crunched as I turned into my parents' driveway. The front door swung open and my entire family spilled onto the lawn before I'd even turned off the car engine.

"Thank God you're okay," Grandpa Max said.

"We heard about it on the news." Uncle Abe gave me a bear hug, then turned and hugged Jordan.

"Stay as long as you like," my mother said. "Both of you. I'd feel a lot better if you stayed here until they catch this lunatic."

It felt good to be home. We walked through the foyer into the family room and I was surprised to see a woman I'd never met before rise from the sofa. A tall blond with broad shoulders and a big chest, she was dressed in a hot pink sleeveless T-shirt and a short pleated white skirt. She had toned muscles that must have taken hours of weightlifting to produce.

Uncle Abe stepped forward and introduced her. "This is Valerie Weinstein. She's the daughter of a friend of mine."

Sometimes Uncle Abe thinks I was born yesterday. His fondness for beautiful younger women was legendary, although I'd never seen him with anyone this young. Valerie Weinstein couldn't have been older than mid thirties - late thirties, tops.

When the introductions were over and we were all comfortably seated with cocktails, Jordan asked Valerie what business she was in.

"Security."

She handed a business card to Jordan and one to me. It said *Bellafusco-Weinstein Security Consultants.*

"Who's Bellafusco?" Jordan asked.

"My partner."

"What do security consultants do?"

"Private investigations, surveillance, personal protection. That sort of thing."

She looked from Jordan to me and smiled brightly. On her cheekbone beneath her right eye was a black beauty mark.

"Your uncle hired me to protect you."

"I never agreed to that," I said.

Valerie and I both looked at Uncle Abe. He just shrugged.

My mother said, "Valerie has excellent credentials, Kate. She's a very experienced security expert."

"Yes, but…"

"I understand how you feel," Valerie interrupted. She had a low, sultry voice that made you have to lean in closer to hear her. "You don't know the first thing about me. Look - I'm a black belt in karate and an ace shot with any kind of weapon. My partner is ex-special forces *and* CIA. We consult for the FBI and local law enforcement departments around the country."

Jordan waited politely for her to finish before asking, "Are there many women in your profession?" She sounded like she was chasing a new story.

"Actually, there's only a handful of us that I'm aware of," Valerie replied.

"Really. How'd you get started?"

Valerie looked at Uncle Abe, who raised his eyebrows as if to say *go ahead.*

"Before I became a security consultant, I was in exotic dancing."

"You mean stripping?" Jordan asked.

"Exotic dancing is more accurate." Valerie's face grew animated. "Most people don't realize it, but exotic dancing is an art form that takes a lot of practice. But some men get looking and touching mixed up, so I learned self-defense to end the confusion."

I was afraid to catch Jordan's eye, so I looked in the other direction where my father was sitting. To my dismay, he was hanging on Valerie's every word.

"In other words," he said, "you learned self-defense to protect yourself against men who tried to force their attentions on you."

Valerie flashed him an appreciative smile and tossed her shoulder-length hair as if she was in the middle of a Clairol commercial. My father smiled back at her, oblivious to my mother who looked like she wanted to kick him in the shins.

"My big break came when Ron King saw my act and asked if I'd give Barb dancing lessons for a new movie she was making about an exotic dancer."

"Who's Barb?" Grandpa Max asked.

"Barbara Wilson," Valerie said.

"An actress," my mother said. "She used to be married to Ron King."

"Oh."

I suspected he'd never heard of either one.

"Anyway," Valerie continued, "Barb caught on so quickly that I invited her to appear with me one night. She was fantastic. But unfortunately some bozo recognized her and jumped onstage. I had the guy pinned before her own bodyguard even knew what happened. Ron and Barb were so impressed they fired him and hired me instead. I felt a little bad about that."

"You gave up exotic dancing?" Jordan asked.

"Not right away. I sort of juggled the two jobs for a while. But I'm a little past my prime for exotic dancing gigs now." Valerie flashed another brilliant smile.

We all assured her it wasn't so. She murmured something demure followed by an awkward silence, which my mother took as her cue to put dinner on the table.

Chapter 20

I was toying with the idea of getting Valerie's take on the letter if I could catch her alone, when the doorbell rang. I opened the door to find Matt Warren holding my script in his hands. He'd spruced himself up and was wearing a blue blazer over a striped shirt that hung partway out of his jeans. He must have seen me look because he stuffed his shirt back into his pants self-consciously before stepping through the doorway and handing me the script.

I invited him in for coffee and cake.

"Great. Through here?" And without waiting for a reply, he led the way into the dining room.

"Matt – so nice to see you." My father rose to greet him and they shook hands. He looked from me to the detective. "Don't tell me you're in charge of Kate's case?"

Matt nodded.

"That's great news." Dad explained to the rest of us, "Matt's been helping us with some problems at the hospital." He went around the table and introduced everyone.

As Valerie's turn approached, she watched the detective with a look of amusement, although he seemed oblivious to her presence. When his eyes finally took her in, he smiled. "My favorite lady security expert. How's it goin', Val?"

Val gave a throaty laugh and rose to greet him. Then she threw her arms around him and kissed him on the mouth.

He draped one arm around her shoulder and said to the rest of us, "This woman helped us catch a serial killer last year. Without her and Sonny, I don't know what would've happened. He gave Val's shoulder a little shake. "Great to see you, Val."

I glanced at Jordan, but she wasn't looking in my direction. She was wearing her reporter-at-work expression and I felt certain she was writing another story in her head – *Valerie Weinstein– Exotic Dancer Turned Security Professional.*

"Who's Sonny?" Jordan asked.

"Val's partner," Matt explained. "Sonny Bellafusco."

My mother placed a piece of chocolate cake on the table for Matt and invited him to sit between my father and Uncle Abe.

Uncle Abe explained that he'd hired Val and Sonny to protect me, but that I didn't want them.

"Why not?" Matt asked.

"I didn't say I didn't want them. I just need to think it through first."

My mother's face relaxed a little.

"I thought you were moving back to the West Coast," Matt said to Val.

"Changed my mind." She winked at him.

Matt grinned. "Oh."

"Val's mother and I are great friends," Uncle Abe told Matt. "So when all this happened," he gestured at me, "I hired Val and her partner to protect Kate."

A light bulb flashed in my head. Uncle Abe wasn't dating Val; he was dating her mother.

"What do you think of the idea, Matt?" my father asked.

The detective's expression turned serious. "I think it's a great idea."

The room grew silent as all eyes looked at me. I tried swallowing the piece of chocolate cake I'd just forked into my mouth and felt suddenly nauseous.

Finally Val said, "Kate, I know what you're thinking. Having me around all the time is an invasion of your privacy. And you're right. But I'm very good at my job. I'm discreet. I stay in the background. But God help anyone who tries to hurt you." Her sultry voice had taken on an edge. I had to admit that despite her flamboyance, she inspired confidence and I found myself liking her.

"Please Kate," my mother said.

"What would I tell everyone at the theater?"

"That's easy," Jordan said. "Tell them she's David's new assistant producer - that she's keeping an eye on things for him."

I had to admit - that could work. But admitting that I needed a bodyguard made me feel so vulnerable.

I said, "This is all so sudden. Please - just give me a day to think about it."

Everyone concentrated on dessert without saying anything. I saw my mother exchange a pained look with my father.

Matt suddenly broke the silence. "How's the kid from the accident?" he asked my father.

"Still doped up. We found traces of PCP in his bloodstream too."

"Like the kid who died," Matt commented.

"Only this kid's bigger so he stands a better chance. The other boy was so small, his heart just gave out," Dad explained.

Jordan looked at my father. "You mean he didn't die in the car crash?"

My father and the detective exchanged a look.

"This is off the record, Jordan," Dad said.

She nodded. "Understood."

"We can't tell without an autopsy, but before we put the family through that, we have to be pretty convinced he died from drugs and not the accident." He took a bite of cake. "I'd give anything to find out how such young kids get these drugs. There's a story for you, Jordan."

I was listening to what they were saying and at the same time trying to remember something that kept floating away. Finally it hit me. "Billy," I said out loud.

"The boy in the hospital with Cy," Jordan said almost at the same time.

"Who's Billy?" Matt asked.

"One of Cy's students," I said. "He's working at the theater for the summer. When Jordan and I went to visit Cy in the hospital, Billy was already there. He's friends with the kids from the accident."

"What's his full name?" Matt had his notebook out. "I'd like to talk to him."

"Billy Cole," I said.

"Why don't you let Kate talk to him?" Val suggested. "She knows him."

"I'll do it," Jordan said. "I can say I'm covering the story – which is true - and that I'm doing a side piece about Cy as an acting teacher."

"I don't know…" Matt said.

"Why not?" Val said. "The kid'll be more willing to talk to a reporter than a cop. He'll think it's cool."

She stood up and looked at me. "I have to go. So do I have a job here or what?"

I said I needed to sleep on it.

Chapter 21

I awoke at dawn with a feeling of dread in the pit of my stomach. The alarm wasn't set to go off for another twenty minutes, so I rolled over and tried going back to sleep, but the negative thoughts in my head wouldn't let me.

Coming to my parents' house had been a terrible idea. Suppose this psycho was hiding nearby and I'd placed everyone dear to me in jeopardy? I considered telling them about the letter, but what good would that do? They'd only worry more.

I reached over and turned on the light. Then I sat up and dangled my feet over the side of the bed before getting up and heading to the bathroom. As I opened the door to the hallway, I paused to hear if anyone was awake, but all was silent.

A half hour later, I was out the door. The sun was rising swiftly and the noise of the cicadas rattled the trees, almost drowning out the birds. I got into my car and lowered the top, but as I was about to turn the key in the ignition, I heard something buzzing. Looking down, I discovered my cell phone sitting in the cup holder where I'd accidentally left it overnight, set on vibrate. The display said I had voice mail.

I recognized the voice immediately.

"Didja sleep well, Kate? Weston's so nice this time of year. You had coffee with that cop when I told you not to talk to the police." He *tsked* twice. "That wasn't nice. And nothing was waiting for me at Cy's." He sighed deeply into the phone before continuing in his raspy, hoarse voice. "Well, give my best to your family – Annie and the doc, Max and Abe. Nice of Jordan to drop by. Tell 'em I'm keepin' my eye on them." His voice cracked. "Bye Kate. See you soon."

I was shaking so badly, I had trouble finding the keys to my parents' house. I held them in my hand like brass knuckles - not much of a weapon, but they were all I had. Vowing to get a gun, I walked cautiously down the driveway to the road. I punched 9-1-1 into my cell phone, prepared to press *Send* if I spotted anyone who looked suspicious. A few cars drove by in both directions, but none of the drivers displayed undue interest as I stood by the side of the road. Retracing my steps to the house, I scanned the property, silently cursing the dense foliage on both sides that provided natural cover for anyone lurking.

A truck screeched to a halt nearby and I stood still, trying to determine its location. Moments later I heard cans clanging and the whine of a compactor crushing garbage. I waited until I heard the truck drive off before continuing. Halfway up the driveway, something moved in the woods to my right. The sound of breaking branches grew louder. A shadow was visible through the trees. At last, a doe burst through the thicket, staring me straight in the eye as she stepped delicately onto the gravel, and then sauntered across the lawn to the back of the house where my mother's flowerbeds were laid out for breakfast. My heart pounded so hard in my chest that I decided to wait for it to calm down before continuing on to the house.

I let Jordan listen to the voice mail.

"My God – he followed you here," she said.

The knot in my stomach tightened. Should I wake up my family and warn them? Or say nothing so as not to frighten them? When I heard my father's knock on the door, I made up my mind.

He listened to the message with a stoic expression - the doctor's trick for dealing with bad news.

"I'll call Matt and let him know what's going on," he said.

"No police!"

"Why not?"

I hesitated before taking the blue envelope out of my bag and handing it to him. "Read this."

The lines between his eyes deepened as he read the letter. He looked up when he was finished. "What's he talking about? What could you possibly have that belongs to him?"

"That's the problem - I have no idea. But I think he's convinced Cy handed something off to me when I went into the actor's lounge that night. He doesn't realize Cy was already unconscious when I got there."

"Please, Kate - call Val and fill her in."

"She might make things worse."

"How?" Dad sounded exasperated.

"He obviously followed me here, so he must know all about her." An idea occurred to me. "Maybe I should let Russell take today's rehearsal and go someplace where he can't find me."

"That's ridiculous," Jordan said. "Where would you go? Hiding won't solve anything. Besides, you don't trust Russell as far as you can throw him."

"But she's safer staying here," Dad said. "Please - let Russell take today's rehearsal."

Jordan shook her head. "I think you're better off going to the theater. You'll figure out what he wants eventually. Then you can decide what to do about it. But for now, just do whatever you'd normally do. You can't let him get to you like this."

She was right. This was no time to lose my nerve. Plus, I'd do my family and Jordan a big favor by getting out of the house. I left for the theater, praying he would follow me to Westport and leave my family alone.

Chapter 22

"Oh my God!" Sparky said when he saw me walking down the aisle from the back of the theater.

"What happened?" Carla rose from the small table at the foot of the stage where she was seated with Sparky and Jake. Even at that ungodly hour, she'd taken the time to sweep her long black curls into rhinestone-studded combs.

Jake poured me a cup of coffee from a pot that had been set up in the corner as I explained what had happened without going into too much detail.

Everyone was there except our stage manager who I suspected would be late on purpose "Anyone hear from Russell?"

"Not so far," Sparky said. "Surprising – the little weasel's usually so prompt." He dipped his chin to his chest and arched an eyebrow. "And underfoot."

Everyone laughed.

We spent the next hour going through the script scene by scene, agreeing on changes that had to be made to lights, costumes, and props. I took copious notes, increasingly irritated at having to do Russell's job for him.

Sparky's team began filing in around eight o'clock. He saw me glance at my watch and said, "Hope you don't mind, Kate, I asked my crew to get here early so we can make some of the changes you and I talked about before rehearsal starts."

I thanked him just as Art Desmond was walking past us. Sparky asked him to join us and Desmond shifted his gaze to me. His eyes widened briefly when he saw the bruises on my face.

"We're changing most of the lighting, Art," Sparky said, "so please - make sure the kids know what to do." He turned back to me and explained, "Art has a young crew – mostly teenage hopefuls from Cy's acting classes."

Desmond smiled. "You can count on me."

We were wrapping things up when Sparky looked over my shoulder and said, "Nice of you to join us."

Russell appeared from behind my chair and stood over me so that I had to look up at him uncomfortably.

"Sorry I'm late." He took his time sitting down and then yawned. "Late night. Did I miss anything important?" His tone suggested this was unlikely.

"Listen Russell," I said quietly as the others dispersed, "when I call a meeting for seven o'clock, I expect you to show up on time."

He regarded me sullenly.

"I know you think you should be directing in Cy's place," I continued, "and I'm sorry you're disappointed. But if you want to continue as my stage manager, I expect you to act professionally. Or go home now and I'll hire someone else."

The sullen expression vanished from Russell's face. "I do want the job – very much." He spoke so softly I had to lean in to hear him.

"Good. I'll walk you through my notes."

Russell and I were still working, when David arrived. Except for the dark circles under his eyes, he showed no signs of the strain he was under. As usual, he was dressed impeccably in a black short-sleeved shirt tucked into what looked like Armani raw silk beige slacks. He apologized for interrupting us and asked me to join him in the lobby, politely acknowledging Russell who had risen to greet him.

"Detective Warren wants to go over some things with us," he said.

We walked up the center aisle towards the back of the theater. David opened the door to the lobby and let me pass in front of him.

Matt Warren greeted me as if he barely remembered who I was. His tone was neutral as he apologized for intruding on our rehearsal time. "I want to question everyone involved with the show. I'll try and work around your schedule. Just let Sergeant Perrone know the minute you can spare someone, and he'll escort them upstairs. I've asked him to stay inside the theater while you're rehearsing and watch over things."

I followed the detective's gaze over to Perrone who was leaning against one of the marble columns by the front door. Perrone saw me and waved.

"You think someone from the production's involved?" I felt the hairs on the back of my neck prickle.

"I didn't say that," Matt said. "But the more questions we ask, the more we're likely to find out. Someone may know something without even realizing they know it."

"May I have everyone's attention please?"

David stood in the center of the stage and looked out at the audience where the entire cast and crew were seated in the first few rows. The house lights were up all the way, so I had a clear view of everyone from my folding chair onstage behind David.

Rationally, I knew Cy's attacker wasn't among the sea of faces staring back at me. For one thing, no one connected with the show had perpetual laryngitis. But what if he hadn't acted alone? That might explain how he always knew where to find me. My stomach tightened. It would have to be someone who knew me well. Otherwise how did he know the names of everyone in my family? Or that Jordan was my best friend? I felt extremely exposed just sitting there all of a sudden, and had to fight the urge to get up and call my family and Jordan to make sure they were all right.

David, on the other hand, looked perfectly at ease. He stood center stage, with his hand on his hip, looking elegant and self-assured. As he spoke, he made eye contact with different people seated in the audience.

"I know you've all been reading a lot of things in the papers over the past few days," he said, "and I wanted to fill you in on what's really going on and give you a chance to ask questions. As I'm sure you all know, Cy was attacked in the Green Room Friday night and he's still in the hospital."

A murmur rippled through the theater. David raised one hand and requested silence. Then he turned and gestured towards me with a sweep of his arm. "Kate walked in on his attacker and chased him away."

A louder buzz broke out this time.

David raised his voice above the din. "Someone beat up Kate on Saturday morning, and then later in the day her apartment was ransacked. The police are trying to determine if these incidents are all related to the attack on Cy."

Everyone started asking questions at the same time. I saw David take a deep breath before continuing – my first inkling that he wasn't as calm as he looked.

"The police are going to talk to everyone here today, one at a time. For those of you who are minors, I've been asked to contact your parents. The police will wait for them to get here before they begin questioning you."

All hell broke loose at that point. Giovanna, the elderly Italian seamstress who worked for Carla, started crying. I later learned that she didn't have a green card and was frightened of being deported. Brad said he didn't like the idea of being questioned without his lawyer present. And a kid on the lighting crew didn't want to talk to the cops "on principal," although I'd have bet large sums of money he was afraid they'd read special meaning into his bloodshot eyes and vacant expression.

"People, people," David said, raising his voice again. "We have a play to rehearse – so please, let's not lose our heads. The police have their work to do and we have ours."

I was deep in my own thoughts, so I didn't hear David introduce me as the show's new director. I snapped to attention at the sound of clapping, mingled with some unsettling boos. I tried to see who was doing the booing, but they'd already stopped.

David motioned me over to the center of the stage and then sat down behind me.

"Jake Ormond has written a fabulous play," I said, "and with the right changes, I know we can make it all the way to Broadway." More clapping, accompanied by a few cheers. "We don't have a lot of time, so I'm going to keep to a tight rehearsal schedule." A few groans. "When you're not working with me, you'll be working with Russell upstairs in Studio A. From now on he'll be playing a dual role as Stage Manager and my Assistant Director."

Those words had flown out of my mouth unplanned. Where they'd come from, I'm still not sure. But judging from how Russell was beaming, my bribing him with a promotion had been a stroke of genius. I was feeling pretty clever.

I remained in the theater to work with two of the actors while Russell went upstairs to rehearse Brad. They deserved each other. Sergeant Perrone took up watch at the back of the theater, sitting unobtrusively near the door to the lobby. David sat one row behind me and, uncharacteristically, stayed for the entire rehearsal. At first, this irritated me to distraction. But who was I kidding? He had a lot riding on me. As a director, I was an unknown.

As the rehearsal progressed, I forgot all about David until he leaned over my chair and whispered, "Have dinner with me tonight?" His lips brushed my ear, lingering near my cheek a bit longer than was necessary. His breath felt warm on my neck and sent a tingling sensation rippling through my body.

I whispered back without turning around, "I have to have dinner with my family." Not strictly true, but it was the best I could come up with on such short notice. I was determined to steer clear of a relationship with my boss.

Concentrating on the action in front of me proved difficult after that. I fought the urge to turn around and see if he was still sitting behind me. Finally I couldn't take it anymore. I stretched, maneuvering my body into a position that let me steal a peek behind me. Still there.

We'd reached a point in the play where Cy's staging was so awkward that I had to completely re-block it. I climbed onstage to show the actors where to expect a new lighting cue and noticed movement at the back of the theater. Shielding my eyes from the glare of the rehearsal lights, I tried to see who was out there without success. My heart beat faster as I looked around for Sergeant Perrone and realized he wasn't there.

Chapter 23

I jumped down from the stage and took a few steps towards the back of the theater. Someone waved. I took a few steps more until three people finally came into focus. Grandpa Max and Uncle Abe were sitting in the back row with Valerie Weinstein sandwiched in between them.

I strode over to where they were sitting and whispered, "What are you doing here?"

Grandpa Max opened his mouth to say something, but Uncle Abe cut him off.

"The family decided it was time to take action."

Val looked resigned. "They wouldn't take no for an answer."

"We want to make sure you're safe, Doll," Grandpa Max said. "Please – just let us stay and watch for today. He shifted in his seat and looked at Val. "We won't get in the way – you have my word."

I was about to object when David came up behind me. "Can we please continue this conversation in my office?"

Grandpa Max lounged comfortably on David's sofa next to Val, carefully balancing a plain green shopping bag on his lap. I sat between Uncle Abe and David at the conference table. My head throbbed as I listened to Grandpa Max and Uncle Abe explain the rationale of having Val Weinstein pose as David's assistant producer.

"Sorry about this, David," I said. I turned to my grandfather. "Look, I know you're concerned, but I'm perfectly safe here. The police are all over the building."

"I know that, Doll," Grandpa Max said.

"If you don't mind my saying so, you need to take this more seriously," Val said.

"I'm taking this very seriously."

She had an annoying habit of playing with her fingernails. When she wasn't clicking them against each other, she was drumming them on top of the end table next to the sofa. I had to force myself not to look at her hands.

David put his hand on my arm. Val looked at him inquisitively and he quickly removed it. "Kate – please. Someone is stalking you. For chrissakes, he's trying to kill you. Besides - your uncle told me he's already paying Val for her services."

I spun around to Uncle Abe. "I thought we agreed that I'd take a day to think about it."

Uncle Abe sat up straighter in his chair. "I'm trying to protect you." He sounded exasperated.

"I know that. But this guy knows every move I make. What if he saw Val at my parents' last night? If he sees her here, it'll make things worse." I looked at Val to back me up. "Don't you think I'm right?"

She thought for a moment before responding. "I don't think he knows about me."

"Why not?"

"Because he rattled off everyone by name when he left you that voice mail. Guys like that are showoffs. If he'd known about me, he would've said so. I'm almost positive."

All eyes were on me. The only sound in the room was the clicking of Val's fingernails.

Finally I said, "All right. You win." I looked at Val. "You can stay."

Grandpa Max and Uncle Abe exchanged smiles.

David relaxed back in his chair, closed his eyes, and rubbed his temples with the tips of his fingers. When he opened them again, he looked around the table and asked, "Anyone hungry?"

Everyone was.

While we were discussing where to eat, David's secretary poked her head in the door. Large and competent looking, she was somewhere in her early forties with round glasses and frizzy reddish-blond hair.

"Sorry to interrupt," she said, "but Miles Triant is here."

Despite his best efforts to pretend that a surprise visit from *Wait Until Tomorrow*'s principal backer was no big deal, David couldn't mask the alarm that had leapt into his eyes.

My face must have mirrored his anxiety because he said, "I'm sure he's just jittery about his investment. Came to see for himself." He smiled reassuringly at me. "Don't worry."

David stood up as Miles Triant came through the door. He was in his late fifties or so with a handsome face that was difficult not to like. His skin was tanned and he had thick silver hair brushed back from his face, revealing a high forehead. Dark, bushy eyebrows formed an arch over intelligent brown eyes. Despite the warmth of the day, he wore a dark blue suit, elegantly tailored, with a crisp, white shirt and red print tie.

Miles scanned the room, looking from Uncle Abe to Grandpa Max and then at me. "You three must be related." He had a pleasant, low voice that bore the trace of an accent.

"How can you tell?" Grandpa Max asked, rising from the sofa.

"The eyes. All three of you have the same eyes."

It was true. The Rosenthals all share the same blue, deep-set eyes – my mother included.

Miles shook hands with each of us as David made the introductions. When it came to Val's turn, David presented her as his new assistant producer.

Miles face registered surprise as he took a seat at the conference table, but he didn't say anything. I had the feeling he was silently gauging what impact Val's job would have on profits. With the pleasantries over, he launched into what was really on his mind.

"I am aware of your gifts as an actress," he said to me, "but frankly, I'm concerned about your lack of directing experience." He said this politely, without rancor.

"Now hold on a second, " David interrupted.

"It's okay, David." I put my hand on his arm, not wanting him to say anything he might regret later.

I sensed Uncle Abe stiffen next to me. Grandpa Max rose halfway off the couch, but settled back down when I signaled I could handle it.

"I'd like a chance to address Mr. Triant's concerns." I took a breath and continued. "I may not have as many years of directing experience as Cy, but I have directed before. And if you've seen me act, then you know I have a talent for bringing characters to life."

Miles inclined his head towards me, a gesture he managed to pull off without condescension.

"A director has to bring all the characters to life while remaining true to the playwright's intentions." I paused, expecting him to say something, but he remained silent. "Look - I'm sorry about what happened to Cy. But that doesn't negate the fact that the show needs a lot of fixing."

I sensed David flinch, but barreled on. "This play can be brilliant. It has real Broadway potential. But not without major changes."

Miles sat there looking thoughtful. "But are you qualified to make those changes?"

"Absolutely. I've already made improvements. Why don't you stay and watch the rehearsals?"

David sat forward in his chair and eyed me warily. Even he hadn't seen all the changes yet. For a moment, I worried that I'd gone too far.

"There's nothing like a demonstration," Grandpa Max said.

Miles crossed his legs and relaxed his expression. "I'd be delighted to watch you rehearse, Ms. Sachs."

"Please - call me Kate."

"With pleasure, if you'll call me Miles."

That settled, the subject of lunch came up again and Miles accepted David's invitation to join us. But as we were settling on a restaurant, there was a knock on the door. David rose to open it and in walked Jordan.

"Sorry to interrupt," she said, glancing around the room until her eyes settled on me. "I'm supposed to be interviewing Billy Cole over lunch. Know where I can find him?"

"He's probably still in the theater," I said.

I introduced Jordan to Miles and explained that she was covering the story of Cy's attack for the Times. Miles stiffened visibly upon hearing this information.

"I'm working on the human-interest side of things," Jordan explained. "I want to talk to some of the kids who take acting lessons from him. Find out what he's like as a teacher."

If she thought she was making Miles feel better, one look at the man's face said she'd done just the opposite. His polite smile froze in place; it looked like only a blowtorch could wipe it away.

David noticed too, because he quickly assured Miles that the article would be great publicity. "People love a mystery. You'll see - it'll be terrific for the box office."

Miles sat so stiffly in his chair, you'd have thought *rigor mortis* had set in. "I never thought about it that way."

"Now - if he died, that would really sell tickets." Uncle Abe pointed out.

David looked like he was going to faint.

As we filed out of David's office to go to lunch, I asked Grandpa Max what was in the shopping bag. A beautifully wrapped package in pink and gold paper was peeking out from the top.

He clasped the handles of the shopping bag together and the package disappeared. "It's a present - for you."

"You shouldn't have!" I reached for the bag, but Grandpa Max moved it behind his back.

"I'll give it to you later. I need to explain a few things about it first." Then he hurried down the hallway to catch up with Uncle Abe.

Miles and I followed at a slower pace. As we were passing by one of the offices, a door opened and Matt Warren emerged carrying a stack of papers. I introduced him to Miles.

Matt glanced dismissively at Miles and said, "I need to speak with you, Kate."

I excused myself and asked Miles to continue on without me, feeling inexplicably responsible for the detective's rudeness.

I followed Matt into an office further down the hall. It was littered with empty coffee cups and paper wrappings containing the remnants of breakfast. He dropped the stack of papers onto the desk and picked up a pink phone message slip. When he was through reading it, he looked up and said, "Want to have lunch?"

This was the last thing I expected him to say.

"I need to ask you some more questions and I figured a restaurant would be a nice change of scenery for both of us."

"I have an important business lunch. Can't this wait?"

"No."

Given the determination on his face, I decided it was useless to argue. How did this man manage to go from Iceman to Mr. Nice Guy and back again within the span of a few seconds?

"Something wrong?" he asked.

"I'll meet you in the parking lot. I have to make my apologies."

Chapter 24

As Matt and I passed through the bar at Skeeters, sunlight slanted through the slats of the wooden shades and bounced off the mirror hanging on the wall behind the bar. An aging hippie with a long black ponytail streaked with gray sat at one end of the bar sipping a beer. A fat man in a business suit sipped something stronger at the other end, his ample belly straining against the buttons of his starched white shirt.

I was standing behind Matt as we waited next to the Plexiglas partition that separated the dining room from the bar. A waitress with long black hair wearing blue jeans and a black Skeeters T-shirt sauntered over.

"Table for one, Matt?" she asked.

"Two," he said, sidestepping out of the way so that she could see me.

She gave me the once-over before leading us to a dark wooden booth set flush against a green wall covered with oil paintings depicting hunt scenes. Ancient scuffmarks and carved initials adorned the tabletop, while a shaded oil lamp reproduction barely cast enough light to read the menu.

"Friend of yours?" I asked.

"Not really," he said, studying the menu. "What're you in the mood for?"

I read through the salad specials and ordered a cheeseburger with fries and a diet coke. No point in wasting calories.

"How do you eat that way and stay so slim?" he asked.

"Genes."

While we waited for our food, we passed the time by making small talk until I finally couldn't take it anymore.

"So what's so important that you couldn't wait to talk to me about it?"

His hurt feelings instantly registered on his face. But in the blink of an eye, his cop look descended. Not unfriendly - just neutral.

"Sorry. That came out a little harsh," I said.

"Not at all. I don't blame you for wanting to cut to the chase."

I said, "Any other time and your invitation to lunch would have been very attractive."

His smile chased the distant expression from his eyes. I felt my face burning; I'd blurted out what I'd been thinking and now it was too late to take it back.

Fortunately, the waitress brought our food to the table. She placed a large Cobb salad in front of Matt, pinning him with a big smile that faded as soon as she placed my cheeseburger in front of me - a bit harder than was necessary, in my opinion. The plate rattled on impact, spewing French fries.

"Sorry," she said.

I doubted it.

Matt reached across and picked a French fry off my plate. He chewed it thoughtfully, and then said, "Do you smoke?"

"No. Why?"

Matt's eyes locked onto mine as he pulled something out of his pocket and held it across the table for me to see. "The police found these in your apartment Saturday night."

I reached for the clear envelope he was holding, but he pulled it back.

"Just look at it."

Inside the envelope was a pack of Marlboro cigarettes.

"Definitely not mine. I told you – I don't smoke cigarettes."

"How about marijuana?"

"What the hell kind of question is that? No – I don't smoke marijuana. And what does that have to do with anything?"

"These aren't cigarettes."

He was watching me so closely that I wanted to look away, but didn't dare.

"They're rolled joints made to look like cigarettes."

"Well whatever they are, they're not mine," I said.

"I'm glad to hear that." He smiled. "And for the record – the prints on the wrapping don't match yours."

"So what are you busting my chops for?"

"Just making sure."

"Well for the record - I don't like mind games." I took a bite of my cheeseburger, willing my anger to subside before finally asking, "Whose prints are they?" If he knew who was trying to kill me, I had a right to know.

"We're still trying to figure that out."

I could feel the vibration of his foot tapping up and down under the table.

"Could they belong to any of your friends?"

"No! I swear."

We were interrupted by the blaring tones of the William Tell Overture on Matt's cell phone. He responded to whoever was on the other end in monosyllables, and I couldn't tell from his expression if he was hearing good news or bad.

When he was through, he snapped his phone shut and looked regretfully at his food.

"I'm sorry to have to do this, but…"

"You have to go," I finished for him.

The waitress wrapped our food to go and then he walked me to my car, having declined my offer of a lift. I left him waiting outside the restaurant for a police car to pick him up and drove back to the theater alone.

Chapter 25

I dragged myself up the stairs to Studio A and quietly opened the door. My understudy, Janice Weller, was rehearsing a scene with Brad. To my relief, he was following the directions I'd left with Russell to the letter. In fact, his performance was magnificent - and he seemed to know it. Russell made the *okay* sign with his thumb and forefinger and flashed a smile. Maybe my new assistant director could be saved. In another hour it would be my turn to be tested. I hoped that Brad would behave himself in front of Miles.

Next door Jordan was finishing up her interview with Billy.

"He's been fantastic," she said as I came through the door. "I could practically write the whole article based on what he just told me."

Billy shoved his long dark hair out of his eyes and smiled. Then he stole a glance at the clock on the wall.

"Don't worry, you still have plenty of time before rehearsals start up again," I said.

"Thanks. I've been keeping an eye on the clock."

I unwrapped my cheeseburger and took a bite. "Fries?" I held the silver container out and they each took some.

"How's your friend in the hospital?" I asked.

"He seems better."

Jordan looked at me and gave a slight nod that Billy didn't see.

"My father said he was pretty strung out on drugs."

"Yeah. I heard that too."

Jordan reached for another fry. "Off the record, how bad is the drug situation in your school?"

Billy seemed startled by the question. "I dunno. Why?"

"It's just that I'm working on another story about drugs in high school, only I can't find enough kids who are willing to talk to me about it. Anything you tell me would be strictly confidential."

"I really don't know anything about that. Sorry." He glanced at the wall clock again.

"Did your friend say where he got the drugs?" Jordan asked.

"No. Like I said, I don't know anything about that." He bit off a hangnail.

Jordan shrugged and looked down at her notes, apparently content to drop the subject for now. I knew she'd bring it up again with him another time. She could be very patient when she had to be.

It felt odd to direct myself. In a few places, I had to stop and rework parts of the action. But my acting instincts told me rehearsal was going well. That is, until I gave Brad Simpson a direction he didn't like.

Instead of simply saying that he disagreed with me and why, he rose from his seat on stage in magisterial defiance and, in his deepest baritone voice, declared that he refused to comply. That it was unconscionable to make me a director. That I had no experience. That he would quit rather than take direction from me.

I looked at him in stunned silence, barely able to think how to respond. I glanced at David who seemed as shocked as I was.

Finally I said, "Brad, I suggest you sit down and listen to me carefully…"

Dismissing me with a wave of his hand, Brad addressed David. "I won't put up with this. I'll quit. Is that what you want?"

It was so quiet in the theater that you could hear the lights humming.

David stood up and walked to the edge of the stage. "You'll honor your contract or I'll see you in court." He paused, as if he expected another outburst. When none occurred, he continued. "Kate is going to tell you the changes she wants, and I expect you to comply."

Brad's momentary silence was apparently due to shock. Fully recovered, he let loose with another tirade.

"You expect me to take directions from this neophyte?" Brad spit out *neophyte* as if it was a curse word.

"I expect you to treat Kate like the talented professional she is," David said. He looked at me. "Kate – want to continue?"

"Thanks, David." I heard the shakiness in my voice and tried to get it under control. "Why don't we take a break." I glanced at my watch. "Let's pick things up in twenty minutes."

I climbed down from the stage and hurried up the center aisle. As I passed by Grandpa Max and Uncle Abe, I couldn't bring myself to make eye contact. Under the best of circumstances, my family is a tough act to follow, but having them witness my total humiliation was more than I could bear.

Miles was seated a few rows behind them. As I brushed past him, I saw him stand up out of the corner of my eye.

"Kate…"

I spun around at the sound of his voice.

"Don't second guess your instincts. You were right."

"Thanks," I said.

When we resumed, rehearsals stayed blessedly uneventful for the rest of the afternoon. To my dismay, Grandpa Max and Uncle Abe remained in the theater with Val like a cheerleading section. At one point, David's secretary called him away with Miles and they didn't return.

I was standing on the apron of the stage talking to Russell and Sparky when they looked past me. Turning to see what had caught their attention, I saw David and Matt standing together in the aisle. Matt's expression was hard and distant. David looked frightened.

Somehow I already knew what they'd come to say.

Cy was dead.

Chapter 26

I stood outside watching the police string yellow crime scene tape across the main entrance. My first day taking over as director had been a disaster. I'd never felt more humiliated in my life. It was almost a relief to hear that rehearsals were being cancelled until a temporary rehearsal space could be located. The police had closed the theater until further notice.

The air felt warming after the chill of air conditioning all day. I thought about Friday night. Maybe if I'd walked into the Green Room sooner, Cy would still be alive. Now he was dead, his killer was stalking me, and because of my own stupidity, my family and Jordan were in danger. If only I hadn't gone to my parents' house last night, he never would have followed me there.

I wandered over by the riverbank and looked at the late afternoon sun sitting low in the sky. Someone grabbed my arm and I yanked it away.

"You shouldn't be wandering around by yourself," Val said. The clouds shifted and her gray eyes seemed to turn blue. Up close, I could see faint crows' feet at the corners of her eyes.

"What happened to my grandfather and Uncle Abe?" I asked.

"The police told them to leave. They asked me to tell you goodbye." She paused and gave me an appraising look. "You look like you could use a rest. Want to go home?"

We walked around to the parking lot where Val's car was parked a few spaces away from mine. I admired her style; she drove a pale blue Jaguar that looked brand new. Her security business was clearly lucrative.

I clicked open my car, got in, and backed out of the space. Then I waited near the entrance until she pulled up behind me and followed me out of the lot.

Twenty minutes later we turned into the alleyway leading to the entrance of my garage. I felt a surge of anxiety driving past the charred wall where the bomb had exploded. At the bottom of the ramp, I put my arm out the window and signaled for Val to drive around to the other side where she'd find visitors' parking.

Slinging my purse over my shoulder, I grabbed my brown leather tote off the passenger seat and got out of the car to wait for Val. A red Ferrari I would have killed for was parked a few spaces away. I looked around to make sure the owner wasn't in sight and then walked over to it and put my nose flush against the passenger-side window.

There were enough dials on the dashboard to navigate a plane. I could almost feel the buttery softness of the beige leather interior through the glass. As I was peering inside, the sound of an idling motor made me jump back. I looked around and finally realized that the sound was coming from somewhere to my right where several empty spaces separated the Ferrari from an old beat-up black Ford. I walked over to the Ford and, sure enough, it was humming away. Inside the dark interior, I could just make out a key ring dangling from the ignition in the *on* position. My heart thumped as I scanned the garage for the owner. That's when I noticed that the door leading from the garage into the building was ajar, and I caught sight of a dark silhouette through the crack in the doorway.

It was like watching a movie - I was there, but I wasn't there. The door inched open and then slammed against the wall. Someone wearing a black mask came hurling at me. A fist caught me in the stomach and I doubled over.

"You bitch," a familiar hoarse voice said, "where the fuck did you put it?"

Clutching my stomach, I lifted my head. "I don't know what you're talking about."

He shoved me hard in the chest with both hands and I toppled over, hitting the back of my head against the concrete floor. He jumped on top of me and yanked my head up by my hair and I screamed.

"Tell me where it is, bitch!" His dark eyes looked furious through the slits in his mask.

I became vaguely aware of running footsteps and a tall blond figure leaning over us. Val dragged him off me and flung him against the black car. I struggled to my feet and watched as he balled his fingers into a fist and drew his arm back. Before I could do anything to stop it, he struck at Val, but she parried his blow with her forearm. Then, balancing her weight on one leg, she raised the other leg off the ground until her knee was practically level with her nose, and let loose one graceful kick that collided with his face. Something cracked.

He let out a piercing howl and reached for his mask. For a minute I thought he would pull it off, but he just batted at it as blood started seeping through the nylon onto the floor.

By now, I was in a crouching position to his left, ready to spring. Val stayed to his right, so we had him covered no matter which way he tried to run. Out of the corner of my eye, I saw Val reach into her purse for something.

He was quick. Reaching into his pants pocket, he drew out a gun and pointed it at Val. But I was quicker. I leaped forward and smashed down on his wrists with my arms locked in front of me like a bludgeon. There was a deafening sound as the gun went off just as it flew out of his hands, skittering across the floor a few feet beyond his reach.

Val had her gun out pointed at his face, but he swung at her, taking her off guard. She lost her footing and tumbled backward.

That was all the time he needed. He snatched his gun off the floor and fired another shot that, mercifully, missed. Val recovered her balance and aimed her gun at him, but before she could get off a shot, he dove into the old black Ford that was still idling away to our right. The tires squealed as he tried to back into us. Val fired a shot at his rear window that made my ears ring. The glass exploded and he must have changed his mind about trying to run us over. His tires squealed again as he shifted into drive and hit the gas, tearing up the exit ramp. We chased after him on foot, reaching the street just in time to see his car skid momentarily, and then disappear over the bridge.

Val took out her cell phone.

"No police!"

"Do you know how guilty you'll look if you don't report this?" Val said.

Before I could respond, a black and white squad car pulled up along side of me. It was O'Brian and Perrone.

"Do you know anything about gun shots in your garage?" O'Brian said.

"News travels fast," Val said. "I was just about to call you."

Chapter 27

I was turning my key in the lock when someone yanked the door open from inside my apartment.

"What are you doing here?" I said.

"We thought we'd surprise you." My mother opened the door wider and looked at me closely. "My God, what happened?"

Hearing this, the rest of my family got up from where they were sitting in the living room and came over to see for themselves.

"A man jumped Kate in the garage while I was parking my car," Val said apologetically.

"Actually, Val saved my life," I said. "She pulled him off me and then broke his nose."

In the living room, Uncle Abe took drink orders with a grim expression. Grandpa Max sat in an armchair looking stunned.

"Bring your drinks to the table," my mother said, "You must be starved."

She vanished into the kitchen as we filed into the dining room. Moments later, she reappeared with steaming platters of crispy fried chicken, barbequed baby back ribs, and so as not to miss any calories, oven fried potatoes and corn bread - all compliments of the take-out department at Stew Leonard's, Connecticut's most revered food store. When we were stuffed beyond capacity, she herded us back into the living room where she served apple pie *à la mode* and coffee.

Before sitting down for dessert, Grandpa Max went to get something out of the front hall closet. It was the green shopping bag I'd seen him with earlier at the theater.

He placed it in front of me. "For you, Katie."

I ripped the pink and gold wrapping paper off the package and discovered a black leather jewelry box.

"Gramps – how beautiful. Thank you."

"Open the box, Katie. The gift's inside."

I lifted the lid. Inside, securely mounted on top of a red velvet cushion, was a shiny silver gun with a black handle and black trim around the barrel.

"A Walther PPK. Do you have a permit for that thing?" Val asked Gramps.

He flashed her his most endearing grin. "Same gun 007 used."

Val looked back at him, apparently nonplussed.

Gramps shrugged. "It takes twelve weeks to apply for a permit. Katie can't wait that long." He turned and faced me. "Pick it up, Doll. See how it feels."

I picked up the gun and examined it more closely. It was small enough to fit in my pocket, so I was surprised to feel how heavy it was. "Is it loaded?"

Gramps rolled his eyes. "What do you think?"

Actually, I thought that anything was possible, but I didn't say so.

"She'll need to learn how to use it," my mother said, looking at Val.

Val walked over to me and held out her palm. I handed her the gun. She pressed a small lever on the side and a black piece of metal slipped out the handle. Then she pulled back on a slide on top of the gun and an opening appeared.

"Is it loaded?" Dad asked, echoing my question.

Val let the slide snap back into place. "No."

A loud sigh escaped from my father.

My grandfather looked at him. "I would never give Katie a loaded gun. You know better than that."

Like me, my father had come to expect the unexpected from my mother's family. He regarded my grandfather apologetically. "Of course - I knew that."

Val reassembled the gun and handed it back to me. Then she turned to my grandfather and said, "It's next to impossible to get a handgun permit in New York City. Did you know that?"

Gramps gave another shrug.

"And each state has its own permit laws," Val continued, "so assuming you bought the gun in the city, carried it with you into Connecticut, and that you don't have a permit in Connecticut or New York, let alone New York City, then you've probably committed at least three felonies - in two states, no less."

"Hmmm." Gramps walked over to the window and looked out at the soft pink sky as the sun set over the Sound.

"Can you teach her how to use it?" Uncle Abe asked Val impatiently. Her objections apparently hadn't made much of an impression on him either.

She rubbed the back of her neck. "Well… as a matter of fact, Sonny owns a shooting range not far from here."

The telephone rang. I started to get up, but my mother beat me to it and ran to the kitchen to answer it.

Uncle Abe stayed focused on Val.

"Okay - I can teach her." Val turned towards me. "But you have to swear you'll apply for a permit."

I nodded. "Sure."

My mother poked her head out of the kitchen. "It's David."

I went into the kitchen and took the phone from her. She stayed glued to my elbow.

I put my hand over the mouthpiece. "'Scuse me a sec, Mom?"

Reluctantly she returned to the living room.

David's voice sounded strained. "I'm glad your family's with you."

I wondered if he'd called to check up on whether I was telling the truth about why I couldn't have dinner with him. For once, my family's surprise visit had actually come in handy. Then I heard the concern in his voice.

"Are you okay?" he asked.

"How'd you find out?"

"Find out what?" he said. "I just called to see how you're doing."

I told him what had happened.

"Oh my God. Thank goodness Val was with you." He was silent for a moment. "This never would've happened if I hadn't asked you to stop by the theater Friday night."

"Don't be ridiculous - it wasn't your fault."

That hadn't come out right; I'd intended to sound reassuring, not snap at him. I made an effort to continue in a friendlier tone. "So what's up with rehearsals?"

David shifted gears. "Remember that kid, Billy Cole?"

"Of course. He must be devastated about Cy. They were pretty close."

"His mother called me. She works for one of the schools." I heard him shuffling through papers. "Soundview High School. They'll let us hold rehearsals in their auditorium for the time being."

"Great."

"Unfortunately," David continued, "we can't get in there until next Monday. Seems the head custodian needs to be there and he's on vacation 'till then."

"But that's a whole week away!" If every rehearsal was going to be as difficult as today's had been, I'd need all the time I could get. "Isn't there somewhere else we can rehearse in the meantime?"

David said no so strangely, I was afraid he'd changed his mind about letting me direct. A few beats went by before he finally explained, "Detective Warren thinks you should lay low for awhile."

"That's ridiculous!"

"I know, but…"

"David, please. Val's an incredible bodyguard. She proved that tonight. Don't take this play away from me."

"I would never do that!" David sounded shocked. "But I'll be damned if I'll let you get killed by some psycho. I'll delay the opening…"

"Don't do that … please. Between Val and the police, there's no need to."

We both knew that postponing opening night could prove disastrous. It would mean refunding tickets and extending everyone's contracts. Even if the show turned out to be a hit, the extra costs could force us to close.

"Maybe by the time rehearsals start up again at the school, the police will have caught the guy." David sounded like he was trying to convince himself. "In the meantime, please be careful."

I went back into the living room to find Jordan there looking as shook up as I felt. In an uncharacteristic display of affection, she threw her arms around me.

"How'd you find out?" I asked.

"I was at the police station when an anonymous call came in about gun shots coming from your garage."

"No wonder they showed up so quickly," Val said.

Jordan sat down on the sofa next to my mother. Her eyes darted to the cocktail glasses on top of the coffee table.

Misinterpreting, my mother jumped up. "Let me fix you something to eat."

"Thanks, Annie, but I'm really not hungry."

"It's no bother." My mother was already halfway to the kitchen. "You have to have dinner."

"Thanks," Jordan said without enthusiasm. She'd known my mother too long to argue. Mom's response to any crisis was food. Even though she was too nervous to swallow a mouthful herself, everyone else was required to eat.

Jordan eyed the drinks on the coffee table again.

Apparently feeling her pain, Uncle Abe walked over to the bar and mixed her a Martini.

She downed half of it. A spot of color returned to her cheeks just as my mother returned with a plate of fried chicken, ribs, and oven fried potatoes. Jordan looked biliously at it, but politely pecked at the chicken.

"Do the police know anything yet?" my mother asked her.

You can't rush Jordan. She finished her drink and studied the empty glass. Uncle Abe rose to get her a refill. She politely waited for him to return before answering my mother's question.

"Their theory is that the killer mistakenly believes Cy passed drugs or money to Kate at the theater."

"That's exactly what I think," I said.

"Do they have any leads?" Uncle Abe asked.

"The forensic guys found hair fibers on Kate's jogging clothes from when she was mugged at the beach. They're hoping for a DNA match. But if not, the blood in the garage should give them what they need." She took a sip of her drink and then looked up abruptly.

"I almost forgot - they still don't know whose fingerprints were on that pack of Marlboros they found in your apartment when it was ransacked."

Chapter 28

The time on the cable box said 11:12 AM. My heart raced as I realized how late I was to rehearsal. Then I remembered that it had been cancelled and started to lie back down again, but the smell of coffee beckoned. I got out of bed and followed my nose to the kitchen.

As I passed through the living room, I ran into Val who was watching *Court TV*. Her bare feet were propped up on my coffee table. I stared deliberately at them, but she didn't take the hint. A pair of embroidered red silk mules lay on the floor nearby.

"Morning," she said. "Feeling better?"

I grunted something and continued on to the kitchen. Cheery people in the morning annoy me. I could see that sharing my apartment with Val wasn't going to be easy.

I poured myself a cup of coffee and sniffed it. Still fresh. Retrieving a carton of milk from the refrigerator, I sniffed that too before adding a drop to my coffee. No little white clumps appeared on the surface; a good sign.

In the living room, I flopped down on a sofa. "Good coffee. Where's Jordan?"

"The city. Hours ago." Val's fingernails were clicking a mile a minute as her eyes stayed glued to the television set. "Said she had a meeting, but may be back later."

I knew Jordan was working on another important assignment but, true to form, that was all she would tell me. The early morning trip back to the city meant something big was going on.

Val and I watched TV in silence. I hated *Court TV*. I thought the point of television was to avoid reality.

Without removing her eyes from the television set, Val reached over and picked up a piece of paper from the coffee table and handed it to me. "Iris Cole called. Said you can call her back anytime."

I didn't know an Iris Cole, but at least I had an excuse to escape *Court TV*.

The telephone barely rang once when Iris Cole picked it up. From the way she said hello, I had the feeling she'd been waiting by the phone for someone's call and that someone hadn't been me.

"Billy's told me so much about you," she said with what sounded like forced enthusiasm. "He's very excited about the play."

At least that solved one mystery. Iris was Billy Cole's mom.

Her voice was soft and high-pitched with a slight lilt to it – possibly the remnants of an Irish accent shed years ago. I pictured a gray-haired old lady in a hairnet.

"I promised Billy I'd inquire about using the high school auditorium for your rehearsals," she said.

"I know. David Sobel told me about it last night. Thanks so much."

"Would you like to see the space?" she asked. "The building manager's on vacation 'til next week, but I'd be happy to show it to you in the meantime if you're interested."

She sounded so eager and, besides, I figured it couldn't hurt to see the place ahead of time. We arranged to meet at the school that afternoon.

I was about to hang up when Iris asked me another question: "Have you spoken with Billy today, by any chance?"

"No."

"He was terribly upset when he came home yesterday afternoon. Then he went out to meet some friends and never came back. I've called his cell phone a million times, but I keep getting his voice mail."

Remembering my own not so sedate youth, I said, "He was probably up all night. It was an upsetting day. I bet he's still asleep on a friend's couch somewhere. Have you called around?"

"Yes, but no one seems to know where he is."

"I wouldn't worry too much. He'll probably show up any minute," I said.

On the other hand, my mother would have called the FBI by now, but I didn't share that with Iris Cole.

Val switched off the television as soon as I walked back into the living room.

"We need to talk."

I hate when people lead off like that.

"I know it's annoying to have me around," she said.

"No, it's not."

"Liar," she said, grinning.

"Sorry. It's just that I'm used to living alone. And I'm not exactly a morning person."

She laughed. "You can say that again. It's almost noon. So technically speaking, you slept through the morning. Believe me, I understand. In my professional dancing days, I wasn't big on mornings either."

She took her feet off my coffee table and sat up straight. "Time to get to work. Let's start with the ground rules."

Great. Just the conversation I craved over my morning coffee.

"Rule number one: anytime you want privacy, you just tell me and I'll make myself scarce." She looked around. "Shouldn't be a problem in this place - there's so much room! My last client lived in a small one-bedroom."

I took another sip of coffee. If I clicked my heels three times, maybe she'd stop talking.

"Rule number two: you don't go anywhere without me. And when you do go out, we stick together like glue."

I started to object, but she raised her hand in the air and interrupted me.

"If you can't agree to that, I'm outta here."

My first impulse was to tell Val good-bye and good riddance. But I didn't dare because, in truth, I was scared. I hated feeling that way because deep down I knew that's exactly what Hoarse Voice wanted me to feel. Of that, I was certain.

"Do you always do that?"

"Do what?" I asked.

"Go off in your head like that. Your face turns real serious and suddenly you're miles away."

"Sorry."

"Do we have a deal?" she asked.

"Sure."

Val spent the next twenty minutes lecturing me on the art of war and self-defense while I sat listening in numbed silence. I needed more caffeine for this.

"This guy's got you by the throat because he knows you're afraid."

That got my attention.

"You're not that difficult to read," she said. "It takes guts to attack a guy holding a gun like you did. Learn how to channel that energy and – wham!" She smacked the back of the sofa with an open palm. "Fear evaporates and in it's place – confidence that can't be shaken."

This all sounded a bit too Zen-like for me.

"You'll see. I can teach you Karate basics fairly quickly. To become an expert, though, it takes years. But you'll be able to defend yourself when I'm through. Trust me."

"What about the gun?" I had a lot more confidence in my ability to shoot the bastard than in fighting him off with my bare hands.

Her expression grew serious. "I can teach you how to shoot a gun, sure. But you have to be certain you're capable of killing him with it if you have to. Otherwise, there's no point. You hesitate and - bang," she formed a gun with her thumb and index finger – "you're dead. Guy disarms you and kills you with your own gun."

Before I could respond, we were interrupted by the sound of the downstairs buzzer.

Val said, "That must be Sonny."

Chapter 29

Val's partner, Sonny Bellafusco, stepped off the elevator and rolled a very buff armless naked male torso into my apartment.

Sonny was short and burly with dark hair streaked with gray and intense blue eyes. When he smiled, even white teeth contrasted nicely with his rugged tan face. He extended his hand and said, "Nice to meet you. Sorry for all your troubles. Val's been filling me in."

Then he walked past me and took Val in his arms and kissed her. "Hey baby." He was a head shorter than she was, but that didn't seem to faze Val.

"Hey," she said, slightly breathless.

It took a while for them to remember I was in the room too. Val disengaged herself and said, "Sonny and I go way back. We worked a case together when he was still with the NYPD."

Sonny winked at me. "Lost track for a while after that. Did a stint in the CIA Val never even knew about. We bumped into each other again after I retired from the Agency. Besides the consulting business, I own a Karate school here in Norwalk."

"And a gun store." Val added. She turned to Sonny and gave him a dazzling smile. "Kate feels safer learning how to shoot."

"Whatever you need, baby I got it," Sonny sang off-key, nuzzling Val's hair.

Val shot him a look and he turned serious.

"Come over whenever you like and use the range," he told me. "We got a big selection of guns you can try out too. But don't discount the Karate. Val's a great teacher." He patted her bottom. "Black belt third degree."

He blew her a kiss on his way out the door.

We nicknamed the naked torso Raoul. Raoul had a painted-on moustache, big muscles, and a glowering face. He was attached to an adjustable pole stuck into a big black stand that looked like a rubber tire. Whenever you Karate-chopped Raoul, he fell backwards. He always recovered, though. And he never hit back.

For the next hour, Val put me through a grueling workout. She taught me simple moves for dealing with any attacker, no matter how big.

"It's all about balance," she said. "Think of your hands and feet as weapons, and make sure you scream *kiaii* before you attack."

She yelled *kiaii* at the top of her lungs and laughed when I jumped back.

"See? It throws your opponent off guard. Always take advantage of vulnerabilities."

Then in one quick motion, she jabbed poor Raoul in the eye with her fingertips .

"It's a great way to immobilize your opponent. Then follow up by slamming the heel of your palm into his nose like this." She demonstrated.

After a while, I started to get the hang of it. I really gave it to Raoul - a right cross, followed by a quick left hook, and then finishing him off with a right upper cut. But without any arms, he couldn't fight back, so it wasn't really fair.

My favorite move was called the round kick - the one Val had used to break Hoarse Voice's nose in the garage. My dance background gave me an advantage here. I practiced kicking out from a one-footed stance that allowed me to leverage the weight of my whole body as I slammed Raoul in the face again and again with my other foot. Unfortunately, I kicked him one time too many, and landed full-force on my rear end.

Val took this as a sign that I'd had enough Karate for one day.

Sonny's gun store was located on the first floor of an old restored building originally built in the mid-1800's. It was wedged in between an ice cream parlor and a clothing store specializing in trendy outfits for the high school set.

We parked the car across the street. Looking up, we saw a group of women, mostly overweight, on the second floor. They were dressed all in white, kicking their legs high in the air. Sonny's Karate school. We crossed over and entered the building through a heavy metal door displaying a white sign with neat black lettering that said *Guns 'N Fun*.

Guns 'N Fun turned out to be bigger than I expected. Inside was a big white-walled room with guns of every shape and size sitting in display cases, and more guns hanging on the walls. The sound of thudding feet reverberated through the ceiling as the Karate lesson continued upstairs.

Val led the way over to one of the display cases where a disinterested black man pointedly ignored us, turning his back on us to dust the wall of guns behind the counter. He was tall with a shaved head and a single gold hoop earring.

We stood directly in front of him so that he finally had no choice but to turn around.

"Hi Val. You know we only allow lessons on weekends."

Val smiled charmingly and pointed to a gun inside one of the cases. "I'd like to see that revolver."

He raised an eyebrow and gave her a sullen stare. Then he slowly reached inside the case and withdrew the gun she had indicated, placing it on top of the counter. He peered at me, as if noticing me for the first time. "You look familiar."

"Now I want to see that Sig 9 millimeter," Val said, pointing, "and that 45 Glock."

When he didn't respond, her charming smile froze in place. Her long fingernails drummed the top of the display case. She leaned across it and spoke in a loud voice, enunciating each word as if he had a hearing problem. "Look. I'm giving a shooting lesson here whether you like it or not. But first I wanna go over some basics. Do you mind?"

I was afraid she might grab him by his gold hoop earring.

He handed Val the guns she'd asked for, while keeping his attention focused on me. Suddenly he snapped his fingers. "Now I know who you are." He smiled. "Julie on *Young and In Love* – right?"

I smiled back. "Right."

"Can I have your autograph?"

"Sure."

Val's fingernails drummed faster on the countertop. She glowered at both of us.

He handed me a pen and paper. "Name's Vincent Thomas."

Val cleared her throat. "Vincent. If you don't mind, we're going to sit over there and take these guns with us." She pointed to a seating area where a beat up coffee table stood between an old sofa and an armchair on the other side of the room.

Vincent stared at her for a few seconds like he was trying to remember who she was. Then he reached under the counter and came up with three small boxes. "Your ammo."

Val grabbed the boxes of ammunition and stomped off towards the seating area without another word.

"What gives with you and Vincent?" I asked when we were out of earshot.

"He's hated my guts ever since Sonny made me a partner." She sat down on the sofa, indicating for me to take a seat next to her. "I didn't realize you played Julie in *Young and In Love.* I love that show."

"You mean I've changed so much, you didn't even recognize me?"

"You were in high school."

"Actually I was in college. I just looked young. Not any more, I guess."

Val rolled her eyes. "Don't be so sensitive. We're all getting older."

She lined up the three guns on top of the coffee table. The largest gun was silver with a black handle. Val picked it up carefully and clicked a small lever. A cylinder with six empty compartments for housing the bullets swung out from the pistol.

"This is a revolver. Every time you pull the trigger, the cylinder revolves around and fires another shot. But it won't shoot unless you cock the hammer back each time. Like this…" she demonstrated, "and squeeze the trigger."

Even though I knew it wasn't loaded, I flinched.

She arched an eyebrow at me while she placed the revolver back on the table. Then she picked up the next gun. It was all black and sleeker than the revolver.

"This one's a semi-automatic. That means it'll keep firing each time you press the trigger. It's called a Sig because that's the name of the manufacturer." She pointed to a similar looking gun on the table. "That one's a Glock. Different manufacturer, but it's still a semi-automatic. So it works the same way."

She pressed a latch on the side of the Sig and a piece of metal slipped out from the heel of the handle. It looked like a giant staple loader.

"Semi-automatics use magazines like this one to load the cartridges." She held it out for me to see. "They're easier to shoot than revolvers and they can hold more ammunition. Some guns can take as many as fifteen rounds at a time."

Val put the magazine back on the table. Then she took one bullet out of each box and placed it under the gun to which it belonged. The bullets all looked like they were made out of the same gold metal, but each one was a different size.

"These are brass cartridges," she said. "The bullet is actually just the tip of the cartridge. The brass casing below the tip holds the gunpowder. In general, the larger the cartridge, the more powerful the ammo."

One by one, she inserted twelve cartridges into the magazine of the Sig. When it was fully loaded, she snapped it back into the heel of the gun.

"If you pull the slide back like this..." She pulled back on the top of the Sig and an opening appeared, revealing a single brass cartridge. "You can see there's a round seated in the chamber ready to fire."

Instinctively I recoiled when she held the gun closer for me to see.

She laughed. "The hammer's down. You lower it by pressing down on the decocking lever." She pointed to it on the left side of the gun. "With the hammer down, the Sig won't fire unless you pull the trigger really hard. It's a safety feature called double action trigger pull." I must have looked confused because she added, "Never mind - you'll understand when you try it on the range."

She pointed to the heel of the gun. "When you run out of ammunition, the gun stops firing and locks in the open position. Now," she wagged her finger at me, "pay attention. Because what I'm about to say is extremely important. When you pull out the magazine, always check to make sure there's no round left in the chamber." She pulled back on the slide again and removed the bullet. "Otherwise you can blow your head off."

I followed Val through a heavy metal door at the back of the store. We wound our way through a labyrinth of narrow corridors until we arrived at another door that opened onto a tiny vestibule leading to the shooting range. Val handed me ear protectors and clear plastic wrap-around goggles and told me to put them on. She did the same. The ear protectors were so tight, I felt like my head was in a vise.

We stepped through the door to the shooting range. A row of cubicles fronted on an open space that resembled a huge cement box. I was surprised to see so many people there.

Val pushed a button on the wall of our cubicle and a metal clip attached to a pulley rolled towards us. She took a paper bull's-eye and attached it to the clip, and then pushed the button again until the bull's-eye receded about twenty feet.

I tried the revolver first. Val stood behind me and showed me how to hold the gun in my right hand while supporting it with my left. Then she told me to extend my right index finger along the barrel above the trigger. I was terrified that I would accidentally shoot us both. She told me to cock the hammer and gently squeeze the trigger. I had trouble getting the hammer to pull back, so she put her hand over mine and showed me how much force to exert. Then she stepped back and told me to fire.

Val reined in the target. I had managed to hit a corner of the paper, far from the group of circles expanding out from the bull's-eye.

"At least you hit the paper," Val said. I could tell from the way she moved her mouth that she was yelling so that I could hear her through the ear protectors.

Next I tried an automatic. Each time I fired, the brass cartridge flew up and some of them hit me in the head. That explained why they wanted you to wear protective goggles. Val had promised the automatic would be easier to handle, and it was. Within no time I was hitting near the bull's-eye. Val picked one of the empty brass casings off the floor and gestured towards the vestibule. I followed her out.

"You're a natural," she said, removing her ear protectors.

"Thanks."

"You've been shooting a .22," Val said, showing me the casing. "See? It's small so it has almost no recoil."

"What's that?"

"It's when the gun jumps back after you pull the trigger."

I was about to learn about this the hard way. We put our goggles and ear protectors back on and went out to the range.

Val handed me the Sig. "The Sig shoots a bigger bullet than the gun you just tried - 9 millimeters - the same caliber as your Walther."

Only the Walther was so small that it fit in the palm of my hand, making it more concealable. But given its relative size, I didn't see how it could possibly be as powerful as the Sig.

Val must have guessed my thoughts because she said, "the size of the gun doesn't matter. The same caliber bullet can be used in guns of different sizes. The Walther may be small, but at 9 millimeters, believe me, it'll get the job done. But because the gun is smaller, you have to aim it more carefully."

I fired six rounds with the Sig. The recoil made my hand jump back and I almost lost my balance.

"Not bad." She took the Sig back and handed me the Glock. "Get ready - this one packs even more punch. Plant your feet so you're well balanced before you pull the trigger."

This time I was prepared. I fired and stood my ground. Bull's-eye. I fired another round and kept pulling the trigger until I ran out of ammunition. I pushed a button and the magazine popped out of the heel of the gun just as Val had described. She looked impressed.

I took the Walther out of my purse.

"Put that thing away!"

"You promised you'd teach me how to use it."

"You don't have a license for it yet," she said.

"I'll get one - eventually. But for now, who's gonna know?"

Val looked like she had a sudden migraine.

I attached another paper bull's-eye to the metal clip and pushed the button on the side of the cubicle to move it further down the range. Looking down the barrel, I lined up the rear and forward sight lines with the target and cocked the hammer. I pictured Hoarse Voice in his black mask. Then I carefully squeezed the trigger and kept on firing.

Chapter 30

We drove to Soundview High School in Val's Jag and she lectured me the whole way about guns. I'd had beginner's luck. I shouldn't get cocky. It was important to practice. Shooting in a life and death situation was nothing like shooting on a range. I nodded and turned up the volume on the radio.

We got hopelessly lost until Val finally turned onto the school access road by accident. A hideous modern building painted blue and yellow with white trim loomed at the top of a steep hill, sprawling in every direction like some giant bug, completely devoid of symmetry.

The door to the main entrance was locked, so we walked around the building to see if Iris Cole was waiting for us at another entrance. The main campus expanded out from the back of the building, dominated by a giant football stadium. Ten minutes later, we'd come full circle just as an old white Buick pulled into the parking lot.

Iris Cole emerged from the car, a small woman with sharp birdlike features. Not exactly the old lady I'd imagined over the phone, but not young either. She had short graying dark hair that curled under in a pageboy, reaching to the top of her shoulders. A fringe of thick bangs hid her forehead, stopping just above her eyebrows.

She greeted us politely with a firm handshake, her hand so tiny that even mine seemed gargantuan by comparison. Hers shook slightly as she turned the key in the lock and held the front door open for us. She made a joke about needing to cut down on caffeine.

We entered a wide lobby. A large glass display case in the middle of the floor exhibited the work of students who had distinguished themselves during the year. It was filled with work by aspiring writers, architects, and future historians. Soundview High clearly had some extraordinary students.

At the back of the lobby, hallways flanked both sides of the main office, which was visible from behind large glass windows. Iris led the way down the hallway on the right past walls covered in memorabilia from the past year. An entire wall was covered in pictures from the Civil War. Beyond that, an astronomy class had recreated the solar system in a glass cupboard using photographs and three-dimensional models. We turned left at the end of the hallway and came to the cafeteria followed by the gym, the smell of old sweat still permeating the air.

As we walked, Iris asked about Cy's murder. She wanted to know if the police had any leads and how the other kids were handling things. It might have been her body language, or maybe it was just her tone of voice, but I developed a nagging suspicion that something was bothering her. I glanced at Val to see if she'd noticed. She must have sensed my gaze because she looked at me suddenly, lifting an eyebrow before turning her attention back to Iris.

We turned left down another hallway, and then right. Val wore high-heeled Pradas that clicked noisily against the tile as she walked along. Heels, nails – she was always clicking something.

I could tell we were approaching the performing arts auditorium from the photographs: actors, dancers, musicians, and designers of every type covered the walls. When we finally got there, I was bowled over. It was huge – built to seat at least 500.

"This is incredible," I said. "It's nicer than Omnibus."

I went backstage and examined the lighting and sound equipment. State-of-the art. I popped my head out. "Val - you've got to see this."

Val wasn't paying any attention. She was standing at the foot of the stage, her eyes darting around the mezzanine where row after row of brand new seats sloped upward towards the back of the theater. All were in an upright position, the natural wood undersides elegantly contrasting with the beige upholstered seatbacks. However, one seat located on the aisle in the second to last row looked different from the others. It was down - as if someone had recently been sitting there.

Val climbed the steps to the mezzanine, her hand casually resting inside her pants pocket. Instinctively I reached for the Walther I had carefully hidden in my own pocket, and was comforted by the feel of cool metal. I wondered if I'd have the guts to use it.

Iris's eyes widened. "Is everything all right?"

I tried to sound unconcerned. "Of course. How about showing me where everything is backstage?"

I followed her into the wings. She gave me a brief overview of the light board and pointed out the ladders to each catwalk. After a while, she seemed more relaxed.

"Watch this." She pushed a button and the front of the stage lowered automatically. "Billy taught me that."

"A real orchestra pit," I said. "Incredible."

"Where'd you guys go?" Val called from out front.

"We're backstage," I said, poking my head out. "Everything okay up there?"

"As far as I can tell."

When we were finished with the tour, Iris led us out through the front of the building. After she locked the doors behind us, we walked her to her car. She slid behind the wheel and rolled down her window.

"I almost forgot to ask you - did Billy come home?" I asked.

Her face fell, grief and fear mingling in her expression. "No."

"Did you call the police?" Val asked gently.

Iris nodded. "They were no help."

"What did they say?" I asked.

"That Billy was upset about Cy. That he'll come home eventually."

Watching her wipe her eyes with those tiny hands, I felt so sorry for her. Val, on the other hand, had stopped paying attention. The way her eyes kept roving around the parking lot was making me nervous.

"Let's find a place to sit down and grab something to eat," I said.

Chapter 31

The Soudview was an old fashioned diner with pale green walls and a long Formica counter stretching along one wall. Near the cash register was a freestanding display of desserts that, according to the sign, were baked on the premises. The chocolate fudge cake had me practically drooling.

"Table ladies?" A bald, thin waiter wearing crumpled black slacks and a white button-down shirt stepped forward. A little white nametag pinned to his chest informed us that his name was George.

The place was nearly empty. George led us to the back of the restaurant and placed us at a roomy booth that could have seated six.

"What'll it be, ladies?"

I ordered the fudge cake.

Val rolled her eyes. "How can you eat like that?" She flashed George her thousand-watt smile and ordered a grilled chicken salad.

George looked smitten. "Anything to drink?"

"Plain water's fine," she said.

George looked expectantly at Iris, his pen poised over his order pad.

"Just black coffee, please."

"Have you had anything to eat today?" Val asked.

Iris shook her head.

It took some coaxing, but we finally convinced her to order a sandwich with her coffee.

When George was beyond hearing range, Val leaned forward and asked Iris if she'd mind answering a few questions.

Iris looked at me and I nodded reassuringly. "It's okay."

"Has Billy ever taken off like this before?" Val asked.

Iris looked like a deer caught in headlights. "Not like this."

"You're afraid something's happened to him?"

Unfortunately, the waiter picked that exact moment to reappear, shouldering a tray of food.

Iris looked everywhere but at Val while George sorted out the dishes.

When he finally departed, Val said, "Iris – if you tell us what's worrying you, maybe we can help."

Iris took a deep breath as if she was trying to steady herself. "When Billy came home yesterday, he went straight to his room and slammed the door. I begged him to let me in." She toyed with her sandwich. "Finally he opened the door and told me Cy was dead."

"They were close?" Val asked.

Iris nodded. "Billy was three when his father deserted us. Since then, it's just been the two of us. I had to work a lot, but we stayed close. Then everything changed when he got to the eighth grade." Iris rested her chin on her hand and stared into her plate.

"What do you mean?" Val asked.

"He grew listless. Distant. He stopped confiding in me. He'd hole up in his room for hours listening to loud music and playing games on his computer." Iris took a sip of coffee and set the cup back on the saucer before continuing. "One day I got a call from the principal of the Middle School. I work at the High School, so we rarely bump into each other. She said Billy had missed a lot of school and she wondered if I knew about it because I hadn't called in any absences."

"So what did you do?" I asked, trying not to sound impatient.

Iris wiped a tear from under her eye. "I confronted him. We argued. But in the end, he finally told me he was in trouble. "

"What kind of trouble?" Val asked.

"Drugs."

"Jesus," I said.

Iris' shoulders sagged. She looked like she wanted to shrink into herself and disappear. "I think it started with marijuana, but then it escalated to cocaine; even heroin. Billy's guidance counselor helped me get him into a rehab program here in Soundview. It's called Amber Hills."

"I'm so sorry," I said.

"He was in their residential program for three months. Then he continued as an outpatient for a year after that. He's been clean for almost two years."

"But now you're afraid he's back on drugs?" Val said.

"I don't know what to think."

"Did he act like he was?" Val asked.

Iris shook her head. "He acted afraid." She laced her fingers together so tightly that her knuckles went white. "I asked him if he had any ideas about who might've killed Cy."

"Did he?"

"He said he didn't."

"But you don't believe him?" Val said.

Iris's voice dropped to a whisper. "He was afraid of something - I'm sure of that. And now he's missing."

"Did you tell any of this to the police?" Val asked.

"No – how could I? They'd want to question him. Dredge everything up again."

"There are worse things, Iris," I said.

Iris looked at me and turned white. For a minute, I thought she was going to keel over. Then the tears she'd been trying so hard to suppress spilled over and she cried as if her heart would break.

Chapter 32

When the elevator doors opened onto my floor, I was surprised to see Jordan coming out of my apartment.

"Hey," she said. "Hope you don't mind me crashing again."

"Course not. What's up?"

"Some kid found a body in the woods near the cliff-jumping rock."

I could barely breathe. "Who?"

"No idea."

"What's the cliff-jumping rock?" Val asked.

"Kids dive off a cliff into a swimming hole," Jordan explained. She turned her attention back to me. "What's wrong?"

"Billy Cole's missing. Can we come with you?"

"How do you know?"

"His mother. Please, Jordan - it's important. I'll explain on the way."

She took another frustrating moment to think about it. Her eyes cut from me to Val, taking in the high-heeled Pradas she was wearing.

"Do you have any sneakers? We're going into the woods," Jordan told her.

"Of course." Val flashed an ingratiating smile, which was lost on Jordan, and disappeared inside. When she reappeared, she had a navy jacket flung over one shoulder and, in place of the Pradas, hot pink Pumas that looked like they glowed in the dark. At least we wouldn't lose her in the woods. Jordan shot her a look she didn't see. Or pretended not to see. I was starting to learn that Val didn't miss much.

Jordan pressed the elevator button. "I'm parked down in the garage."

"Let's take my car," Val said.

Jordan bristled. "Why?"

"I get nervous when other people drive." She tried another Val smile. "Besides, if I drive, you can concentrate on your story."

Located in Weston, the cliff-jumping rock was a teenage rite of passage. Thrill-seeking kids – Jordan and me among them – dove off the rock, plunging twelve feet below into a narrow pool of water. By the time we got there, the sun was setting quickly, transforming the trees into black silhouettes against a dark blue sky.

A cop stopped us as we drove up. Jordan leaned over from the passenger seat and passed him her press badge through Val's window. He examined it carefully, giving Val and me a cursory glance before waving us on to a makeshift parking area under some trees.

We crossed the road on foot and positioned ourselves near the edge of the cliff. It took a while to adjust to the eerie glow of floodlights that had been positioned around the area. Arcs of light beamed in different directions as dark shapes moved through the woods below us.

Jordan spotted a group of cops and charged off in their direction, leaving Val and me to our own devices.

"Jesus," a male voice whispered near my elbow.

I almost fell off the cliff. A firm hand grabbed my arm and pulled me back from the ledge.

"Kate! Sorry. Didn't mean to scare you." Peter Robinson, a photographer from the Times, was looking at me apologetically. I knew him through Jordan; they'd worked together on a number of stories. He was tall and lanky with dark hair highlighted with bleached-blond streaks. A painful looking silver stud pierced the flesh of one eyebrow.

I introduced him to Val. He acknowledged her briefly, and then went back to snapping pictures of something I could barely make out at the bottom of the cliff.

Then I saw what he was photographing. A pair of pale naked legs extended out from yellow swim trunks. He was lying on his back and even at that distance I could tell that he was young. His arms were flung at odd angles; his face hidden in the shadows.

God, please don't let it be Billy. I reasoned with myself that he looked younger than Billy. But in truth, I had no idea who he was as I strained to see below me in the gathering darkness.

"Let's go," Val said.

We walked off in the direction of where we'd last seen Jordan heading and spotted Matt Warren huddled in the middle of a group of men and women - some in uniform, others not. Val and I stepped closer to the trees so he wouldn't see us.

Just then, my cell phone vibrated in my pocket. I took it out and flipped it open.

"Kate?" a female voice said.

"Yes. Who's this please?" I said quietly.

"Iris Cole." She sounded upset.

"What's wrong, Iris?"

Val motioned for me to follow her further into the woods.

"A man has Billy." Iris started to cry. "He says you stole something and if you don't give it back, he'll kill Billy."

I tried to speak, but the words stuck in my throat. Finally, I managed to say, "Iris - I don't know what he's talking about."

"Please!" Iris shouted. "You have to help me."

"Calm down, Iris. I want to help you. But I haven't stolen anything."

Val lowered her palm through the air and mouthed a warning *shush* for me to lower my voice.

I put my hand over the mouthpiece and whispered to Val, "Billy's been kidnapped."

"Oh my God. Ask her if she spoke to him."

I asked Iris the question. Val placed her ear next to mine and I held the phone so that we could both hear the response.

"No - he wouldn't let me!" Iris' voice turned shrill. "You can't tell the police anything. He'll kill Billy if they get involved. You haven't told anyone he's missing, have you?"

"No. No, I haven't." I said.

Iris seemed to have forgotten that she'd already called the Soundview police herself, but she was so hysterical that I didn't think now was a good time to remind her. Val mouthed the word *meeting* and I nodded my head in agreement.

"Iris, let's talk about this in person," I said. "Can I come to your house?"

"No. He could be watching my house." Her voice dropped as if it had suddenly occurred to her that he might be listening in on our conversation.

"There's an all-night diner on Route 1 in Westport," I said.

"Too public," Val whispered.

"On second thought," I said, "Maybe it's not private enough. Do you know how to get to Weston Center?"

"Yes, but it'll take me a half hour or more to get there."

"That's okay. Let's meet at ten. That should give you plenty of time, and by then all the stores will be closed. Drive around to the back behind the post office and stay in your car. I'll come find you."

I snapped the phone shut, not having the heart to tell her I was looking over a cliff at a boy who might be her son.

"What time is it?" I asked Val.

She looked at her watch. "Almost eight."

"We can't meet Iris without knowing for certain if it's Billy down there."

"Let's find Jordan," Val suggested. "Maybe she knows who it is by now."

We found her with a crowd of reporters shouting questions at Matt Warren, which for the most part, he refused to answer. I motioned for her to come over to where we were standing, but she waved me away.

We decided to stay hidden until she could join us. The last thing we needed was for Matt to spot us and ask what we were doing there. I kept my eyes glued to the spot where he was holding court with a group of officers, obviously the person in charge. One of them – a man – shifted his position so that suddenly his face became visible in the floodlight. Art Desmond from Sparky's lighting crew was listening attentively to what Matt had to say, clearly a member of the inner sanctum.

This evening was growing more bizarre by the minute.

I grabbed Val by the arm, "There's a hidden path Jordan and I used to take when we were kids. We used it to sneak up on people diving off the cliff. With any luck, the police haven't discovered it yet."

We headed up the hill and walked north, staying close to the trees lining the perimeter of the road. After a quarter-mile or so, we came to a small rock formation that provided a natural bridge over the stream. The rock wasn't as slippery as usual thanks to the dry summer we'd been having, and we crossed over to the other side easily. The path was overgrown with brush and looked like it hadn't been used in years. We threaded our way back until the stream widened into a pool.

Only a few feet of water separated us from the boy who lay on the opposite shoreline. In the harsh white light, he looked like a marble statue on display in a museum. His hair was caked with mud. Muscles had begun forming around his arms and chest, beginning the transformation into manhood that now he would never know. The boy wasn't Billy.

"The police wouldn't give out his name. They have to tell his family first," Jordan said.

We walked towards the car in single file, staying as close to the trees as possible.

"You didn't tell anyone Billy's missing, did you?" I asked.

"No, but maybe someone should."

"If the police get involved, Billy's as good as dead," I said.

"I agree with Kate." Val looked back at Jordan who was walking behind her. "Where do you want us to drop you?"

It was too dark to see her expression, but I could feel Jordan seething.

"I'm not letting go of this story," she said in a quiet voice. Her eyes cut to me, "Tell her."

"Jordan brought us along, Val. It's her story. She knows the risks." I hoped that was true. She was my best friend and I would never go against her. But if she got hurt, I'd never forgive myself either.

Val tsked. "You're the client."

We reached Val's Jag and got in without arousing anyone's curiosity. Val pulled out onto Valley Forge Road and drove the short distance to Weston Center while Jordan and I navigated. As we drove, we came up with a plan.

Chapter 33

We parked in the school bus lot across from the Center, out of sight from the main road.

"Put your cell phones on silent mode," Val ordered. She fumbled in her purse and withdrew her Glock.

Jordan said, "What's that for?"

"In case he's following her."

Val rummaged some more in an oversized tote and extracted a brown leather holster that she strapped around her waist, shoving the Glock inside. Next came the navy jacket, which hid the gun and disguised the holster as an innocent looking belt. She got out of the car and took one last look around. Then she got back behind the wheel and maneuvered the car forward.

Instead of driving directly into Weston Center, we drove past it and headed north until we came to a small road that let us loop around and drive back towards the Center on a street running parallel to the main road. When we were certain we weren't being followed, we turned back onto the main road and approached the Center from the south, entering through the gas station.

The station sat in between the post office and a large circular drive lined with stores that provided all of life's necessities: food, hardware, liquor, and pharmaceuticals. All errands could be completed without ever having to move your car. Fortunately the stores were all closed at this hour - even the Lunch Box, Weston Center's only eatery.

Val backed into a space on the northern side of the gas station between two other cars. To the average passerby, we looked like just another automobile waiting to be serviced first thing in the morning.

We had a clear view of the Post Office and, most importantly, a straight escape out to the main road. Although we couldn't see the circle from where we were parked, we'd hear if anyone drove in from that direction.

Val turned to Jordan. "Okay - you can get out of the car now. Remember to walk slowly and stay close to the wall. Then hide behind the dumpster and don't say a word."

I had a knot in the pit of my stomach. My best friend was about to put her life on the line for a story.

"Maybe you should stay in the car."

"Let's stick to the plan," Jordan said. "If something happens, I can either stay hidden behind the dumpster or – plan B - run like hell and jump back in the car and drive away with you." She paused. "Kate, I'll be fine. It's my job. I know what I'm doing."

"If anyone approaches the Center – and I mean anyone – send me a text message," Val told Jordan. She stretched out her arm. "Here - give me your cell phone. I'll program my number into it."

When Val finished entering her number, she handed the phone back to Jordan. Then I took the wheel and Val jumped into the back seat. Jordan got out of the car and eased her way along the wall until she reached the dumpster and disappeared.

At five minutes before ten o'clock, we heard a car approaching from the south. Then a big white car came into view and signaled left before slowly turning into the Post Office and nosing into a parking spot along the southern wall of the building. The sound of the engine cut out and, moments later, the headlights went out too.

"Do you see anything?" Val was talking to Jordan over her cell phone. The answer must have been negative because shortly after that, Val instructed me to get out of the car and convince Iris to switch vehicles.

The distance between the two cars couldn't have been more than a few yards, but it felt like I'd been walking forever by the time I reached Iris' white Buick. I tapped on her window and she jumped.

I motioned for her to roll down the window while I looked in all directions for any signs of movement. "I'm parked over there," I whispered. "We're better off talking in my car in case he's tailing you."

Iris said, "How do I know I can trust you?"

"Iris - I've been attacked twice, someone tried to blow up my building, and now Billy's been kidnapped." I looked behind me to make sure there was nothing moving in the woods. "We need to figure this out together because I have no idea why all this is happening."

Iris got out of her car. She timidly followed my lead and clung to the side of the building until we were close enough to jump into the Jag. She climbed into the passenger seat, glancing dubiously at Val in the back.

Once inside the car, her courage returned. "What have you stolen?" Her tone was accusatory.

"Iris – you have to believe me. I haven't stolen anything."

"He says you have."

"But it's not true!"

We heard a car turn into the circle. "Get down," I whispered, lowering myself below the dashboard.

Iris ducked down.

Wheels crunched against the tarmac as the car rounded the circle. The sound of the motor grew louder the closer it came to the post office. Finally it stopped, somewhere in the vicinity of Iris' car. We heard a car door slam, followed by footsteps. I held my breath and begged God to keep Jordan safe. I started to poke my head above the dash, but Iris pulled me back down with a force I never would have expected.

The footsteps stopped. A few seconds later, the blare of Iris' cell phone shattered the silence.

"Turn that damn thing off!" Val popped up from the back seat and grabbed it out of Iris' hand. She hit the silence key on the side of the phone and the ringing stopped. Iris grabbed her chest.

We heard running footsteps, followed by someone pounding on the window. Val swung the door open and Jordan dove in head-first.

"Did you get a look at him?" I asked.

"It was too dark," Jordan replied.

Val had her Glock out and was pointing it at the back window. "Go!"

She didn't need to tell me a second time. I hit the accelerator pedal and the Jag took off. Two shots rang out, bouncing off a tree to our left.

"If he hits this car, I'll kill you myself," Val said.

I wasn't sure if she meant Iris or me.

"Head back to the cliff-jumping rock," Jordan said. "If you can't lose him, he might back off when he sees all the cops there."

"No police!" Iris was still clutching her chest.

"You having a heart attack Iris?" Val asked.

Iris shook her head and tried to catch her breath. "You tricked me," she said looking at me.

"No." In my rearview mirror, I saw headlights gaining on me. "He tricked you."

I pressed down harder on the accelerator pedal and the Jag sped up. As we drove past houses lining both sides of the road, I started worrying that some residents might have heard the shots and called the police. I glanced at the speedometer. I was doing sixty on a winding country road. Any faster and I'd get us all killed.

"We're trying to protect you," Val told Iris.

"You're not a producer?"

I glanced in the rearview mirror and thought I saw Jordan suppress a smile.

"I'm a security consultant," Val said. "Kate's family hired me to protect her."

"Who are you?" Iris asked Jordan.

"Jordan Hollis. I'm a reporter for The New York Times."

"None of us want anything to happen to Billy," I said.

Iris didn't say anything, but out of the corner of my eye, I saw her slump in her seat. Headlights behind me loomed nearer.

"Shit. He's catching up," Val said. "Step on it."

I accelerated and the Jag took off. His lights receded in the distance. I'd been driving these roads since childhood and felt certain I could lose him.

"Turn here," Jordan said.

"You're reading my mind." I barely moved the wheel; the Jag responded like it was part of my hand.

His tires squealed as he almost missed the turn.

"Damn," Jordan said. "Go faster."

A road came in from the left, and I waited until the last minute to turn onto it. His reflexes were fast and he followed just in time, inches off my bumper.

"Hold on guys." I pressed the accelerator pedal to the floor. The road twisted and turned. We skidded through one of the turns just as a shot rang out. It missed. I clenched the steering wheel tighter and rounded another sharp curve. Val cursed as our tires scraped against a boulder on the side of the road.

We were speeding north on winding roads that led out of town towards Easton. We rounded the reservoir and this time when I looked in my rearview mirror, blackness stretched behind us.

"Did we lose him?" I asked.

"Not sure," Jordan replied.

His lights winked on and another shot sounded like it hit one of our taillights. He was bearing down on us.

"My car!" Val said. "Go faster."

Iris hadn't said a word in a long time. I glanced over at her. She was slumped in her seat with her eyes tight shut.

"Iris – you okay?" I said. "Somebody take a look at Iris."

Jordan leaned forward and shook her shoulder. Iris groaned.

Val said, "We need to get her to a hospital."

"Okay," I said. "Hold on."

I turned the wheel to the left and his headlights disappeared. Then he made the turn too and they reappeared, although I'd put some distance between us. We were on a main road leading to the parkway, but with any luck, he didn't know that. I glanced at the speedometer; I was clocking eighty.

"Cut your lights," Val said.

"Are you crazy? I can't drive onto the parkway without lights."

"Just do it," Val said.

I turned my lights out, grateful that the road had straightened out. In my rearview mirror, I saw his headlights way off in the distance. The road ended, and I made a sharp right without slowing down and somehow managed to merge onto the Parkway. Glancing in my mirror, I expected to see him following, but there was only blackness.

When we'd gone about a half-mile up the Parkway, I turned my lights back on, scaring the hell out of an SUV driver who narrowly missed plowing into us. He moved into the left lane, giving me the finger as he passed. I was doing ninety-five; he had to be going well over a hundred.

Suddenly a siren blared. Red revolving lights pierced the blackness that stretched behind me.

"Dammit," I said. "Police."

"Take the ticket," Val said, "and say as little as possible."

The tires squealed as I braked to a stop. In my side mirror, I saw the police car stop and extinguish its lights. A dark shape got out of the car and approached us on foot.

"Why isn't he wearing a uniform?" Jordan asked.

"Good question," Val said.

As he got closer, I saw that he was wearing a short dark jacket and no hat. There was something familiar about him. He stooped down to peer into my window, and I recognized Art Desmond.

"Evening ladies," he said.

I cracked my window and immediately got a whiff of tobacco. "Art?"

The lit tip moved through the darkness as his hand reached his mouth and he dragged deeply on the cigarette. "The same," he said, exhaling a cloud of smoke.

I lowered my window the rest of the way.

He pulled out his wallet from inside his jacket and opened it, passing it through the window so I could see his badge. Detective Art Desmond.

"Traffic violations are not usually my thing, but do you realize you were driving ninety-five miles an hour – and part of the time without lights?"

Iris groaned as if on cue. I put a reassuring hand on her arm and said, "I was on my way to the hospital. I think she's having a heart attack."

Desmond's face fell. "My God. Let me pull out in front of you. I'll give you an escort to the hospital. I'll radio ahead so they expect you."

His sirens blared the whole way there. I followed as closely as I dared, glancing frequently behind me.

"He's gone," Val said. "He never got onto the parkway."

Iris was moaning in pain by the time we arrived. Two medics hoisted her onto a gurney and wheeled her into the ER through double glass doors that sprang open automatically. Jordan went with her while Val and I parked the car in the underground garage.

Art Desmond removed the red revolving light from the top of his car before following us to the garage. After we'd nosed the Jag into a parking space, he stepped out of his vehicle and held the rear door open for us. "Get in, ladies. I'll drive you back to Emergency."

The car looked like a regular Chevrolet now that he had removed the light from on top. But in order to get out of the car, someone had to open the doors from the outside; there were no door handles in the back seat. My palms started sweating as my claustrophobia took over. I tried taking deep breaths, but that only made me hyperventilate.

Art drove us back to the Emergency Room entrance and finally let us out. I breathed in the cool night air and felt better.

"Does Billy know about his mom?" Art asked. "I can call him for you if you'd like."

I tried not to react to hearing Billy's name. "Thanks, but I think I'd better do it."

He looked relieved and started to go, but turned back around as if he'd forgotten something.

"One thing - I'd appreciate it if you didn't tell anyone at the theater that I'm a cop."

"Your secret's safe with us," I said.

He smiled and got back in his car.

Chapter 34

It was two o'clock in the morning by the time we got back to my apartment and discovered my answering machine blinking. I tried ignoring it, but finally gave in and pressed the *Play* button.

"Kate, it's Dad. Call me whenever you get in. It's important."

He picked up on the first ring.

"What's wrong? Is someone sick?"

"No. No. Everyone's fine."

The tension in my shoulders eased up a little.

"Something happened at the hospital tonight I thought you should know about."

I sat down at the kitchen table. Jordan and Val had followed me into the kitchen and sat down also.

"Do you remember the two kids they brought in the other night? One died?" my father asked.

"Sure."

"The kid that pulled through – Andrew Barnes – claims someone came into his hospital room and threatened him. He's been ranting ever since about warning Billy Cole. Isn't that the kid who works at the theater?"

I drew in a sharp breath. "My God."

"Do you know what he's talking about?"

"I think so."

Jordan and Val were watching me intently

"Dad – Billy Cole was kidnapped tonight."

"How do you know that?" The distress in Dad's voice made me sorry I'd blurted it out that way. I told him about Iris Cole minus the chase through Weston.

"Kate, maybe you should stay here for now."

"I'll be fine, Dad. Honestly."

He stayed silent. I could almost feel him worrying through the line.

"Please don't worry. Jordan and Val are both with me."

"Okay." He didn't sound convinced.

I let a moment go by before asking, "Did Andrew say what the guy looked like?"

"Not really. He wore a surgical mask."

"Damn."

"What the hell does this guy want?" Jordan said, more to herself.

"Drugs. Money. Maybe both," Val said.

They looked at me.

"How the hell do I know?" I was exhausted and couldn't think straight anymore.

"One thing's for certain," Jordan said. "He didn't get what he wanted from you, so he's expanded the search."

"So where does that leave poor Billy?" I asked.

"Maybe Billy led him to Andrew," Jordan said.

"Or the other way around," Val said.

Chapter 35

Andrew Barnes was in Room 416, across from the nurse's station. It was breakfast time and the aroma of eggs and bacon almost masked the stench of cleaning fluid and antiseptic. Nobody seemed interested in where we were going or whether we belonged there. Attila the Hun could have swept in with his entire army and no one would have stopped him. Thank goodness Soundview Hospital wasn't high on terrorist hit lists.

When we walked in, Andrew was propped up on pillows, eating breakfast and watching *Smallville* on a tiny TV screen fastened to a moving metal arm that stretched over his bed. His eyes stayed glued to the TV as he forked scrambled eggs into his mouth, oblivious to the bits of egg that were spilling onto the front of his hospital gown. He was a hefty boy with spiky red hair and a round face covered in freckles. He had some cuts and bruises on his face too.

We hovered over his bed for a while before he realized we were there. Finally, he acknowledged our presence, peering at us through glazed eyes that seemed to be having trouble focusing. He rotated his head a few times as if trying to rid himself of a kink in his neck, then clamped his eyes shut. When he opened them again, he squinted at us like he couldn't decide if we were really there in the room with him or if we were a figment of his imagination.

Jordan stepped forward. "I'm Jordan Hollis from The New York Times."

"Cool." Andrew tried to focus on Jordan's face, then gave up and turned back to *Smallville*.

"How are you feeling?" Jordan asked, trying to get his attention again. A few beats went by. "Andrew?"

"Huh? Oh yeah. I feel fine."

He looked at Val and me, but didn't ask who we were.

"Mind if I ask you some questions for the paper?" Jordan asked.

Andrew broke into a smile, momentarily lucid. "Sure."

"What happened to you?" asked Jordan.

"I was driving my mom's car and hit a tree."

"Were you by yourself?" Jordan said.

He shook his head and his eyes clouded over, as if trying to remember something. "Luke was with me. Do you know Luke?"

We all said no; we didn't know Luke. I wondered if he even knew that Luke was dead.

"We know Billy Cole, though," I said. "Do you know him?"

What little color Andrew had in his face drained completely away. He blended in with the sheets so thoroughly that I was reminded of a pet chameleon I once owned.

"Billy's in a lot of trouble," he whispered.

"Why's that, Andrew?" Jordan said quietly.

"He and Cy were real tight."

Andrew tried to pull himself up by the bed railing. His face flushed with the effort and he groaned. "A man said he's gonna kill me if I say anything."

"Say anything about what, Andrew?" Jordan asked.

"I don't know!" He fell back onto the bed and buried his face in the pillow.

"What else did the man say?" Jordan asked.

"He said he's gonna kill every kid who worked for Cy." Andrew's voice sounded muffled through the pillow.

"Worked for him at the theater?" I asked.

Andrew lifted his face up from the pillow. "Yeah."

Anxiety shot through me as I tried picturing the six or seven kids who worked at Omnibus. I was certain Andrew wasn't one of them.

"Have you ever worked at the theater?" I asked.

"Unh-unh."

"So how come he came after you? Did you take something?"

"No - I swear."

"Andrew." I put my hand on his arm, careful not to disturb the IV. "This is important. Did Billy steal something?"

"I don't know!" He wound the top sheet around his finger so tightly that his finger turned purple. "Maybe."

"What did he steal, Andrew? Drugs?"

Panic filled his eyes. "I don't know. I swear I don't."

I tried a different approach. "Is there someone else who might know?"

Andrew looked at me and gave a slight nod, as if a bigger gesture might put him in greater danger.

"Who can tell us, Andrew?" I said. "Please. We want to help you."

"Justin Reed," he whispered. "Billy's best friend."

"Do you know his address?"

"He's back in rehab. Hiding."

"From who?" Val broke in. "The man who threatened you?"

Andrew closed his eyes like he hoped it would make us disappear. When he opened them again, he looked Val in the eye. "I don't know. Maybe."

"What's his name?" Val asked.

"I don't know." Andrew's voice dropped to a whisper.

"What's the name of the rehab?" she asked.

"Amber Hills. Val bent closer to him. "What did the man look like?"

Andrew looked at Val for a few moments as if he was trying to place her. "Who are you?"

Val flashed her most dazzling smile. "I'm Val."

"Cool," Andrew said, obviously charmed.

She leaned over the bed railing and took his hand gently. "I'll kick anyone's butt who tries to hurt you."

Andrew gave a small smile, but the fear never left his eyes.

"What'd he look like?" Val asked again.

"A doctor. I couldn't see his face 'cause he had a mask on."

"What'd he sound like?" Val asked.

Andrew closed his eyes and for a minute, I thought he'd fallen asleep. But when he opened them again, they were a little less glazed. "He had a sore throat. Kind of hoarse, like."

"You rest now," Val said soothingly.

Chapter 36

Matt Warren stepped off the elevator just as we were getting on. He stuck his arm between the closing doors and they sprang back open.

"Kate - got a minute? Save me a phone call."

A short plump Asian nurse with a stethoscope draped around her neck eyed me impatiently. She wore a white uniform dress that was hemmed just above her round stumpy knees.

I stepped off the elevator.

"I'll come with you," Val said.

The nurse gave a loud *tsk* as Val tried to maneuver around her, but the elevator doors closed in Val's face before she had a chance to get off.

"What brings you here?" Matt asked me.

"One of my father's patients is a big fan of *Young and In Love*. He thought it might cheer him up if I stopped by."

We walked down the hall and found an empty waiting room.

"We can talk in here," he said.

I sat down on a sofa and he pulled up a worn plastic chair facing me. He was so close that our knees were almost touching. Part of me wanted him to push his chair back; the other part didn't. He seemed happy leaving it where it was. I wondered if Art Desmond had told him about Iris and the night before. In case he had, I decided it was better to bring it up myself rather than risk having him think I was hiding it from him.

It would have been a relief to confide everything in him, but that wasn't an option. Still, I had to warn him that kids' lives were in danger. Like a soldier carefully crossing a minefield, I told him about the conversation with Andrew. I told him about the connection between Cy and the kids at the theater, careful not to mention anything about Justin Reid hiding out in rehab or Billy Cole having been kidnapped. I owed that much to Iris.

Matt shifted in his chair. I could tell something had clicked in his mind, but without warning his cop mask descended: expression indecipherable, eyes wary.

I decided to force the issue. "Who was the boy that died in Weston last night?"

"I thought I spotted you. What were you doing there?"

"Jordan needed a ride. Who was the boy?" I repeated.

"I can't tell you that."

"Did he work for Cy?" I asked.

His expression softened. "Look, Kate, you can't get involved in this."

"I'm already involved."

Matt hesitated, as if struggling with something. "I don't know if he worked at the theater or not. I never thought it was important – until now. I appreciate the heads up." He smiled, but his eyes were still wary. Whatever was on his mind, he wasn't sharing.

"What did you want to talk to me about?" I asked.

Matt took a moment before answering my question. Then he said, "There's a boy on your crew - Billy Cole…"

I could tell from his expression that he'd seen how startled I was. He paused, as if waiting for me to explain.

"His mother had a heart attack last night. We brought her to the hospital." I thought I'd recovered nicely. "Didn't Art Desmond tell you?"

It was his turn to be startled. "What about Art Desmond?"

"Come off it, Matt. I know he's a detective. He was with you at the cliff-jumping rock. But don't worry, I won't tell."

Matt shook his head and grinned. Then his expression turned serious. "Did you tell Billy about his mother?"

"Of course."

"That's a relief. She reported him missing earlier in the day," he said.

I was numb with guilt. For all I knew, I'd just sentenced Billy to death by not telling Matt he'd been kidnapped.

He sat back in his chair and watched me intently. "Cy's autopsy results came in. He suffocated to death, but not right away. We think Cy came out of the coma, and then someone disconnected his oxygen tank and moved the call button out of reach. Nasty way to die."

I held his gaze. "If you're trying to scare me to death, you're doing a great job."

"That's exactly what I'm trying to do. We're dealing with a homicidal maniac who has you at the top of his hit list. And you're running around the woods like it's a damn movie instead of a homicide investigation."

I stood up, feeling shaken.

He stood up also and blocked my way. "Kate, someone wants you dead and I want to know why."

"And I already told you – I don't know why! Now, if you'll excuse me, I have to go."

He shook his head and stepped out of my way.

"I know you want to help, but please – for now just stay away from Andrew and anyone else connected to this case. I can't protect you otherwise."

Val and Jordan caught up with me at the main entrance. I walked with them towards the car, still upset as I tried to explain everything that had happened.

"He's right, you know," Val said.

I frowned at Val and tried to think of a retort when my cell phone went off.

"You're not being reasonable, Kate." His hoarse voice was calm, almost friendly. "Give back what you stole and I'll let Billy go. It's as simple as that."

I stopped in the middle of the parking lot.

"How do I know you even have Billy?" My shoulder blades felt like they'd turned to steel.

Val and Jordan moved in closer, trying to hear.

I heard muffled noises, as if he'd put his hand over the receiver. Then he said clearly, "Billy? Someone wants to talk to you."

My body went rigid as I waited for Billy to take the phone.

"Kate?" Billy sounded frightened.

"Billy?"

Then I heard three high-pitched screams.

Scraping noises were followed by Billy's voice, high and pleading. "Don't. Please don't." Another scream.

I clutched the phone so tightly, my fingers cramped.

Finally he came back on the phone. "I wouldn't mention any of this to the police if I were you." Then, as if I'd asked for his address, he said, "998 Fifth Avenue."

Only it was Max and Abe's address.

Several moments passed before I realized he'd hung up.

Chapter 37

"If only I could figure out what he thinks Cy gave me at the theater, I'd have something to trade for Billy." I placed a bowl of tuna fish on the table next to a loaf of rye bread and motioned for everyone to sit down. Val ladled Minestrone soup into bowls while Jordan poured the coffee.

I sipped my soup and thought about Grandpa Max and Uncle Abe. I imagined Gramps pressing the intercom button and telling the doorman to send up the deliveryman. I pictured Uncle Abe opening the door and the look of fear on his face when he saw the gun. In my mind, I heard two shots puncture the silence, and watched as first Uncle Abe and then Grandpa Max sank to the floor, blood flowing freely; eyes widened in surprise for eternity.

"Earth to Kate," Val said. "Snap out of it!"

I looked at her. "I was thinking about my family. You can't be everywhere."

She spooned some tuna fish between two pieces of bread and took a small bite, apparently thinking about what I'd just said. Finally she said, "Sonny's finishing up an assignment today. Maybe he can help out."

"Would he be willing to stay in the city with Max and Abe for a while? They have an extra bedroom in their apartment."

"I can ask." She walked over to the telephone, pulled a stool out from underneath the countertop, sat down and dialed. Her nails clicked against the granite until Sonny finally picked up, at which point she cooed something incoherent into the phone.

Jordan rolled her eyes and I shot her a look to cut it out.

Val's conversation with Sonny only lasted a few minutes. She returned to the table smiling. "He'll do it."

Jordan took a small bite of tuna. "What about Annie and Jeff?"

My mood sunk lower. Breaking into my parents' house would be child's play. They never turned on their alarm system; the basement was always unlocked; and the deadbolts on the door were pointless since he could just break a window and get in that way. Convincing my parents to be more careful would be next to impossible.

"Matt should be able to assign someone to protect them," Val said.

I started to object, but Val interrupted. "All Matt has to know is that he threatened your family again. This has nothing to do with Billy."

The downstairs buzzer rang and I jumped up to answer it.

Val said, "Were you expecting anyone?"

Shaking my head, I ran to the intercom and pressed the *Talk* button. "Yes?"

No response.

"Who is it?"

Still no answer.

I turned around and saw Val holding the Glock in her hand. She positioned herself behind the front door with her eye flush against the peek hole.

The buzzer rang again. Val motioned for me to answer it.

"Who is it?"

"It's David. Is this a bad time?"

"Come up."

I punched the door release and saw Val hide the gun in her pocket.

David stood in the doorway. He looked like he wasn't sure if he wanted to come in.

"Did you see anyone else ring Kate's buzzer?" Val asked.

He shook his head. "That might have been me. I rang once, but then my cell phone went off and I stepped outside to answer it. Sorry."

"What are you doing here?" I asked.

"I thought I'd take a chance you'd be in and see how you're feeling. But if this is a bad time…"

"It's fine." I opened the door wider. "Come in."

I led the way into the living room. Val flopped down on one sofa and I sat next to Jordan on the other. David took a seat in one of the armchairs. He was neatly dressed in white linen slacks, a black button down, and brown penny loafers with no socks. Not exactly a blue jeans and sneakers kind of guy. A strained silence ensued.

"Did you see the rehearsal space?" he asked.

It took me a moment to realize what he was talking about.

"Yes, thanks. It's beautiful."

"I'd love to see it while I'm up here."

I must have reacted strangely because he quickly added, "If you're too busy, I can always take a taxi up there. Or maybe Iris Cole can pick me up."

David noticed Val stiffen and exchange a look with Jordan.

"What's wrong?"

Val gave me an encouraging nod.

"Iris had a heart attack last night," I said.

David's eyebrows shot up. "Is she okay?"

I stood up, realizing that I had no idea.

"I'm not sure. Excuse me – I'd better call the hospital."

I waited on hold for Patient Information to pick up while Jordan and Val fixed lunch for David, setting it up for him in the dining room. I heard him excuse himself and move towards the bathroom near the bedrooms at the back of the apartment.

Val and Jordan joined me in the kitchen just as Patient Information finally picked up. I hit the speaker button so they could hear. A woman's voice, cool and indifferent, asked how she could help me.

"I'd like to know the condition of Iris Cole, please."

"Are you a relative?" she asked.

"Her daughter," I said without hesitating.

She didn't say anything further while she consulted her computer, but I heard the *clickety-clack* of a keyboard in the background. When she came back on, she said that Iris Cole was in satisfactory condition.

David wandered into the kitchen and placed his dirty dishes in the sink. He joined us at the table and I poured everyone a cup of coffee. It was almost one o'clock. We weren't going to find Billy by sitting around my apartment.

"You all seem a bit edgy," David said. "Is something going on I should know about?"

"You mean beyond Cy's killer thinking I have something that belongs to him?"

David glanced around the table at us like we were actors he was having trouble casting. "It's obvious something else has happened. Please – let me help if I can."

An idea occurred to me. "Okay. Can you help us get back into the theater without the police knowing?"

"What for?" he asked.

"Whatever he thinks Cy handed off to me has to be there."

"And you think the police might've missed it?" Jordan said.

"Maybe." I looked at Val for support.

She shrugged. "It's worth a try."

David stayed silent for a while, tugging on his ear as he seemed to consider this.

The telephone rang, but we were all so focused on David that no one moved to answer it.

"There's a back door that leads into the basement," he said.

The phone rang again.

"Aren't you going to answer that?" David asked me.

"Of course," I said, getting up.

Before I could reach it, the phone rang once more and then the answering machine switched on.

"Billy and I are still waitin' here, Kate. Isn't that right Billy?" His gravelly hoarse voice sounded strangely loud in the quiet of my kitchen.

We heard some shuffling, then: "Please Kate..." Billy's voice sounded young, pleading. It disappeared abruptly as if someone had yanked the phone away. Then the phone clicked off and we listened to the drone of the dial tone until the answering machine finally switched off.

David's face paled. "You knew about this?"

I nodded. "Iris told us before she had the heart attack."

"Did you call the police?" David asked.

Val touched his arm. "If we go to the police - and he finds out - Billy's as good as dead."

Chapter 38

Grandpa Max must have looked more worried than he sounded over the phone because Uncle Abe picked up an extension and asked me what was wrong.

"He knows your address," I said.

"Big deal," Grandpa Max said. "So he knows where we live."

I took a breath. "Sonny's on his way into the city to stay with you."

"That's ridiculous," Uncle Abe said. "Believe me, no one is coming near us."

"Not unless he wants to get shot," Gramps said.

"If anything ever happened to you…" my voice broke.

"Katie, Katie," Grandpa Max said in a quiet voice.

"You don't understand how dangerous he is! He kidnapped a boy from the theater."

"My God," Uncle Abe said.

I put my hand up to my mouth, realizing that I'd said too much. I took another deep breath before continuing in a calmer voice. "You can't tell anyone. Especially not the police or he'll kill him. Please - you asked me to hire Val and Sonny and I'm glad I listened to you. Now I'm begging you to let Sonny stay with you in the city so he can protect you too."

They conferred with one another in muffled voices. I traced my finger around the rim of an empty glass on the counter, willing the panic I was feeling to subside. I hadn't felt this powerless since Robert's plane disappeared. Day after day I waited for his call, refusing to accept that he was dead. My family and Jordan closed ranks and pulled me back from the brink of despair and I vowed never to allow myself to sink that low again. This was no time to allow my emotions to cloud my judgment; keeping my family and Jordan safe was all that mattered. I was not willing to lose them too.

"Okay Katie," Uncle Abe said at last. "But just for a day or two."

I didn't argue; a day or two was better than nothing.

"What about your folks?" Uncle Abe said.

"Val thinks I should ask Matt Warren to assign someone to protect them."

"Great idea," Grandpa Max said.

Matt Warren sounded pleased to hear from me.

"I was going to call you," he said.

Given the testy conversation we'd had in the hospital, the warmth in his voice was surprising. I told him about the call from Hoarse Voice, leaving out all mention of Billy.

"When did this happen?" he asked.

"Right after I left you at the hospital."

He exhaled loudly. "Where's your family now?"

"My father's probably at the hospital; but he goes back and forth between the hospital and his office a lot. I'm more worried about my mother. She roams around all over the place."

"I'll put someone on both of them right away." As if anticipating what I was about to say next, he added, "Don't worry - they'll stay inconspicuous. Trust me."

"Thanks."

We were both silent a moment.

Finally I said, "I'm sorry if I was rude earlier."

"That's okay. You can make it up to me over dinner."

"Excuse me?"

So I wasn't imagining things - Matt Warren was definitely hitting on me.

"You heard me. Dinner – you and me. The price of protection."

"Oh." I imagined him grinning on the other end of the phone.

He continued in a more serious tone, "I can't do much about your grandfather and great-uncle though; the city's beyond my jurisdiction. But I'll work something out with NYPD."

I told him about Sonny.

"You're all set then. Sonny's better than the whole New York police force combined." He paused. "Is Val around? I have some news you'll both want to hear."

I called Val into the kitchen and waited for her to sit down before pressing the *Speaker* button.

She arched an eyebrow at me and then focused on the phone. "Hey Matt."

He said, "We ID'd the fingerprints on that Ipod. You know - the one we found in Kate's apartment Saturday night after the break-in."

Val and I exchanged a look.

"Who?" Val asked.

"Billy Cole."

I almost fell off the stool. "Are you sure?"

"Boy's got a record," Val commented.

"Selling," Matt said.

"How'd you find out?" Val asked.

"Called in a favor from a guy in Juvie. I want to talk to that kid, only I can't find him. Are you sure he knows about his mother?"

"I told him myself," I said.

I felt as if I'd hammered a nail into Billy's coffin.

Jordan and David broke off mid-sentence and looked at us expectantly the minute we walked back into the living room.

We told them about Billy.

"This whole kidnapping thing could be a big hoax," Jordan said. She untangled herself from the afghan she was lying under and stood up. "I have to go."

"You're not coming to the theater?"

She shook her head. "The forensics lab called while you were on with Matt. The DNA tests are in, but they won't tell me anything over the phone. I've got to go up there before the News and Post scoop my story." She grabbed her handbag off the floor and headed for the door. "Call me and let me know what happens at the theater - okay?"

Chapter 39

We were in Val's Jag trying to turn out of my garage. I sat in the passenger seat next to Val. David had the backseat to himself. A stream of cars prevented us from turning right onto Water Street.

The sidewalks were clogged with people heading to the bridge on foot for a food festival in Veterans Park. Why they had to start the damn thing on a Wednesday, I had no idea. The weekend was inconvenient enough.

A group of teenagers walked by, joking with each other in loud voices. They almost knocked over an elderly man, but one of the boys caught him just in time. A young mother, roughly the same age as me, pushed a little girl in a stroller and I felt the sudden ping of my biological clock ticking away.

The little girl sat upright in her stroller and stretched both arms out in front of her. A bright smile spread across her face as she wagged all ten fingers at someone. I followed the direction of her gaze and saw that a woman in blue jeans and a red T-shirt was taking her picture. I recognized the photographer immediately, but she lowered her camera and looked right at me without any sign of recognition. I smiled to myself. My mother was so caught up in her work that nothing else registered.

I shifted my eyes to the right and noticed that a disheveled man with long oily hair and a stubbly beard was hovering way too close to her. I lowered my window and called out to her, but she didn't hear me. The man moved even closer. A feeling of panic jarred me into action and without thinking, I jumped out of the car and darted into the street, oblivious to the two-way traffic. A car screeched to a stop as I reached the centerline. The driver flipped me the finger and swore through his window.

I glanced at the traffic in the other direction, making eye contact with an elderly gray haired woman at the wheel of a Honda who looked like she'd just come from a perm. She stopped and let me cross, but by the time I reached the sidewalk, my mother had vanished. I picked my way through the crowd, moving as fast as I could towards Veteran's Park until I finally caught sight of her again where she'd stopped to take a picture of a man with red-tinted hair.

He was too busy scanning the crowd to realize he was being photographed. His skin was stretched taut across high cheekbones and he had a full mouth and slightly hooked nose. His black eyes moved methodically from point to point, as if he needed to find someone urgently. He was dressed all in black – jeans and a T-shirt. I pegged him for Russian, maybe even Yugoslavian, but definitely Slavic. He had a dancer's body, tall and lithe. Something about his expression made him look snarly and mean. But he had an arresting face and I could see why my mother found him intriguing.

I hung back, not wanting to draw his attention to my mother or myself. Finally, he gave up on whomever he was trying to find and started walking again. I watched until his back disappeared into the crowd.

"Mom!"

My mother turned around. "Katie!" She looked behind me. "Where's Val?"

"I'm meeting her at the theater."

"I thought the police closed it down," she said.

"I'm just taking a look around."

"Katie…" she said, frowning.

"Never mind that – do you realize a man was following you?"

"No." She looked around with a sudden wariness. "Where is he?"

I scanned the area. "I think he's gone now."

"How did you see him?"

I shook my head and smiled. "I was trying to get out of my garage. You were taking that little girl's picture across the street."

Her eyes widened. "I didn't see you."

"No kidding. I jumped out of Val's car to warn you."

Just then my cell phone vibrated in my pocket. I raised it to my ear.

"Where the hell are you?" Val said.

"With my mother. Where are you?"

"The other side of the bridge. We're almost to Westport."

"I'll go back and get my car and meet you at the theater," I said. "You'll never find me in all this mess."

"I can drive you to the theater," my mother said. "I'm parked in the municipal lot."

Mom wasn't fooling me. I knew she was dying to take pictures of the crime scene.

"Thanks - that'd be great." I glanced around the area, making sure that the man I'd seen hovering near her earlier was nowhere in sight. I had to suppress a smile when I noticed that a good-looking guy in his late thirties or so was ogling her. Then I realized that I had my own admirer – an overweight guy in a sweaty looking T-shirt that said, *Kiss me - I'm Irish.*

"Are you still there?" Val said over the phone.

"Yes." I glowered at the guy in the T-shirt and he looked away. "My mom's giving me a lift to the theater. I'll meet you inside."

Mom and I walked over to Washington Street where the stores and restaurants were unusually busy for a Wednesday afternoon. A group of young mothers attempting to hang onto energetic toddlers were lined up outside of the Cold Creamsicle. A dark haired little boy was bawling his eyes out over a glob of chocolate ice cream melting at his feet on the sidewalk. He held his empty cone up for his mother to see.

We started to turn into the alleyway leading to the parking lot. Out of the corner of my eye, I saw a huge red thing come flying at us.

"Remember me?" The red thing had a voice.

"Matilda!"

"The pizza lady - right?" she said.

"Right."

Dressed in a plus-size red T-shirt and red spandex leggings, Matilda looked like a Christmas Elf who had failed Weight Watchers.

She gave me a loopy smile. "Who's this?"

"This is my mother, Annie Rosenthal. Mom, meet Matilda."

"Nice to meet you, Matilda."

Matilda gave my mother a big gapped-tooth smile and then turned her attention back to me. "Where your boyfriend at?"

My mother's eyebrows shot up.

"He's not my boyfriend."

"Oh," Matilda, said. "That's too bad. He be good lookin'."

"Who does she mean?" my mother asked.

"Detective Warren. He and Matilda are good friends."

"Matt's a detective?" Matilda sounded suddenly anxious. Then she saw my mother's camera and brightened. "Will you take my picture?"

"Sure I will." Mom raised her camera to her eye.

Matilda stared directly into the lens and smiled woodenly, holding a stiff pose until my mother lowered her camera.

Mom took a small notebook and pen out of her camera bag and told Matilda, "I'll send you the picture if you give me your address."

A genuine smile appeared on Matilda's face this time. She slowly spelled her last name – Destry - and gave my mother an address in Norwalk. Then without saying goodbye, she skipped away down the street.

My mother and I continued walking towards the parking lot. When we got there, a workman in dust-covered overalls was climbing out of a black truck parked at the far end, while a young woman wearing a navy and white striped dress walked towards the pedestrian exit, twirling her keys. Mom clicked the locks open on her car, relocking them as soon as we were safely inside.

I could tell my mother's mind was elsewhere as she drove by the way she fiddled with her hair. Like me, she had thick strawberry-blond hair and freckles across the bridge of her nose. She looked a lot younger than fifty. Convincing her to stop wandering around all by herself was not going to be an easy sell.

My mother was no stranger to danger. The night before she left for Kuwait to cover the first Gulf War, I'd asked her if she was ever afraid.

"Of course," she'd told me. "But I don't let that stop me. Courage means doing what you think is right in spite of being afraid."

But my father and I were afraid for her. We'd sit glued to the television set watching the news, praying she'd come back alive. And now I was afraid for her again, only this time it was my fault she was in danger. She wouldn't like the idea of police protection, but I had to tell her about what I'd set in motion.

"Detective Warren is going to assign someone to watch over you and Dad."

She glanced at me quickly before turning back to the road. "Oh no he's not. I can't work with someone hovering over me."

I laughed. "Yes you can. That's why I jumped out of the car and ran after you. A man *was* hovering over you, only you were too absorbed in your work to realize it!"

My mother smiled in spite of herself. "I promise to pay more attention from now on."

Mom could be infuriatingly stubborn. I decided to drop the matter for now and let her think she'd won the argument.

We drove the rest of the way to the theater chatting about nothing in particular, purposely avoiding the one topic that was on both our minds: namely, who killed Cy and why did he think I'd taken something?

Chapter 40

Yellow crime scene tape was draped across the front entrance of the theater. With the motor idling, Mom got out of the car and snapped a few pictures. I looked around for signs of the police, but other than the crime scene tape, I didn't see any. We drove around to the rear of the building and parked next to Val's Jag, which was almost hidden under some trees.

We walked down three steps leading to a plain black door. I turned the knob, but the door wouldn't budge. I knocked gently. No response. I rapped harder. Still nothing. Finally I leaned into the door with my shoulder and shoved. It gave way with a rusty squeal.

I felt along the wall until my fingers connected with the light switch. I flicked it on and instantly heard the buzz of fluorescent lighting overhead.

My mother snapped a few more photos.

"We must be directly under the stage," I said. "There should be a door that leads to it somewhere."

We walked down the hallway, passing a narrow door marked *Maintenance* three-quarters of the way down. At the end of the corridor, a flight of cement steps led up to another door that, sure enough, said *Stage*.

I gave it a shove and the door opened onto total blackness.

"One sec," Mom said.

She rummaged in her purse and came up with a small penlight. Dozens of blackouts while on assignment had taught her never to go anywhere without one. She flicked it on and shined the light around the area in front of us.

We were standing backstage between the rear wall of the theater and a large flat suspended from the ceiling. Muffled voices came from out front, presumably Val's and David's. We pushed our way past one black curtain after another until we were finally standing in front of a flat that had been painted to look like a winding street disappearing over the horizon. A scrim was all that separated us from Val and David, although it was unlikely that they could see us. I lifted the scrim high enough for my mother to slip underneath.

A male voice I didn't recognize said, "Stay right where you are. Don't make another move." I heard the click of something metallic.

Mom and I froze.

I said in a loud voice, "It's Kate Sachs. I'm with my mother. We're here to pick up some things I need for rehearsal."

A hairy hand jerked the scrim higher and the voice ordered us both to step forward. Detective Art Desmond looked like he wanted to shoot us on principle. Instead, he clicked the safety back on and holstered his gun.

He looked closely at my mother and grinned. "This is your mother? Nice to meet you, ma'am."

Desmond's reaction was by no means unusual. Men have always – to my intense embarrassment while growing up – been bowled over by Mom. So I wasn't surprised when she convinced him to let us all go upstairs without him.

Upstairs in the Green Room, more yellow crime scene tape blocked the door. We ducked underneath and entered the room. White powder covered the surfaces of most of the furniture.

"Fingerprint powder," Val explained.

My mother took photos of the front room and asked to see where we had found Cy's body. I led the way down the narrow corridor to the back where the open closet alcove faced the sliding doors to the deck.

"He was hiding here," I said, pointing to the closet, "and he chased me out onto the deck." I turned right into the kitchenette and pointed again to a spot on the floor. "Cy was lying over there."

My mother snapped a dozen or so more photos. I was starting to feel guilty that Jordan hadn't come with us too.

I looked around the room trying to find whatever it was that Hoarse-Voice thought I had stolen. But the only thing visible was a coffeemaker half-filled with brown sludge. David joked that he'd have to cough up the money for a new one or convince everyone to start drinking tea.

"As long as we're here," he said, "I really do need to get some papers out of my office. Excuse me a minute – I'll be right back."

When he'd gone, Mom asked me, "Anything strike you?"

Everything seemed so much less ominous than the night Cy was attacked. I shook my head, disappointed that we'd wasted so much time for so little gain.

"Mrs. Sachs…," Val said.

"Please - call me Annie."

"Annie. My partner is on his way to New York to stay with Abe and Max. Detective Warren is setting up protection for you and your husband."

My mother rolled her eyes at me before turning her attention back to Val. "I appreciate everyone's concern, but I can take care of myself. Really."

Val looked at me. "I see where you get it from."

Mom laughed.

"We're dealing with a psychopath, Annie, " Val said. "You should have protection and so should your husband."

My mother's smile vanished.

Val continued, "I don't know if Kate told you this, but some guy dressed up like a doctor has been parading around your husband's hospital threatening to kill people."

Mom digested this for a moment. Finally she said, "So long as Detective Warren assigns protection for my husband, and has someone watching our house, we'll be fine. Honestly. I can't work with someone hovering over me."

Val ran her hands through her hair and gave a loud sigh. "You're the client." She shot me a look that wasn't lost on my mother.

"Can we please change the subject?" Mom said, smiling.

I took one last look around the Green Room and then suddenly remembered something.

"What is it?" Mom asked.

"Cy wasn't in here when I overheard him arguing with that maniac. He was in one of the offices."

I darted out of the Green Room and rushed down the hall with my mother and Val following close behind. The door to the office Cy had been using was open, but other than a telephone on top of a desk and some shelving, the room was empty.

Mom stepped into the room and was framing shots when she almost slipped on something. She bent down and picked up a piece of paper and placed it on the desk. It was a flyer from a company called Tower Self-Storage in Norwalk.

Val shook her head. "Another dead end."

"I'm sorry, Kate," my mother said.

David appeared in the hallway carrying a stack of paper.

"There you are. I was wondering where you went." He paused and examined us more closely. "Find anything?"

I shook my head.

He handed me some papers. "Well, maybe this'll cheer you up – it's a director's contract. My lawyer insists that we need to make you official."

Despite the ludicrous circumstances, I felt a surge of excitement. If only this nightmare would end, I could get on with my life.

David glanced at his watch. "We'd better get out of here." Then he added, "Sorry this turned out to be such a bust. At least you tried."

Chapter 41

David insisted on coming with Val and me to the hospital where Iris was in cardiac intensive care. She was only allowed to have two visitors at a time, so he stayed in the waiting room while we went in to see her.

Val and I entered Iris' cubicle through a curtained opening. She seemed a lot older than she had when we'd first met her at the high school. Her dark hair was fanned out against the pillow, with coarse strands of white visible along the hairline. She was asleep.

Val motioned towards the door, but I didn't think it was right to leave without letting Iris know we'd been there. I reached over the bed railing and lightly touched her arm. She opened her eyes. When she recognized us, she smiled and tried to rouse herself. She seemed genuinely glad to see us at first, but then reality came crashing in on her.

"Billy?" she asked in a weak voice.

I hesitated for a split-second trying to think of something positive to say without telling her an outright lie. "He's all right. We even spoke to him briefly, so we know he's okay."

Val gave me a sharp look.

I said, "You need to concentrate on getting better. Let us worry about Billy for now."

Iris grabbed the bed railing tightly and tried to sit up, which seemed to cause her pain. She fell back against the pillow and closed her eyes. I glanced anxiously up at the monitor over her bed. The green line moved steadily across the screen, although I had no idea what it meant.

"Hello ladies. How's she doing?" Art Desmond said quietly from the doorway.

Iris' eyes fluttered open at the sound of his voice. She seemed calmer.

Val waved him over. "This is Detective Desmond. He helped us get you to the hospital. Remember?"

Desmond leaned over the bed and smiled at Iris, who didn't seem to recognize him. "That's okay, Mrs. Cole. You were pretty sick by the time I got there. How're you feeling now?"

Iris rested her fingers on her cheek and studied Desmond's face for a moment. "How thoughtless of me. Of course I remember. Thank you." Her eyes darted from Desmond's face to Val's and then to mine. "Thank you all. If it weren't for you..."

"No thanks needed," Desmond said. "You just concentrate on getting well." Then as an afterthought, he added, "How's my pal Billy doing? That's some great kid you've got there."

Iris' face fell at the mention of her son's name.

"Art knows Billy from the theater," I explained to her quickly. "It's a good thing he drove by when he did."

Desmond didn't seem to notice the change in Iris' expression.

"Which brings up a delicate point," he said. "I've been working *undercover* at the theater, Mrs. Cole. I'd appreciate it if you kept that to yourself and not mention it to Billy." He gave Iris a wink and then looked over at Val and me and smiled. "As far as anyone's concerned, I'm just one of the stagehands. Okay?"

Val smiled back. "Don't worry – we won't say anything."

Suddenly Iris clutched her chest. Her face looked contorted with pain. Her monitor went haywire with green lines galloping across the screen and alarms clanging.

A young woman in green scrubs came rushing into the room, shoving the tips of a stethoscope she had draped around her neck into her ears. Two nurses clad all in white came running in behind her and chased us out.

We sat in the waiting room, expecting the doctors to give us an update on Iris' condition any moment. After a half hour or so, we ran out of things to say to one another. I was too fidgety to sit there any longer and excused myself to search out someone who could tell us what was going on.

The young woman who'd rushed into Iris' cubicle was in a huddle with an older man with spiky gray hair and a beard to match. He too was dressed in green scrubs and had a white surgical mask dangling under his chin.

I asked how Iris was doing. The older man smiled sympathetically and explained that they were running some tests. His nametag said he was Dr. Olander.

"Are you a relative?" he asked.

"Friend."

"Does she have any family we can contact?"

My heart started to pound. "A teenage son."

Dr. Olander grabbed one of the charts off the desk and scribbled something inside. "What's his name?"

"Billy Cole."

I saw him write Billy's name in the chart.

"Thanks," he said.

The woman – Dr. Silverstone according to her nametag – had been eyeing me closely. "Aren't you Kate Sachs?"

"Yes." Taken off guard, I tried to think how I knew her, but I couldn't place her.

"I'm a big fan," she explained. "I was so excited when they put *Young and In Love* back on the air."

"Me too," I said, smiling.

Dr. Silverstone was around my age and had probably been in college when the show had run in prime time. I was surprised she still found time to watch it.

"You're Jeff Sach's daughter," Dr. Olander said, snapping his fingers.

"I am."

"Does he know you're here?" he asked.

"Probably not."

"I'm almost certain I saw him wandering around here a little while ago," he said, reaching for the phone. "Want me to page him?"

"Thanks."

"I'll tell him to look for you in the waiting room."

My father appeared in the doorway looking exhausted. His face brightened as soon as he saw me. He wore a white doctor's coat over a blue Oxford shirt and striped tie that had tumbled to half-mast. The coat was too small for his six-foot frame and I couldn't help laughing at the way his arms stuck out past the sleeves.

"Nice coat," I said.

He laughed too, running his hand through the unruly crop of curls sprouting chaotically around his head. "I know. Either mine shrunk or this coat belongs to someone else."

He greeted Val and David. I introduced Art Desmond who had risen to his feet when my father entered the room.

"We've met. Matt's got him trailing after me like a bloodhound." Dad peered at me over the top of his reading glasses. "Your doing, I hear."

"Now if you could only talk some sense into Mom."

My father creased his brows together. "What do you mean?"

"She doesn't want anyone around while she's working," Val said.

He groaned as he collapsed into an upholstered armchair next to me. "I'll talk to her."

"You look exhausted," I said. "What's going on?"

"They brought another boy into the ER last night. DOA." He exhaled a loud sigh and shook his head. "Broken neck."

"The boy at the cliff-jumping rock?" I asked.

Dad's eyebrows shot up. "How did you know that?"

"Jordan's covering the story. We drove her over there. Who's the boy?"

"I can't tell you that until the police notify his parents. They're having trouble reaching them on vacation."

"What's the cliff-jumping rock?" David asked.

My father leaned forward with his arms resting on his thighs. "It's a cliff over a watering hole. He turned to Desmond. "Got to be – what? A twelve foot jump?"

"At least," Desmond said. "These kids are crazy."

"Come on," I said. "It's not that dangerous. Jordan and I did it lots of times."

My father threw back his head and laughed. "There really are some things parents are better off not knowing."

"Were drugs involved?" Val asked

Dad's expression turned serious. "The police aren't sure." He looked at his watch and stood up. "They won't know if Iris had another heart attack until her blood work comes back. That'll take some time, so you might as well come back later. Sorry I can't buy you a cup of coffee, but I've got a lot of patients to see."

We walked with him down the hall to the elevator.

"I almost forgot," he said, turning to me, "That kid Andrew's done nothing but talk about you since you went to see him."

I held my father's gaze and shook my head slightly, chancing that Detective Desmond wouldn't catch the exchange. From his expression, I knew that my father had understood. The last thing I needed was for Desmond to find out that there was a link between Billy Cole and Andrew.

We followed my father and Desmond onto the elevator. They got off one floor below while we continued down to the main floor. My cell phone vibrated the instant I stepped off the elevator into the lobby.

"Hello?"

"How's it going?" Jordan asked.

"You're not supposed to use a cell phone in the hospital! Go outside!"

I looked up and saw an elderly woman with slitty eyes boring into me. I was trying to think of a snappy retort when I spotted the old man next to her who was seated in a wheelchair. He was propped up with pillows and had an IV attached to his arm. The snappy retort died on my lips when an unexpected image surfaced of Grandpa Max with my grandmother right before she died. I shut my mouth and stepped outside.

It was so hot out that I stood under the canopy to avoid the sun. Val and David had followed me outside and were standing a few feet away.

"Do they know who attacked me?" I asked Jordan.

Val and David came a few steps nearer.

"No. There was no DNA match in any of the databases."

"Damn." I looked at Val and David and shook my head.

They seemed as disappointed as I was.

"Is David still with you?" Jordan asked.

"Yes. Why?"

"Can he hear you?"

"No," I said, forcing myself not to look at him.

"You can't tell him what I'm about to say."

I tried to sound casual. "Fine."

"About six months ago, Narcotics was staking out a warehouse in Bridgeport. A bunch of kids were seen going in and out of the place at weird hours."

"Anyone we know?"

"They wouldn't give me names. But right after that they put Desmond undercover at Omnibus."

I turned completely around so that my back was to Val and David and spoke softly. "Are you saying David's involved?"

"No, but the point is that I don't know for sure."

"Was Cy?" I asked.

"I don't know that either. But that would explain why he was murdered."

"Maybe he was trying to break it up," I said.

"Maybe." I heard her thumbing through her notes. "The kid who died at the cliff-jumping rock…"

"My father just told us his neck was broken. Apparently they won't release his name until they locate his parents."

"They just did - Gregory Reid."

The phone almost slipped out of my hand. "Justin's brother?"

"Correct."

"He must've known Billy too," I said.

"Not only that – he studied acting with Cy at Omnibus." I heard her thumbing through more pages. "I have some questions for David. How about meeting me back at your apartment?"

Chapter 42

David cradled his coffee cup in both hands and took a sip. He told Jordan, "Cy and I met around five or six years ago. He directed my wife...I mean my ex-wife - in a show at Player's Theater. Allison – my ex-wife – introduced us at a cast party on opening night."

Player's Theater was a well-known Off-Broadway house on West 42nd Street. It was known for showcasing new works that lacked the commercial appeal to make it to Broadway.

Jordan's pen was poised over her notebook. "Do you know if Cy was worried about anything?"

David shook his head. "I didn't know him that well on a personal level. Just professionally. So he wouldn't have confided anything like that to me." He blew on his coffee and took another sip. "But I got a call – actually I got several calls - complaining about his behavior. I didn't think that much of it at first - actors call me all the time with complaints about directors."

That shocked me. I'd never think of calling my producer to complain, especially not about my director.

"But when Jake called – he's the playwright," David explained to Jordan, "I knew I had to do something. He was threatening to pull his play out of production."

Jordan's pen was flying across her notebook. She stopped writing and looked up. "Had anything like this ever happened before?"

David shook his head. "Never. And Cy directed a lot of plays for me. He directed the first show I ever produced. In fact, when I took over at Omnibus…"

"When was that?" Jordan asked.

"Two years ago - almost three. I made him Director-In-Residence." David rubbed his temples. "And head of the acting school."

"Do you know anything about his personal life?" Jordan asked.

"He was very private," David said.

"Girlfriends?"

"If he had one, I never met her. Actually, I always thought he was gay. But as I said, I really didn't know him personally."

"Did you speak to Cy about the complaints?" Jordan asked.

"Yes." David looked into his coffee cup as if he was thinking about something.

"What did he say?" Jordan asked.

"That he was under a lot of pressure. Brad wasn't cooperating. That Brad was making it hard for the other actors. All things that made a lot of sense at the time."

"And now?" Jordan asked. "You think there was something else going on?"

David leaned forward and placed his cup down on the coffee table. "I think that maybe Cy was on something."

"You mean drugs?"

David nodded. "He seemed so twitchy lately whenever I talked to him. He was like another person."

I was so upset by what David had just said that at first I didn't hear my cell phone ringing. Then I realized everyone was looking at it and I snatched it off the table and flipped it open.

"Kate? It's Russell. Hope I'm not interrupting anything."

I pressed the phone into my chest and mouthed the name of my newly appointed Assistant Director.

"Everyone's been calling me," he said. "They're anxious to get back to rehearsals."

"They've been calling you?" I instantly regretted the irritation in my voice.

"Well…they didn't want to bother you." He sounded apologetic. "They figured…you know…the attack and everything."

"Oh." I continued in a friendlier tone, "Soundview High School is letting us rehearse there starting on Monday. Sorry - I forgot to call you."

"That's okay." He paused. "Do you want to get together for a production meeting before that? You can use my apartment in Stamford if you like. It's only a small studio, though."

The man was making it harder and harder for me to go on disliking him.

"That's a great idea. But you don't need that headache. We can use my loft in South Norwalk." I hated the idea of having my privacy invaded, but I couldn't think of anywhere else.

"Great!" He sounded relieved.

We agreed on eight o'clock the next morning and that he would notify Carla and Sparky.

I snapped my cell phone shut and informed the others about the meeting

"Do you want me to come?" David asked.

"No."

He looked a little hurt. "Why not?"

"Because it's not necessary." I smiled. "Don't you trust me?"

"Of course."

Jordan had taken out a train schedule and was examining it. "If you hurry, you can catch the four thirty-seven back to the city."

"I'll give you a lift to the station," I added.

Here's your hat - what's your hurry?

Chapter 43

Val and I timed our arrival at Amber Hills to coincide with visiting hours, which began at seven. We drove onto the property behind a stream of cars and proceeded up a steep road flanked by sweeping lawns dotted with oaks and maples. After a quarter-mile or so, a cluster of buildings came into view. Pink and purple flowers were artfully arranged along the perimeter and a trellised walkway led from one building to another, creating a campus-like environment. In the center, there was a red-roofed white colonial with a sign above the door that said *Administration.*

Most of the cars turned left into a large parking lot adjacent to the Administration building. We turned right and followed another sign that said *School.* Eventually we came to a long red brick building separated into two wings, one with a door marked *Boys,* the other with a door marked *Girls.* We parked around back in a small lot.

Some teenagers were shooting hoops in the fading light. A tall skinny black kid caught the ball and halted the play over his friends' protests. "Hey," he called out to us, "you're supposed to check in at *Administration.*"

Val and I walked over to the basketball court where three boys and two girls were playing. One of the girls was Asian. A head shorter than the others, she had a small, bow-shaped mouth and long black hair tied back in a ponytail. A couple sat on the grass watching the game. The boy had a thin face with intelligent brown eyes partially obscured by his long hair. His arm was draped around the shoulders of a young girl with coffee-colored skin and huge black eyes.

"We're looking for Justin Reid," I said. "Any of you know where he is?"

The skinny black kid shrugged and turned to his friends. "Anyone know him?"

None of them did.

We started to leave when one of the boys on the court, a muscular kid who looked like he was bulked up on steroids, stepped forward. His eyes were so hostile that Val took a step closer to me.

"What do you want him for?" he asked.

"Do you know him?" Val met his gaze head on.

They stared each other down like that until finally the boy turned away, a sneer still on his lips.

"What are you being such an asshole for?" the Asian girl said. "If you know the dude, say so."

The muscle-bound kid tensed. You could see the veins pulsing in his neck. After several moments, he dropped his head and looked at the ground. He took a deep breath as if he was trying not to lose it. When his head came back up, he looked at Val with a neutral expression, the menace gone from his eyes. "Yeah. I know who he is."

"Do you know where we can find him?" Val asked in a friendlier tone.

"Boys' dorm." He tossed his head towards the brick building.

"Thanks," Val said.

As we were walking away, the girl on the grass called out, "Hey, lady! You ever been on TV?"

I turned around, not anxious to attract that kind of attention.

Val nudged me with her elbow and whispered, "Tell her."

"Yes."

The other girl on the playing court, chubby with freckles, smiled. "I knew you looked familiar. "*Young and In Love* – right?"

"Right."

The boy on the grass snapped his fingers. "Julie!"

"That's right." I said with a smile.

"What happened to your face?" he asked.

"I fell," I said, waving good-bye. "See you later."

I pretended not to hear the muscle-bound kid say how much older I looked in person. When we entered the building, the first thing that hit us was the lingering smell of perspiration. It took a while for our eyes to adjust to the dim light.

Small rooms lined both sides of a narrow hallway. In the first room we came to, a small iron cot made up with white sheets and a scratchy-looking green woolen blanket took up most of the space. One small window with black bars on it looked out onto the basketball court. The building was only one story high, so the bars couldn't have been put there to prevent anyone from committing suicide. I figured they were there to prevent patients from sneaking in and out, although there didn't seem to be any guards around to stop them from marching out the door.

We didn't see anyone in the first room we passed. The room opposite was empty also and we were about to continue past it when I thought I detected movement. I looked in again, but still didn't see anyone. As I was about to leave, a face showed itself from under the bed.

It was a teenage boy with wild dirty-blond hair worn Rastafarian style.

"Hello," I said, trying to sound friendly.

He stared at us for such a long time from under the bed that I started to think he hadn't heard me.

"Can you speak?" Val mouthed at him as if he was hearing-impaired.

"Whaddayou – nuts? Of course I can speak." His adolescent voice had just started to change, leaving him somewhere between a tenor and a soprano. It cracked on the word *nuts*.

"I'm not the one hiding under the bed," Val pointed out.

I nudged her in the ribs to be quiet.

The boy crawled out from under the bed and stood up. He was almost as tall as Val. "What do you want?"

"We're looking for Justin Reid," I said. "Know him?"

He couldn't prevent the glimmer of recognition that showed in his eyes. He stared at us for a moment. "No."

I didn't believe him. I stared back at him without flinching, expecting that he'd cave. He didn't.

"Thanks anyway."

The next few rooms were empty. I made sure to check under the beds. We got lucky when we reached a room off the middle of the hallway. Two boys were sitting on the bed talking to two girls who were stretched out on the floor. They jumped when they saw us.

"You gonna tell?" a little blond girl no older than thirteen asked.

"Tell what?" I asked.

She looked at me as if she was trying to figure out if I was being sarcastic. Seated next to her was a Hispanic girl who looked a year or two older. They exchanged glances.

"Girls aren't supposed to be in the boys' rooms," the Hispanic girl said.

"Oh that," I said. "We won't tell," I turned to Val, "Will we?"

"Nope," Val replied.

One of the boys was looking at me intently. He had dark hair and a nice face, with round glasses that made him look like an owl. "Are you on television?"

"Yes."

He broke into a sweet smile. "Julie on *Young and In Love*. Wow. I love that show."

He and his friends all wanted autographs. I asked them their names so I could write something personal.

Val glowered at me, but I ignored her. I wasn't about to refuse a bunch of kids stuck in a hellhole for psychos.

The boy in the glasses told me his name was Peter; his friend was Jamal; the little blond was Debbie, and the young Hispanic girl was Marisol.

"Don't show the autographs to anyone or you'll get us in trouble," Val said. "Okay?"

"You can trust us," Debbie whispered.

"We're looking for a boy named Justin Reid," I said. "Do any of you know him?"

The girls shook their heads, but the boys gave each other a sidelong glance.

Jamal had light brown skin and curly black hair cropped close to his head. He was so emaciated that I wondered if he had an eating disorder. He dangled his feet back and forth over the side of the bed, keeping his eyes focused on the floor.

"Why are you in here, hon?" Val asked him.

Jamal kept his eyes down and didn't answer.

"My parents made me come," Debbie said.

"Why's that?" I asked.

"I got kicked out of school for marijuana. I can't go back unless I go through rehab."

I had to force myself not to react. Who would sell drugs to such a young child?

Val looked at Peter and waited expectantly.

He smiled sheepishly. "I sold marijuana in school. For me, it was jail or rehab, so I chose rehab."

Marisol's face turned stony. "Jail don't frighten me."

"No?" Val said. "How come?"

"I visited my mamma in jail plenty of times."

I watched Val struggle to keep her face neutral.

"Why are you here?" she asked.

"Judge said if I don't come here he was puttin' me in foster care. My mamma can't handle me," she said matter-of-factly.

"Is it helping?" Val asked gently. "Rehab, I mean."

Marisol nodded. "I'm all through with that shit."

"Me too," Peter said.

"Same," Debbie said.

Only Jamal remained silent with his eyes downcast throughout the entire exchange.

"How about you Jamal?" Val asked.

We all looked at him, waiting for him to respond.

Finally Marisol said, "He don't like to talk about it. He's seen some bad shit."

"He saw a head in a bucket," Debbie said.

Jamal lunged at the little girl. "Shut up!"

Val stepped in between them. "Did you tell the police?" she asked Jamal.

Jamal said, "You nuts lady? Why you think the dude's head got chopped off in the first place?"

Marisol spun around on Debbie. "What you open your mouth for?"

Debbie's lip trembled and then she ran from the room.

"Shit - she's such a baby," Marisol said. She looked anxiously at the door and stood up. "I better go find her." She left the room shaking her head like a weary mother tired of chasing after her kids.

"Did you two know each other before you got here?" I asked.

Peter and Jamal shook their heads. Jamal's eyes were focused back on the floor.

"Do either of you know a boy named Billy Cole?"

Jamal's head came up sharply.

"Billy a friend of yours, Jamal?" Val asked.

Jamal looked trapped.

"We think Billy may be in a lot of trouble," I said.

Jamal abandoned the subterfuge. "What kind of trouble?"

"He's missing," I said. "We're trying to find him so we can help him."

"I don't know where he is," Jamal said, looking down again.

"How do you know him?" Val asked. She put her hand under his chin and raised his head up until their eyes were level with each other.

"Everyone knows him," he replied.

"Why's that, hon?" she asked.

He shrugged. "Billy's the moneyman."

"What do you mean?" I asked.

"We gave Billy the money, he gave us our cut and more drugs to sell. That's how it worked."

"What did Billy do with the money?" Val asked.

"I dunno. Maybe give it to that fag friend of his. Older dude. A real fudge-packer." Jamal stole a glance at Peter and the two of them snickered.

I struggled to keep the irritation out of my voice. "You've met him?"

Jamal shrugged again and said, "Nah. Justin met him and he told me."

"So you do know Justin?" Val said.

Jamal and Peter were caught out and they both knew it.

"We really need to talk to him," Val said. "Can you help us find him?"

Peter said, "He's probably downstairs at the Meeting." He glanced at his watch and jumped up. "Shit - we gotta go!"

Jamal jumped up too. "What time is it?"

"Seven-twenty." Peter looked over at Val and me. "If you wanna come, I can point him out to you."

"Will they let us in?" I asked.

"Anyone can come. It's a 12-step Meeting," Peter said. He shoved his glasses back onto his nose.

"You mean AA?" I tried to sound nonchalant.

"Not just alcoholics. Addicts too," Jamal said. "Some people have issues with both."

An image of his therapist in tortoise-shell glasses and a three-piece suit popped into my head and I almost burst out laughing.

Jamal and Peter started to leave, but Val stood up and blocked their way. She flashed them her Val smile. "We never had this conversation. Understood boys?"

From the look on their faces, it was clear they would rather die than betray her confidence.

The boys led the way down a steep flight of steps to the basement. We entered a large room at the end of the hall. At least thirty people – mostly kids – were seated around a long rectangular table. Another twenty or more were seated on folding chairs against the walls. A coffee pot had been set up on top of another table along with platters of cake and cookies.

Peter whispered to me, "There's Justin."

I looked in the direction of where he was pointing and saw a boy seated at the far end of the table. He was tall and slim with blond hair and regular features. He looked straight ahead as if he wanted to avoid eye contact with anyone. "I'll introduce you when the meeting's over," Peter said. Then he took a seat at the table next to Jamal.

Val and I helped ourselves to coffee and cookies and found seats against the wall. We deliberately sat at the far end of the room so that we could observe everyone without being obvious.

A kid with dark curly hair – eighteen or nineteen max - called the meeting to order. He introduced himself saying, "Hi - I'm Dave and I'm an alcoholic and a drug addict."

The others in the room chanted, "Hi Dave."

It took a while to get going, but Dave was a patient moderator. He called on people who raised their hands, encouraging them to share whatever was bothering them. One young girl talked about how frightened she was to be leaving Amber Hills. Her father was abusive and she was terrified of the beatings. I sensed Val tense up beside me. A few hands shot up and, one by one, people offered solace and advice, reminding her to take it one day at a time. I was amazed at how kind they were towards one another.

As the hour drew to a close, Dave looked around the room. "Any newcomers today?"

His eyes landed on Val and when she didn't respond, he moved on to me. I stared at the floor until I felt him look away, turning his attention to the people sitting at the table. Finally, his gaze fell on Justin.

Justin took a deep breath and said, "My name's Justin and I'm an addict and an alcoholic. This is my second time at Amber Hills."

Dave smiled encouragingly and said, "This is my third time, so don't think you're special."

Justin smiled back and relaxed in his chair. An older man sitting next to him patted him on the shoulder.

Then Dave said, "I remember you now. You were here with a buddy last time."

Justin's smile froze, his body suddenly so rigid that he looked like a marionette. "Yeah," he said quietly. "He's not here this time."

At the end of the meeting, everyone stood up and joined hands, and said the Lord's Prayer out loud. When it was over, they dropped hands and shouted, "Keep coming back - it works if you work it!"

The room emptied slowly; some people lingered to chat. Peter came over to where we were sitting and walked us over to Justin who was stuffing papers into a backpack at the table.

"Recognize her?" Peter asked him, pointing at me.

Justin wasn't in the mood for *Guess Who*. He barely glanced at me and then scowled at Peter.

"This is *Julie*. From *Young and In Love*. Don't you recognize her?" Peter asked.

Justin could have cared less.

Peter shrugged. "Suit yourself." Then he waved goodbye to Val and me and left.

Justin pushed past us.

"We're friends of Billy," I said. "He wanted to come himself, only he couldn't make it."

Justin turned around. The sullen expression had changed to wariness.

"Who are you?"

The room was almost empty now, save for a few people seated at the table deep in conversation.

"We have to find Billy," Val said. "Please – it's urgent. Is there somewhere we can talk in private?"

Justin sized us up for a moment before motioning for us to follow him back up the stairs. When we reached the first floor, he led us out through the rear of the building. Facing us was a wooded area with picnic tables where a few kids sat chatting with relatives and other visitors in the twilight.

Val pointed to a table set well apart from the others. "Let's sit over there."

Justin took a seat across from us.

"Billy's in a lot of trouble." I said.

"What do you mean?" Justin asked.

He saw me glance at his hands. They were shaking. He crossed his arms over his chest and stuffed his hands under his armpits.

"No one can find him," Val said. "His mother had a heart attack."

Justin's eyes registered shock, but the fear had drained away and he relaxed a little. "Jesus. Is she all right?"

"We hope so. She's still in the hospital," I said.

"I don't know where he is - I swear." He uncrossed his arms.

"We know you came here to hide," Val said.

Justin turned pale. "That's bullshit."

Val spoke quietly, "I don't think it is." She leaned in closer to him. "Want to know why?"

Justin looked so frightened that I was afraid he might run away.

"You know too much." Val's fingernails made a staccato sound as she drummed them on top of the picnic table.

"What do you want from me?" Justin whispered.

"I want to know who you're running away from," she said.

Justin searched Val's eyes as if he might find the answer there. "I don't know his name, but he's killing all the kids who work for Billy."

Chapter 44

Justin's eyes darted around the wooded area as if he expected something terrible to jump out at him.

"Justin?" Val struggled to get back his attention.

"What?" he said, looking behind him again.

"How do you know this?" Val said.

His eyes made a sweep of the area one more time before finally cutting back to us. "Huh? … This guy … called my brother."

I was about to say how sorry I was about his brother's death when I glanced at Val and saw the almost imperceptible shake of her head and wary expression. Suddenly it dawned on me; Justin didn't know his brother was dead. He started to twist around again, but stopped when Val touched him lightly on the arm.

"Who was he?" she asked.

Justin shook his head. "My brother didn't know."

"What did he say?"

"To keep his mouth shut or …" He stopped speaking and cleared his throat.

"Or?"

"Or he'd wind up dead … like… "

He stopped talking and sat there staring at us.

"Like who?" Val asked.

Justin didn't answer right away. Finally he found his voice again. "Like Terence. Terence Brown. My brother's friend."

"Come on," I said. "Something like that'd be all over the papers by now."

Val gave me a warning tap under the table.

"Fuck you, lady!" Justin started to get up.

Val rose halfway and grabbed his arm. "Sit down and tell us what happened."

Justin responded to the authoritative tone in her voice and sat back down. He took a moment to compose himself before continuing. "Like I said, this guy called my brother..."

"When was this?" Val cut in.

"Sunday morning." His voice cracked and he took a breath before continuing. "He said he'd kill us one by one if he didn't get his money."

"By us, you mean the kids selling drugs for Billy?" Val asked.

Justin paused a moment before answering. "Yes."

"Do you have it?" Val asked.

"No! I swear!"

"Does one of the other kids?"

"No!"

"What about Billy?" Val asked.

"He'd never double-cross us like that."

Honor among drug dealers, I thought to myself. "What did this man sound like?"

Justin's eyes widened. "Hoarse! He sounded hoarse ... like he had a cold or something. Do you know him?"

Val and I exchanged a look. She turned back to Justin and said, "A man with a hoarse voice has been threatening Kate."

The pieces were starting to fall into place. Hoarse Voice thought I'd stolen his drug money out of the Green Room that night. But where was it? The police hadn't found it. Or if they had, they weren't telling me about it. Nor had we found it when we'd gone back to the theater and searched the Green Room ourselves.

If I could just get my hands on the money, I'd at least have a bargaining chip for getting Billy back.

Val poked me in the ribs and I brought my attention back to the conversation.

"What happened after the phone call?" she asked Justin.

"There's this game room up in Bridgeport. We hang out there sometimes. Greg … my brother … went into the bathroom and … and he found Terence's head."

"Just his head?" Val asked.

Justin folded his hands on top of the table and stared at them. "Stuffed in a bucket."

If where I lived in Norwalk was Fairfield County's poor relation, Bridgeport was its bad seed. Despite valiant attempts to take the city back from the pimps and drug dealers, Bridgeport's housing projects were still rife with crime. I could see how a head turning up in the wrong Bridgeport neighborhood might not make the papers.

"Were you there too?" Val asked.

Justin shook his head. He was so tightly wound that you could see the muscles in his face contracting. His eyes started roving around again. Val reached over and grabbed his face, yanking his head around so that he had to look her in the eye.

"Think, Justin. What else did your brother say?"

Justin's eyes darted to something over my shoulder and a look of alarm spread across his face. I turned to see what he was looking at. A squat middle-aged woman with a frizzy perm in blue jeans and a blue-check button-down shirt that barely closed around her ample chest was coming down the path. Despite her casual attire, she walked with an air of authority and, from the way her lips kept moving, she seemed to be taking a head count. Some people at the other tables nodded at her as she walked by. Taking my cue from Justin who had lowered his head, I turned my back to her. Only Val nodded hello as the woman walked by our table.

"Who was that?" I asked.

"Sue Ann. She's the night supervisor for the dorms," Justin said.

"The staff doesn't wear uniforms?" I asked.

"They think we'll relate to them better if they wear regular clothes." Justin smiled for the first time since we'd sat down.

Val brought the conversation back on topic. "How many kids are involved?"

Justin took a few seconds to think about this. "Six."

"Including Terence?" Val said.

Justin nodded.

That left only four boys alive: Billy, Justin, Andrew, and Jamal.

"What kind of drugs?" Val asked.

Panic leapt into his eyes.

"We're not here to get you in trouble. But we can't help you unless we know what we're up against."

Justin leaned in closer and whispered, "Pretty much anything - marijuana, heroin, coke. Some pharmaceuticals." He shrugged. "Whatever's in the shipment that month."

"Where do the shipments come from?" Val said.

He shook his head. "No idea."

"Who does Billy give the money to each month?" she asked.

Justin shrugged again. "Don't know that either."

"Who?" Val said.

He rolled his eyes without answering.

"Look, Justin," Val said, "Terence is dead, Billy's missing, and you and Jamal are scared shitless."

"You know Jamal?" he said, surprised.

Val ignored his question, "If you want help, you've got to fill us in on how this thing works and tell us who's running the show."

Justin scowled at her. "Fuck you, lady. I said I don't know."

He stared at us across the table.

Suddenly I remembered something Iris had said.

"Does Billy know who killed Cy?" I asked.

"I don't know … maybe."

"Did Billy help whoever did it?" I said in an angrier voice than I'd intended.

"No!"

Val put a restraining hand on my arm. "How can you be so sure?"

Justin brushed his hair out of his eyes with a shaky hand. "Billy and Cy were real tight." His voice caught in his throat. He cleared it and continued in a quiet voice. "He'd never hurt Cy."

"How tight were you and Cy?" Val asked.

"I knew him, but we weren't close or anything. Not like him and Billy."

"Did Cy sell drugs?" Val said.

Justin's eyes widened. "Not that I knew about."

Maybe Cy was killed because he tried to get the kids away from drugs. I wanted this to be true with every fiber of my being.

"Who did Billy get the drugs from?" Val asked again.

He leaned forward and spoke earnestly. "I swear I don't know. Billy would never tell me. I asked, but he always said the less I knew the better."

"Who's in charge now that Billy's not around?" Val asked.

"I don't know."

"Bullshit!" she snapped.

"Why won't you believe me?" His voice rose to a wail.

I looked around to see if anyone was looking at us. Justin was in such a state of panic that I was afraid someone might notice and call Sue Ann, the night supervisor. I leaned forward and spoke softly. "Justin, pull yourself together. We need you to help us. Think. Billy disappeared right after Cy was killed."

Justin licked his lips as if he was badly parched. Beads of perspiration had formed on his forehead and were starting to trickle down his face. "Cy was friends with this guy. Billy was afraid of him."

"What's his name?" I asked.

"I don't know."

Val frowned. "Billy told you all about him, but never said his name?"

Justin flicked the perspiration off his forehead with a finger. Val was going to push this kid over the edge if she wasn't careful. It was my turn to tap her under the table. She ignored me.

Justin said, "Billy always called him the fag."

"Why was Billy afraid of him?" Val asked.

On the other side of the picnic area, a young girl and her family were laughing loudly at something. Justin gazed at them as if he wished he could join them. Reluctantly, he turned back to us. "Billy saw him beat the shit out of Cy once," he said.

"Did he say what the fight was about?" Val asked.

Justin shifted in his seat, crossing his arms in front of his chest. "The guy acted sort of… like … jealous. Like he and Cy were more than friends – know what I mean?"

"You mean they were homosexuals," Val said.

"Yeah."

"Being homosexual is not a crime, you know," I said.

Val shot me a warning look.

"Billy said the guy was like … pawing him. And when Cy tried to… like… shake him off, the dude got mad. Beat the crap out of him." He leaned across the table and focused on me. "Isn't that a crime where you come from lady?" he said belligerently.

"Easy," Val said. "We're on your side – okay?"

She turned up the charm, flashing him a bright smile. The boy was visibly mollified. I was convinced the woman could charm snakes.

Justin was putty in her hands after that. He explained how on the third Saturday of every month, Billy sent a text message to the other kids telling them where and when to meet.

He said, "We gave him the cash from our drug sales that month and he paid us ten percent of whatever we sold. Then we divided up whatever new drugs came in and took them with us to sell."

You would have thought he was talking about Tupperware.

"When's the last time you met?" Val asked.

"A week ago, I think. Yeah - last Thursday night."

"Where'd you meet?"

"Rest stop on 95. Near Fairfield."

Which meant that each boy had a stash of drugs hidden somewhere. And possibly more cash that Billy hadn't even collected yet.

"When's the last time you saw Billy?" Val asked.

"He came over after he found out Cy was dead."

That meant Monday. The same day Iris had last seen her son.

I looked up to see Sue Ann bearing down on us. She was frowning and muttering something about Justin and no visitors. Val and I got up hastily and moved towards the dormitory. We slipped through the side entrance with Justin following close behind.

We were about to slip out the front door to the parking lot, but I had to ask one more question.

"Do you know David Sobel?"

To my great relief, Justin had never heard of him.

The basketball court was deserted as we walked to the car and got in. My cell phone went off as Val backed out of the space. I reacted to the sound like Pavlov's dog, with my heart instantly starting to pound.

Fortunately it was only my mother. She sounded extremely stressed.

"Want to come over for Chinese?"

I said, "Thanks, but I'm all the way up in Soundview with Val."

"We can wait. Bring Jordan too if she's around."

"What's wrong?"

Mom could be annoyingly cryptic. "You can see for yourself when you get here."

I heard the click of the receiver as she hung up without saying another word.

Jordan sounded happy to hear from me. She'd been holed up in my apartment cranking out an article for tomorrow's paper and badly needed a break. We pointed the car towards Norwalk so we could pick her up. Dark clouds had gathered overhead as we merged onto I-95 into a stream of traffic.

"Think that kid really was decapitated?" I asked Val.

"Damned if I know."

"You'd think the police would know about it by now." A shudder ran through me as I thought about what a severed head might look like sitting in a bucket. Shriveled no doubt. Not to mention the smell.

Jordan was waiting for us in front of my building. It had started to drizzle. Her sculpted features and dark hair were partially hidden by the hood of the navy rain jacket she was wearing.

We filled her in as we continued up to Weston.

"Maybe Cy was trying to convince Hoarse Voice to leave the kids alone," I said.

"Maybe," Val said.

"Or else they were partners," Jordan said with a shrug.

We heard a crack of thunder followed by the plop-plop of heavy raindrops hitting the windshield. By the time we rolled into my parents' driveway, rain was streaming down with a steady patter. I raced towards the house and almost collided with the black and white squad car that was parked under some trees. Sitting like bookends in the front seat were O'Brian and Perrone.

Chapter 45

Sonny Bellafusco stood up to his full 5'6" height as we entered the family room. Val swept past me and rushed into his arms, stooping down to kiss him while the rest of us stood by awkwardly waiting for their lips to unlock.

Grandpa Max, who had been sitting next to Sonny on the beige love seat, rose to give me a hug. Uncle Abe got up from the matching sofa and hugged me as well. Judging from the luggage sitting in the corner and the pained expression on my mother's face, it appeared they were here for an extended stay.

Grandpa Max saw me glance at the luggage. "We thought we should stay here and keep an eye on things until this mess gets cleared up."

I wasn't sure, but I thought I heard my mother mutter something under her breath.

It wasn't until we were all settled comfortably with drinks in hand, balancing little plastic plates on our laps piled high with dim sum and sushi, that I noticed the electronic paraphernalia on top of my parents' coffee table.

"What's all this?" I asked.

Uncle Abe had a satisfied gleam in his eye. "Sonny went shopping with us in the city today."

All eyes shifted to Sonny who seemed extremely pleased with himself.

"He took us to buy state-of-the-art tracking equipment. The CIA uses the same stuff," Grandpa Max said.

Val was seated in one of the armchairs on the other side of the room. She looked across at Sonny and beamed. "He's so knowledgeable," she said to no one in particular.

"We're not taking any chances," Uncle Abe said. "We bought new cell phones for everyone with the latest tracking technology built right into them."

"What's wrong with my iPhone?" I said.

"These are more advanced."

He handed each of us a box, which according to the big red lettering across the front, consisted of one cell phone fortified with internet and email access plus the latest satellite technology - whatever that meant.

"Bought one for you two as well." Abe handed a box to Val and another to Jordan. "If anything happens to prevent you from calling or emailing for help, the police can find you." He scanned the room, making eye contact with each of us. "Make sure they're always charged and always turned on."

"And don't give the number out to friends. They're only for staying in touch with each other," Grandpa Max said.

Always on? I looked at the package on my lap, not sure I wanted to open it.

Uncle Abe picked up a small black box the size of his palm from the center of the coffee table and held it up for us to see. "This is a tracking device for under your car. If you're carjacked, the police can follow."

"Is that legal?" Jordan asked.

"Of course," Sonny said.

Jordan removed her cell phone from the box and started flipping through the manual. She pushed a few buttons on her phone.

"I don't get how this thing works." I could tell she had a new article running through her head.

"Allow me to explain…" Sonny said.

"Wait one sec' please." Jordan took out her pen and black notebook and opened it to a blank page. "Go ahead - I'm ready."

"Once I set it up for you, the phone does all the work. All you do is dial 911, and the phone tells us where to find you." Sonny waited for Jordan to finish writing. When she looked up again, he continued. "Now this gets a little complicated. As you probably know, GPS stands for Global Positioning System…"

"It was developed for the military," Grandpa Max said. "Same technology that maps out travel routes in your car."

Sonny nodded. "That's right. There are twenty-four satellites floating around in space that can pinpoint a location anywhere in the world." He smiled at Jordan and for a minute I thought Val was going to rip Jordan's heart out. Sonny didn't seem to notice. He retrieved his own cell phone from the coffee table and held it up for us to see.

"The beauty of this baby is that it transmits a signal to the GPS satellites up in space. Then the satellites figure out where the phone's located and transmit the location back to the phone. So when you call a number - like 911, for instance - the phone transmits its location to the 911 website. That's how the cops know where you are. But I can also make it dial into another website that lets *me* know where you are."

"Incredible," my father said.

Sonny paused and looked around the room to make sure we were all still with him. Except for Dad, I doubted any of us were.

Sonny said, "To find you, all I have to do is look at the website. See?"

No one really did, but we all nodded.

"So what do I have to do?" Jordan asked impatiently.

"You don't have to do anything," Sonny said. "Just make sure the phone has unobstructed access to the sky. Otherwise it can't communicate with the satellites."

Val blew Sonny a kiss from across the room and smiled. "You're so smart." She was practically cooing.

Sonny smiled back at her. Then he turned to face Uncle Abe and his expression turned serious. "We're thinkin' about expandin' our surveillance business."

Uncle Abe stroked his chin thoughtfully. I could tell he was thinking about how much risk he'd be taking if he backed Sonny's new venture. Even in a crisis, Uncle Abe couldn't stop thinking about the next deal.

I picked up the little black box for under the car.

"That works along the same idea," Sonny said. "Your grandfather was worried what would happen if you forgot your phone or if someone took it away from you. With that thing," he thrust his chin at it, "I can still track you, assumin' you're in your car."

Which reminded me that Jordan's car and mine were back in Norwalk parked in my garage. I mentioned this to Sonny.

"It's easy to install," Sonny said. "Once you watch me attach it to Val's car, you shouldn't have any problems. But if you need help, stop by the range tomorrow. I'll be in and out all day, so call first to make sure I'm there." He swiveled his head around to look at Jordan and smiled. "You too."

"Thanks. I'd love to see your setup anyway. Kate's told me all about it."

"My pleasure," he said with a little nod. He seemed momentarily mesmerized by her beauty, but quickly looked away.

Val narrowed her eyes at Jordan.

"Which reminds me," Sonny said turning back to me, "How you comin' with the Karate and gun lessons?"

I explained there'd been little time to practice.

"You gotta take this thing seriously, Doll," my grandfather said with a note of disappointment. "I don't know what I'd do if anything happened to you."

He exchanged a look with my mother that sent a pang of guilt traveling from the top of my head out through my toes.

"The range is open 'till eleven at night seven days a week," Sonny said.

"No kidding." Jordan was definitely in the throes of writing a new article.

"I didn't know that," I said. "I'll start coming regularly. For certain."

Jordan popped a spicy tuna roll into her mouth and asked me in a casual tone, "So - how'd it go with Justin Reid?"

I couldn't believe my ears. The last thing I wanted to discuss in front of my family was my probably illegal adventures at a rehab center. I looked at Val expecting help, but she just shrugged. I was on my own. So against my better judgment, I launched into a disjointed description of our visit to Amber Hills.

"Billy seemed like such a nice kid," Jordan said after I'd finished speaking. "Full of plans for the future and all that."

Val's eyebrows shot up. "Nice kid? He's running a teenage drug ring!"

"According to the kids *we* talked to," I said.

"Oh really? Tell 'em about the head," Val said.

I stared at her in disbelief. I'd intended to leave Terence Brown and his unfortunate decapitation out of the conversation.

"We don't know if that's even true," I said. "Justin never saw it. Only his brother did."

"Who happens to be dead," Jordan said.

"Jamal saw it," Val said.

"Who the hell is Jamal?" Uncle Abe asked.

I described the emaciated young black boy we'd met who had been so traumatized by what he'd seen.

"Jesus." Sonny's eyes had hardened into an inscrutable expression I'd come to associate with cops in general and with Matt Warren in particular. It was jarring to see it on Sonny; he'd seemed so amicable up to that point.

My father regarded Sonny with a worried expression. "This could be part of the teenage drug abuse case the hospital's been working on with the police."

Sonny's eyes mirrored my father's unease as he turned towards Val. "Are you sure you shouldn't tell Matt about this?"

"No!" I said. "If he finds out we went to the police, he'll kill Billy. Or go after my family." I looked at Val. "Please. I thought we agreed on this."

Val's eyes softened. "It's okay, Kate. Calm down. No one's going to the police unless you agree to it."

"They should know about the head, Kate," Jordan broke in impatiently. "And the phone call Greg Reid got. The cops think his death was an accident. That's not right." She paused a moment before continuing. "Look – let me call Matt. I'll tell him I found out when I started researching the drug story. He knows I can't reveal my sources."

Before I could respond, my mother stood up abruptly. The expression on her face told me that she'd had enough.

She said, "Let's talk over dinner. The food's getting cold."

We followed her into the dining room where the table was covered in little white cartons and round black containers with plastic lids clouded by steam rising from the hot food inside. You could always tell my mother's stress level by the type of cutlery she put on the table. Her stress was clearly maxed out tonight; she'd set out clear plastic forks next to heavy white oval-shaped paper plates and red plastic cups.

My father took his usual seat at one end of the table with Sonny on his left and Val on his right. My mother sat at the other end with my grandfather and Uncle Abe on either side. Jordan and I sat facing each other in the middle.

I helped myself to large servings of Szechwan chicken, shrimp with black bean sauce, moo shu pork, and vegetable fried rice. As an afterthought, I grabbed an egg roll and spooned hot mustard and duck sauce over it.

Val stared at my plate.

"I'm hungry. " When I'm stressed I eat.

Jordan took an egg roll and a few shrimp. "I cornered Art Desmond at the station today."

"And?" Val said.

Jordan took a bite of egg roll, chewed it thoroughly, and swallowed before answering. "He was tailing Cy."

"What for?" A part of me didn't want to know the answer.

"He wouldn't tell me."

"Does he know who killed him?" my father asked.

"Or why?" Sonny said.

"He wouldn't say," Jordan said.

"He didn't say much, did he?" I said.

Uncle Abe eyed me sympathetically.

"I think Cy was trying to get Billy away from drugs," I said.

My father looked up thoughtfully. "It's possible."

Everyone but Jordan nodded in agreement.

"You don't think so?" I asked her, annoyed.

"We don't know all the facts yet."

"I wouldn't start speculating at this point," Val said, her tone solicitous.

Sonny nodded. "I agree. The cops look at everyone in the beginning. Then they rule people out one by one."

"That sounds logical," Gramps said.

A period of silence seemed to stretch interminably. The scratching of plastic cutlery on paper was the only sound in the room. It felt like everyone was avoiding looking at me.

Finally my grandfather guided the conversation to more mundane topics as everyone polished off the Chinese food. Everyone, that is, except my mother who barely touched her plate. She sat there saying little, looking worried and distracted.

When everyone had finished eating, I retrieved a plastic trash bag from under the kitchen sink, and passed it around the table so that everyone could toss in their dishes. The ideal cleanup.

By the time we were settled back in the family room waiting for the coffee to brew, my mother still hadn't said much. All this talk of killers and drugs and undercover cops had obviously taken its toll. My father caught my eye and tilted his head in her direction.

"How did the photos from the festival turn out?" I asked her.

"Okay I guess," she said.

"Can we see them?" Jordan asked.

My mother smiled. She knew exactly what we were up to. "Sure. Why not."

She went downstairs to her studio in the walkout basement. When she came back, she placed a box down on the coffee table.

I scooted over so she could sit beside me on the sofa. She reached into the box and took out a stack of 4" x 6" glossies and handed them to me.

In the first photo, I recognized the little girl in her stroller. I passed it to Jordan and looked at the next one. A clown was juggling for the crowd, his face in rapt attention as he watched the balls he'd flung into the air moments before.

We passed the pictures around, intrigued by the street life my mother had managed to capture. Flipping through them, I paused to look more closely at one in particular. It was the man with red-tinted hair and high cheekbones she had been photographing when I'd first caught up with her in the street. His lip was curled in a sneer that jolted me into remembering how I'd stepped back into the crowd so as not to draw his attention to my mother or me.

"How would you like to win a date with him?" I asked, passing the photo to Jordan.

She looked at the picture, placing it side-by-side with another one she was holding in her hand. "Here he is again," she said. "He looks like something out of the Russian mafia."

Jordan handed me a photo of a crowd of people watching a bicycle daredevil flying through the air off a steep ramp.

"That's not him," I said.

Jordan craned forward to see. "Not him." She pointed. "Him."

Sure enough, there in the corner of the photograph was the man with the red-tinted hair. But the real surprise came when I saw the woman he was with. Matilda Destry, my large pizza lady friend, was cowering in fear. His right hand was raised as if to strike her and his mouth was wide open, yelling at her. Poor Matilda looked like she wanted to run away; only she was too hemmed in by the crowd to escape.

"My God, Mom - look at this." I passed the photo to my mother.

She looked at it and said, "What kind of lowlife abuses a mentally handicapped woman?" She handed my father the photo. "Look at this jerk."

"I know her from my neighborhood," I explained. "Actually, Matt Warren knows her. He introduced me."

Mom took the picture back from my father and passed it to Sonny. "Can't the police do something about this?"

Sonny looked at it and sighed. "I doubt it. There's nothing to charge him with unless she lodges a complaint."

Mom got up without another word and went into the kitchen to get dessert. In my mother's house, stress is a signal to serve more food.

I was halfway through my second piece of blueberry-peach pie topped with Haagen Daas vanilla ice cream when we heard tires crunching over the gravel in the driveway.

"Expecting company?" I asked.

"No," my mother replied gloomily.

The doorbell rang and my father rose to answer it. A male voice I didn't recognize returned my father's greeting and a few beats later, Matt Warren followed him into the family room.

I glanced at my watch. It was past 9:30. I wondered if Matt worked this late every night. He was wearing what I presumed to be his work clothes: gray slacks and a crumpled navy blazer over a blue shirt that poked out from between the lapels. He looked tired and his thick dark hair needed combing. He greeted Sonny enthusiastically with some kind of male bonding handshake ritual.

"Sorry to interrupt your evening," he said to the rest of us, "but I wanted to make sure you're all okay."

My father pulled a chair over and gestured for him to sit down.

"Thanks, but I can't stay."

"Nonsense," my mother said. "You look like you could use a cup of coffee and some pie."

Matt Warren sat down and smiled. A dimple appeared on each cheek. He had a kind, open face with the type of cheeks old ladies like to pinch - broad without being fat, angling off at the jaw line. He was very handsome, although he didn't seem to know it.

"I see you've met Officers O'Brian and Perrone," he said.

"Will they be out there all night?" Grandpa Max asked.

"Just for tonight. After that, they'll drive by the house periodically." Matt flashed a smile at Sonny. "You're plenty safe with this guy. No need to worry."

My mother came back from the kitchen with a tray laden with coffee, cream and sugar, and a huge piece of pie *à la mode* that she placed in front of Matt.

He had just taken a bite when Abe asked him how the investigation was going. Matt swilled some coffee and let the pie go down before answering.

"Takes time, but we're making progress." He dabbed at his mouth with a cocktail napkin my mother had given him that looked too delicate in his enormous hand.

"Did you get anywhere with the DNA samples?" Abe asked.

Matt shook his head. "So far nothing."

"I thought you said having DNA samples was a big break," Grandpa Max said.

Matt looked longingly at his pie, but refrained from taking another bite. "It still might be. We ran the samples through Connecticut's database, but nothing turned up. Now we're running them through the FBI's. But if he has no criminal record, his DNA won't turn up in their database either." He looked around the table. Satisfied that there were no more questions, he dove into the pie. "This is great," he told my mother.

"Any news about the kid who died the other night?" Dad asked.

"As far as we can tell, it was just a freak accident."

Dad glanced quickly at Jordan before turning back to Matt. "Not related to the drug case you've been working on?"

"Doesn't look that way. At least not so far." He took another bite of pie and seemed to suddenly realize he was the only one still eating. He looked down at his jacket self-consciously and brushed some reddish-blond hairs away. "Damn dog. Sheds all over the place."

"What kind is it?" I asked.

"Golden retriever," he said, grinning. "Arnie."

"Speaking of the drug case," Jordan said, interrupting, "I did a little research. Do you know anything about a decapitated head up in Bridgeport?"

Matt looked up from the pie and he was all business again. "How did you find out about that?"

"So it's true?" she said.

Matt shifted his weight and the chair creaked. His eyes darkened as the cop mask descended. "Yes. But how do you know about it?"

Jordan said, "You know I can't reveal my source. But thanks for the corroboration."

"Damn," Matt said under his breath.

I glanced at Val. She put an index finger to her lips and mouthed *shush*, at which point Sonny frowned at both of us.

Honor among cops and former CIA agents.

"If I were you, I'd rethink the freak accident angle," Jordan said.

"Why?" Matt said.

"Apparently right before he died, Greg Reid got a phone call. A man with a hoarse voice threatened to kill him."

Matt looked astonished. "Who told you this?"

Jordan stared at him, the embodiment of journalistic integrity. "Again - I can't reveal my sources."

He looked so frustrated that he was practically gnashing his teeth. "What about Billy Cole? You were supposed to talk to him."

I was startled at the mention of Billy's name and hoped that Matt hadn't noticed.

Jordan, on the other hand, looked positively serene.

"I did, but he was no help. He barely knew the kids in the car crash."

"More pie?" I asked Matt.

He stared at me as if expecting me to shed some light on the conversation, but all I had to offer was the pie.

"Thanks."

While Matt ate, Jordan watched him with an expression that made me uneasy. Finally she asked, "Is David Sobel a suspect?"

"Where did you hear that?"

"Detective Desmond."

Matt stared back at her for a moment. Then he said, "Sorry – can't confirm or deny."

"Touché," Jordan said.

Chapter 46

I stepped off the elevator and immediately spotted the package sitting in front of my door. It was a small brown box professionally wrapped with sealing tape tightly wound around both ends and across the top. The label said that it was from Tiffany, and from the size of the box, I guessed jewelry or possibly a small house gift for my apartment. I bent down to pick it up, but was swiftly intercepted by Val.

"Careful," she said.

"You think…?"

"Could be," she said.

I glanced at Jordan who eyed the package dubiously.

Although my experience with gifts from Tiffany was limited, I thought the label looked legitimate and the likelihood of a bomb ticking inside seemed unlikely.

"This is ridiculous," I said. "What do you expect me to do – phone the police and tell them I'm afraid to open a Tiffany box? They'll think I'm insane."

I swooped down and picked up the box before either of them could stop me, tucking it under my arm while I unlocked the door.

A part of me wanted it to be from David. But given what Jordan had said, the other part was afraid to go there. Besides, accepting an extravagant present was probably out of the question. Then again, maybe all he'd sent was an inexpensive key chain – the cheapskate.

As we stepped through the doorway, Jordan sniffed the air. "Do you smell something funny?"

"Oh no - not another mouse," I said.

One of the disadvantages of living in a converted loft building originally constructed in the late eighteen hundreds was the ongoing battle with rodents. No sooner had I defeated them with glue pots and d-CON trays placed in strategic corners, then the damn things found their way back into the apartment again. Everyone in the building complained about them. It was enough to make me consider getting a cat.

I tried prying the carton open with my fingers, but the job called for a knife. Grabbing a steak knife from the kitchen, I slashed at the packing material until it gave way, revealing the understated blue box for which Tiffany is famous. I placed it on the kitchen table and started to untie the white ribbon. I stopped. The smell was coming from inside the box.

Val grabbed my arm and pulled me back from the table. "Do you have a big scissors?" she asked.

I pulled one out of a kitchen drawer and handed it to her, carefully holding it by the blades until she had a firm grip on the handle.

She snipped the white ribbon and pushed it out of the way, careful not to touch the box with her hands. Then she closed the scissors with a snap and used the point of the blades to lift the top of the box.

The stench was so bad that I covered my nose and mouth with my hand.

Slowly, Val used the scissors to dislodge the white tissue paper covering the contents of the box.

She jumped back. "Jesus!"

Inside was something small and narrow that I couldn't identify. It was covered in a brown crust that had spread all over the white tissue paper lining the box.

"What is it?" Jordan asked.

"Not sure," Val replied.

I forced myself to examine it closely. It was shriveled and smelled like the mouse that had died in my walls last summer. Something hard and brittle was attached to one end. A wave of nausea almost sent my dinner hurling as I realized what I was looking at. A finger. The hard substance was the nail.

Val moved to the phone on top of the counter and lifted the receiver.

"You can't call the police," I said. "They'll find out it's Billy's."

"You're jumping to conclusions again," Jordan said.

"For chrissake, how can you say that?" I said.

"We don't know anything for certain right now," she said. "Maybe it's Billy's, maybe not. The only thing that's clear is what a sick bastard we're dealing with. You can't hide this from the police. It's wrong."

I said, "And if it is Billy's? And we tell the police and he tortures him some more? Or – worse - kills him? Is that right?"

"Stop arguing," Val said. "Now's not the time to lose our heads. Anyway, you're both right." She started to dial the phone.

"No!" I yelled.

"Relax. I'm calling Sonny."

Twenty minutes later, Sonny walked through the door. He gave Val a peck on the cheek and asked to see the finger.

He recoiled as the smell hit him. "Damn. This is one sick fuck."

"We can't go to the police," I said. "If he finds out, he'll take it out on Billy."

Sonny stared at me for a moment without saying anything. He seemed to be mulling something over in his mind. Up close, it was hard not to notice the massive muscles bulging under his T-shirt. The sprinkling of gray in his dark hair only contributed to his air of authority.

"Okay," he said at last, "no police – for now. Can I have some rubber gloves and a plastic bag? A grocery bag would be fine."

All I had was a pair of clumsy-looking yellow rubber gloves. He put them on and carefully reassembled the Tiffany box. After covering the finger with the white tissue paper, he replaced the top of the blue box. Then he put the whole thing back in the carton and placed that inside a plastic Chang Chung grocery bag. I'd never be able to eat takeout from Chang Chung again.

"Where are you taking it?" Jordan asked.

"I know a guy." He took off the rubber gloves and tossed them into the Chang Chung bag as well. Then he chucked Val under the chin, blew her a kiss, and walked out the door.

Chapter 47

The next morning my alarm went off at six just as I'd finally fallen asleep. None of us had slept much during the night. I'd gotten up every half hour or so and each time I'd heard Jordan and Val moving around in their rooms. I was tempted to hit the snooze button and go back to sleep, but Carla, Sparky, and Russell were due at eight for our production meeting. So I rolled out of bed instead and put up a pot of coffee.

Russell arrived first, a half hour early. Despite an awkward greeting at the door when he tried to peck me on the cheek and I stepped back to avoid it, his behavior was strictly professional. He was neatly dressed in a pair of black jeans and a pale yellow shirt with the sleeves rolled up to just below his elbows. A brown leather briefcase dangled from a strap on his shoulder, bulging to capacity and forcing his small frame to lean slightly to the left. He remained standing in the middle of the room with a wooden smile until I invited him to make himself comfortable. He sat down stiffly in an armchair as if he wasn't sure how I'd react to his choice of seating. I gave what I hoped was an affable smile and went to get him some coffee.

We had just started to discuss the staging for scenes that still needed more changes, when I heard someone trying to get in my front door. There was no time to get my gun out of the bedroom, so I grabbed a heavy glass bowl off the coffee table.

Russell sprang to his feet, alarm turning his face a pasty white. "Kate, what's wrong?"

Without answering, I kept my eyes on the door. I heard a key slide into the lock and engage. I watched the doorknob turn slowly. Like a pitcher winding up, I threw my arm back clutching the bowl, ready to hurl it at the intruder's head. I knew I'd only get one chance; I didn't want to blow it by acting too soon. The door opened partway. I inched closer, forcing myself to wait until he stepped into the room. A large black sneaker with white stitching appeared between the doorjamb, and the door slowly opened the rest of the way.

"What the hell are you doing?" Jordan said from the doorway.

I lowered the heavy bowl just in time, my heart banging in my chest. "You're supposed to be asleep in there." I pointed to the bedroom.

"I heard you up all night, so I snuck out to the Healthy Bagel. I figured you'd never have time." She held up two plastic bags.

I collapsed into a chair. "My God - you scared me to death."

"Sorry."

"Thank you for the bagels," I said apologetically. "I really appreciate it."

Russell was still standing, looking confused.

Jordan waved hello. "It's a long story."

The confusion on Russell's face deepened when Val entered the room wearing skin-tight pale blue pajamas.

"Morning," she said. "Is there coffee?"

I nodded. "You know Russell?"

"Sure. How's it goin'?"

"Val was worried she'd be late, so she stayed over last night," I explained to Russell.

Half asleep, it took Val a while to catch up. Finally the penny dropped and she remembered she was supposed to be David's Assistant Producer. "Oh right. David asked me to stand in for him. Afraid I'm not a morning person."

Russell seemed at a loss for words. He sat back down.

"Why don't you grab some coffee and get dressed so you can join us," I told Val.

Val grunted something and headed towards the kitchen.

"I'll put the bagels in a basket and set out some plates," Jordan said, following her.

Russell and I got to work, but ten minutes later the downstairs buzzer interrupted us. Carla and Sparky were early too.

I wanted to shoot myself.

Carla swept into the room laden with garment bags draped over both arms. Her big hair was bigger than ever and tumbled to the shoulders of her blue print dress that billowed as she moved. She'd recruited Sparky to carry in an enormous carton of accessories she wanted me to see. He held the box out in front of him, careful not to dirty his clothes. After he'd set it down on the floor, he examined his orange polo and white slacks, almost expiring at the sight of a black smudge at his waistband.

"Oh my God! Look at my pants!"

"Relax, you old queen," Carla said. "It's only dirt."

"Who are you calling an old queen, you brazen harlot!" Sparky said, bursting into high-pitched laughter.

My head was starting to throb.

"Speaking of queens," Sparky said, dropping into an armchair, "Did they catch Cy's killer yet?"

I must have looked appalled because Sparky added, "Oh Kate - don't be such a prude." He threw his bottle-dyed straw-colored head back and gave another high-pitched squeal.

"The police don't know anything yet," Val said from the sofa.

Sparky snorted. "I don't see what's so difficult. Just find out who he gave AIDS to."

Jordan had been having coffee and a bagel in the dining room, reading the paper. Cup in hand, she walked over to the arched opening that separated the dining room from the sunken living room and sat down on the top step.

"What do you mean?" she asked.

Sparky flapped a bejeweled hand at her. "Cy was a notorious crystal meth user. Surfed the net for parties. Found them too. In some pretty chic New York hotels - you'd be amazed." He curled his lip in disgust. "If you call three dozen men on drugs humping themselves to death chic."

"Sparky!" I couldn't help myself. Cy had been a friend and a mentor and I couldn't stand to hear him talked about like this.

"Do you really think Cy had AIDS?" Jordan asked.

"Who knows? But nothing would surprise me." Sparky folded his hands in his lap and sat there looking prim.

Jordan sipped her coffee thoughtfully.

"Was he ever in a relationship?" Val asked.

Sparky arched an eyebrow at her. "How would I know? We hardly traveled in the same circles. But I doubt it. Monogamy was never his thing." He must have seen me wince. "Sorry, Kate. I know you two were friends, but you didn't know the real Cy."

"Do you know for a fact he was into drugs?" Jordan asked.

"I most certainly do. He was forever trying to get me to take them. I'm telling you – that man would screw anything that moved – even old queens like me."

I wondered if Sparky had known Cy better than he admitted. I glanced over at Jordan and suspected she was thinking the same thing. But Sparky was small and portly, somewhere in his late sixties, early seventies. It was hard to picture them together.

Russell glanced at me sympathetically. "This isn't getting us anywhere, is it? And it's eating up time we should be spending on the play."

Before I could respond, Jordan's cell phone started ringing. She listened attentively for several moments and then moved towards the bedrooms at the back of the loft where she completed the call out of earshot. We had just resumed working when she reemerged to say that she had to go out for a while.

She didn't say where she was going, but I had a gut feeling she was on her way to Sonny's range to find out who belonged to the finger wrapped in the blue Tiffany box.

Chapter 48

When the production meeting finally ended, I headed straight for the medicine cabinet, downed two Tylenol, and collapsed on the couch. I closed my eyes with the intention of drifting off to sleep when my tranquility was shattered by something rumbling inside my apartment. Reluctantly, I opened my eyes to see Val pushing Raoul, the armless naked male torso, into the room.

"Karate time, Kate. Get up!"

I buried my head in the sofa. "Not now. I have a headache."

Val wouldn't take no for an answer. She made me stretch first and then practice a variety of kicks and strikes. Strikes are a kind of whipping action you do with your fists thrusting out from your body. I got good at the hammerfist strike, a particularly lethal move executed with the heel of the palm. The object is to land on different body parts: temple, spleen, groin, face. Poor Raoul.

With every kick or punch, Val made me yell *Kiai* at the top of my lungs. She said it would help me focus my energy, but I liked it because it was bound to scare the hell out of anyone within hearing distance.

After forty-five minutes of this, I'd had enough.

Val pushed Raoul against the wall. "Good warm-up. Now stand back a little and face me. I'm gonna teach you how to spar."

The woman was relentless.

We stood facing each other and did this little dance. Then she'd jab at me with her fists, managing to just miss hitting me. The kicking part got a little dicey. A few times I thought I was dead, but she always came within an inch of my body without actually connecting.

She wasn't so lucky. I was okay with the punching part, but I lost control with my first kick and landed one right on her solar plexus. Val looked pained, but she was still standing. Then I executed a pretty good roundhouse kick that unfortunately connected with her kidneys and she went down. She lay there for a full minute without moving. I thought we should call it quits, but she was hell-bent on continuing.

"Stand behind me and grab me around my neck," she said.

I'm barely five-feet four inches tall, whereas Val's a shade under six feet. So when she told me to grab her from behind, I had to stand on tiptoes and even then it was a stretch. I should have paid more attention to the look in her eyes because two seconds after I grabbed her, she yelled *Kiai* and flipped me over her shoulder.

I landed face up in front of her on my rear end.

"I said I was sorry for kicking you. What'd you do that for?"

"I'm teaching you to defend yourself. Think an attacker's gonna stand there and dance with you? No! He's gonna freakin' try and kill you. Now get up and grab me again."

I hesitated.

"I promise I won't flip you again. Don't be such a baby."

My whole body tensed as I moved behind her and got back up on tiptoe.

She said, "If someone grabs you from behind, the first thing you do is throw him off balance. Watch."

She stepped forward with one foot and I almost toppled over.

"Next you throw your arm up to break his grip and turn towards him like this." She turned her whole body and faced me. Then she grabbed my wrist and yanked it down, twisting it behind me while she pressed on my shoulder with her other hand and shoved me to the floor. Pleasant exercise.

"Now you try," Val said.

The word Karate means "empty hands." It relies on movement and balance for defeating your opponent instead of weaponry. According to Val, my smaller size didn't matter. It took several tries, but I finally succeeded in flipping all five feet, eleven-and-a half inches of Valerie Weinstein over my shoulder. I was starting to get the hang of this. Surprisingly, I liked it.

The last move Val taught me was how to defend myself against someone sticking a gun in my face. By then it was after one o'clock and I was famished.

"There's no time to eat," Val said. "I reserved time at the shooting range. We can do a drive-through at McDonalds."

"I don't eat McDonald's. It's junk food."

"Oh, excuse me - I should have realized. You eat everything in sight *except* for McDonalds." She rolled her eyes. "Give me a break."

Chapter 49

Val drove up to McDonalds' drive-through window and a teenage boy with acne in a striped shirt and matching hat asked us what we wanted to eat. Val ordered a grilled chicken salad with light Caesar dressing. I considered having the same, but decided that a Big Mac with fries and a chocolate shake was more in keeping with my mood. I scarfed down most of it in the car and was feeling a little nauseous by the time we pulled up to the range.

We climbed upstairs and Vincent greeted me like an old friend. He was dressed in khaki cargo pants and a sleeveless black mesh shirt that showed his rippling arm muscles to full advantage. A diamond stud gleamed against the dark brown skin of one ear. As usual, he ignored Val.

We grabbed a paper sheet with Osama Bin Laden's picture on it and headed for the range. It was almost deserted, save for a man giving lessons to a woman several practice cages away.

Val watched as I loaded cartridges into a clip that I slid into the butt end of the Walther with a click. My gun fully loaded, I aimed at the target and squeezed the trigger, firing one shot after another until I ran out of ammunition. The gun locked open and I reined in Osama.

"Not bad," Val said.

I did an eye roll. "Not bad?" I pointed to the cluster of holes centered on Osama's forehead.

I was loading more cartridges into the clip when a familiar voice called my name. I turned around to discover Matt Warren staring at me in disbelief.

"What are you doing here?" He took a step backwards, his eyes never wavering from the gun I held pointed at the floor.

"Learning to shoot," Val told him. She handed me her Glock. "Here - try this one." Then she turned back to Matt. "We're trying to decide which gun she should buy."

I engaged the safety lever on my illegal Walther and handed it to Val, which she pocketed nonchalantly.

"I like the Glock," Matt said. "We use it on the force. I have a SIG too. The CIA uses them, but you probably know that from Sonny." Matt glanced from Val to me and added, "The Glock may be too hard to sight for a beginner."

That was the wrong thing to say to me. I faced the range and fired off three shots with the Glock. When I reined in the target, I was disappointed to see that they'd gone wide, landing in the upper-right corner of the paper.

"Here, let me help you sight that thing." He turned towards Val. "Mind waiting behind the wall? Sonny'd never forgive me if I let you get shot."

She raised an eyebrow at him and went behind the Plexiglas window in the observation area.

Matt put his hand over mine as I held the gun. "You want to compensate for the kick by aiming low."

He dipped his head to see the target through the sight lines of the gun. Our cheeks were almost touching. It was difficult to ignore the spicy scent of his aftershave. I took a quick breath and pulled the trigger. Bull's-eye.

"Impressive," he said.

"So they tell me."

Matt wanted to talk to us about something and I needed caffeine, so the Daily Grind seemed like the perfect place. We brought our cappuccinos to a table in the back where the lunch crowd had thinned.

"So what's up?" I asked.

He added two sugars to his coffee and stirred his cup absentmindedly. "The DNA tests came back. The hair on your jogging clothes from the guy who attacked you at the beach matches up with the blood from the guy who attacked you in the garage." He flashed his dimples. "You're a disaster magnet."

"Who is he?" Val asked.

"We're still working on that."

"I already told you it was the same guy," I said. "His voice gave him away."

"But now we have evidence that will hold up in court." Matt raised his cup to his lips and took a sip of the cappuccino. "Plus we can link him to Cy's murder in the hospital. Apparently Cy woke up and tried to defend himself. We found tissue under his fingernails." He paused, carefully placing his cup back down on the table. "We think Cy knew him."

"Why?" I asked.

"We tested the saliva on two glasses we found in Cy's living room. The DNA on one of the glasses matched your attacker. The other belonged to Cy."

"They had a drink together," Val said.

Matt nodded.

"So what's the holdup over his identity?"

"There's no match in any of the databases so far."

"What's that mean?" I asked.

"Unless he has a record," Val explained, "there's no way to ID him."

Seeing that I was still confused, Matt explained further. "The way you use DNA to identify someone is by comparing the unknown person's DNA with the DNA of someone whose identity is known. The FBI and CIA maintain separate DNA databases of known and suspected criminals. Each state keeps a database as well. When there's no match with any of the databases, it means the person you're trying to identify probably has no record."

"So in other words, the police are nowhere," I said.

Matt tapped his foot underneath the table, making it vibrate. "That's not completely true. We may not know *who* he is, but we know some things about him now that can help us find him." He took another drink.

I was getting impatient. "Such as?"

"We can estimate his age between twenty and forty. Also, one of the scientists at the FBI has been doing research on using DNA to identify ethnic origin. But it's very experimental. He thinks there's a strong probability our guy's of Slavic origin, possibly with a trace of Asian in his background."

Val drummed her fingernails on the table and looked gloomy. "Terrific. That narrows it down. A youngish oldish guy with slanty eyes and high cheek bones."

Something Matt had said was tugging at my memory. Slavic. Why did I think that meant something?

"Did he ransack Kate's apartment too?" Val's voice jarred me back to the present.

Matt shook his head again. "No. Forensics thinks it was someone much younger. Possibly a kid, which fits in with the iPod."

An image of poor Billy leapt into my head. Had Billy ransacked my apartment? But what had he found? Or not found? Maybe that's why he'd been kidnapped.

"Did you want to say something?" Matt asked.

"No."

"She goes off in her head like that every once in a while," Val said.

Suddenly the idea that had eluded me clicked into place. The man my mother had photographed at the fair. He'd been tall and slim-hipped with high cheekbones and arresting almond-shaped eyes. When I'd first laid eyes on him, he'd reminded me of a dancer from Russia or somewhere in Eastern Europe. My mother had photographed him with Matilda as she cowered away from him. I wondered if Cy had known him as well.

I tried to sound casual when I told Matt that I'd run into Matilda Destry on the street.

"Got talked into another pizza," I said.

Matt laughed, but Val eyed me warily.

I said, "I was thinking that maybe I could do more than just buy her pizza. Maybe I could find her a job at the theater. Then she could buy her own pizza."

Matt grinned. "That's a great idea!"

"Can you give me her address?" I couldn't remember the address Matilda had given to my mother the day she'd taken her picture.

"Sure. She lives in a group home called Applewood Gardens." He gave me the address and waited patiently as I wrote it down.

Chapter 50

"Let me get this straight," Val said. "You think the guy in the picture with Matilda is Hoarse Voice because he looks Russian?" She darted her eyes away from the road and looked at me like I was crazy.

"Not necessarily Russian," I said. "He could be Polish. Or Yugoslavian. You know - Slavic. I just want to feel her out about him."

"It's a waste of time," she said. "We're better off checking out Cy's house first. Maybe we'll find something the police missed. Come on."

"Okay," I said after a few beats. "We can use the key hidden near the door."

"If it's still there," Val said, turning into the parking lot of a drug store.

"What are you doing?" I asked.

"Trust me."

Ten minutes later we got back in the car with a package of washcloths and a box of latex gloves that Val tossed into her oversized handbag. Then we shot up Route 1, arriving in Fairfield fifteen minutes later.

Cy lived in a small gray and white Cape Cod on a tree-lined street a few blocks in from Route 1. The houses were close together with tidy backyards and tasteful shrubbery that faced the street. Val did a sweep of the area, driving past the house and around the block. Not a living soul in sight. She rounded the corner back onto Cy's street and parked behind a blue Volkswagen two doors down.

I looked for the fake rock Hoarse Voice had described in the letter he sent before exploding the bomb outside my building. It was exactly where he said it would be - under the bushes to the right of the door. Unfortunately the key was missing. The only reason I could think of is that the police had found it and taken it with them. Fortunately Val had a contingency plan.

She motioned for me to follow her up the three wooden steps to Cy's front door. Glancing casually in both directions, she ripped the yellow crime scene tape down the middle. It drooped to the ground on either side of the door like streamers left over from a party. Then Val withdrew a little tool resembling an ice pick from her bag and grabbed the doorknob with one of the wash clothes we'd just purchased at the drug store.

"Hey there. You two! What are you doing?"

We spun around towards the street, but didn't see anyone.

"Over here."

A thin woman with a sharp nose and iron-gray hair swept back into a bun was standing on the porch of the house next door, regarding us with a shoot-to-kill expression. Her lips were drawn into a narrow line and her bony shoulders were thrust back so far that we could see her pointy boobs pushing against her white blouse. She must have been watching us from her window because we hadn't seen anyone when we did our drive through of the area before parking the car. She held a portable phone in her hand, probably so she could dial the police quickly if necessary.

"No one's home," she said. "What do you want?"

Val gave the woman a dazzling smile and strode over to her, hand outstretched. I went back down to the sidewalk and stayed there.

"I'm Alexandra Sellers," Val said. "Poor Cy's cousin. Thank you for keeping an eye on the house. It's all so tragic, isn't it?"

The woman let Val pump her hand, but didn't say anything.

"This is Kate Sachs. You've probably seen her on TV."

I glared at Val in disbelief.

The woman eyed me more closely without a shred of recognition, but had the decency to pretend. "Uh-huh - I thought you looked familiar." She turned back to Val and spoke in a less frosty tone. "I'm Doris Offenbach. I've never seen you around here before."

"I'm from New Jersey," Val said as if that explained it. "I'm here to close up the house.

The woman thawed the rest of the way and offered condolences.

Val thanked her and, motioning for me to follow, proceeded back up the steps to Cy's front door. Inserting the pick into the lock, she turned the knob with the wash cloth carefully concealed in her other hand and threw open the door, all under the watchful eye of Doris Offenbach.

The door opened onto a tiny foyer. Ahead of us was a stairwell that curved around to the left and a short hallway leading to the back of the house. To our right, was a small living room dominated by a fireplace and mantel covered in photographs.

Val handed me a pair of latex gloves and waited for me to put them on. "Let's start upstairs."

I could feel my heart pumping. "What are we looking for?"

"Insights."

Upstairs, two rooms faced each other on opposite walls of a narrow hallway. The room on the left was used for storage. A bare mattress atop an iron frame was shoved against one wall. Brown corrugated boxes were piled on top of each other, and old sheets covered in dried paint lay crumpled in a corner. There was a single window in the room covered with a brittle shade yellowed with age. I pushed it to one side and saw that it looked out onto the side of the house into Doris Offenbach's yard. I quickly dropped the shade back into place. All the surfaces in the room were covered in the same fingerprint powder that we'd found at the theater.

We crossed the hall into what had apparently been Cy's bedroom. I jumped at my reflection in a mirror hanging on the wall over a wooden dresser. The bed was unmade with a tangle of white sheets and a blue duvet falling onto the floor. We searched the room thoroughly, but other than pictures, found nothing.

There were photographs on top of the bureau and on top of a small table next to the closet. I appeared in a few shots that had been taken recently at Omnibus. One picture showed Cy when he was a teenager standing between what were presumably his parents. In another photo, they looked much older - late seventies, maybe even eighties. My eyes welled up thinking about the pain they must be feeling. Did Cy have brothers and sisters? I didn't even know.

We descended the stairs to the living room. An upright piano sat by itself against one wall. There were more photographs on top of two lamp tables situated on either side of an overstuffed purple velvet sofa opposite the fireplace. The sofa was backed against French windows that overlooked the front of the house. Sunlight slanting through the panes cast shadows around the room and reflected off a mirror hanging over the fireplace. Except for fingerprint powder, the room was neat and tidy and, despite our methodical search, we found nothing besides more photographs.

There was even an old picture of Cy and me at the OBIE awards smiling for the camera. I picked it up and examined it closely. Cy looked much younger, but then again, so did I. When had he gotten into drugs? Surely not then. I slipped the picture, frame and all, into my bag.

"What the hell are you doing?" Val said.

"It's a picture of Cy and me years ago. What's the big deal?"

"Put that back! The cops could prove breaking and entering if you're caught with that thing."

I hadn't thought of it that way. I fished the photo out of my bag and placed it back on the table where I'd found it.

I wandered around the room looking at the other pictures. I recognized Andrew, Billy, and Justin together with another boy – tall and lanky with blond hair making a goofy face. The hairs on my arms prickled when I realized it was Greg Reid, the boy we'd seen lying dead at the cliff-jumping rock.

Tucked away behind some other photos was another picture of Cy as a teenager. His hand was draped around the shoulders of a friend. Something about him looked familiar. He was a head taller than Cy, with a dancer's body – tall and lithe. He had dark eyes and medium-brown hair with a flared nose and high cheekbones. For a minute I forgot to breathe. I could feel my heart thumping. I'd seen that face before, only he'd been much older. He was the man yelling at Matilda in my mother's photograph.

Val came up behind me and saw what I was staring at. She sucked in her breath. "Holy shit. You were right."

A shadow darkened the mirror over the fireplace. I jerked my head up to see what was causing it and for an instant saw the reflection of a man. It happened so quickly that I would have put it down to my imagination had Val not grabbed me by the arm and pulled me low to the ground.

"Take out your gun," she whispered. Her Glock was already in her hand. Glancing at the photo, she reached up and snagged it and dropped it into her bag.

"But you just said..."

"*Shhh.* Follow me and stay low."

So much for getting caught with evidence.

We ran out of the living room and took the hallway to the left off the foyer, following it to the back of the house. We passed a bathroom and another bedroom before coming to the kitchen at the end of the hall. Val put her hand up to stop me from going any further. The kitchen had windows on three sides and a door leading out the side of the house.

I held the Walther out in front of me with both hands, tightening my grip to make them stop trembling. We remained in the cramped hallway and listened. My breathing felt ragged.

"On the count of three," she whispered.

We stayed low to the ground as we dashed across the kitchen and crouched by the door. We stayed that way so long that my knees started to ache. Finally Val reached for the doorknob and turned it. She slowly pushed the door open and waited. Then she stood up and motioned for me to do the same. We went outside and huddled near the side of the house before venturing further. No one appeared. Val closed the door gently behind her and turned the knob, making sure it was locked. She took off her rubber gloves and waited while I removed mine. Then she linked her arm through mine and we sauntered through the door set into the white picket fence that led from Cy's yard to the street. We strolled to the car. Just a couple of girlfriends out for the afternoon.

Chapter 51

"Stop turning around and sit still," Val ordered. "See anyone?"

Val glanced in the rearview mirror for the hundredth time and shook her head. We were stopped at a light on Route 1.

Even though I knew it was ridiculous, I felt like a sitting duck. After all, who would be stupid enough to start shooting at us in broad daylight on one of the busiest thoroughfares in Connecticut?

The light changed and Val accelerated.

Vivaldi's *Four Seasons* blared from my cell phone and we both jumped. I examined the display. Jordan.

"The finger's Billy's," Jordan said.

"Wait a second and I'll put the phone on speaker," I pushed a button. "Go ahead."

"Sonny pulled out all the stops on this one," Jordan said.

At the mention of Sonny's name, Val cut her eyes to the phone. "You talked to Sonny?"

"Yes. And the finger definitely belongs to Billy. Poor kid."

Val's eyes were fixed on the road ahead. She seemed to be struggling with something.

I filled Jordan in on our breaking and entering excursion. "We're on our way to talk to Matilda now."

"Not without me you're not," she said. "I'll meet you. Where does she live?"

"In Norwalk not too far from my place. We should be there in another twenty minutes or so. Where are you?"

"The shooting range. Sonny gave me a lesson."

The car swerved and I braced myself against the dashboard. "Watch it."

"Sorry." Val said in a strained voice.

Jordan's voice sounded loud over the speaker. "If you give me Matilda's address, I can meet you."

Val glanced at the phone. "Meet us at Kate's garage." Her tone was chilly. "We should stay together."

"Fine," Jordan's said.

"See you in a few," I said as brightly as I could.

But Jordan had already disconnected.

Chapter 52

Val thought she could get a better sense if we were being followed if we walked over to Matilda's, so the three of us trekked over to Belden Avenue and headed in the direction of the train station.

We walked past the housing projects, a row of nondescript off-white apartment buildings that took up the entire block. A group of teenage boys were huddled on a patch of grass near some broken swings. A few of them wore do-rags; others had caps with the brim pulled in all directions except front. Someone let out a catcall. "Yo, ladies! What you fine bitches up to today?"

Jordan and I walked faster, pretending not to hear, but Val turned around and flashed a smile. "You watch your language in front of us fine ladies, hear?"

The boys couldn't resist that smile. They shoved each other and howled with laughter. I heard one of them say something about a foxy lady as we passed.

Past the projects, the avenue ended at a T-intersection. We crossed over to the other side and continued for another block.

Suddenly Val started moving like she was on high alert - posture straight, arms swinging purposefully at her sides. A tan Honda with a white roof whizzed past us, and she kept her eyes on it until it disappeared from view.

"Something wrong?" Jordan asked.

"I thought that car was following us. The driver looked vaguely familiar."

Jordan said, "Well he's gone now."

We turned off Belden onto Cranberry Lane. It was a residential street with small houses set on tiny lots with patches of green. They weren't shabby exactly, just tired-looking, as if it was a struggle for their owners to maintain them.

Halfway down the block we came to a sprawling green clapboard house that was bigger than the others on the street and better maintained. It had a large front porch lined with chairs facing the street. No one was sitting in them. Except for the number on the mailbox, there was no way to identify the house as Applewood Gardens.

I rang the doorbell and stood in front of the peephole so that whoever answered could see I was harmless. The door swung open and a middle-aged black woman surveyed me cautiously with a smile.

"Yes?" she said, looking past me to Jordan and Val.

"We're friends of Matilda Destry. Is she home?" I asked.

"How do you know Matilda?"

"Through Matt Warren. I see her from time to time around my neighborhood and buy her pizza. I promised I'd visit." I hoped I sounded convincing, and introduced Val and Jordan.

She smiled warmly and opened the door wider. "How nice of you. I'm the house manager, Denise Campbell. Please - come in." She spoke with the lilting cadence of the islands. "Matilda doesn't get many visitors. Excepting Matt, of course. He's a nice young man."

"Yes he is."

She led us into a large living room with pale peach walls. In the middle of the room was a plush oversized couch with matching chairs on either side covered in a pastel print fabric. A glass coffee table in front of the couch held a navy porcelain vase filled with silk flowers. Off to the side was a dining area. A modern light fixture hung from the ceiling over a rectangular white wooden dining table with enough seating for ten.

The layout of the house was wide open, with arched wall openings leading from room to room. From where we stood, I could see into another room with a widescreen TV inside a built-in against the wall.

Denise turned towards the TV room. "Matilda, you have a visitor." Then she turned back to us with a friendly smile and said, "Come on in. Everyone's inside helping me get dinner ready."

We followed her into the TV room. Adjoining it was a bright kitchen with a microwave, state-of-the-art chrome refrigerator, and two ovens built into the walls. Two women and two men were seated around an island in the center peeling carrots and chopping greens for a salad.

When Matilda saw me, she sprang up and ran towards me, throwing her arms around me. "The pizza lady." She turned to Denise. "This be my friend. She buy me pizza and she knows Matt too."

I laughed.

"These be my other friends," she told me, indicating the others seated around the island. "This be Jake," she said, pointing to a young man with pale white skin and a balding head. His features told the tale of Down's syndrome. Shy, he barely looked at me as he waved and said an almost inaudible "Hi."

"This be my best friend, Claudia," Matilda said, indicating a black girl around her own age.

Thin and gawky, Claudia looked at me through thick glasses. She gave me a bright smile and giggled.

Next Matilda introduced a young Asian man who forced himself to meet my eye. "Hiya," he said, waving.

"And that's Delinda," Matilda said, indicating a wispy woman in her forties. Delinda said hello and smiled, revealing gray, overlapping teeth. I noticed she was wearing a hearing aid.

I was trying to figure out how to get Matilda alone when Denise told her, "If you'd like to take your guests out on the porch, you may be excused."

Matilda threw her arms around Denise and almost knocked her over, which Denise reacted to good-naturedly.

When we were seated on the porch, Matilda said, "How's yo' boyfriend?"

"Which boyfriend would that be, Kate?" Jordan asked.

Matilda looked at Jordan and then back at me. "She don't know?"

I laughed. "I told you - he's not my boyfriend. He's just a friend."

"Oh." Matilda seemed disappointed.

"He says to say hello to you, by the way," I said.

Matilda's face brightened. "I love Matt. He's my friend. He meet me after school sometime and buy me pizza."

"Where do you go to school?" I asked, genuinely surprised.

"On Washington Street. Near yo' house."

"How do you know where Kate lives?" Val asked.

Matilda looked confused and got up suddenly.

"It's okay, Matilda," I said. "You can come over to my house after school one day. Would you like that?"

She nodded.

"We can get a pizza. Come on – sit with us." I patted the chair and she sat back down.

"I love pizza."

"I know you do," I said.

Val reached into her bag and pulled out the photo she had taken from Cy's house and handed it to me.

I said, "I was wondering if you could help me out with something. But you can't tell anyone. It'll be our secret – okay?"

"Okay," Matilda said solemnly. "I promise."

"Can you tell me who this is?" I showed her the picture of Cy as a boy with his arm draped around his friend.

Matilda shook her head, a puzzled look on her face. She clearly wasn't able to link the teenager in the picture to the man who had yelled at her.

"Do you remember the day I saw you at the fair with my mother?"

Matilda smiled. "I like your mother."

"She likes you too. I'll have to show you the pictures she took of you that day. Do you remember?"

"I remember."

"She even got a picture of you watching the juggler."

Matilda kept smiling.

"But the strangest thing turned up in that picture." I watched Matilda closely to see if she had any recollection of that day.

She stared back at me expectantly, waiting for me to finish the story.

"You were standing in a big crowd, and a man was yelling at you. He looked just like the boy in this picture, only he was all grown up." I held the photo out for her to take another look.

Matilda's smile vanished. Her skin turned gray. She looked at me with so much fear in her eyes that I reached out to steady her.

"It's okay, Matilda. I won't let him hurt you. I promise."

She ran off the porch. We chased after her. By the time we caught up with her, she was halfway down the street, crying. I looked around to see if anyone was watching.

"Don't cry Matilda," Val said. "Tell us what happened and we'll make it all better. I swear."

Val flashed her a smile. Matilda visibly relaxed as Val put her arm around her shoulders and led her back up the street.

Chapter 53

"Who's the man in the picture, Matilda?" Val asked.

Matilda rocked her chair back and forth so furiously that the porch shook. She turned towards me and stared at me with frightened brown eyes.

"It's okay, Matilda," I said. "He can't hurt you."

She hiccupped and threw her arms around my neck, almost knocking me off the chair. "I sorry."

"It's okay." It was like talking to a 280-pound child who understood every third word. "Please - tell us who he is."

Matilda looked at the floor and continued rocking. "He a very bad man. If I don't do what he say, he hurt me bad."

"Has he hurt you before?" Val asked, an edge in her voice.

Matilda looked at me with an uncertain expression.

"It's okay. You can tell us," I said.

Matilda stopped rocking and began swinging her feet back and forth instead.

"He beat me very bad." Her voice dropped nearly to a whisper.

"When?" My voice came out an octave higher than I expected.

"When I don't give his package to the boys on the corner."

"What corner?" I said.

"Around the corner from my school," Matilda said. "Bus'll leave without me if I not there. Then how I supposed to get home? I tell him, but he don't listen."

"What was in the package?" Jordan asked.

Matilda shrugged.

"What about his voice?" Jordan said. "What did he sound like?"

Matilda shrugged again. "I don't know. He be sick all the time."

"What do you mean?" Jordan asked.

"He always has a cold. So he be like whisperin' all the time.

"You mean he's hoarse?" Val said.

Jordan rolled her eyes. "Do you mind letting her answer?"

"What did you do with the package?" Jordan asked.

"He tell me to give it to the boys 'round the corner or I in trouble. Then I supposed to bring somethin' back to his house."

"You know where he lives?" I said.

Matilda smiled at me. "Uh-huh. He write down his address on a piece of paper."

"Can I see it?" I asked.

She stuck her thumb in her mouth and sucked on it.

"Matilda?" I said.

"I thinkin' where I put it." She removed the thumb and her face brightened. "Now I remember. It in my jacket upstairs. I go get it." She stood up.

"Wait a second," Jordan said. "What about the package? Did you give it to the boys?"

Matilda looked at her shoe. "Bus come so I took the package home."

"Do you still have it?" Val asked.

Matilda shook her head, still watching the floor. "He was waitin' for me the next day."

"In front of school?" I asked.

"Uh-huh."

"And?" I said.

"I give him the package back. Then he say I not have to wait for the bus. He take me home in his car." She lowered her voice so that we had to strain to hear what she said next. "But he take me to his house instead. He hit me here." She placed her hands on her buttocks. "And here," she said, touching her face. "And he punched me here." She grabbed her stomach.

Val put her arm around Matilda. "He's gonna be sorry he did that."

"How did you get home?" Jordan asked.

"He drive me," she said in a whisper. "I tell him I not wanna get in his car." She wrapped her arms around her body. "He slap me and kick my behind. Say if I tell anyone he kill me." She clapped her hands over her mouth. "I not supposed to tell you. He gonna kill me now."

"No he's not," Val said. "Not if he wants to live."

Matilda's looked at Val for a moment. Then she laughed and sat back down in the rocker.

"Did you see him again after that day?" Jordan asked.

Matilda studied her sneaker. "He waitin' for me after school sometime."

"What for?" Jordan asked.

Matilda glanced up at me, but as soon as our eyes met, she looked back down at her sneaker. "He make me deliver packages."

"To whom?" I said.

She kept her eyes down. "Man in yo' building."

"You mean my super? Mr. Rosario?" I said.

"I dunno his name."

"In apartment 1A?"

She nodded, her eyes still fixed on the floor.

Val kneeled in front of her and lifted her chin. "Tell us his name, Matilda - the man who hurt you."

Matilda rocked back and forth and covered her ears.

Val stayed where she was. "Please, Matilda. Tell us his name."

Matilda stopped rocking and looked at Val. "Nick. His name be Nick."

"What's his last name?" Val said.

"I don' remember."

"Is it on the piece of paper he gave you?" I asked.

Matilda shrugged.

"Would you get the paper for me?" I asked.

She looked from me to Val as if she couldn't decide what to do. Val said, "Please, Matilda - show us the paper."

Matilda threw her arms around Val and hugged her so tightly that Val looked like she'd stopped breathing. Then Matilda sprinted inside and we heard her trample upstairs.

We'd been waiting for her for about ten minutes when Denise walked out onto the porch.

"Everything okay out here?"

"Great," I said. "Matilda went to get a school project she wants us to see."

Just then Matilda came bounding back and saw Denise. "Dinner ready? I'm very hungry."

Denise laughed. "You're always hungry. Dinner will be ready very soon - I promise." She invited us to come back into the house.

"Thanks, but we need to get going soon," I said.

"It was nice meeting all of you. I hope you come again soon," Denise said, going back inside.

"Please come again," Matilda said. "Pretty please."

"You bet we're coming again," I said. "Next time we'll go for pizza. Would you like that?"

Matilda jumped up and down, making the porch shake. "Goody-goody. Thank you, thank you." She paused; then, "When you comin'?"

"Next week. I promise. Do you have that paper for me?" I held out my hand and forced a smile.

"Oh yeah. Here." She handed it to me.

I read it carefully. *Nick D., 1485 Enders Street, Apartment 4F* was written in a scratchy scrawl. I was certain it was the same handwriting that had been on the blue envelope Matilda had left for me in front of my super's door. From the expression on Jordan's face, she recognized it too. I copied the address onto a slip of paper I dug out of my bag. Then I handed the note back to Matilda.

Chapter 54

It was almost six o' clock by the time we drove over to U-Haul. A man with a shaved head, big ears, and squinty brown eyes asked us what we wanted.

"I need a small truck," Jordan said.

He turned his head and spat into a wastebasket a few feet away. "All I got now is that panel van." He pointed to a white truck sitting in the garage on the other side of a glass partition. "Want it? I gotta close up, so make up your mind quick."

Jordan looked like she was about to say something venomous back, but she must have decided he wasn't worth it because, instead, all she said was, "I'll take it."

Val and I drove the Jag back to my garage and walked over to Washington Street to meet Jordan. In case Nick D. was lurking somewhere, we'd decided Jordan should park the van in a public lot in the middle of Restaurant Row.

We stopped off at Ralph's Pizzeria and bought one plain, one pepperoni, and a large salad to go. Then we stopped at Dunkin' Donuts and bought a bag of donuts and three containers of coffee. No use cooking if you don't have to.

"I think we should turn this over to the police," Jordan said. Grease dribbled down the front of her shirt. "Damn." She tried to wipe the grease up with a napkin, but only made it worse.

"No," I said. "We've almost got him now. We just have to wait until we see him drive away and then sneak into his apartment and get Billy out of there."

Val sipped her coffee and stared at the pizza. "If he's there."

"Have another piece. It won't kill you," Jordan said.

Val threw willpower to the winds and indulged in another slice of pepperoni.

"It's after seven," I said. "If we're going, we need to get ready."

"We can get ready now, but we shouldn't leave until it's completely dark outside," Val said, drumming her fingernails on the arm of the chair.

Jordan glared at her. "Please stop that."

To my surprise, Val obliged.

"Thank you." Jordan seemed surprised too. She nibbled on a slice of plain pizza. "Maybe you should call Sonny for backup."

Val's eyebrows shot up. "Meaning?"

"Meaning maybe you should call Sonny for backup." Jordan shook her head.

"Sonny's got better things to do with his time than traipse after us."

"Suit yourself," Jordan said.

"I'll do that."

They were both getting on my nerves. I got up and went into my bedroom. After rummaging around in my closet, I found what I was looking for and brought it into the living room. I set it on top of the coffee table and opened the lid.

"My God," Val said. "You have more makeup than Macy's."

"It's not just makeup," I said. "It's theatrical makeup. And hairpieces." I held up a skein of hair. "See? Real human hair. I'm about to turn you both into men."

"God, I hope not," Val said.

I glanced at Jordan's chest. "You're no problem." I turned to Val. "But you'll need to bind yourself up with an ace bandage.

Here." I shoved one into her hands. "Wind this around your boobs. Tight. Sort of flatten them out. And while you're at it, put on something masculine. Jeans and a loose shirt would do it."

Val shot me a look and disappeared into her bedroom.

When she was out of earshot, Jordan said, "I doubt that woman owns anything that could even remotely pass as masculine."

"Shsh! She'll hear you."

The phone rang.

Val shot out of her room as Jordan and I raced to pick it up. I got there first and saw David's name on Caller ID.

"Hello David," I said.

"Hi. How'd the meeting go?"

"Fine."

"I'd really like to come up tomorrow and go over some production things with you."

"Sorry, but I'm busy tomorrow."

"Where will you be?" he asked with a trace of annoyance.

"I have to take care of something."

Neither of us said anything for a few moments.

"Kate, I'm so worried about you. It's all I can think about. Has he called again?"

"No."

"Iris' doctor called me looking for Billy," he said.

I'd forgotten all about poor Iris!

"How's she doing?" I asked, feeling guilty.

"Not great. The doctor says she'll be in the hospital a long time. It's bad. Every time she wakes up, she asks for Billy and no one knows what to say."

"What do they tell her?"

"That they can't find him. It's not helping her any, believe me."

I almost told him that we thought we knew where Billy was, but stopped myself, remembering Art Desmond's suspicions. *Please don't let there be any truth to them.* "I have to get going now, David."

"Wait! Please tell me where you're going."

"I can't tell you that."

Several beats went by before David said, "Will you have dinner with me tomorrow night?"

"If I get back in time. Can I let you know?"

David's voice brightened. "Sure. Is Val going with you tomorrow?"

"Yes."

"Please be careful."

We agreed that Jordan would remain in the van. Since no one would see her up close, all I had to do was create the *illusion* of an older man. I darkened her skin tone with foundation and deepened the lines around her mouth and eyes with contour makeup. I tucked her hair into a short gray wig I'd worn years ago in a play. Then I attached a coarse gray moustache to her upper lip with spirit gum.

I stepped back and asked Val, "What do you think?"

"That's amazing!"

Val's disguise was more difficult. Someone might see her up close, so she actually had to be able to pass for a man. I hid her blond hair under a dark hairpiece I'd worn last summer for a production of *Twelfth Night* in Central Park. After darkening her complexion to an olive tone, I filled in her heavily tweezed eyebrows with strands of dark hair. The hardest part was creating a five o'clock shadow. First I chopped up strands of hair into tiny pieces and placed them in a bowl. Then I applied wax to Val's face wherever a man's beard line would be. Starting near the ear, I used a tongue depressor to apply the wax to her cheeks, lip line, and chin, moving down her neck to where a man's Adam's apple would be. I pressed a piece of special makeup lace into the wax, and using a powder brush, dabbed tiny pieces of hair onto her face through the lace.

"Look even?" I asked Jordan.

"A little more over here." She pointed to Val's chin.

I brushed on a bit more hair.

"Perfect," Jordan said.

After carefully removing the lace, I told Val to look in the mirror.

"Holy shit!"

"You definitely need a shave," Jordan said.

"Now for a hat to complete the ensemble." I placed a New York Yankees cap on her head and pulled the peak down low over her eyes. "Sonny should see you now."

It was my turn. I struggled into tight black jeans and threw on a black crewneck T-shirt. In the bathroom, it took me several tries before I finally got the brown contact lenses to stay in my eyes. I put on a long dark wig and tied it back in a ponytail, making sure that none of my red hair was showing. I used greasepaint to darken my skin several shades so that anyone looking at me would see a light-skinned Black or Hispanic. Not bad. I stepped into the family room.

No one spoke.

"Well?" I said.

"You're a genius with that stuff," Val said.

Chapter 55

Enders Street was on the other side of town. There was a Catholic school on one side of the road and a public school on the other. Halfway down the street we came to an apartment complex with a sign on the front lawn that read, *Beauview Apartments, 1485 Enders Street.* Jordan drove in between two stone pillars flanking the entrance and continued around back to the parking lot. White globe lights on top of black iron posts were evenly spaced around the area, giving off a lot of light. We parked away from them in the darkest corner we could find.

The back of the building was made out of white cinder blocks. It had no decoration save the odd flowerpot on a windowsill here and there. I counted six stories high and eight windows across on each floor.

I glanced at my watch. It was a little past nine. "I don't see his car. Maybe we should take our chances and check out his apartment now."

"I blew out his rear window for chrissake," Val said. "His car's probably still in the shop. Let's wait awhile. He's probably driving a loaner."

"How nice," Jordan said, "we get to bond overnight in a van."

"Look," Val said, "you didn't have to come. If you're gonna bitch about it all night, you should've stayed home."

"I wasn't bitching," Jordan said. "I was making an observation."

A dark sedan drove in and parked three rows in front of us. We heard the engine cut out and the car door slam, followed by the chirp-chirp of the doors being locked remotely. I couldn't make out what the driver looked like, but I was pretty sure it was a woman. She walked briskly towards the front of the building, her eyes darting around the lot as if she was nervous.

An hour passed and no one else had driven in or out. My legs were starting to cramp and I was trying hard not to think about how badly I needed a bathroom. We amused ourselves by playing a game. It was Jordan's turn.

"I'm thinking of the initials A. E.," she said.

"Is it a place?" I asked.

"No."

"Person?"

"Shhh," Val warned.

We heard footsteps through the window. They stopped, and then a match flared and we saw the burning end of a cigarette moving through the dark. I couldn't tell if it was a man or a woman, but whoever it was raised a wrist closer to the street lamp to see the time. My need for a bathroom intensified when the light caught the red-tinted hair. He moved forward and the light fell directly onto familiar high cheekbones and almond-shaped eyes.

"It's him," Jordan said.

"Shhh," Val warned again.

I tried to quiet my breathing as I watched him walk over to his car.

"The window's all fixed," Jordan whispered.

"Shh!!!!" Val hissed.

His engine made a sputtering sound and died. He revved it a few times more until it finally turned over and he drove towards the front of the building. I strained to hear which way he was turning, but it was impossible to tell.

Jordan's hand was on the key in the ignition. "Should we follow him?"

"No," Val said. "If Billy's here, we need to get him out." She slid out the back door and waited for me to climb out the passenger side. "Call my cell if he comes back," she told Jordan.

We entered a small vestibule that was separated from the main lobby by heavy glass doors that were locked. On a wall perpendicular to the doors was a silver panel with black buttons next to each apartment number and the name of the tenant who lived there. The name written next to apartment 4F was N. Dimitrov. Russian. The DNA sample had told the right tale.

Val pressed the button.

"What'd you do that for?" I said.

"Don't you want to know if anyone's home? Or would you rather go bursting in there and get your head blown off?"

As it turned out, no one was home. Or at least no one was answering. Val rang Apartment 2A.

"Who's there?" a female voice said over the intercom.

"Pizza delivery," Val said.

"We didn't order anything. You've got the wrong apartment."

Val tried two more buttons. The first didn't answer, but the second buzzed us in, no questions asked. One shove and we were through the doors and into the lobby.

The lobby was shabby and poorly lit with linoleum flooring and green and gold wallpaper lifting up at the seams. We turned the corner and waited in front of the elevators. There were two of them and the display said that one was on the third floor and the other one was in the basement. The only sound was Val's nails clicking against each other.

We stepped onto the elevator. I smiled at our reflections in the mirrored wall. Val looked like a thirty-something guy who needed a shave and I looked like a petite Hispanic woman with Gothic taste in clothing. I counted the floors as the elevator rose to the fourth floor. When the doors opened, there was no sign indicating whether 4F was down the left or right corridor. We tried the left. The lighting was so dim that I had to squint to see the apartment numbers on each door. We found 4F at the end of the hall. I put my hand in my pocket and wrapped my fingers around the Walther.

Loud voices came through the door. We listened intently until we satisfied ourselves that it was only the TV. Val inserted her pick into the lock. Nothing happened. She tried again, but the lock held. From inside of an apartment several doors down, we heard what sounded like the rattling of a chain. Strain showed on Val's face as she inserted her pick again. The door down the hall opened but before anyone emerged, the tumblers on Nick's lock finally yielded to Val's pick.

We stood back-to-back with our guns out in front of us, scanning opposite sides of Nick's living room. The TV was in front of the window on a rickety iron stand that looked like it might collapse if you touched it. The bare wood floor was badly scratched and the only furniture in the room was a stained yellow-gold velvet sofa next to a fake wood coffee table. Old newspapers were piled on top of the coffee table next to empty Budweiser cans and a large round ashtray brimming with butts from what had presumably been Marlboros, judging from the empty cigarette box nearby. The place reeked of stale smoke and perspiration, and the remnants of a sandwich sitting on top of the paper in which it had been wrapped at the deli.

To the left of the living room was a small kitchen. Val motioned for me to stay in the doorway while she checked it out. She kept her gun out in front of her as she moved forward, disappearing momentarily inside. Her face reappeared through a serving window that looked out from the kitchen to a dining alcove. She shook her head; no one was there.

We moved down a small hallway towards a partially open door through which we could see a toilet and a sink. To the left was a closed door to another room. Val motioned for me to keep my gun pointed at the door while she checked out the bathroom. She opened the bathroom door the rest of the way and swiveled right. I couldn't see what she did after that, but I heard her move the shower curtain aside. Seconds later she emerged from the bathroom, shaking her head again. She pointed to the closed door and mouthed the words *on the count of three*. She threw it open and we stepped inside.

Empty.

We moved silently towards the closet doors to our right, crouching down so that we couldn't be seen through the window on the opposite wall that looked out at the parking lot.

"Billy?" I said softly, staring at the doors.

Val slid them open.

A few shirts and jeans on hangers were the only things there, plus a tweed jacket and lots of stacked up boxes on the floor. But no Billy.

Val surveyed the room, hands on hips. "What a shithouse."

It was. A faded comforter and filthy white sheets that looked like they hadn't been washed in weeks were falling off the bed. The room smelled of old sweat and the unmistakable sicky-sweet smell of marijuana. Discarded underwear and other clothing were piled up on the floor, and in every corner of the room there were more corrugated boxes piled one on top of another. Opposite the bed, there was a folding chair and a small square card table holding a scale, rolling papers, an open box of clear plastic envelopes, and enough marijuana to mellow out a small country. In addition to the corrugated boxes, dozens of cartons of Marlboro cigarettes were piled up on the floor. Either this guy had one bad smoking habit or the packs were filled with joints like the one the police had found in my apartment.

The corrugated boxes were all sealed except one. Val pushed a flap back and removed a clear sandwich bag filled with white powder.

"I'll be damned, " she said.

"Heroin or cocaine?"

Her phone rang and she dropped the bag back into the box.

"What the hell?"

She pressed her cell phone to her ear and listened for a moment. Then she snapped it shut and moved quickly towards the door, motioning for me to follow. By the time we got to the elevators, one of them had started to climb. I watched the floor indicator change from one to two and then stop.

"Where's the stairs?" I started to turn down a hallway to the left of the elevators where I'd spotted an exit sign.

"Shit!" Val said. "You dropped your gun!"

I spun around. "Where?"

"There!" She said, pointing. She darted down the hall, picked up my gun, ran back and handed it to me. I finished shoving it into my pocket just as the elevator doors opened.

He glanced at us with disinterest. Val stretched her arm across the opening to prevent the doors from closing as he stepped off.

"Thanks," he said in a hoarse voice.

I kept my eyes down as I followed Val onto the elevator. She reached in front of me and pressed the button for the lobby. When she dropped her arm, I looked up and found him staring at me with a flicker of recognition that faded when he seemed unable to place me.

I tried to control my breathing until the doors finally closed.

Chapter 56

Jordan was on her cell phone when we climbed back into the van.

"Who are you talking to?" I asked.

"Sonny."

"What?" Val said.

"Here. He wants to talk to you." She handed the phone to Val in the back seat.

Thank God it was too dark to see the look on Val's face.

As Jordan drove back to Washington Street, Val gave Sonny a rundown on what we found in Nick Dimitrov's apartment. It sounded like he was taking notes because at one point, she repeated something she'd said more slowly.

"Did he see you?" Jordan asked quietly.

"Yes and no."

"What does that mean?" Jordan asked.

"He saw a man in work clothes with a short Hispanic woman," I said.

Val closed her phone. "For a minute, I thought he recognized you."

"I thought so too. But then he changed his mind."

"Are you sure?" Jordan asked.
"Pretty sure," I said.

By the time we drove into the lot on Restaurant Row and parked, it was almost midnight and the attendant had gone off duty. We locked the van and walked towards the entrance to the lot where Sonny was sitting on a bench. He glanced at us and then looked away. He leaned back and crossed his legs with both arms sprawled across the back of the bench.

Val approached him. "Wanna buy me a drink?"

"Sorry bud. You're not my type."

"Sonny, it's me!" Val said, laughing.

He jumped up and examined her more closely. "Jesus. You gotta be kidding me."

Val tried to put her arms around him, but he pushed her away with a grin.

"Later. When you look more like yourself."

Back in my apartment, we filled him in on our plans for the next day.

"You remember how to activate the tracking device?" he asked Jordan.

"Yes."

"And you attached it to the van?"

"Not yet," Jordan said. "We'll do it in the morning."

He spun around to Val. "You mean you drove over to that psycho's apartment without the tracking device? You got a death wish?"

"Don't yell," Val said. "It was an oversight."

Sonny took a deep breath. "Tell you what. I'll go do it and bring you back the keys. Mind if I borrow the one that's attached to your car?" he asked Jordan.

"Be my guest. I'm parked in Kate's garage." She described the Mini Cooper and handed him the keys.

Sonny started to leave, but turned back to Jordan. "Give me your cell phone and I'll program all my numbers into it. Just to be on the safe side."

Val sat up straighter in her chair; Sonny didn't appear to notice.

"I'll be monitoring the tracking device," he said, "but if anything seems even the slightest bit off, you call me."

Chapter 57

We were back in Nick Dimitrov's parking lot by 5:50 the next morning, parked in the same spot as the night before. It was already too warm to sit in the van without opening the windows. Nick's old black Ford was in the same parking space at the rear of the building where he could see it from his bedroom window.

We remained in disguise, figuring that even though he'd seen Val and me the night before, it was better than having him recognize us as ourselves. Besides, even if he spotted us in the van, he'd just think we were on our way to a job.

We didn't have long to wait. At 6:25, he appeared. We ducked down until we heard him pull out. Then Jordan turned the van's engine over and we rolled out of the lot not far behind him. He turned onto Main Avenue and after a half-mile or so, turned into McDonald's. Keeping up with him at that point became a challenge since we didn't want to risk getting too close. We got lucky when the two cars in front of us turned into McDonald's as well, and we followed them in. Fortunately, he didn't use the drive-through lane or we'd have lost him by the time we got through the line. Instead, he parked in a space near the entrance and went inside. We parked near the exit so we wouldn't miss him when he left. After twenty minutes, he came back out carrying two large bags. He got in his car and drove out of McDonald's, heading north on Route 7. Jordan stayed close behind, allowing only one other car to get in between.

She started to follow him onto the Merrit Parkway.

"Wait! You can't drive a van on the Merrit," I said.

Ignoring me, Jordan sped up the entrance ramp. "It's either that or lose him."

The Merrit was the usual rush hour parking lot – stop and go, dodge and weave. We almost lost sight of him when a motorcycle followed by two SUV's jumped in front of us.

"Shit. You're losing him," Val said from the back seat.

Jordan leaned in closer to the windshield without saying anything. A small opening appeared in the left lane. She turned the wheel sharply and moved over. I braced myself against the dashboard. The driver she'd cut off honked his horn and I glanced behind just in time to see a man giving us the finger.

"Do you see him anywhere?" Jordan asked.

"I think we lost him," I said.

The traffic eased up and we started moving again.

"There!" Val said.

Jordan put her right blinker on and eased over behind a tan Chevrolet just in time to follow Nick off one of the exits in Fairfield.

"Back off," Val said. "He'll see us."

Jordan let a pickup truck turning out of Starbucks pull out in front of us.

Nick Dimitrov drove north past the downtown area and it became easier to follow him. Luckily it was rush hour or it would have been impossible to stay hidden as we climbed further into the country.

"Where the hell is he going?" Val asked.

"Easton would be my guess," I said.

Jordan agreed.

We drove along in silence past the reservoir. The morning air coming in through the windows smelled fresh and clean. At first, the water just peeked out here and there between the trees. But eventually the road straightened out and ran along the water's edge for several miles. As we approached the town, houses appeared on either side of the road. Suddenly a black and white squad car drove out of a side road and followed behind us.

"What does he want?" Jordan said.

"Probably just patrolling," I said.

We approached a town green and were forced to stop at a t-intersection. Nick turned right, but then the car behind him let a stream of cars go by before finally turning out of our way.

Val said, "We're gonna lose him. Go!"

Jordan braked briefly at the stop sign and turned right. The squad car had to let several cars go by before also turning right, so at least he was no longer directly behind us.

"I think this road leads back to the parkway," Jordan said.

The traffic thinned out after about a mile and we could see the black Ford directly in front of us. Jordan eased off the gas pedal so Nick wouldn't see us.

"Where is this guy going?" Jordan said.

We drove past a string of tree farms where tourists picked apples in the fall and cut down Christmas trees in the winter.

"This town is too quaint to be real," Val said.

"Wait 'till you see the cemetery," I said. "Poe himself would be inspired."

"Speaking of which," Jordan said.

Up ahead, Nick turned into an empty parking area. It was next to a white wooden church. Beyond the church was an old cemetery.

"We can't follow him. He'll see us," I said.

"Turn and park over there," Val said.

We turned onto a small country road bordering the cemetery on the side opposite the church and parked under some trees.

"How can I keep watch from here? I can't see anything but the damn leaves," Jordan said. "I'm going with you." She started to open her door.

"No," Val said. "Stick with the plan. If anything happens, we'll call your cell or text message you. Keep the doors locked."

Val and I pushed our way through the trees and entered the cemetery by climbing over a wrought iron fence.

"Our luck, we'll be arrested for loitering." I lifted my shirt to examine my midriff for blood where I'd almost impaled myself on one of the stakes.

"Or indecent exposure," Val whispered. "Put your shirt down and hush."

The cemetery grounds were sprawled over a flat wide area. The church steeple poked through the trees at the northern end. Most of the headstones were from the early 1800's, worn thin and covered in moss. They were too small to offer any cover. I looked around for a tall monument or mausoleum, but the local farmers must have been too poor or too modest to rest eternally surrounded by that kind of opulence.

We proceeded cautiously, taking cover behind trees as we made our way to the church entrance. There was no sign of movement, not even around the few houses across the road. He had to be inside; there was nowhere else he could have gone. His car was still parked in the church lot.

Val motioned towards the door of the church and started to rise.

I yanked her down, pointing to the back of the building. "Rear entrance," I whispered.

Nodding, Val led the way, staying low to the ground and close to the shrubbery that bordered the cemetery. We waited another ten minutes before slipping into the darkened church through a side entrance that led to a side aisle extending the entire length of the building. We were at the end nearest to the altar, hidden by the overhang of the second story gallery. Along the opposite wall, three small recessed chapels had been erected beneath blue and rose-colored stained glass windows.

My eyes swept each row of wooden benches covering the floor of the nave, beginning at the main altar and methodically moving back towards the entryway. Without thinking, I stepped out from underneath the overhang in order to get a better look at the seats in the choir loft over the main entrance. Val pulled me back with so much force that my back slammed against the wall.

"What are you doing?" she mouthed.

I'd forgotten about the gallery overhead. My heart pounded as we stood still, our backs flush against the wall, waiting for him to make the first move.

It was so quiet inside the church that we could hear birds chirping outside. By process of elimination, there was only one place where he could have disappeared: behind the altar, there was a small door.

We crept along the side wall until we were almost level with the altar. Val turned to me and whispered, "Cover me."

It took me a few seconds to realize that she wanted us to split up. My arms felt heavy, as if I was moving underwater, as I lifted my gun and aimed at the door, waiting for Val to reach it.

She ran out from underneath the protective overhang of the gallery and slipped behind the large marble lectern. Then she waited several moments before moving again, this time taking cover behind the wooden benches to the left of the altar. She was almost at the door. Squatting behind a marble baptismal font, she reached up and slowly turned the brass doorknob. When the door was open wide enough for her to slip through, she closed it behind her and disappeared.

I was completely alone. The only sound I heard was the chirping of the birds outside, even louder than before, and my own ragged breathing. I thought about taking the same circuitous route as Val, but hadn't the patience. Instead, I sprinted towards the altar and slipped through the door.

I found myself standing near Val in a dark paneled room dimly lit by a small tassel-shaded lamp on top of a rectangular oak table against the wall. Uncomfortable looking Victorian chairs with straight wooden backs and red velvet seats lined the perimeter of the room. On the left wall, a partially open door led to a darkened room that turned out to be an empty bathroom.

There was only one other door in the room on the right hand side of the wall. I put my ear up against it, but didn't hear anything. I stepped back so that Val could listen. Nothing. She opened the door and, instead of another room, we stared down a flight of steps.

"What is this?" Val whispered.

I am my mother's daughter and she has taught me never to venture forth without a flashlight. Fishing into my bag, I dug out a small penlight and twisted the head once. It turned on, giving off just enough light to see down the stairs.

"I've read about this," I said. "Some old churches have underground passages leading to smaller chapels. The Underground Railroad used them to transport slaves during the Civil War."

We descended the long flight of stairs that ended at a small cellar with a dirt floor. An opening in the wall led to a narrow tunnel that was just wide enough to walk single file. I went first since I had the flashlight. The air smelled damp and after we'd walked a while, my breathing felt labored. My claustrophobia mounted and I began to worry about how strong the walls were, and if they collapsed, how long it would take before anyone found us.

"Maybe we should let Jordan know where we are," I whispered, fighting back the panic.

"Text message her," Val whispered back.

I took out my cell phone. There was no service, which meant the 911 tracking feature wouldn't work either. I tried not to think about it.

Instead, I concentrated on putting one foot in front of the other, breathing in and out – anything to keep myself from giving into my claustrophobia. We walked along in silence until my nose slammed into something hard.

"Shit," My eyes stung from the pain and I put my hand up to my nose. I pointed the flashlight at my fingers, but didn't see any blood.

"What's wrong?" asked Val.

"I think I walked into a wall." I moved the flashlight around the area in front of me and discovered an iron door.

"Now what?" I said.

"Give it a shove and see if it opens. But turn out the light first."

I pushed and nothing happened. Then I used my shoulder to shove harder and the door gave way a few inches, enough for a shaft of light to stream in from the outside. It took a few moments for our eyes to adjust to the brightness.

Chapter 58

We were in the woods facing a small gray stone building. A plaque attached to the front identified it as the *St. Jerome Chapel, circa 1697*. I turned around and saw St. Mary's Church behind us only a hundred or so feet away - tall, white and mockingly near.

"He's here." Val pointed to footprints in the grass.

We entered the chapel quietly, opening the door just wide enough to slip through. Wooden chairs in neat rows took up most of the interior. On either side of the altar, dark wooden benches faced each other. In the apse, a table draped with a white cloth held a large gold crucifix. Behind it, a painting of St. Jerome hung on the back wall, lit only by the light coming in through the stained glass windows.

It was so dark inside the church that we almost didn't see the door behind the altar. It was slightly ajar and as we got closer we heard someone talking in a raspy voice that made my heart start pounding in my chest.

"Eat up. I made a special trip to McDonald's for you."

Several moments of silence went by.

"That's enough."

"Please," a young voice said. "I didn't finish."

We heard a slap followed by a sharp cry.

That was enough for me. I moved forward, but Val grabbed me back. She pointed to the entrance and motioned for me to follow her.

Outside, I lost it. "What the hell did you do that for? We could have gone in and stopped him. Didn't you hear what was happening?"

"You can't risk bursting in there. All he'd have to do is pump one round into Billy and that'd be the end of it."

I hadn't considered that. "So what do you propose?"

"Wait for him to leave. Then call the police to go after him. Once we're sure he's gone, we'll go in and get Billy."

We walked around the building and checked for other doors through which he might exit. When we were satisfied that no other doors existed, we waited behind an old stone wall, watching the entrance through uneven cracks in the wall. Fifteen minutes later he exited the chapel. He looked around cautiously and then walked over to the entrance to the tunnel and disappeared.

We waited a full ten minutes before making our move. We kept our eyes on the tunnel as we moved towards the chapel and slipped through the door. Then we ran to the door behind the altar and opened it.

The first thing that hit me was the smell of urine and feces. I waved the flashlight around the room. It was more like a closet than a room, barely large enough to hold all three of us. Billy was tied to a wooden chair, naked from the waist up. His hands were tied behind his back, his feet trussed together in front of him. His mouth had been taped shut with a wide piece of silver duct tape.

I tried to untie his hands, but the rope was too tight.

Val fished a Swiss Army knife out of her bag. "Here, let me."

Billy moaned as I removed the tape from his mouth as gently as I could.

"Can you walk?" Val asked him.

"I don't know," he said.

We lifted him under his arms and he whimpered. When we got him out of the room and into church, I saw why. At first I thought the light through the stained glass windows was playing tricks on me, casting weird shapes along his torso. I moved the flashlight up and down his thin chest. It was covered in red sores.

"Cigarette burns?" Val whispered.

Billy nodded. His eyes were almost swollen shut. It was obvious that he couldn't walk far on his own.

I pulled my cell phone out of my pocket and made a deal with God that if he'd let me have service, I'd devote the rest of my life to doing good works. A single bar rose on the screen, but it was enough. I dialed Jordan. She answered on the first ring.

"We've got him," I said.

"Where?"

I tried to remember my directions. "A stone chapel in the woods just in back of St. Mary's on the northeast side. Nick's around, so be careful. There's a tunnel leading here from a room in the church behind the altar. Nick may be hiding there."

"Call Sonny?" Jordan asked.

"Sonny. Matt. Also an ambulance. Billy's in bad shape."

Val and I debated what to do next. Stay inside and wait for help?

"He could come back for something," Val said. "Let's get him outside. We can wait behind the stone wall."

Billy and I were standing behind her as she flung the door open. A crack rang out and it wasn't until Val clutched her stomach and lurched forward that I realized what it was. Val was laying face down, her body wedged in the door. All I could see of Nick through the opening in the door was his arm pointing at Val; I couldn't even see the gun I knew he was holding.

I let Billy sink to the floor and looked around for a hiding place. "Go behind the altar," I told him. "Stay there until help comes."

I didn't see what he did next because another shot rang out and I saw Val's body shudder through the opening in the door. I grabbed her by the legs and pulled her inside, letting the door shut.

"Get up, Val. Please."

It was no use. She didn't respond.

I pulled her out of the doorway and dragged her across the aisle over to the side wall. Then I called 911 and prayed I had enough service to make the call. A woman picked up after three rings.

"Please help me," I said. "My friend's been shot and a boy's been badly hurt. The killer is outside."

I tried to concentrate on what the woman was asking me.

"I'm in an old stone chapel in the woods. Behind St. Mary's Church. It's in Easton next to a cemetery."

The door swung open and I dropped the phone. I could hear the woman asking me what was going on. He heard her too and started to move towards me, although I could tell that he was having trouble adjusting to the light. I grabbed my gun in both hands and tried to remember what Val had taught me. If I aimed for his head, there was a good chance I'd miss. So I aimed at his chest and waited for him to get closer. I had the advantage of being able to see. He stumbled forward and when he was no more than a few feet away, I held my breath and gently squeezed the trigger. He dropped to his knees, rolled over on his side, and lay still. I could hear the 911 operator pleading with me to come back on the phone and tell her what was going on.

Chapter 59

My hands were shaking so badly that I could barely hold the gun, but I kept it pointed at his body. I got up and walked closer to him. He was curled on his side in a fetal position and I couldn't see his face. I stayed far enough away so that he couldn't grab me if he was faking, but I was close enough to observe the rise and fall of his breath. There wasn't any. I stared at him a few moments to make sure. He was completely inert. I took a step closer. Blood was pooling around him, streaming from his chest and out his mouth. His gun was inches from his hand and I kicked it beyond his reach before picking it up just in case.

I knelt down next to Val. Her eyes were open partway, but she didn't seem to see me. She was lying in her own pool of blood, perfectly still. Each time she took a breath, she made a gasping sound, as if most of the air had escaped without doing her lungs any good. Her stomach was bleeding badly. I placed the guns next to me on the floor and tried to stop the bleeding by applying pressure to the wound. Then I realized she was also bleeding from her chest beneath her left shoulder. I tried to stop that too, but it was hopeless. I picked the guns up from the floor, feeling safer with them in my hands, and started to stand up. I must have accidentally squeezed the trigger of Nick's gun because it fired a round into the thick stone wall to my left with a deafening noise.

Instantly the doors to the chapel flung open and light streamed in for a moment before they closed again. I slid back down to the floor and aimed both guns at a man crouched in the doorway holding a gun out in front of him. I stretched in front of Val, shielding her body as best I could while holding both guns out in front of me.

He moved forward, scanning the area from side to side with his gun pointing ahead, not aiming at anything in particular, but moving in line with his body. It had never occurred to me that Nick had a partner. I stayed still with the guns leveled at his chest and waited for him to get closer. Seconds later the doors opened again, but this time someone held them open and I had to shut my eyes against the glare.

"Hold it right there."

For a minute, I thought he meant me and I froze without saying anything. Then I opened my eyes and saw that two more men were standing in the doorway with their guns aimed at the first man's back. One of them was a head shorter than the other and wore what looked like a baseball cap on his head. A third person came up behind him and it didn't register that he was a policeman until he pushed the brim of his uniform hat back.

The first man froze and slowly raised both arms into the air.

"Turn around," the tall man sai.

The man did as he was told.

"For chrissake, Sonny. I almost shot you." Matt Warren lowered his gun. "Jesus."

I made some kind of sound to let them know I was there, but I couldn't manage a coherent sentence.

Matt Warren and the guy in the baseball cap came towards me and stopped a few feet away. Then Matt moved closer while the guy in the cap kept a safe distance. Both carried guns that they pointed at me. Matt shined a bright flashlight in my face with his other hand and I cringed, but didn't dare move. He roamed the light around and let it linger on my hands for a moment until he saw Val stretched out behind me. He pressed the barrel of his gun against my right temple.

"Put the guns down," he said.

I looked at my hands, surprised to see them holding two guns. They were covered in blood. I carefully laid the guns down in front of me one at a time.

The guy in the cap stepped forward and picked them up.

"Are you hurt?" Matt asked in a gentler tone. He aimed the flashlight at my hands again. "Habla Inglese?"

I'd forgotten I was wearing a disguise. As far as Matt could tell, I was some Hispanic girl he'd never seen before and Val was a guy in need of a shave - probably my boyfriend.

I shook my head and smiled. "Matt, it's me. Kate."

"What the hell…" he lowered his gun. He shined the flashlight in my face and then roamed it up and down Val's body. "Who's the guy?"

"It's Val. She's been shot."

Hearing Val's name, Sonny ran up beside Matt and saw her. "Oh my God. Oh my God." He crouched down and cradled her in his arms.

"Ambulance should be here any minute," Matt told him. He looked at me as if he still couldn't believe it.

"Billy." I was having trouble getting full sentences out.

"Where?" Art Desmond appeared next to Matt.

"Behind the altar," I said, pointing towards the front of the chapel.

The guy in the cap still hadn't said anything, but he'd holstered his gun and was squatting beside Nick. His cap and bulky vest had FBI written in large white block letters.

"Recognize him?" Matt asked him.

The FBI guy shook his head. "No."

"His name's Nick Dimitrov," I told Matt. "He kidnapped Billy. And shot Val."

Matt stared at me for a minute. Then he gently helped me to my feet. "Are you hurt?" He was staring at my hands.

I shook my head. "No."

From the front of the church, Art Desmond yelled out, "He's here." Something sounded like it was being dragged. Then, "Sweet Jesus, Son of Mary."

"What's going on?" Matt said sharply.

"Kid's in bad shape," Art said. "I'll wait with him until the ambulance gets here."

I swayed slightly and Matt grabbed me around the waist. Then he helped me over to one of the chairs in the nave.

"I think these are antiques. You're not supposed to sit on them."

"Screw antiques," he said. "Sit."

A figure called from the doorway, "Kate." I recognized Jordan's voice. "Kate." She was practically shouting.

"You can't come in here," someone said.

"The hell I can't," Jordan said.

"It's okay," Matt said. "Let her in."

Matt waved his flashlight so she could find us. As she got closer, my bloody hands caught the light and Jordan screamed.

"I'm not hurt," I said. "He shot Val and I tried to stop the bleeding."

"That answers the first question I was going to ask you," Matt said.

He may have said something else, but the sound of sirens drowned it out. An army of police and paramedics burst through the doors and by the time they carried Val and Billy away on stretchers, I felt able to stand up on my own.

"What happened here?" the FBI man asked me. He had a square jaw and steel gray hair cut short. His face was unlined and didn't go with the gray. He wasn't actually short either, except in comparison to Matt. Standing next to Jordan, I realized he was around six feet tall.

"Who are you?" Jordan said.

"Special Agent Hank Baxter," he said. "FBI."

"I can see that. It says so on your hat. What do you want?" Jordan said.

"Knock it off, Jordan," Matt said. "We're trying to find out what's going on here. Kidnapping is a federal crime. You know that."

Jordan held her tongue.

The church was flooded with police and FBI agents who kept knocking into us.

"Why don't we step outside so we're not in everybody's way," Baxter said.

Matt guided me by my elbow as we stepped outside. I blinked against the glare and let myself be led over to the stone wall where I sat down on top of it.

"Why don't you tell us what happened?" Matt said.

I took a deep breath. "We followed him here. Then we waited for him to leave. As soon as he did, we called Jordan so she could alert you and Sonny. Then we went in to get Billy. Only he must've known we were here because the minute Val opened the door to leave, he shot her. Twice."

"Then what did you do?" Hank asked.

"I pulled Val back inside and told Billy to hide behind the altar. Nick came after us and I shot him."

"Jesus," Matt said.

"Is he dead?" I asked.

"Yes," Matt said.

"Good."

Chapter 60

"How did you know Billy Cole had been kidnapped?" Hank Baxter asked me.

We were in the police station, seated in the same stuffy room where Matt had questioned me after I'd discovered Cy's body. My claustrophobia got the better of me and I glanced anxiously at the closed door. Matt got up and opened it.

"Better?" he asked.

I nodded. "Thank you."

Baxter looked annoyed. "Do you mind?" he said to Matt.

Matt locked eyes with him for several seconds before taking his seat again at the table. I didn't want to be the cause of any friction; I figured I needed them both on my side.

"Billy's mother," I told Baxter. "She called and said if I didn't give back whatever I'd stolen, he'd kill Billy." I looked at Matt. "She called me on my cell that night at the cliff-jumping rock. When the boy died at the swimming hole."

"Gregory Reid," Matt said.

Baxter nodded.

"What did Nick think you'd stolen?" Baxter asked me.

"I didn't steal anything," I said.

"I didn't say that you had," Baxter said. "I asked what he *thought* you'd stolen."

"I don't know for certain, but I'm pretty sure it was drug money."

I looked at Matt, but he just stared back with that inscrutable expression of his.

"Why didn't you go to the police?" Baxter asked.

"Because he set a bomb off near my building," my voice rose in spite of myself. "He threatened to kill my family. Christ, what would you have done?"

"So you decided to find Billy on your own," Baxter said.

"Yes," I said. "Especially after he sent me Billy's finger."

From the expression on both their faces, it was obvious that they hadn't known about that.

"When did *you* find out Billy'd been kidnapped?" I asked Baxter.

He took so long to answer that I thought he wasn't going to. "Mrs. Cole told Detective Desmond in the hospital." He waited for me to say something and when I didn't, he switched gears. "When you started investigating on your own, what did you find out?"

I hesitated.

"It's okay," Matt said. "Trust us."

I drew in my breath and exhaled. "Cy was using an army of kids to sell drugs for him. Billy was the ringleader."

"And you know this because?" Baxter said.

"Because Andrew Barnes said so and Justin Reid – Greg's brother - confirmed it."

Baxter flipped through some notes. "Barnes is still in the hospital, right?" he asked Matt.

Matt nodded.

"What's Justin Reid's part in all this?" Baxter asked me.

I said, "He's Billy's best friend."

Baxter nodded at Matt who jotted something down in his notebook.

"When did you talk to him?" Baxter asked me.

"About a week ago. Andrew told us Justin was hiding out in a rehab." I sighed, trying to remember the name. "Amber Hills. Val and I went to see him there."

"Jesus." Matt said.

Baxter glanced at him with an annoyed expression, and then turned back to me. "What else did you find out?"

I considered the question for a moment. "For one thing, Cy and Nick go way back."

"What makes you say that?" Baxter asked.

"Cy had an old photograph of the two of them together. They must've been in their late teens."

"Where did you see this photo?" Baxter said.

My voice stuck in my throat. "Cy's house."

"Jesus, Kate," Matt said. "You broke into his house?"

"Not exactly," I said.

Baxter glanced at Matt and smiled for the first time. He tried to suppress it, but there it was just the same. He said, "I really don't care how you found out, so let's move on."

Matt rolled his eyes.

"What else did you find out?" Baxter asked.

"Well… He terrorized Matilda into running drug errands for him," I said, looking at Matt.

"What's Matilda got to do with this?" Matt said.

I explained about the photograph my mother took with Nick yelling at her.

"He abused her," I said. "He forced her to leave the letter in front of my super's door. And Billy's finger."

"My God," Matt said. "Did she tell you that?"

I nodded.

"Val and I did a little investigating."

Chapter 61

Val was in surgery for nine hours. Sonny, Jordan, and I took turns pacing the waiting room. My father was on duty in the ER and came and sat with us whenever he could get away, assuring us that Val was in good hands. When at last the surgeon came out and told us that he was cautiously optimistic, Sonny burst into tears. We tried to convince him to come get something to eat with us, but he wouldn't budge from the waiting room.

Jordan and I grabbed a bite in the cafeteria. On our way back, we stopped in to see how Billy was doing. Art Desmond was sitting at his bedside reading the papers. Billy was asleep with his head burrowed into the pillow so that all we could see was one eye, purple and swollen. He was lying partially on his side, one arm tucked underneath him, the other stretched across the bed, bandaged and attached to an IV.

"How's he doing?" I whispered to Desmond.

"They keep giving him pain medication, so he's pretty knocked out. He's lost a lot of blood. Plus he's dehydrated; they're giving him fluids through the IV."

"Did he tell you anything?" Jordan asked.

Art looked at her cautiously. "Not really."

"Meaning?" Jordan said.

"It means I'm not ready to give statements to the press," he said.

"So talk off the record," Jordan said with a smile.

"Actually, I have some questions for you," he said, meaning me. "Pull up a chair."

I started to sit down, expecting Jordan to pull a chair over from the empty bed next to Billy. Instead, she remained standing in the doorway.

"I don't think you should answer any more questions without a lawyer present," Jordan said.

She was right. Matt and the FBI had already taken my statement. Although it had been self-defense, I'd still killed a man no matter how you looked at it.

"Hey, this is no big deal," Art said to me, smiling. "I just wanted to ask how you figured out where he was."

I looked at Jordan. She shrugged, and then walked across the room and pulled up the other chair. We gave Desmond a quick rundown on how we'd staked out Nick's apartment.

A young doctor appeared in the doorway and asked us to step outside. Jordan and I wanted to get back to Sonny anyway, so we excused ourselves and headed towards the elevator.

"I'll stay with Billy a while longer," Desmond said. "In case he wakes up."

"Can't you wait until he's better before questioning him? He's been through hell," I said.

Art looked surprised. "I'm not doing it for that reason. The poor kid's got no one. His mother's in here with a heart attack and he doesn't even know it yet."

I apologized.

It had been a very long day.

Chapter 62

The next two weeks went by in a blur. By some miracle, Val survived. Unfortunately, her doctors predicted it would take the better part of a year for her to fully recover, and they transferred her to a facility that specialized in rehabilitation. But as Sonny kept saying, Val was one tough lady.

Billy recovered slowly. Not only had Nick nearly tortured him to death, but he'd pumped him full of heroin as well. Consequently, Billy floated in and out of consciousness, making it difficult for the police to determine if what he told them was the truth, or if he was being delusional.

According to Billy, millions of dollars in drug money had gone missing. Nick was convinced that a group of kids must have stolen it, so he went on a rampage to get it back. When that didn't work, he realized they didn't have it. He figured Cy must have stolen it and was hiding it somewhere. He tried to beat it out of him in the office, only I interrupted them when I rapped on the door. When I walked into the actors' lounge that night and interrupted them again, he was convinced I was in on it. But when nothing he did to me produced the money, he decided that Billy was double-crossing him and knew where it was hidden; hence the kidnapping.

Billy insisted that he didn't know anything about the money, let alone where it was hidden. The police tended to believe him. As Sonny pointed out, even trained CIA agents have their breaking point. Wouldn't Billy have talked after Nick sliced off his finger? Even sooner would have been my guess.

Iris Cole, Billy's mother, made a full recovery from her heart attack. She accepted a plea-bargain on her son's behalf, thanks to the clever negotiating skills of a court-appointed lawyer. The state agreed to drop all charges in exchange for Billy undergoing residential treatment at Amber Hills as soon as he was well enough to leave the hospital.

As for me, I had a lot to be thankful for. The show opened to rave reviews in the local press. Jordan even convinced the Connecticut section of the New York Times to review the show and they loved it.

My only problem was that I couldn't stop thinking about everything. I had nightmares that Nick had somehow managed to survive without anyone knowing it, and that he was stalking me. In my waking hours, I worried endlessly that Nick had been working with a partner who would turn up at any moment like a bad penny looking for his money; assuming, that is, that Billy was right about drug money having gone missing. I found myself looking over my shoulder all the time, certain that someone was following me. I stared rudely at strange men who stopped me for my autograph or who merely glanced at me in the street. I lay awake at night, imagining what it would be like if I had to kill someone again.

Jordan kept telling me I needed to get away, but with eight performances a week, I couldn't afford the time. So when David called to invite me to dinner at a posh restaurant in the city, I figured it might be just the diversion I was looking for. Besides, it was Monday night, the theater was dark, and I hadn't been out on a date in a very long time.

Chapter 63

David sat next to me on a red banquette against a wall that had been faux-painted with scenes of Villefranche on the Riviera. He'd spared no expense. The restaurant was old New York, the food French *haute cuisine.* Spotlights on the ceiling were aimed at red and purple flowers artfully arranged in painted vases along the walls. David wore a navy blue suit, starched white shirt, and pale pink tie. We were more than halfway through a bottle of Dom Perignon and I was feeling no pain.

"Here's to Val," I said.

"And to Cy for introducing us."

"Poor Cy," I said.

"I think you're being sentimental. The man pushed drugs - on kids!"

We were both silent a moment. I thought I'd known Cy. It turned out he was someone else entirely.

"Do you think Cy really took the money?" I asked.

David looked startled. "Of course."

"Then where is it? What'd he do with it?"

David regarded me cautiously. "Kate – what are you saying?" He looked like he was considering the possibility that he might be having dinner with a crazy person.

I felt suddenly foolish. I hadn't shared my fears with anyone except Jordan until now. "I know - it sounds nuts. But I can't shake the feeling that someone's still out there - looking for it. I even turned my loft upside down – in case it was hidden somewhere that no one had thought to look."

"And?" David's tone was incredulous.

"And nothing. It's not there. Don't you see? That's the point – it's nowhere."

David leaned forward. "Kate – you have to stop thinking about this." He smiled in an obvious attempt to lighten things up. "Suppose you had found the money? Then what would you have done?"

"Turned it over to the police, of course!"

He shook his head, smiling. "You really are special. Most people would take it and run off to the Caribbean."

I laughed. "David! Is that what you would do?"

"Absolutely." He raised his champagne glass. "To a carefree life in the Caribbean!"

We clinked glasses and sipped our champagne.

"So what's this big meeting at Miles' office on Wednesday?" I asked.

"What meeting?"

"Miles called about some new show he said you're thinking of doing and wanted my take on it. I thought you were supposed to be there too."

David tinkered with his champagne glass without saying anything. He seemed suddenly upset. "You're holding a meeting without me?"

"Of course not. Miles must've forgotten to call you."

"I'll be in California on Wednesday. I leave tomorrow," he said.

"So we'll pick another day when you can make it. It's no big deal."

His expression relaxed. "No – it's okay. Have the meeting. I'll call Miles tomorrow."

He smiled and then he took my hand and kissed it.

Chapter 64

David gave the taxi driver an address in Greenwich Village. "That's not Grand Central Station," I said.

"No it's not."

We pulled into the circular driveway of a large white building on the corner of Eighth Street and Fifth Avenue. The doorman opened the taxi door and waited for us to get out before ushering us into the building. We took the elevator to the twenty-eighth floor. When the doors opened, there were only two apartments on the floor, one to the left and another to the right. David lived in 28A to the right. He fished his key out of his pocket and unlocked the door, at which point a shaggy white sheep dog jumped me. He stood on his hind legs with his front paws on my shoulders so that we were eyeball to eyeball.

"This is Shakespeare," David said. "He's a puppy. No manners."

Shakespeare shoved off and almost knocked me over as he turned to greet his master. Then he lifted his leg and peed on David's mahogany table in the hallway. David disappeared inside to find something to mop up with while I looked around.

It was not your typical man's apartment. Either he'd hired a decorator or the ex-wife had had a hand in things. The large foyer had expensive marble flooring with a multicolored earth-toned medallion in the center. A Louis XIV table was flush against a wall decorated with a giant mural depicting Ancient Greek ruins. A small ratty-looking Persian rug was strategically placed beneath the table. According to Uncle Abe, who was an expert in such matters, the rattier the rug, the more expensive it tended to be.

To the left of the foyer was an immense living room. High ceilings were painted white and contrasted prettily with pale green walls and floor to ceiling silk brocade curtains in a matching shade. The room felt like it had no furniture, which wasn't technically true. There was a small white silk sofa, two matching wing chairs, and a dark wooden coffee table, all of which seemed dwarfed by the vastness of the room. I had the impression that the furniture was beside the point since the room was rarely used anyway.

I was thinking that coming here had been a bad idea and that I needed to go home when David and Shakespeare reappeared. David cleaned up the pee with some paper towels and Fantastic.

"Sorry about this," he said. "Come in the kitchen while I get rid of this mess. Want a glass of wine?"

"Sure."

David's kitchen was spectacular. He had a black granite island in the center and chrome and black appliances against the walls. A round glass table and natural wood chairs were tucked into an alcove near a window that overlooked lower Fifth Avenue.

"Nice," I said, admiring the view.

"Yes it is."

David had crept up behind me and wrapped his arms around me. He turned me around and kissed me gently. His lips moved from my mouth to the nape of my neck and down my arm. He gently slipped the straps of my dress off my shoulders. By the time his hands cupped my breasts, whatever remaining resolve I had to go home and sleep in my own bed had flown out the window.

We skipped the wine. He swept me up in his arms and carried me to the bedroom. I felt mildly ridiculous playing Scarlett O'Hara to his Rhett Butler, although I had to admit it was a turnon.

In the bedroom, he lowered me to my feet and I caught sight of myself in a gilded mirror opposite the bed. I adjusted my black silk dress and pushed the straps back on my shoulders where they belonged. My hair looked redder than usual and was falling out of the rhinestone barrettes I'd spent half an hour getting to stay in place before leaving my apartment. David convinced Shakespeare to lie down on a doggie cushion that matched the color of the walls - a vile shade of green that reminded me of pea soup. Heavy cream-colored satin drapes with green velvet trim blocked all light from the outside.

"Who decorated your apartment?" I asked.

"The ex," he said, kissing me. "Why? Don't you like it?"

"I do. It's beautiful. So tasteful."

David unzipped the back of my dress, and it fell to the floor. He kissed me as he undid my bra, gently caressing me with his fingertips. I practically ripped his shirt off as he struggled out of his pants. He eased me down onto the bed and I put my arms around him, enjoying the intimacy.

The phone rang and I lifted my head, but David ignored it.

It rang a second time.

"Shouldn't you answer it?" I asked.

"Whoever it is will call back."

The phone rang three times more and the answering machine on his night table kicked in.

"David – are you there?" a female voice said.

David turned his head towards the machine, his eyes rounded in horror.

"Shit. It's my ex-wife."

"Sweetheart? Please? Angel, I need to talk to you. I'm soooo lonely," the voice said.

He sprang off me and grabbed the phone. "What?"

"Can I come over?" Her voice was still coming over the answering machine.

"Let me turn the damn machine off." He fiddled with some buttons and the machine made a squealing sound.

I got up quietly and accidentally stepped on Shakespeare who let out a pathetic cry. I nuzzled him by way of an apology, and he flopped back down again. David motioned for me to wait, but I shook my head. I was gasping with laughter and put my hand over my mouth so the ex wouldn't hear. Then I picked my things up from the floor, went into the bathroom, and closed the door.

"Please, Kate, don't go. We're divorced," David said through the door.

Fully clothed, I opened the door. "This was a bad idea anyway. We have to work together."

David stood blocking the doorway, scowling. "You're being ridiculous."

I tried to get past him, but he wouldn't let me go by. At first, I thought he was kidding, but then I saw the anger in his eyes. I tried to get around him again, only this time he grabbed me by both arms and shook me.

"Stop that!"

"You can't just walk out on me like this!"

He shook me again and I banged my head on the doorframe.

"Stop it! You're hurting me," I said, pulling away.

David dropped his arms to his side, but he didn't move out of the way. The fury on his face was frightening.

"Get out of my way."

Finally the anger in his expression subsided and he looked contrite as he stepped aside.

"I'm sorry. Don't leave."

I pushed past him and left the apartment.

Chapter 65

It was three in the morning and I'd missed the last train back to Connecticut. From David's lobby, I called Jordan on my cell phone and woke her up to let her know I was coming over. She lived nearby on Bleeker Street on the other side of Washington Square Park.

David's doorman offered to call me a cab, but I needed to calm down, so I decided to walk. Despite the hour, there were still a few people strolling along lower Fifth Avenue. The big white arch at the entrance to the park was all lit up and I thought about whether to walk through the park or around the perimeter. I walked south from David's building and started to enter the park when I noticed groups of homeless people asleep on the grass on both sides of the arch. Two elderly men in short sleeves were sitting at a stone table playing chess. The scene looked harmless enough, but I decided to play it safe anyway and take the long route around the perimeter.

I walked east on Fourth Street, still upset over David's violent outburst. When I got to the corner, a tall man came up next to me and waited for the light to change. I glanced over at him and an irrational panic swept through me. The light changed and I waited for him to cross the street ahead of me. I slowed my pace behind him. He seemed to deliberately slow down too. Then he stood in the doorway of a brownstone halfway up the block. He was facing the door with his back to the street. I walked as slowly as I could and thought I saw him turn around and look at me. I stopped and fiddled with my watch under a street lamp. He was definitely staring at me. I waited under the light, trying to decide what to do, when suddenly he threw open the door and disappeared inside.

By the time I got to Jordan's building, I was out of breath from walking so quickly. Her doorman knew me, so he didn't bother to ring her before letting me take the elevator upstairs.

I rang Jordan's doorbell and she opened the door.

"You look like you've seen a ghost. What's wrong?"

I explained about the man in the street.

"Have you seen yourself in a mirror? Your hair's a mess and your dress is on inside out. You look like you got mugged."

I looked down at myself. "Oh."

Jordan was wearing pink baby doll pajamas.

"Is Ned here?" I asked. "Am I interrupting?"

Ned Winslow was a political science professor at Columbia University who was twelve years older than Jordan. They'd been on again, off again for years, having met when Jordan was a Columbia journalism student.

"He left an hour ago. Come sit down."

Jordan lived in a gorgeous one-bedroom apartment overlooking Washington Square Park. Her furniture was sleek and modern without looking austere. In the living room, she had a black leather sofa that opened into a bed and bright red chairs around a glass and bamboo coffee table. The walls were decorated with large oil paintings that she'd bought from some of the galleries in lower Manhattan, and in other cities where she'd traveled on assignment.

"I think I need alcohol before I hear this story. I'll get you something to sleep in first."

She disappeared into her bedroom and emerged with an oversized T-shirt that said Grateful Dead across the front.

"How retro," I said, going into the bathroom to put it on.

When I came back out, Jordan was in the kitchen putting cheese and crackers on a plate. As New York kitchens go, Jordan's was enormous. She'd designed an eating shelf herself that was built into the wall, cafeteria style. Three tall chrome stools with bright red seats sat side-by-side under the shelf. Hanging from the ceiling was a red and black Calder-esque mobile - the only other spot of color in an otherwise all white room.

Jordan rummaged in the refrigerator and pulled out a bottle of white wine. "Pinot Grigio?" She held the bottle up for me to see.

"Sounds great." I grabbed two glasses from the cabinet, snatched a bag of potato chips off the counter, and followed her into the living room.

She stretched out on the floor with a pillow. "Now explain to me slowly why you're eating cheese and crackers in my apartment instead of making wild, passionate love in David's."

Chapter 66

The telephone woke me up from a sound sleep.
"Rise and shine!" Jordan sounded unbearably cheerful over the phone. "It's nine o'clock already."
"Where are you?"
"At the office." Meet me at the garage by ten and I'll give you a lift back to Connecticut."
"Are you throwing me out?"
"Billy Cole's finally regained consciousness," she said. "I want to drive up and talk to him."

It was almost noon by the time Jordan dropped me at the Westport train station so I could pick up my car. I had an eight o'clock curtain and wanted to take a nap, but I hadn't been to the cleaners in ages and it was on my way home.
Myron, the owner, greeted me from behind the counter. He glanced at my dress. I was still wearing my cocktail dress from the night before - a little over the top for errands.
"Haven't seen you in ages," Myron said. "Congratulations. We saw your show last Saturday night. You were terrific."

"Thanks." I handed him four cleaning tickets. "You should've let me know you were coming. I would've arranged house seats."

"Thanks. I'll remember for next time." Looking at the numbers on the tickets, he pressed a lever on the wall that made the cleaning move around a carousel. When he found my clothing, he hung it on a silver rod over the counter.

"The raincoat had some things in the pocket," Myron said. "I put them in an envelope and stapled it to the plastic cover. Sorry. I meant to call you. Hope none of it was important."

I handed him my credit card. "No problem."

I was putting the cleaning away in my hall closet when I spotted my raincoat already hanging there. I lifted the plastic bag off the cleaning. Myron had accidentally given me a man's trench coat. I lay it across a chair in the living room so that I wouldn't forget to take it back to him and headed for the bedroom.

I flopped down on the bed and closed my eyes. Why is it that sleep is so elusive whenever you need it most? I rolled over on my side and started thinking about the raincoat. David had placed a man's trench coat around my shoulders the night Cy was attacked. I must have taken it to the cleaners by mistake.

There was no point trying to sleep anymore until I looked at what was inside the envelope. I got up, walked back into the living room, and ripped it off the plastic bag. The contents were a big disappointment. Inside were a five dollar bill, three ones, and a key. The key was big and heavy – like a hotel key that you're supposed to leave at the front desk before going out. A picture of a tower was etched onto the background with the number 2581 overlaid on top. Something about the picture looked familiar, but I was too exhausted to even think about where I'd seen it before. I put the key and the money back into the envelope and stuffed it into the pocket. Then I went back into my bedroom and fell asleep almost instantly.

I dreamt that I was onstage with a packed house out front. I couldn't remember any of my lines and the other actors were standing around staring at me. People in the audience were mur-

muring to one another. I wanted to run off stage, but my legs were too heavy to move. Someone's cell phone started ringing and wouldn't stop.

I opened my eyes and sat up. The cordless phone on my night table was blaring.

"Hello?"

"Sorry I woke you again," Jordan said.

"How'd it go with Billy?" My muscles were so tight from the bad dream that my back hurt.

"He seemed pretty with it." She sounded pleased with herself. "Get this - he admitted he was the one who ransacked your apartment."

That brought me fully awake. "Why?"

"When Nick found out Cy was double-crossing him, he beat the shit out of him until Cy finally admitted he was stealing. Two million dollars in drug money to be exact. Hidden in a public storage room. Only Cy claimed he forgot the key at the theater."

"Good Lord," I said.

"Billy claims that's what Nick and Cy were doing in the Green Room that night – looking for the key. Only it wasn't in the drawer like Cy said it was. Then you walked in and interrupted them. After that, Nick decided you had it. He made Billy break into your apartment to look for it by threatening to kill his mother. When Billy came up empty-handed, Nick went ballistic."

It was like a giant jigsaw puzzle with all the pieces falling into place. I ran to the living room, taking the cordless phone with me. I grabbed the envelope out of the raincoat pocket and looked at the key again.

Where had I seen that tower before?

And then it hit me. My mother had slipped on a flyer the day we'd snuck back into the theater. On the flyer, there had been a drawing of the same tower. I closed my eyes and tried to picture the words underneath. Finally my memory released them: Tower Storage.

"Jordan - I do have the key."

A half hour later, Jordan was in my apartment.

"I think we should hand this over to the police," I said.

"Please, Kate. This is a once in a lifetime story."

"You say that about every story," I said.

"Let's open the storage room first and then we'll call the police. With Nick dead, what's the risk?"

I looked at my watch. "I can't go now. It's almost 5:30 and I have to get into costume and makeup before the curtain goes up."

"First thing tomorrow then," Jordan said.

"I have a meeting in the city at Miles Triant's office. I told you that."

Jordan look annoyed. "I can't hang around waiting for you to get back. I have to be in my office tomorrow afternoon."

"Tell you what," I said, "I'll meet you in the city when you're finished working and we can take the train back up here together. Then we can drive over to the storage place in my car straight from the Westport station."

"I suppose that'll have to do."

"Don't be so grumpy, Jordan. We'll go tomorrow. I promise."

Chapter 67

I arrived at the Westport train station before eight o'clock the next morning. Commuters were already lined up at intervals along the platform. From years of practice, they knew exactly where the front and rear doors of each car would open. I walked to the imaginary back of the train, hoping I'd find a seat when the real train finally arrived. I rushed past a friend of my parents who waved hello, and avoided eye contact with a man I'd known in high school. Commuting at this ungodly hour was making me decidedly unsocial.

We boarded the train like lemmings plunging into the sea. Two briefcases, one handbag, and The New York Times took up the only vacant seat I could find. A blond woman in a navy pantsuit with short hair slicked back with gel sat in the inside seat, staring out the window, pretending I didn't exist. An impeccably dressed man with silver hair and a smug expression sat on the aisle staring resolutely ahead of him as if I were invisible.

"Excuse me," I said, addressing them both. "Would you mind moving your things?"

Neither said a word. The woman rolled her eyes and let out a loud *tsk* as she yanked her handbag, briefcase, and The New York Times onto her lap. The man was more politic; he smiled as if he'd just noticed me, removed his briefcase from the middle seat, and stood up so that I could slide inside.

I realized what a mistake I'd made the minute I sat down. Our seats were next to the bathroom; the strong smell of urine wafted from under the door. A person would really have to go desperately to open that door and venture inside. I closed my eyes and tried not to breathe.

The train arrived at Grand Central Station exactly one hour and ten minutes later. I joined the throng of people headed down a long flight of stairs leading to the North Corridor. Everyone turned left at the bottom, so I did too, making the assumption that they knew where they were going.

It was a long walk to the exit and I couldn't shake the feeling that I was being followed. At one point, I stopped and pretended to read an ad on the wall, glancing around as the crowd rushed by. But people walk fast in New York; slow down and you're likely to get trampled. I rejoined the flow, moving as quickly as I could until I hit the street at 47th and Madison Avenue. There were thick rain clouds overhead. On the corner, a bottleneck of people waited for the light to change; when it did, we moved forward in a wave.

Miles Triant's office was on Broadway and 51st Street. I walked west on 47th and turned up Fifth Avenue, stopping to look in Saks' windows. I was admiring a sleek brown dress when a man's reflection appeared next to me in the window. It took me a moment to realize he was staring at me. I spun around to look at him, but he was already gone. *Get a grip*, I told myself, *he's probably a fan*.

I crossed Fifth Avenue and continued down the long promenade leading to the skating rink at Rockefeller Plaza. During the summer, the ice was replaced with outdoor restaurant seating, so I had to imagine the skaters. I skirted security personnel cordoning off crowds that had gathered to watch *The Today Show* broadcasting live on the plaza. I headed west on 49th street, walking the long block over to 6th Avenue, renamed Avenue of the Americas for no good reason that anyone can remember. I passed NBC Studios where I'd once reigned over the teenage set as their nighttime drama queen. I felt old.

When I got to 6th Avenue, I walked north to 51st Street and turned left, continuing west towards 7th Avenue. By the time I got to the middle of the block, it had started to drizzle. The crowds had thinned and I started to feel edgy again. I looked behind me, but saw nothing more sinister than two women strolling along together and a man some distance behind them.

Triant Industries was in an old building on Broadway sandwiched between two of the newer, glitzier ones. I took the elevator to the 22nd floor and followed along a winding hallway until I found Suite 2207. A polished oak door was set into a glass wall through which I could see an empty reception desk. I spotted a numeric keypad on the wall and pressed the call button. I was fishing in my bag to find Miles' extension when David opened the door.

"Surprise – my trip to L.A. got cancelled." He was dressed in a beautifully tailored suit and tie; but there were dark circles under his eyes as if he hadn't slept, and apparently he'd forgotten to shave.

I decided to follow his lead and pretend that the incidents of the other night had never happened.

"Why don't we talk in Miles' office? It's more comfortable there."

He led the way down an open corridor past several glass-enclosed offices with a view of Broadway out the windows.

A wall clock said that it was almost ten.

"Where is everyone?" I asked.

He smiled. "Miles gave them the morning off to attend an importers' conference at the Hilton."

"Nice boss. Is he here yet?"

"Actually, that's another reason I'm here. Miles isn't feeling well. He asked me to stand in for him."

David led the way to Miles' corner office. He walked in ahead of me through the open door. To my surprise, he ignored the couch and comfortable looking wing chairs, and continued around the massive wooden desk, taking a seat behind it. He gestured for me to take a seat on one of the straight-back chairs in front of the desk.

"It's good you're early. It gives us a chance to clear the air," he said.

"Let's not even talk about it, David. I like you a lot, but we have to work together. I just want us to stay friends. Okay?"

"Okay."

He was staring at me so intently that I began to feel uncomfortable. I couldn't decide if he was about to apologize or if I'd made him angry again.

I looked away at the built-in shelves lining the walls. There was a doorway near the desk at the back of the room. Miles owned an eclectic collection of books ranging from *The Olive Oil Connoisseur* to *Great Moments In American Theater*. Instead of books, the top shelves were crammed with cartons of Marlboro and Camel cigarettes.

"Miles sells cigarettes?" I asked, changing the subject. "Sorry - nothing worse than a reformed smoker."

I smiled, but he didn't smile back. Instead, he stood up abruptly and took a carton of Marlboros down from one of the shelves. He wasn't his usual relaxed self. His body language seemed stiffer somehow.

"These are special cigarettes. You might like them." He opened one end of the carton and removed a pack. "Here – take a look."

"No, that's okay. I gave it up. My grandmother died of lung cancer a few years ago."

He tore open the pack of cigarettes as if he hadn't heard me and offered it to me. His expression was devoid of friendliness; almost menacing.

"No - really. I don't smoke," I said.

"Go on. Take one, Kate."

He reached across the desk and shook the pack of Marlboro's in my face. I felt the hairs on the back of my neck rise as I recognized the neatly rolled marijuana joints. Like the ones the police had found in my apartment the night it had been ransacked.

David stood up and laughed as if I'd missed the joke. He stretched his arm out towards me. "Come. There are some people in Miles' conference room that I want you to meet." His eyes cut to the doorway on the right wall near the desk. When I didn't move, he said, "Please – I insist. After you."

Reluctantly, I got up and walked in front of him. He opened the door and held it for me.

Grandpa Max and Uncle Abe were seated at the far end of a wooden conference table. Their mouths were sealed shut with silver duct tape and an image of Billy bound and gagged in the chapel flashed through my mind. Their arms were tied behind them so that all I could see was their elbows bent back uncomfortably.

"What the hell…" I spun around towards David. He was pointing a gun at my chest.

"Take a seat."

Chapter 68

I remained standing, surprised at how quickly my mind had switched into a higher gear. I moved to the opposite end of the table from where Max and Abe were seated, making it impossible for David to see all of us at the same time without turning his head back and forth. For the time being, his attention was on me.

Out of the corner of my eye, I saw Uncle Abe trying to signal me. I glanced at him as he tossed his head at the coat draped across the chair next to him. I looked away quickly, but David had caught the exchange.

His face twitched for an instant. "Don't try anything foolish. Now – give me that key."

The last piece of the puzzle clicked into place. Nick and Cy had only been foot soldiers. David was the silent partner I'd been dreading.

"I don't have it."

His face twitched again and he took a step closer. "Don't fuck with me, Kate. I have your conversation with Jordan on tape. Wanna hear it?"

I felt like I'd been slapped. David had played me. He must have bugged my loft during one of his visits.

"I waited around yesterday to see if you'd call and tell me about the key," he continued. "But you were going to just hand my money over to the police, weren't you?" His eyes were black with fury and he took another step towards me. "Or maybe you planned on stealing it from me…"

I backed away from him. Out of the corner of my eye, I saw Gramps staring at me wildly, shaking his head.

"I don't want your money. You can have the key. But it's not here – I swear. It's in Connecticut. You should know that if you heard my conversation with Jordan."

David's smile never reached his eyes. "Then I suggest we go up there together and get it."

I gestured towards Max and Abe. "Let them go first. You have me. You don't need them anymore. And they're not about to tell anyone if I'm with you."

"Once I have my money, one of my associates will set them free. You have my word." He smiled and tilted his head towards the door. "After you."

He dug the barrel of his gun into my back as I crossed in front of him, and I arched involuntarily. Grandpa Max and Uncle Abe made protesting noises, but when I tried to turn around and look at them, David upped the pressure of the gun against my back.

"I wouldn't make any sudden moves." The man had obviously seen one too many B-movies.

We crossed the threshold into the office. I felt some relief at hearing the door close behind us, although I couldn't stop worrying about his "associate" who was likely to be another sociopath like Nick.

"I need my handbag. It's on the chair," I said, pointing to it. "My car keys are in it."

"Get it." He shoved me forward with the muzzle of the gun.

Val's voice whispered in my head. *Size doesn't matter. Throw your opponent off-balance.*

I moved to the chair. *Focus.*

David followed close behind, digging his gun into my back again.

You can do this. I grabbed my bag by the strap. *Concentrate. Breathe.* In one fluid motion, I swung the bag at the gun, yelling *kiai* at the top of my lungs. He looked surprised as his arm flew up in the air and the gun fired into the ceiling.

He moved his arm down and tried to take aim again, but I grabbed his wrist with one hand and pushed his shoulder in the opposite direction with the other. Then I stepped back the way Val had taught me, and pulled him off balance, forcing him onto the floor face down. But he kept hold of the gun and fired another shot into the floor this time before I finally wrenched it away. It flew out of his hand and skittered beyond his reach along the carpet. He turned on his back suddenly and tried to sit up, reaching for it. I slammed my knee up under his chin and heard a nasty crack as his head snapped back and then bounced off the side of the desk. I brought my leg back like I was about to kick a soccer ball – aiming for his ribs this time - but stopped when I realized he was no longer moving. I grabbed his gun off the carpet and stood over him, pointing it at his chest. *Aim for the widest target.*

"Get up."

He stared up at me through glazed eyes.

I kicked him hard in the thigh. "Did you hear me? I said get up."

Actually, he didn't hear a thing because he was out cold.

Chapter 69

I backed over to the conference room door and opened it with the gun still pointed at David. Grandpa Max had tears streaming down his face. I ran over to him and removed the duct tape as gently as I could.

"I heard that gun go off and my heart stopped. Untie my hands, Doll." They were shaking uncontrollably.

"What are you doing here?"

"David called." Gramps was having trouble catching his breath. "Said to come right away. You were in trouble. Not to tell anyone."

I was struggling to untie the rope from around Grandpa Max's hands when Uncle Abe began making noise. I turned to him and carefully removed the duct tape from across his mouth.

He said, "You'll never get that rope untied with your bare hands. There's a penknife in my pocket. Take it."

I used the knife to untie Gramps first. He grabbed his raincoat off the chair and fumbled for something in the pocket as I cut Uncle Abe free. Abe massaged his wrists, but then looked up suddenly.

It sounded like David had recovered and was moving around the office. I thought I smelled stale cigarette smoke.

Uncle Abe whispered so softly I could barely hear him, "Let's see what he's up to."

I got to the doorway leading from the conference room into the office and stopped abruptly.

"Whoa. Put that gun down." Detective Art Desmond kept his gun pointed at me until I lowered David's gun. "You can give that to me now," he said, reaching for it.

I handed him the gun. He checked the chamber before shoving it into the waistband at his back. His blue cotton zip-up jacket covered it nicely.

David was on the floor lying on his side with his hands cuffed behind his back. He looked like he was still unconscious.

"You knew about David?" I asked.

"And Miles." He tilted his head and grinned. "I'm a detective."

"Well your timing stinks." Uncle Abe stepped out from behind me followed by my grandfather. "He almost killed all of us."

Desmond's expression turned serious. "Is everyone all right? What happened?"

"We got here first," Uncle Abe told him. "David's little plan."

"He grabbed Abe," Grandpa Max said. "I should have put up a fight, but he had a gun…" Grandpa Max stumbled.

"Max!" Abe shouted.

"Gramps!"

"Lie down on the floor," Desmond said, rushing over to help. Desmond grabbed a pillow off the sofa and gently placed it underneath Grandpa Max's head. Then he stood up and removed a cell phone clipped to his belt. He dialed and waited momentarily until someone picked up on the other end. Then he requested an ambulance.

I knelt down next to my grandfather.

"I'm fine, Doll, really. It's the excitement, that's all."

Uncle Abe placed my grandfather's raincoat on top of him and knelt down on the other side. Desmond went out front to wait for the ambulance drivers.

Within ten minutes, a team of medics followed by Desmond burst through the door with a stretcher. A young black woman wearing white cotton trousers and a matching short-sleeved shirt saw David first and hurried over to him.

"He'll be fine," Desmond told her, flashing his badge. "NYPD's on its way." He gestured towards my grandfather. "There's your patient."

A young, barrel-chested Asian man in his early twenties rushed over to my grandfather. He had a stethoscope around his neck and got busy attaching a blood pressure cuff to my grandfather's arm. The woman gave my grandfather a reassuring smile as she replaced the raincoat with a light blanket.

"I'll take that for you." I hugged my grandfather's raincoat to my chest like it was a security blanket.

"I'm fine. Really," Gramps said. He tried to sit up.

"Better to be safe than sorry," the woman said. She helped him lie down again. "Get you checked out at the hospital."

"What happened here?" she asked Desmond.

Desmond gave her a brief rundown of the situation and helped them ease my grandfather onto the stretcher. My grandfather gave them his medical history as best he could, with Abe and me filling in some of the details.

When the medics lifted the stretcher off the floor, I rose to go with them.

"I need you to wait here," Desmond said to me. "NYPD will have a lot of questions. It would be better if you were here to answer them."

Uncle Abe started to protest, but the medics were already halfway down the hall with my grandfather. "Don't answer anything without a lawyer," he said, running after them. "I'll get you someone."

"Where are you taking him?" I called after them.

The medics stopped and turned around. "Roosevelt Hospital. It's the closest," the woman said.

"But his doctors are all at New York Presbyterian," Uncle Abe said. "Please."

The medics looked at one another.

"Okay," the woman said. "It's not that much farther. We'll take him there."

After they left, the office seemed very quiet.

"So," I said. "How did you know where to find me?"

Art Desmond walked over to Miles' desk and picked up a paperweight. He grinned and said, "I heard him set up the meeting."

He turned it over for me to see. A tiny piece of metal was embedded into the surface. "Microchip," he explained.

I was flabbergasted. "Did you suspect Miles all along?"

Desmond shook his head. He seemed pleased with himself. "Not really. I was just covering all the bases in the beginning. Miles is quite the businessman. Whatever people want, he's happy to sell them: shoes, olive oil, canned goods. And of course - drugs. His importing business made it easy to move anything around the world." Desmond glanced at the cigarettes lining the shelves before continuing. "It took me a long time to figure it out, but I finally realized that he was smuggling drugs inside legitimate shipments - everything from marijuana and ecstasy to heroin and cocaine. Used his own ships and cargo planes to transport the stuff out of Latin America, the Middle East, *and* the Far East. Very diversified."

I glanced at David who showed signs of stirring.

"But I could never figure out how he fit in," Desmond said, jutting his chin out at David. "Then one day I realized what was going on. Miles was just the supplier. This one was in charge of distribution and sales. He used the kids at the theater and their friends to do the selling. And don't think he didn't know about Nick's killing spree."

"He knew Nick was torturing Billy?"

Desmond nodded. "He's one sick fuck."

There was a lull in the conversation. Desmond looked at me as if he was waiting for me to say something. He seemed to have something on his mind.

"What's taking the police so long to get here?" I asked.

"They're not coming."

"What?"

"I didn't call them," he said.

"But I heard you."

"You heard me call for an ambulance. You never heard me call for police backup."

He unlatched his holster and took out his gun, pointing it at me.

"The key, Kate. I want it – now."

Chapter 70

At first I was confused. But then I looked in his eyes and saw how dead they were. A shock ran through me. I felt like I'd touched an electric coffee pot that had shorted out with wet hands. My mouth went dry and I backed away.

"Don't fuck with me!" he shouted. "You think you can deal with me like lover-boy? Don't even try."

I hugged my grandfather's raincoat closer to my body as Desmond stepped closer.

"Billy searched for it in your apartment, but he didn't find it." Desmond took another step towards me.

I backed away further. I was standing in the doorway, my back to the hall.

Desmond said, "That's because it's been at the cleaner's all this time."

I felt my eyes widen in surprise. There was no way for him to have known that unless he'd bugged my loft too.

"I'm very good at my job, Kate. I know all about you. I planted a few listening devices around your apartment. Very enlightening. You and Jordan have a date to see what's inside that warehouse.

Only good old Detective Desmond will be there too. For protection."

David groaned. Desmond walked over to him and stopped a foot or so away from where he lay in front of the bookshelves. Closing one eye, Desmond pointed his gun at David's head and pulled the trigger.

David made a *whoosh* noise that sounded like air escaping from a balloon. A small hole appeared in the center of his forehead. Then his head lolled to one side and I saw that the back of it had blown out. Blood seeped into the plush carpet. Some of the books had tumbled off the shelves behind him. Bits of red and pink matter were splattered along the lower shelving. I wanted to run, but couldn't put thought into action.

Desmond winked at me. "You're better off without him." Then he walked up to me and rammed his gun into the middle of my forehead. "Turn around."

I flinched, but held my ground; not saying anything for fear my voice would betray me. *Never show fear if you can help it,* Val's voice whispered.

My silence made him angry. He shoved me hard and I flew backwards out the door, slamming into the wall on the opposite side of the hallway.

Desmond stood in the doorway of the office with his gun pointed at me. "I don't want to hurt you, Kate. Why do you think I let Max and Abe go? I just want the key to that storage room and then I'll disappear. By tomorrow at this time, I'll be sunning myself where no one can find me."

I clutched Grandpa Max's raincoat tight against my chest and felt something hard in the pocket. I suddenly remembered Abe's face as he'd tried to signal something to me about the coat; how my grandfather had reached for it as soon as he'd been cut free. I slipped my hand inside the pocket and wrapped my fingers around Grandpa Max's gun. Gently, I released the safety and cocked the gun.

The blast ricocheted off the walls in the hallway. Desmond looked shocked as his eyes traveled to his thigh where blood was streaming down his leg.

He lunged at me. "You bitch."

I sprinted down the hall to the reception area and was fumbling with the locked door when he grabbed me by the hair. I raised the gun, but he grabbed my wrist and almost yanked it away before I could pull the trigger. I shoved my shoulder into his chest and jammed the thumb of my other hand into his eye. He stumbled backwards and let go of my hair. I raised the gun again and took aim, but my hand was shaking so badly that the shot went wide and hit the wall. As he steadied himself, I finally got the door open and ran down the hall towards the elevator. I passed another office where people were huddled around a reception desk. A woman was on the phone, her mouth moving rapidly. All heads turned to look at me; their eyes locked on the gun in my hand.

"Call the police," I shouted.

I looked behind me and saw Desmond trying to catch up. The pain must have gotten to him because he was moving slowly, dragging his leg.

I frantically pressed both elevator buttons, not caring if I wound up going in the wrong direction so long as I put some distance between Desmond and me. When the elevator finally arrived, I leapt on, jamming my thumb against the *Lobby* button until the doors were almost closed. But an arm sliced between them and they sprang back open. Desmond started to get on and I kicked him in the groin and he fell backward. I fired another shot at him, but it missed. Then I pressed *Lobby* repeatedly until finally the doors closed and the elevator descended.

I examined myself in the smoked mirror, smoothing my navy dress back into place and straightening the lapel on my white blazer. As far as I could tell in the dim light, no blood had splattered my clothing. But just in case, I put my grandfather's raincoat on and belted it so that it didn't drag the ground. With shaking hands, I placed his gun back in the pocket. I tried to look nonchalant as I got off the elevator and walked past the uniformed doorman seated behind the circular desk. He was busy on the phone and didn't look up as I walked out the door.

Chapter 71

It was drizzling outside and the traffic on Broadway was all snarled. The gun was still hot inside the right pocket of my grandfather's raincoat. I worried about shooting myself with it since I'd forgotten to engage the safety, but I couldn't just pull a gun out of my pocket on the streets of New York. I managed to put the safety back on by feeling my way.

There were no taxis, so I started walking uptown, fumbling in my bag for my cell phone.

Sonny picked up after the first ring.

"Where are you?" I asked.

"With Val," he replied. "What's wrong?"

I explained briefly what had happened. "Desmond will go after them again in order to get to me. They're sitting ducks in the hospital."

"I'm on my way. In the meantime, I'll call a buddy on the NYPD. I'll call Matt too and let him know what's going on."

"No – don't."

"What?" Sonny sounded shocked.

"How deep do you think this thing is?"

"You mean Matt? You gotta be kidding. No way." He was silent for a beat. "Everything's gonna be fine, Kate. Whatever you do, don't turn your phone off. I need to be able to track you."

After I hung up with Sonny, I called Uncle Abe's cell phone repeatedly, but it kept rolling over to voice mail after the first ring. It finally hit me that he'd turned it off in the hospital. I left a message warning him about Desmond and to be careful until the NYPD or Sonny got there.

I continued up Broadway to 57th Street and turned east. The streets were clogged with people dodging the rain. The traffic was a mess in both directions, but at least there was no sign of Desmond. I saw a woman getting out of a cab on the corner of Madison Avenue and 57th Street. In my frenzy to nab it, I collided with an old man and almost knocked him over.

"You must be in a big hurry, lady," the driver said in a disapproving tone.

He spoke with a clipped accent and had thick dark hair and a light brown complexion. I studied his photo attached to the Plexiglas partition that separated the passengers from the driver. His name was written underneath the photo: Mustafa Feenjah.

"New York Presbyterian Hospital," I said. "67th and York."

"Very good, lady. You can relax now. I know where it is." He looked at me in the rearview mirror. "Is it an emergency?"

"Yes."

He peeled away from the curb. Spotting an opening in the traffic to our left, he moved over quickly and then slammed on his brakes to prevent us from plowing into the car in front of us. We traveled a few feet in the left lane when another opening appeared to our right. He changed lanes again, charging into that space too. We dodged in and out of cars the whole way across 57th Street. I clung to the strap over the door as the taxi lurched from side to side. By the time we turned north on York Avenue, I felt grateful that I had nothing in my stomach to give back. By the time we reached the hospital, I was so happy to be alive that I gave him an extra tip.

A young man in a business suit held the door open and politely waited for me to get out of the cab. He seemed worried when I looked him in the eye and shook my head in warning before heading towards the entrance. The last thing I heard before going inside was Mustafa yelling at him, "Well - are you getting in or not?"

As I walked through the doors, a burly guard with a Spanish accent stopped me and demanded to see inside my handbag. My heart skipped a beat as I opened it for him and remembered the gun that was hidden in the pocket of my grandfather's raincoat.

He looked at my face for a moment longer than seemed necessary, finally letting me pass into the interior of the hospital. I tried not to look nervous as I walked down the long marble hall past the nondenominational chapel and a small coffee shop with the lousiest food on the planet.

When I lived in the city, I'd worked as a volunteer in pediatrics. My job had been to pick up children from their rooms and escort them to a large playroom that had been donated to the hospital by a toy company. It gave the kids a few hours of normalcy in an otherwise grim world of sickness and scary test.

I approached the information booth in the center of the main lobby. A friendly grandmother type asked if she could help me.

"I'm looking for my grandfather, Maxwell Rosenthal," I said.

She squinted at her monitor as she typed something into the computer.

"He's in Starr Pavillion, Room 408. Go down that hallway," she said pointing, "and turn left."

I walked in the direction she pointed me to and was struck by how much busier New York Presbyterian was compared with Soundview Hospital where my father practiced. So many people were rushing through the halls that I had to force myself to slow down so as not to trample anyone.

The corridor dead-ended at an intersection where I stopped to read a color-coded sign and get my bearings. My limbs felt suddenly heavy as I examined the sign more closely and realized that my grandfather was on one of the cardiac floors. Forcing myself to put one foot in front of the other, I proceeded to the elevator.

I was a bundle of nerves as I stared up at the floor display, willing the elevator to come more quickly. When I got tired of waiting, I looked around for a stairwell. That's when I spotted Art Desmond limping purposefully down the hallway I'd just come from. His leg was wrapped in something white with nasty red stains. Next to him was an overweight middle-aged security guard in uniform. Desmond saw me and yelled for me to stop.

I didn't dare pull out the gun inside the hospital. Instead I bolted around the corner past a woman in a white lab coat and slipped through the door to the stairwell. I had two choices. I could run down to the basement and try finding an exit to the street, or I could run upstairs and take cover on one of the floors above me. I picked the latter, reaching the second floor just as footsteps clattered onto the stairs below me. I yanked open the door to the second floor and followed a maze of hallways that I remembered led to an older building housing maternity. I doubted that Desmond would think of looking for me there.

I jumped in front of a large Hasidic family crowding the hallway, and was instantly hidden by the horde of women in calf-length dresses and men in wide-brimmed hats. Desmond and the guard would have a hard time locating me. That is, assuming they'd even followed me to the second floor.

The family peeled off into one of the rooms and I continued towards the visitors' lounge. Fortunately it was empty so I decided to flout hospital rules and use my cell phone. But as I was dialing Uncle Abe's number, it hit me that if Sonny could track my cell phone, the police undoubtedly had access to the same technology and could do the same. Desmond was a cop; ergo so could he. I shoved my phone back in my pocket and went in search of a pay phone, debating whether to turn my cell phone off altogether. I opted to leave it on, praying that Sonny would find me before Desmond.

A computer-generated voice told me to deposit $5 in change to complete the call, which I didn't have. I banged the phone down so hard that the booth rattled. I dialed Uncle Abe again – collect this time.

He sounded relieved to hear from me.

I said, "Desmond killed David. He's in the hospital. He'll try and use you to get to me. Sit tight - Sonny's on his way."

"Slow down, Kate. We're fine. The police are already here. Sonny called them."

"Thank God. How's Gramps?"

"They think it was just an anxiety attack. Kate, where are you?"

Before I could answer, a deep voice came on the phone. "This is Detective Julian LaMott, NYPD. Sonny's friend."

I gulped some air and explained as quickly as I could about Desmond again. "He must've convinced hospital security that I'm dangerous."

"How do you know that?" LaMott asked.

"Because he and a security guard are chasing me. Look – I don't have time to go into details. Just don't let him near Max and Abe."

I poked my head out of the phone booth. Desmond and the guard were standing in the hall talking to one of the Hasidic men who was gesticulating wildly.

"They're here," I whispered into the phone.

"Where's *here*?" LaMott asked sharply.

"Second floor maternity. I'll try and lead them away from the building." I hung up.

I tried remembering the layout of the floor from my days as a volunteer. At the end of the hallway, another one branched to the left. Halfway down that corridor was a stairwell I could take to the main floor of the 70th Street building. Then I'd play it by ear.

Desmond and the guard spotted me the minute I stepped out of the phone booth. I darted down the hall and around the corner and dived into the stairwell. I ran down one flight and exited the building on 70th Street. Then I crossed over to the other side of the street and hid behind a column along the drive-through that cut over to 71st Street in front of Hospital for Special Surgery. I watched them emerge from the building and look up and down 70th. They didn't see me. The security guard said something to

Desmond and then went back inside the building. At least it was no longer two against one.

The air was heavy with humidity, but it had stopped raining. The sun drifted in and out of the clouds and I was hot inside my grandfather's raincoat. But I was afraid to take it off in case I needed to grab the gun out of the pocket quickly. I poked my head out from behind the column just in time to catch Desmond heading west on 70th in the direction of York Avenue.

I crossed back over to his side of the street and followed him at a safe distance. The streets were crowded, but I had no trouble keeping Desmond in my sights until an ambulance came racing along, sirens blaring, and parked diagonally across 70th with the front wheels up on the sidewalk. I had to wait until the medics removed the patient from the back before I could maneuver around the ambulance. Then I ran the rest of the way down the block.

When I reached the corner, Desmond was nowhere in sight. He'd either turned north on York Avenue, continued west on 70th, or returned to the main entrance on 68th Street. I followed my instincts and headed south towards the main entrance.

I walked quickly down York Avenue and caught sight of him again halfway down the block. He stopped to light a cigarette and casually glanced around. As he looked backwards in my direction, I slipped under the awning of a greengrocer and pretended to study a display of peaches. I was sure my instincts were right. The bastard was headed back to the hospital where he planned on doing God knows what to Grandpa Max and Uncle Abe.

Desmond was at the curb looking in both directions as if he intended to cross the avenue, when a northbound black sedan made a sudden left in the wrong direction onto 68th Street and blocked the crosswalk. A young man who had been pedaling a delivery bike along the sidewalk, stopped short. He toppled over the rectangular metal storage bin attached to the front of his bike and landed on top of the trunk of the black sedan. Furious, he banged his fist against the car's rear window.

"Where the fuck you goin' man?" he shouted at the driver.

A huge man in a dark suit emerged from the car. The boy took one look at him and ran off, but the man hardly seemed to notice. His eyes were fixed on Desmond.

Desmond turned his head to see what the commotion was about and a flicker of recognition crossed his face when he saw the man. I looked too, more closely this time. For a second our eyes locked and then the man looked away as if he'd never seen me before. Stunned, I stayed where I was as Matt Warren moved forward.

Desmond's hand flew under his jacket near his waistband. He started to close the distance between him and Matt when a little girl on a tricycle careened into him. He glared at her and she started to cry. Her mother rushed over and, seeing the fury on Desmond's face, snatched her daughter away and hurried off.

Desmond reached inside his waistband again, only this time he pulled out a gun. Someone screamed as he pointed it at Matt.

I crept up on Desmond from behind and pulled Grandpa Max's gun out of my pocket. There was another scream and Desmond spun around and knocked it out of my hand like he was swatting away a fly. He yanked my arm behind my back and jammed his gun against my temple as people on the sidewalk ran in all directions, screaming.

Matt stopped moving and raised both arms over his head. "Easy, Desmond."

I felt like I'd stopped breathing. Everything moved in slow motion until I grew conscious of a droning noise overhead. Desmond relaxed his hold for a moment as he glanced up at the helicopter hovering overhead. Springing to life, I stomped on his foot and jammed my elbow into his ribs as hard as I could. Matt was a blur as he ran towards us and grabbed Desmond, punching him hard in the face until he crumpled to the cement sidewalk. Hank Baxter appeared from behind me wearing an FBI vest. He stood over Desmond with a gun pointed at his chest while another agent put him in handcuffs. Then they yanked him to his feet and shoved him into a police car that had appeared at the curb.

Matt held the door of the sedan open for me and I climbed into the back seat. Then he slid in beside me and slammed the door shut. Hank sat up front next to the driver, a young guy with freckles and red hair that stuck out from underneath a navy blue cap that said FBI across the peak.

"Where are we going?" I asked Matt.

"Connecticut. To open that storage room."

"How'd you find out?" I asked.

"I have my sources," he said, smiling. "Which reminds me - Sonny told me you were afraid for him to call me – that you thought I was in on it with Desmond?" Dressed in a suit and tie, he looked more like an investment banker than a cop.

"How the hell was I supposed to know? Desmond seemed like a nice guy too – until he tried to kill me."

He grinned at me. "A thank you for saving your life would be nice."

"You didn't save my life. I saved yours."

"He was *trying* to save your life," Baxter said from the front seat, "before Desmond grabbed you."

Baxter had a point.

"Thank you," I said to Matt. "What're you all dressed up for?"

"Job interview."

"Which you interrupted," Baxter added.

"With whom?" I asked.

"FBI," Matt said.

"You?"

"Why not me?"

"Sorry," I said. "I thought I read somewhere that you need to be a lawyer. Or a forensics expert."

"I am."

"Which?"

"Both."

"I'll have to call you Super Cop from now on," I said.

"Do you always have to have the last word?"

"Yes."

My cell phone rang.

"I just got out of the subway." Jordan sounded out of breath. "I'm walking across 68th - almost to Second. Are you okay?"

"I'm fine. Who told you?"

"Val called me after Sonny left to see Max in the hospital."

Val and Jordan. Who would have thought?

"How's Max?" she asked.

"They think it was just an anxiety attack."

"Thank God. Where's Desmond?"

"On his way to jail where he belongs. It's a long story. I'll tell you everything later."

"Where are you?" she asked.

"In a car with Matt Warren and Hank Baxter. Not far from you. Walk over to 68th and First. We'll pick you up."

I ended the call and told Matt we had to pick up Jordan so that she could come with us.

He looked like he was about to argue.

"I'm not opening that storage room unless she's there too," I said.

Matt threw his head back and laughed.

"You can't be serious?" Baxter said to him.

"She saved my life," Matt said. "How can I refuse?"

Chapter 72

"Did you read Jordan's article in today's Times?" Grandpa Max sounded especially chipper over the phone.

I was becoming convinced there was a conspiracy going on to prevent me from ever getting a full night's rest. I tried to rouse myself. "How do you feel?"

"Fine. They're letting me out later."

"That's great," I said, stifling a yawn.

"Sorry, Doll. They wake you up so damn early in this place; I didn't realize it was only 6:30. But wait 'till you see the paper! Jordan should win a Pulitzer for this one. Listen to this, Doll. 'Actress-director Kate Sachs was instrumental in bringing down an international drug ring that relied on an army of teenagers to sell millions of dollars in heroin, cocaine, and other drugs. In a stunning display of bravery, Sachs faced off against David Sobel, the mastermind of the operation, and a corrupt narcotics detective, Arthur Desmond.'"

"Wow! I'll have to go out and buy the paper," I said.

"Wait – there's more. Listen to this: 'A Broadway producer, Sobel was the alleged head of a drug trafficking cartel operating under the guise of a legitimate import-export enterprise owned by Sobel's partner, Miles Triant. A favorite money-laundering scheme was to invest in theatrical productions and films. One of Sobel's productions was *Wait Until Tomorrow*, a show starring Sachs that is currently running at Omnibus Playhouse in Westport, Connecticut. Police speculate that two weeks ago, Sobel ordered the killing of the show's director, Cy Williams, for attempting to steal several million dollars in drug money. While working undercover, Desmond found out about the double-cross and tried to steal the money himself. Sachs saw Desmond shoot Sobel to death as Sobel lay on the floor of Triant's New York City office in handcuffs. Missing from the scene was Triant himself, a diabetic who was found dead in his Upper East Side apartment from an apparent insulin overdose. There is some speculation that Sobel murdered Triant by administering the overdose himself.'"

"Some story," I said, stifling another yawn.

"Go back to sleep. I'll call you later." Gramps blew me a kiss and hung up.

After that, I was too revved up to go back to sleep. I brewed some coffee and brought a cup with me into the living room and switched on the TV. I channel-surfed through the morning news programs and saw my face staring back at me from every station.

That night, the audience went wild with applause the minute I stepped on stage. I doubted that it had much to do with my talents as an actress, but it felt great anyhow and I sailed through the performance with more energy than I'd had since opening night. When the curtain came down, the applause was deafening and, as far as I was concerned, well deserved.

I was taking my makeup off backstage when someone knocked on the door to my dressing room.

"Kate – you decent?" Russell asked through the door.

"Yes. Come in."

He opened the door partway and stuck his head in. "You were amazing out there tonight."

"Thanks."

"Detective Warren's here to see you. Okay to send him in?" Russell asked.

"Now what? Sure - send him in."

The door opened wide and the tall frame of Matt Warren filled the doorway. He was holding a bouquet of flowers and had a dismayed look on his face.

"I didn't think you'd mind."

He was all decked out in a blazer and slacks. His unruly black hair was neatly combed.

"You mean this is a social call?" I asked.

"Of course. What'd you think?"

It was my turn to be embarrassed. "I heard the word *detective* and thought…"

"Strictly unofficial," he said, thrusting the flowers at me. They were an assortment of pink and yellow roses nestled between sprigs of baby's breath and green ferns. "These are for you."

"They're beautiful. Thank you."

He'd made a reservation at an Italian bistro on the water in Fairfield. It served dinner until 1 AM – unheard of in Fairfield County where most restaurants stopped serving at nine even on the weekends. We ate linguine Bolognese and tiramisu for dessert, and polished off a bottle of Chianti. When we were through eating, the owner brought over two glasses of Sambuca.

"Compliments of the house," he said with a wink at Matt.

We sipped in comfortable silence.

"Did you get the job?" I asked.

Matt's face fell. "I did."

"You don't seem very happy about it."

He swirled the clear liquid around his glass absentmindedly. I waited for him to decide if he wanted to discuss it.

"I've wanted to join the FBI for as long as I can remember. Just goes to show you – be careful what you wish for."

"Why? What's wrong?"

He stared at his drink for a moment longer before looking up at me. "They've given me my first assignment."

Something about the way he said this made me sorry I asked. "And?"

"It's in Chicago."

"Oh." I tried to keep the disappointment out of my voice. "Permanently?"

"No. Just 'til the assignment's over."

"How long will that be?"

He shrugged. "Could be as much as a month. Maybe longer."

For a split second, it felt like all the air had been sucked out of the room.

"Well if you need any help, give me a call. After all, I own a gun," I said.

Matt grinned. "Which you're in the process of getting a license for – right?"

I'd forgotten all about that.

"Kate?"

"Right."

He took a sip of his drink and set it down on the table. Then he took both my hands in his own. "There's something else."

"Oh?"

"I'm crazy about you."

"You're crazy about me?"

He leaned forward and kissed me.

"Yes."

Chapter 73

The door to my apartment banged shut as he swooped me into his arms and kissed me. He lowered his arms and drew me closer, his fingers tickling the backs of my thighs. His hands felt for the waistband of my white skirt as he continued to kiss me. He gave a gentle tug and the skirt fell to the floor. Then he lifted my blouse over my head and tossed it on the floor next to the skirt.

We moved to the bedroom, leaving a trail of clothing through the apartment. I pushed him down on the bed and climbed on top of him, enjoying the feel of his hands exploring my body as we rocked with pleasure, climaxing together in one big wave; then rolling through aftershocks until the early hours of the morning when we fell asleep, exhausted.

It was early September and I was on my way to rehearsal, heading west on 21st Street. It was still warm and I was enjoying the quiet of the morning. Up the block, a man in a black trench coat was walking in the same direction and I wondered why he needed a coat on such a beautiful day. Then something in his gait jarred my memory. I quickened my pace and shortened the distance between us.

"Robert?" I called out to him. "Robert – stop! It's me, Kate."

He stopped abruptly and stood with his back to me. I stopped moving too, barely breathing, waiting for him to face me. He turned around slowly and at first I didn't recognize him. He was tall and thin, balding with a black beard streaked with gray that hid the features of his face. But when he smiled, the years fell away and the old Robert I'd known emerged.

"Robert!" I started to run towards him, but stopped, halted by the dead stare.

He reached inside the black trench coat and at first I thought my eyes were playing tricks on me. It looked like a machine gun. He pointed it at me and fired.

I sat up and had trouble catching my breath, as if I'd been running. I drew the covers back and slipped out of bed and got a drink of water from the bathroom.

"Kate?" Matt's voice was thick with sleep.

"Just getting some water," I said, returning to the bedroom. "Sorry I woke you."

He patted the bed. "Come back."

I climbed back into bed and he pulled me close. I liked the feel of his chest hair against my cheek as we cuddled. He stroked my back and then moved his hand lower. He smelled of after-shave.

"What's wrong?"

I told him about the dream.

He kissed the top of my head. "It's okay. You're safe."

"I know."

"I have something for you." He hoisted himself out of bed and looked around the room. "I was going to give it to you over brunch, but I think now's a better time."

In the light, his body looked even better than it had the night before. I liked the way the muscles on his back rippled as he moved. I even liked the slight love handles that reminded me of a football player gone to seed.

He saw me looking at them. "I know. I need to work on these." He pinched the extra flesh at his sides.

"I like them. What are you looking for?"

"My pants."

"In the living room."

"Oh yeah." He grinned.

He disappeared for a few moments and returned with his pants draped over his shoulder. In his hand was a blue box from Tiffany's with a white ribbon wrapped around it. He got back into bed and sat up straight, his head against the headboard. "Come here." He opened his arms and I snuggled into them.

"This is for you."

"It's not a finger, is it?"

He threw his head back and laughed. "No – I swear." He pulled me closer and kissed me. "Go ahead – open it."

Inside was a gold chain link bracelet. Dangling from one of the links was a gold charm embossed with the masks of comedy and tragedy.

"Matt – it's beautiful."

"See what it says on the back."

I turned it over and read, *For Kate – my light and my star.*

"I'm sorry about Robert, Kate." He kissed me lightly on the mouth.

"I never think about him anymore. Honestly. Then all of a sudden I'll have a nightmare, and when I wake up – just for a moment – there's this ghost lurking in the corner." I forced myself to smile. "But then he goes away and I forget all about him. How's that for strange?"

Matt hugged me closer. "I like strange. And I'm not afraid of ghosts. I can even help fight him off if you let me. But you have to be willing to let him go."

I looked into Matt's eyes and realized how badly I wanted to let Robert Bennett rest in peace.

"I'm ready to move on, Matt. It's time."

"Yes it is."

And he kissed me again.

About the Author

M.K. Perkins has been a non-fiction and commercial writer for most of her life, including her early years as an actress when she wrote articles on the side. Like her protagonist, Kate Sachs, she knows what it's like to be a struggling actress, having appeared on stage and in dozens of soap operas and movies as an extra. Thanks to the research she did for this book, they're both pretty good shots with a handgun too. She lives in Connecticut with her husband and daughter. **Deadly Play** is her first novel.

Please visit her at www.mkperkins.com